SOMETHING
MORE
TO SAY

TONY J FORDER

A DI Bliss Novel

Also by Tony J Forder

The DI Bliss Series
Bad to the Bone
The Scent of Guilt
If Fear Wins
The Reach of Shadows
The Death of Justice
Endless Silent Scream
Slow Slicing
Bliss Uncovered
The Autumn Tree
Darker Days to Come
The Lightning Rod
What Dies Inside Us

Standalones
Fifteen Coffins
Degrees of Darkness

The Mike Lynch Series
Scream Blue Murder
Cold Winter Sun

The DS Chase Series
The Huntsmen
The Predators

TWO

JIMMY BLISS WAS DELIGHTED to be first into the office on Monday morning. He hoped his presence there proved to those due to arrive that he took his leadership role of their newly established group of retired detectives seriously. If things didn't work out that way, he could be a team player; provided the others in the side played the right kind of game. Bliss wasn't a 'credit for taking part' sort of man. He was there to do a job, and to do it to the best of his ability and as effectively as he had when he carried a warrant card.

He had avoided stepping inside Peterborough's Thorpe Wood police station for over a month, and staying away had been agonising. Absence hadn't suffocated either his enthusiasm or desire. His spirit, however, was another matter entirely. Its pulse had slowly weakened before gasping that final terminal breath. He'd passed the time in a variety of ways: long walks with Max, his rescue Golden Labrador; putting his feet up in the garden; his turntable stylus had tasted a lot of vinyl; he'd played his guitar more extensively than he had in decades, forming heavy callouses on the fingertips of his left hand; he'd also fallen back on aimless night drives to divert his attention to the simple basics of life;

8

ONE

BIG MOFO AND LI'L Mofo bobbed their heads in unison to Cypress Hill as they cruised the city streets in their tricked-out BMW. Big was six-four and twenty stone of pure muscle sculpted by pumping iron in the Definition Gym located in the Woodston district of Peterborough. He wore a lime-coloured Under Armour wife beater that showed off his powerful physique and shiny ebony skin to great effect. A foot shorter, Li'l was portly and bald, wearing a thin hoodie and a sheen of sweat over his doughy face.

The big black man and the little pink dumpling beside him made for an odd couple at the best of times, but with Big's dreads flapping in time to the heavy beat and the dull city lights reflecting off Li'l's shiny smooth dome, they were bound to draw attention with the Bimmer's soft top down, even without the booming music emanating from a new set of Bose subwoofers.

Neither occupant gave a flying fuck about being seen together or what others thought about them, both young men being supremely confident in their ability to handle any situation between the two of them. With good reason they regarded themselves as a formidable partnership. Big had the athleticism

5

and raw brute strength. He was also as visually intimidating as The Predator. And while Li'l looked as if he'd be hard pressed to tackle Bambi caught in a bear trap, he was one sick motherfucker whose reputation alone terrified others.

The moment they slipped into the Old Fletton area, Li'l killed the sounds. Shortly afterwards, Big tapped his partner on the arm and pointed ahead. On the Duke Street corner, opposite the post office, stood that evening's entertainment. Li'l slowed and eased the car to the kerb in front of two young boys, keeping the engine idling. Big looked over, jerked his head and made a beckoning gesture. One lad held back while the other stepped forward. He raised his chin after first scanning the road both ways.

'What's the word, bruh?' he said.

Big knew he wasn't being asked what was happening on the streets or what their plans were. The Soke line drugs gang enforced a daily codeword, which allowed authorised members working in small cells to know it was safe to interact with select strangers. It was a clever tactic, provided its secrets could not be bought or beaten out of somebody. He made the shape of a gun with one hand, clicked his tongue, and winked. 'Good for you, little man,' he said. 'You ain't ask me I might've pulled my piece just to fuck wit your head, you feel me?' All the brash attitude of a New York gangsta despite having been born and bred in Norfolk.

Again with the chin raise. Another with the same unwarranted arrogance.

The big man showed two rows of dazzling white teeth. 'Dozer,' he said solemnly.

The dumb kid laughed as if he hadn't been sweating bullets. 'What's up, bruh?' he asked, this time actually wanting to know what was going on.

'You got yourselves a new corner coming your way. Big earner, too. No more weed for youse guys. So get yourself together

because the man himself wants to meet wit you. He impressed wit your work and wishes to parley in person. Between me and you, kid, you're moving up the ladder. Both of you. That ain't no small thing.'

The lad grew excited. He licked his lips, no doubt already tasting the money and the adulation from the streets. He turned to tell his fellow runner, then looked back at Big. 'We coming with you two?' he asked.

'Yeah. S'why we here.'

The pair bumped fists and climbed into the back of the car. 'Man, these wheels are lit.'

'They fire, man,' his partner agreed with a heavy nod.

Li'l revved the engine by way of encouragement. The exhaust crackled like electricity.

'Where we meeting the man?' the second boy asked.

'You'll see,' Li'l said from behind the wheel, releasing the handbrake stamping down on the accelerator. They took off in a pall of smoke, leaving black streaks of rubber on the road. He turned his head to check out his partner. Big grinned and winked.

It was time to go to work.

shares in Guinness had to have risen tenfold, but he'd paid for that in blood, sweat, and tears in the boxing ring. Well, sweat and tears, at least. Gentle sparring wasn't going to leave too many splashes of claret over the worn canvas. In theory, doing nothing ought to have been easy. Plenty of people consumed their lives with inactivity. Not Bliss, though. He'd found it impossible, a task best performed by the aimless and the brainless. His old friend and colleague, Lennie Kaplan, had suggested he start writing a memoir. But the thought of labouring over a notepad or a computer without being compelled to do so by the specifics of an employment contract made him feel queasy.

His disdain for enforced leisurely pursuits was one reason why he'd been the first to arrive in the freshly aired room recently designated to house the new Unsolved Cases Team. Having risen earlier than usual, he'd walked Max, handed over the dog to his volunteer carer for the day, and without any real idea of what to expect had eagerly driven to work.

For Bliss, it was more than a return to the familiar. It was a new beginning.

The beginning of the end?

Of sorts.

But if his mind and body held out, he was determined to make sure there was plenty of distance between the starting gun and the finish line. Handing in his warrant card, together with his rank of Detective Inspector, had been a tough experience. He'd taken it much harder than he cared to admit. Without the police credentials, Bliss felt naked and vulnerable. He was a civilian for the first time in forty years, and he'd forgotten how to be one. The new job was a step in the right direction, and he was grateful for the opportunity to start afresh as a Senior Investigating Officer in addition to working unsolved cases. But no longer being a serving police officer was like hiking with a pebble in his sock.

He realised he'd been fingering his collar. He hadn't been suited and booted for a while, and he could feel the material rubbing against his neck. Fortunately, the shirt was a good decade old, so any initial stiffness was a distant memory. He didn't really know why he'd decided against more casual attire, but assumed he was feeling a familiar sense of professional duty. He yanked his hand away and took a deep breath to settle himself.

It came as no surprise to him when, less than ten minutes after he'd taken a seat in his new surroundings, Detective Sergeant Penny Chandler popped her head in to wish him well. He'd not laid eyes on his ex-partner since retiring; partly by design, partly because she'd been away on annual leave. They had exchanged several texts, during which she had informed him of her decision to stay in the city rather than move to mainland Europe with her boyfriend. Chandler appeared to have made peace with their separation. Indeed, she looked refreshed; younger, leaner, fitter, a tanned glow sculpting the contours of her pretty face.

'Bloody hell,' he said with an admiring shake of the head. 'How many paintings in how many attics do you have?'

'I'll take that as a compliment,' Chandler replied, offering a haughty sniff. 'Though I'm amazed a muppet like you has even heard of Oscar Wilde.'

Not half as surprised as Bliss was that she had recognised the Dorian Gray reference.

'As much as it pains me to say so, Pen, you look bloody good. Fit.'

Chandler mockingly flicked her hair back. 'Fit as in physically, or fit as in ravishing?'

'If you held a knife to my throat, I'd have to say both.'

'Oh, believe me, Jimmy, if I held a knife to your throat, you would never utter another word again.'

He dismissed the threat with a roll of the eyes. 'Yeah, yeah. You're all mouth and trousers. And when I say you're fit, I do of course mean for your age. It's all relative.'

'Have I ever told you you're a dick?'

'I believe so. Many times. And how come I don't see a hot drink with my name on it in your hand?'

Chandler pointedly glanced over at the room's two large windows, bright sunlight streaming through the glass. 'Are you kidding? It's muggy and steamy outside even at stupid o'clock.'

'A cold one, then?'

'Bugger off, Jimmy. I'm not your lapdog anymore. Fetch your own or persuade one of your new workmates to do the honours.'

Bliss grinned. 'Give me time to work my magic, Pen. It's early days.'

Chandler's features became less sanguine. 'We haven't had a chance to chat about that aspect of the job. You and your new colleagues. Do you know any of them? There are four of you in the team, right?'

'No, and yes. In that order. We all had a meeting with the boss last week at area HQ. She had us sign for our new credentials and phones, then we got together to discuss the first case.'

'Anything interesting?'

'Could be. It dates back to early 1999. A family man who worked for the county council was shot and killed near his home in Alwalton. With no evidence and not a single suspect, it looks like a tough investigation.'

'Intriguing. And the team?'

'They seem decent enough. Two blokes, one woman.'

'Oh, the poor cow. Three toddlers to take care of, and her in the prime of her life.'

'There's a good chance she won't be far off my age.'

'Which is the prime of life for a woman. Men become old codgers as they age.'

Bliss huffed. 'Given you didn't bring me a drink, did you come here just to take the piss?'

'No. I came to tell you to break a leg, you old git.' Chandler visibly softened. 'Seriously, Jimmy, I do hope this is everything you wanted it to be. The SCU is never going to be the same without you as our DI, but at least we've not lost you entirely.'

'You'll hardly notice the difference once we're at it. But I'm trusting you to keep me in the loop. Unsolved cases alone won't hold my interest. I need the immediacy, the urgency of a live case, so I want to be useful wherever else I can be.'

'I'm sure that between us, Diane and I will do what we can.'

DCI Diane Warburton had been holding down the fort while the unit waited for an inspector on temporary placement, with DI Foster the favourite to move across from CID.

'Actually,' Chandler continued, 'I think we have something on the go. I don't have any details, but we'll be on our way out later when Diane gets back from a meeting. I know for a fact that they haven't assigned an SIO yet. I'll have a word with her to see if she has any thoughts as to who to bring in, and if not I'll suggest you.'

He frowned. 'I'm surprised she hasn't already approached me about it. What's that all about?'

Chandler cocked her head. 'It's your first day back, Jimmy. Perhaps she thought you might want to get your feet under the desk over here before taking off again to rejoin the SCU. Plus, like I said, we only just got the shout and she's being briefed on the details as we speak.'

'I suppose. Forget about it. Listen, Pen, I'm sorry about you and Shrek. Don't get me wrong, I'm pleased you didn't sod off abroad. Selfishly, I wanted to carry on working with you. But not at the expense of your own happiness.'

After a short pause and a lengthy sigh, Chandler said, 'You know, I'm not sure Graham ever truly appreciated why you gave him that nickname. He couldn't see the resemblance and so was unable to grasp the humour. I'm not even sure we were entirely compatible or on the same wavelength. But the truth is, he wanted that job, and I didn't want to leave. He chose it over me, and I think he was right to. We were happy enough together up to a point, but neither of us was devastated by the thought of breaking up.'

Bliss leaned forward and took hold of his friend's hand. 'Things mostly turn out the way they're supposed to, Pen. And I'm here for you if you ever want a shoulder to cry on.'

'I know that,' Chandler told him with a smile. 'And you'll always have mine if you need it.'

'Big boys don't cry,' he said with a chuckle. '10cc said as much in *I'm Not In Love*.'

'Yes, and they were wrong. We could all do with a bloody good sob at some stage in our lives. My own shoulders may be narrow and soft, but they're here if you want them.'

Bliss gave a clipped nod. He loved Chandler in every way it was possible to love a person. She was so much more than his best friend, and the truth was – though he would never have admitted it to her – that if she had moved away, he wouldn't have returned to Thorpe Wood to do this job. He would have felt her presence in every room, every corridor, in every meeting, at every moment. All of which would have been too much to bear. He needed her in his life far more than she needed him, which was yet another truth he would never confess to.

'So, what are your plans here for the day?' Chandler asked him.

'I've no idea, but whatever happens by lunchtime I reckon I'll be able to make myself available to Major Crime.'

'You're a sneaky bugger,' she said, a gleam in her eye. 'You've got it all planned out, haven't you?'

Bliss shrugged. 'Just staying one step ahead, that's all. You don't get as far as I did in the job without having a few tricks up your sleeve.'

Chandler grinned. 'And you have more than most. Mind you, I have a feeling you're going to need every single one of them in your new gig.'

THREE

AFTER A BRIEF WELCOME and introduction from the recently
promoted Superintendent Alicia Edwards, Bliss and his three
new colleagues took the first tentative steps towards examining
their unsolved investigation in greater detail. The recent discovery of a handgun with a ballistics match to the weapon that had
killed their victim back in February 1999, was the biggest factor
in this particular case having been selected as the team's first.

'Having been part of the Major Crime Unit here in the city,
this being a Peterborough-based case is of obvious interest to
me,' Bliss admitted.

'I take it you were not part of the initial op?' Guy Foley asked.
He had retired at the rank of Detective Sergeant from CID in
Northampton earlier in the year. He looked younger than his
retirement age suggested, though Bliss wondered if the ex-DS
had altered his appearance; the lack of grey even in the temples
of his thick jet-black hair implied as much and his teeth gleamed
as if irradiated.

Bliss shook his head, meeting the man's inquisitive gaze. 'No,
it was long before my time.'

'How about your pals in the MCU?'

'I'm pretty sure it was the Major Investigation Team back then, and no, none of my colleagues worked this one. Why? Did you think I might have a particular interest in this one because of them? A bit of favouritism, perhaps? Protection, even?'

'Not saying that,' Foley said innocently. 'Just wondering if we were going to be upsetting people working here in the same building.'

'We went through a case review not so long ago. My colleagues were professional about it. If one of theirs happens to come up, I have no problem reviewing.'

'Nor reinvestigating?'

Bliss began to bristle. 'You seem to have a bee in your bonnet about this, Guy, so let me make myself crystal clear. I'm prepared to look at any case, even my own. Is that acceptable to you, or do we have a problem here?'

Foley shrugged. 'No problem, Jimmy. Just finding out where we stand.'

'Well, now you know.'

'Jimmy, why don't you start by giving us your thoughts on this case?' Beth Greenhill suggested, perhaps trying to take the heat out of the discussion. She had been out of the game for three years before applying for the job, having been a DI in Cambridge city centre. She came across as forthright and direct, which Bliss liked.

He was more than happy to oblige. The case had remained unsolved for considerably longer than two decades. In February 1999, neighbours discovered thirty-seven-year-old Justin Nolan, who worked for Cambridgeshire County Council and lived in the village and civil parish of Alwalton approximately five miles west of Peterborough city centre, murdered not far from his home in the grounds of a small cemetery. He had been shot twice, the second bullet slamming into the middle of his face from close range as he lay on the ground according to the pathologist's report. If there were any eyewitnesses, they had not come forward, although several residents admitted to hearing gunfire. 'The majority of them claim to have heard four or five loud cracks,' he said without referring to notes. 'The original investigation team initially believed the discrepancy was due to people hearing echoes of just the two shots. However, SOCO discovered a third bullet wedged into a nearby wooden fence post. This could have been crucial because, unlike the bullets found inside the body, it was relatively undamaged. It gave ballistics something positive to work with. All they needed was the murder weapon, which sadly never materialised. Until recently, that is. After some cleaning and test firing, the ballistics unit in Birmingham were able to positively identify the unearthed revolver as the gun that fired the shots that took the life of Justin Nolan.'

'What else did that original investigation turn up?' Ben Corry asked. 'Or not turn up, I suppose. After all, a lack of evidence and suspects is surely why we're here re-examining the case.'

'I'll give you both,' Bliss said. Corry had served his entire career as a DC, the last seven years of which he'd worked out of the county HQ at Hinchingbrooke. Both men had expressed their surprise at not having met before. 'The first list is short and sweet. They turned up literally nothing worthwhile in terms of evidence. Despite the lectures we've all heard about every contact leaving behind a trace, SOCO bagged and tagged very little, and not a thing of any consequence upon forensic examination. We all know that can happen in the real world, so there's no blame to attach there. Not unless we find something glaringly obvious missed by the original team. At first glance, however, it seems to me they did the best with what little they had to go on. Which was bugger all. No eyewitnesses, no stranger sightings before or after the shooting, no unknown vehicles spotted in the vicinity, and no suspects. Mr Nolan apparently led a simple and honest life. He held down a decent job, was a respected family man with a seemingly loving and faithful wife, no enemies, no skeletons tucked away inside dusty cupboards, and no problems at work. An ordinary man going about his ordinary day cut down for no reason so far as the investigating team could find.'

'How unlikely is that?' Guy Foley asked, eyes narrowed sceptically. 'He'd have to be one unlucky bastard to be shot dead with no explanation at all.'

Bliss nodded. 'Agreed. One hypothesis the team came up with is that Nolan could have been the victim of mistaken identity. They never could put their finger on why or how that might have occurred, but using the same reasoning you just did, Guy, they couldn't accept his murder as being the result of some madman firing off shots at random. The main reason for having doubts was because they found no similar incidents before or afterwards, which is what you'd expect to uncover. Somebody who pulls the trigger and puts another person down for the thrill of it doesn't stop after one successful kill.'

'Sounds like a tough case to have worked,' Greenhill said sympathetically. 'We have to hope the firearm provides us with a lead. Is there any news on that?'

'A DS submitted the bullet to NABIS as part of the ten-year cold case forensic review. Until now, they couldn't match it to a weapon other than to suggest it was likely to be a .38 special. They became popular here around the late eighties, before the ex-Soviet hardware started rolling in. Now that they've officially linked the spent round with the actual gun, they are hoping to connect the revolver to other shootings. That's where things stand to date.'

The National Intelligence Ballistics Service, known by all as simply NABIS, was little more than a year old when they sent the bullet for forensic examination. It had been physically stored there ever since as an evidentiary item, along with its digital profile awaiting additional information. After receiving the unearthed Smith & Wesson from Cambridge police, NABIS examined the result of a test fire which they later matched against existing examples, resulting in a confirmed link between weapon and projectile.

'Confirmation alone isn't going to take us much further,' Corry stated. 'We need that weapon to be linked to another incident. Without a break, I'm not sure what our next move should be.'

Bliss felt all eyes on him. It was his case to run with. 'As you rightly point out, identifying the weapon without also finding an owner, related crime, or potential shooter doesn't achieve a great deal. It's good evidence for making a charge stick, perhaps, but that's for later and for others to make progress on. For the time being, and just to get a feel for it, I'm in favour of a visit to the scene of crime. I don't think that requires all four of us, so I suggest Beth comes with me. Ben and Guy, I'd like you to examine the case file in detail and draw up a list of interviews we might undertake. If you can find a lead for us to follow while you're delving, that would be great. Also, as this is a reinvestigation and not just a case review, we're going to need all the documentation and exhibits drawn from storage. Everyone okay with that?'

There were no dissenters. Corry did, however, raise a pertinent issue. Given the age of the original case, the volume of paperwork it and subsequent reviews would have generated, he suspected the amount of paperwork alone might be too great for them to fit inside their office. Bliss realised his new colleague was right and suggested Corry made contact with records to arrange an inspection. Satisfied, he allowed Greenhill to lead the way out.

FOUR

RAFFIC WAS LIGHT, SO it took less than ten minutes to reach
Alwalton. A tiny parish of no more than 300 inhabitants, the
village straddled both Huntingdonshire and Cambridgeshire.
Bliss knew it best for its lone pub, the Cuckoo. Stone built and
used primarily as stables in the seventeenth century, the pictur-
esque setting was just one of the qualities Bliss enjoyed during
the summer months especially. He'd never really taken much
notice of the village itself, although he had on occasion visited the
post office opposite the pub. After parking outside St Andrew's
Church, the pair navigated their way along a well-maintained
grass path that ran between houses to a cemetery that looked to
be the final resting place for perhaps a hundred souls.

A stone wall surrounded three sides of the perimeter, and the
lawned areas were neatly mown and strimmed. The gravestones
came in all shapes and sizes, but each had been degraded by time
and weathered by climate. Water-stained, pock-marked, etched
wording faded due to spalling and many decades of accrued
grime, they stood to sombre attention, some determinedly erect,
others appearing to wilt in the heat. At the far end a line of trees
loomed over the only fence, creating deep pockets of shadow.

The first thing Bliss noticed was how snugly nearby homes bounded the quiet patch of green. Judging by the build and appearance of the dwellings themselves, they had to have existed on the night of 11th February 1999.

'How many people came forward to give statements about hearing the shots?' Greenhill asked, seeming to draw the same conclusion he had upon seeing the location for themselves.

Bliss checked his memory. 'Seven in total, I think.'

'Hmm.'

'I assume you're wondering the same thing I am.'

'Why so few?'

'Exactly. As I recall from the case notes, the unknown gunman shot our victim just after six-thirty in the evening. By all accounts it was a pretty miserable and cold day, with frost lying thick on the ground, which to me suggests the majority of people along this street were most likely tucked up indoors eating a hot meal at the time.'

'Agreed. Seven people from this many homes? That doesn't sound right to me.'

Offering a non-committal shrug, Bliss said, 'I'm not about to argue. It does feel as if there ought to have been more. It might be worth checking to see how many local residents living here in early 1999 are still with us. Perhaps a fresh door-to-door enquiry will jog a few memories, or guilt those who stayed silent all those years ago into speaking up.'

'Where exactly was the body found?' Greenhill asked.

They were standing at the end of the pathway at the point at which it merged into the cemetery grounds, and it was there that Bliss stamped his feet. 'Right here,' he said.

'Interesting. Where was Justin Nolan living at the time?'

'Did you notice the road forking further along from where we parked?' When Greenhill nodded, he continued. 'You go right, it becomes Water End. You turn left and you're in Mill Lane. That's where the Nolans lived.'

'Did the original enquiry learn why Mr Nolan was here that evening?'

Bliss nodded. 'He was walking the family dog. Usual time according to his wife. Her husband's customary route was to cut across the unused section of the cemetery just to our left and exit through a second opening.'

'So, it was his routine, then. Possibly not a chance encounter, after all?'

'Possibly not.'

Frowning, his new colleague looked around, turning a full circle as she took in their surroundings. 'Where's the fence post?' she asked. 'You told us the stray bullet found its way into a fence post, but I'm not seeing a wooden one anywhere nearby.'

Bliss took a moment to carry out his own visual search. Greenhill was correct. 'Nice catch. We'll need to see the case file records, check the crime scene diagram and photographic evidence. I assume it's been removed since.'

'So, who do you think we should interview first?'

'That's an easy one. The SIO, or at the very least their deputy from the original investigation. Also, the last person to have reviewed the case before us.'

Greenhill nodded. 'Good call. I doubt if anyone from that original team is still in the Job, though.'

'Why not?' Bliss queried. 'I did forty years.'

She looked at him askance. 'You never did.'

'Yep. Way past the age I could have retired at. In the end it was compulsory.'

'That's amazing. How many of those years have you been at Thorpe Wood?'

Bliss told Greenhill about his two stints, including why he had left, why he had returned. Filled in a few of the blanks. His new colleague seemed genuinely interested, and happily chipped in with a few of her own background snippets. He got a sense she was a little reserved, perhaps even shy. Or possibly just wary of being on his stamping ground. But she had a pleasant way about her, and he found himself enjoying her company.

As they strolled through the church grounds, making their way via a different route back to Bliss's vehicle, a thought occurred to him. He took out his personal mobile, apologising to Greenhill for making a call.

'I'm a bit busy, Jimmy,' Sandra Bannister said. 'Is it urgent?'

'If I wasn't so thick skinned I'd be offended,' he said dolefully.

'You're not missing me, then?' Bannister was a journalist for the city newspaper, the *Peterborough Telegraph*, and had proven to be a good source of information for him in the past.

'Sorry. Under pressure to make my deadline.'

'Fair enough. I won't bother you right now.'

'No, no. It's fine. I can spare a minute or two for my favourite ex-police officer.'

Bliss smiled as the reporter's tone softened. 'I'll keep it short and sweet, and we can catch up when you have time. The intel I'm after came before your time at the paper. We're talking early 1999. Name of Justin Nolan. Murdered. Shot dead. I'd appreciate anything you can come up with, Sandra.'

He knew he might be able to find the story via a web search, although he wasn't sure when the newspaper first went online. But he also knew that whatever ended up in any article would have earlier been subject to the editor's red pen. Bannister would have access to all the relevant files, including any additional notes that had not made the cut but might prove invaluable now.

'Got it,' she said brightly. 'I'll call you back. It won't be until late afternoon.'

'No problem. Cheers.'

Aware that his partner had heard only his side of the conversation, Bliss explained his relationship with Bannister. Close fraternisation between police officers and the media was frowned upon, but Bliss never gave up more than he ought to in exchange for information. In his experience, journalists, and newspaper reporters in particular, were often able to winkle out intelligence for their articles that the police simply had no legitimate means of accessing. He wondered what Greenhill made of it, but she admitted to having had similar contacts when in the Job.

'It's a fine line,' she said. 'I'd often worry about being played, but never discussed anything on the record.'

'Me neither. I would never have wanted to give anybody the ammunition to take a run at me over information exchanges.'

'What kind of intel are you hoping for?'

Bliss shrugged. 'In this instance, not a great deal. I don't think they went much deeper than we did, and I very much doubt they returned to the story in later years.'

They'd reached his vehicle, and Greenhill paused with a wry grin on her face. 'Do you worry that people might see this motor and wonder if you were on the take?' she asked.

He took the question in the spirit in which it was intended. 'My retirement gift to myself. I've had money sitting in the bank from house sales and insurances and rarely treated myself while I was in the Job. I needed a car, and I remember having a loaner Volvo SUV after I drove my own wheels into a lake, and I liked the way it handled. To be honest, driving around in a big, black SUV, I'm more concerned about people thinking I'm a drug dealer.'

His colleague put back her head and laughed, a delicate yet throaty sound. 'I never thought of that. But you're right. You'll get a pull in this motor, that's for sure. Still, I can see why you need a huge SUV, what with all the hills and mountains around us.'

Chuckling, Bliss said, 'Okay, smartarse. It's an age thing. Frankly, these days I'd much rather step up into the driver's seat than down into one.'

Greenhill nodded. 'I can understand that. I'm not as supple as I used to be, either. I do have one more question, though.'

'Go on. Fill your boots.'

'Did you mean I *am* a smartarse, or I *have* a smart arse?'

Bliss shook his head and waved both hands across his face. 'Oh, no. I'm not going there, Beth. Whichever offends you the least is my answer.'

'Do you really think either would offend me?'

'The sad truth is, I have no idea what the rules are anymore. If I joked about my old partner's arse, she'd be more likely to moon me than complain about what I said. But times have changed and I'm not taking anything for granted.'

She squinted at him. 'I get that. But for future reference, I'm not that easily offended. Oh, and by the way, if you think I'm letting go of that driving the car into a lake business, you have another thought coming. That's one story I really do have to hear.'

Bliss chuckled. 'No problem. I'll tell you all about it one of these days.'

They climbed into the vehicle and Bliss drove back to Thorpe Wood, unable to shake the feeling that there was far more to this investigation than met the eye.

FIVE

ACK AT THE STATION, Foley and Corry were working the lap-
tops in the Unsolved Cases Team office. They paused to listen
as Bliss and Greenhill provided a brief account of their murder
scene exploration and ensuant impressions. Corry picked up on
the matter of the missing fence post, querying its significance.

'We can check the exhibits log to see if SOCO removed the
post,' Bliss said, without a great deal of enthusiasm. 'But I suspect
that will be a dead end. I'm betting they were able to extract the
bullet cleanly with it still in place.'

'Perhaps somebody replaced the entire fence at some point.
We are talking more than twenty years, after all.'

'Much more likely,' Bliss agreed. 'How about checking out the
diagram drawn up by the original scene of crime investigators?
They would have identified the location of the evidence findings.
From that, we should be able to pinpoint the relevant property
and make further inquiries if we think the post itself is at all
relevant. I'm not so sure it is. Meanwhile, I see a list of names
written on the whiteboard. I assume these are the people you
think we should reinterview?'

Foley nodded, stood, and walked across to the board, indicating each name in turn. 'Justin Nolan's wife is a no-brainer. The following seven names belong to those who admitted to hearing the gunshots. Then we have Jeff Smalling and Carrie Lott. The original team identified them as Nolan's closest work colleagues. Smalling was his manager, Lott his assistant. Next, we have the couple listed as being Justin and Sarah Nolan's best friends. Those are our priority reinterviews, but we've also added a name. We did a bit of research, made a few calls and discovered that Iain Houseman was the St Andrew's Church Reverend. As far as we're aware, he is still alive and we're in the process of tracing him.'

'That's great work you two,' Greenhill said, eagerly. 'I'm surprised nobody thought to interview him before.'

'I suppose there's no reason why he'd have any information for us,' Foley said. 'But we asked ourselves who else might have seen or heard something without being aware of its relevance, and the church came to mind. The Post Office, too, but we've struggled more with that one.'

'Don't forget the pub on the corner,' Bliss said. 'The Cuckoo. They've probably changed owners and staff multiple times, but worth making enquiries.'

'Sure. I'll check the review updates to see if anyone has already tackled that angle.'

Bliss was pleased. 'Are you both happy to work your way through the list and progress them as far as you can?' he asked. 'Beth and I want to speak with the original SIO if possible. Somebody who worked the case, at least. Plus, the last officer to review the case.'

'I have to admit,' Corry said, 'it's possibly the smallest murder case file I've ever seen. I'm not saying the initial investigators weren't thorough, they simply had little to go on.'

'We're so fortunate having access to digital data these days. Consider how little or actually non-existent it was two decades ago. Security camera tech – even if present – was generally of poor quality. No doorbell cams, no dashcams. Think of how much we can discover from extracting phone data now compared to then.'

'Yeah. Most we could find were call logs, and nothing of interest in those.'

'So, what can we rely on?' Greenhill asked.

Bliss thought about it. 'We can work our way through the TIE, actions, and statement logs. The exhibits reference book could be useful in identifying priorities. Forensically, we'll want to re-examine results of tapings, bloodwork, DNA, prints. It might also be worth having a look at any recorded media interviews. I think spending time on becoming familiar with all of those elements will give us a real grounding for the investigation ahead. Remember, we're in no rush. This case is cold and we're just trying to warm it up over time.'

The others nodded in agreement. 'You mentioned prints,' Corry said. 'I'd like to chase up NABIS to see if they've managed to pull any off the weapon. I realise it's unlikely after all this time, but it'd be our best lead so far if they found just one.'

'Yeah, crack on with that,' Bliss said. 'And while you're at it, find out if the cartridge casings were dusted for prints. If not, let's arrange to have that done. The NABIS techs will have focussed on the casings toolmarks when matching the spent bullet to the revolver, but whether they will have printed it, I'm not sure.'

'Will do. I'd expect the same result as the gun itself given how long it's been in the ground. I realise it was wrapped in a cloth, but even so.'

Nodding, Bliss said, 'Okay. We have work to get our teeth into. I'll admit it doesn't look promising at this stage, and I'm not banking on the new evidence in the shape of the weapon find breaking open this case. But let's get some actions sorted and agreed. Ben, you want to handle the assignments?'

Corry nodded.

'TIEs for you, Guy?'

Foley was agreeable. The Trace, Interview, and Eliminate part of an investigation was crucial, and in addition to following up on the original case and its subsequent reviews, he also required a TIE sheet for his fellow investigators.

'One more thing,' Bliss said. 'How far did you get with records for this case?'

'We're waiting for a call back,' Corry said. 'Looks as if the best way to view everything is at the main storage office, but I'll confirm as soon as.'

While the two men got stuck in to their list of jobs, Bliss and Greenhill delved into the case file. Bliss popped his reading glasses on and checked back all the way to the beginning. He was startled to discover the name of the SIO: Detective Superintendent Sykes. The man had been Bliss's first boss following his transfer up to Peterborough in 2002, and the pair had despised each other from the off. Sykes had passed away some time ago in a nursing home following a lengthy spell of illness, so Bliss read on to identify the deputy SIO.

Matthew Cleland had been the Major Investigation Team's DCI. He would know as much about the case as the SIO, possibly more. Bliss made a note of the name, but then continued on until he'd identified a DS who also worked the case. Sergeants might not feature heavily when it came to ultimate decision making, but they knew the investigation inside out. With the name of Edward Battersby also in his notebook, Bliss put his glasses away and checked the time. He turned to Beth Greenhill.

'Do you have plans for lunch?' he asked. 'Only I'm meeting up with my ex-partner if you'd like to join us.'

'No, that's fine thanks. I'll sort myself out.'

'Okay. If you try the canteen, I'd suggest you stick with the all-day breakfast and have a bottled drink. The hot chocolate is also decent enough from the vending machine. As for this afternoon, my old team might have an SIO job for me. If that's the case, are you okay to follow up on the previous case review yourself?'

'Of course. You want me to track down whoever you have on your own list?'

'To be honest, I'd rather be there when you speak with them. I think they are the ones with the real knowledge to tap. But, yeah, if you can locate them that would be a great start.'

Greenhill was agreeable and seemed happy enough with the arrangements. Bliss told both Foley and Corry that he might be unavailable to them after lunch, but knew they had plenty to be getting on with. Before leaving the office, he had something to say to them as a group.

'I realise it's early days for us as a team,' he said. 'People have preferences and quirks and we're all long enough in the tooth to be set in our own ways. That said, from what I've seen so far, the four of us are more than capable of ironing out any wrinkles. There's work to be done and if I am taken away by my other job for the remainder of the day, just know I won't be doing any second guessing when we next meet. You're all highly experienced, so go about your business and we'll review and see where we are first thing in the morning.'

'Might this second job of yours pose problems for the rest of us?' Foley asked.

Bliss frowned. 'In what way, Guy?'

'Only that it's day one for us in this team, and already we might be losing you to an active case. It sounds to me as if we might become less of a priority.'

'You will be. An active case will always take precedence. None of which means you three can't do your jobs without me. The workload is there, but there's no pressure. Yes, we want to find out who murdered Justin Nolan, but we're in no hurry. Take each lead, each fresh action as far as you can. Carry out the interviews and log them. When I walk out that door, I'm not leaving for days or weeks. I could be back later – in fact, this is where I will be doing all my paperwork at the end of each day, so we may well catch up this evening. Otherwise, as I said before, I'll be here first thing in the morning for a meet and a chat and a look at where we are and where we're going.'

Bliss looked around. 'Anyone else?'

Greenhill and Corry shook their heads.

'Any*thing* else?' This time, he looked hard at all three of them.

He nodded. 'As I said before, it's early days. If my shooting off to work as SIO on other cases is a wrinkle we have to iron out, then we will. Let's just see how it goes this week, and then come Friday afternoon we can all lay our cards on the table. Fair enough?'

Happy with the response this time, Bliss marched out of the room and left them to it.

SIX

BEFORE HE'D EVEN LEFT the corridor in search of DS Chandler, Bliss received a call from DCI Diane Warburton. From her he learned that his Major Crime Unit colleagues were attending a crime scene, and the DCI wanted to know if he was available to appear as the SIO. He readily agreed, obtained the location, and grabbed a bacon roll from the canteen before heading out to join them.

The officer who signed him in at the scene had come to be a good friend and was responsible for Bliss getting back into boxing. PC Griffin looked up at his approach, grinned and said, 'Meet the new boss. Same as the old boss.'

Bliss stopped in his tracks. 'Have you been saving that one up for when you next laid eyes on me?'

'Possibly,' Griffin admitted.

'Not a terrible effort, but not good enough. The Who. *Won't Get Fooled Again*, from the album Who's Next. You need to up your game, pal.'

The two men shared a love of music and often tried to outdo each other with their knowledge. Griffin had lobbed him up an easy one upon his return to the fold, so he hit back with, 'Where did the band Danny Wilson take their steam trains to?'

The uniformed officer puffed out his cheeks, handed a clipboard over for Bliss to sign, and shook his head dejectedly when he took it back. 'Nope. You've got me with that one.'

'The Milky Way,' Bliss told him. 'I'm disappointed in you, young man. I thought you knew your stuff. Anyway, do yourself a favour and get the album.'

'Will do. Oh, and welcome back.'

'Cheers. Let's see if I remember how it's done, eh?'

Once he was beyond the police cordon, Bliss found himself with plenty of spaces to choose from in the Orton Lock car park. Police and crime scene investigation vehicles stood idle, their occupants either at the scene itself or scouring the immediate surrounding area. Over the years he'd visited Orton Mere frequently, to walk dogs or spend time on his small boat moored nearby. He had crossed the footbridge spanning the River Nene on numerous previous occasions, but had always veered left alongside the golf course rather than take the path in the opposite direction towards the rowing and canoeing course.

This time he did head right, lured as if by siren song towards flashes of yellow fluorescence and white forensic suits congregated underneath the Nene Parkway flyover. The space occasionally hosted musical events, whose sonorous bass and drum beat he could hear from his own back garden if the wind blew in the right direction. The well-trampled soil directly beneath the vast concrete structure was firm underfoot, and Bliss's shoes kicked up baked dirt as he made his way over to the white and yellow tent that had been erected over the two bodies – both of which had subsequently been whisked off to the mortuary in the bowels of the city hospital as soon as the crime scene manager had given permission.

The air was redolent of dust, heat, and blood. The latter might have been imagined, but the odours were thick and heavy enough to feel like a physical entity brushing against his exposed flesh. The day screamed high summer and bright sunlight, but lurking in the shadows lay cold, dark chambers mirroring the bleakest hearts of mankind.

As he encroached upon the wider scene, Bliss studied his surroundings more closely. Each of the flyover support pillars bore low level markings some might describe as art, but the graffiti artists and taggers hadn't yet taken to defacing the columns above their natural reach. The incident tent traversed a gravel border that ran between the flat soil and ankle-high grass close to one of the rectangular supports. A group of familiar faces in animated conversation huddled together outside the zipped entrance flap. For reasons he couldn't immediately identify, Bliss felt a brief pang of anxiety as he approached them. There was no good reason why he should feel any unease; these were his friends and colleagues, after all. He quickly shook off his vague concern, swallowed thickly and continued on, forcing a wide grin as one by one his old team noticed him drawing closer.

'Well, I never,' DS Bishop said, extending a hand for him to shake. 'If it's not the venerable Mr Bliss himself. Or are we still allowed to call you Jimmy?'

'Only if I'm still allowed to call you a dozy twat,' Bliss said, winking as their grips tightened. 'How're you doing, pal?'

'I was doing very nicely, thank you, until we got called out to this shitshow.'

'Bad one, is it?'

Bishop grimaced and sucked between his teeth. 'A couple of mid-teen lads, by the look of them. Both sliced to ribbons in addition to having something corrosive poured over their faces.'

'Ouch. That sounds like overkill.'

'Yeah. Possibly hit with a stun gun as well. Looks professional and pre-planned. Oddly, though, they were both found with their phones resting on their chests.'

Bliss nodded as if the peculiarity made perfect sense. 'Drug dealers? Runners, maybe?'

'We all had the same thought. The level of violence and the use of acid on two young males during the same incident is unusual outside of the drugs business. You weren't slow in picking up on that, Jimmy. Lost none of your skills since you've been gone, my friend.'

'It's only been a few weeks, you berk.' Bliss shook his head then turned to exchange a few words with the rest of the team. DCs Ansari, Gratton, and Virgil seemed pleased to see him, each of them offering wide smiles of appreciation. Chandler, who had been deep in conversation on her phone, ended the call and nodded in his direction.

'The boss says hello again and welcome back,' she said, referring to DCI Warburton. 'She also said to tell you that if this is too big too soon on top of the cold case, just say the word and she'll bring in another SIO.'

'I think we'll be all right,' he answered quickly. 'My new colleagues have plenty to be getting on with in my absence.'

'What are you looking into?' DC Ansari asked him. 'Anything interesting?'

'A murder from 1999. Shooting. Bit of a puzzle, but then it wouldn't be an unsolved if it wasn't. Takes time to wrap your head around it, though. We're all used to active cases and working under extreme pressure, so taking our time and reviewing what's gone before doesn't feel quite right. But it'll come. Anyway, who wants to do the honours by filling me in about this one?'

Bishop stepped up. He looked better than he had in some time, having taken a few weeks off work to get his mind right following a breakdown during Bliss's last few days as a DI. 'Obviously we're going to have to wait on the post mortem to firm up on the time of death, but crime scene indicators suggest some time on Saturday night. As you'd anticipate if they were dealing or even just running, neither had any ID on them. But then there's the phones to consider.'

'Yeah, that's unusual. You'd expect whoever killed the boys to have pinched them.'

'Precisely. Both are Nokia 106 burner-type devices, which suggests the possibility they were involved in a county lines operation. Presumably, whoever topped them had a good look at the contacts and messages before leaving them on display for us.'

'Whoever did this is sending a message,' Bliss said, glancing across at the tent. 'Same goes for the overkill. I dare say we'll eventually find the pair of them were running for a gang. My money is on them being murdered like this as a warning to others. Leaving the phones is part of the same message.'

'Which would be…?' Chandler prompted him.

'Our offender, or more likely offenders, killed the lads to let a rival know how serious they were. In leaving the phones, they were letting whoever ran the victims know they've had access to contact information, calls and messages going in and out, and that others can expect to go the same way.'

'But how? They couldn't be certain how much of this scene we'd reveal to the media.'

'I'm betting they took photos. Possibly even filmed it. Whatever they shot has probably already been sent to every number on those two phones.'

'Shit!' DC Virgil hissed. 'I hope that didn't include family members.'

Shaking his head, Bliss said, 'I doubt it, Alan. Not on their burner phones. Even kids their age will have had it drummed into them not to save any personal identifiers.'

'Yeah, you're probably right. Besides, if they had, I dare say we'd have heard about this sorry mess long before they were found.'

'Who did come across them?' Bliss asked, looking around for any anxious civilians being corralled by uniforms.

'A couple of canoeists,' Bishop told him. 'They were taking photos for a website they're building. One of them crossed the bridge and came close to the scene to get a decent distance shot of his mate over by the mere. He spotted the bodies and called it in.'

'This was this morning?'

'No. Yesterday evening. Evidently, the lighting was ideal for the photo shoot. Which reminds me, the scene isn't quite straightforward on our part. The responding officers requested a duty inspector, but nobody was immediately available, so they put in a call to their own sergeant. He eventually handed it off, leaving Diane to take the shout. She said it was obvious from speaking to the response team and CSI that there was nothing the rest of us could do until today, because the scene was still being secured and SOCO had only just begun to collect evidence. She figured there'd be no worthwhile access for us until daylight.'

DCI Warburton had made a judgement call. The right one as far as Bliss was concerned. He didn't see a problem with the escalation issues, either. The first responders had acted appropriately and delays in getting an inspector on scene were not unheard of.

'Okay, so tell me where you lot were on this when I arrived. Consensus?'

'Pretty much the same as your initial instinct,' DC Ansari told him. 'Going by the way they were murdered and the burner phones, most likely a couple of runners topped by another gang. Letting other lines know who the boss is in the city.'

'Not in our fucking city they don't,' Bliss shot back with a snarl. 'Not without a fight from us, anyway. From what I understand, there have been a number of threats, a few stabbings, but no outright warfare in quite a while. This is a serious escalation.'

'We're agreed,' Bishop said with a nod. 'Our first task is to ID both victims and go from there.'

'Did the use of corrosive include their hands?'

'No. Faces only.'

Bliss turned to DC Virgil. 'Alan, have a word with the crime scene manager. Ask them to put a rush on the prints they pulled from the bodies. Pretty please with a cherry on top, if that's what it takes. Cheers. Oh, and while you're at it, let them know there's the same urgency in dusting the mobiles for prints, swabbing them for DNA, and then getting them across to digital forensics.'

Turning back to the others, he said, 'As soon as they release those phones back to us we can go through the messages to see if any of them provide us with some useful intelligence.' He then opened up a discussion regarding routine procedures. DS Bishop was the first to react.

'You're much more familiar with this area than most of us, Jimmy,' he said. 'So, you'll know it isn't exactly the best for CCTV. We'll grab what we can from the car park, but that'll be it.'

Bliss pointed beyond the flowing expanse of water. 'You're forgetting the tracks you crossed before you reached the bridge. The Nene Valley railway runs alongside the opposite embankment, and the Orton Mere station is just over the river. You can't see it from here because of the trees on the other side, but it could have its own security cameras, possibly covering its own small car park as well, so you never know what else it might have captured.'

The DS jabbed a finger in his direction. 'That's why you're the boss.'

Bliss smiled. 'Ex-boss,' he reminded Bishop. 'But if CCTV

doesn't give us anything notable, then we may be scuppered. Likely candidates to have done this?'

'Nobody leaps out,' DC Gratton said with a shrug. 'We're aware of the use of knives and machetes in the recent past, but these two kids were sliced open to an extent we've not seen before. As for using acid, I've never encountered that in my entire career.'

'There was an acid attack on a Wisbech woman a few years ago,' Ansari said. 'And if I remember rightly it was also used in a burglary, again a good few years back. There was a dealer who threw ammonia in a woman's face back in 2019, but that's about it as far as I can recall. Nothing like we've seen with this one.'

Bliss nodded. 'We're going to need a word with the drugs squad, the intelligence team, and CID. If this sort of frenzied attack is unprecedented, then we might well have a new gang operating in the area. Either that or an existing one making a play. These two lads might not be the last, and that's something none of us wants.'

'I'll mention it to Diane when we get back,' Chandler assured him. 'She might want to organise a meeting.'

Bliss shook his head. 'You forget, I'll be coming back with you. If Diane wants me as SIO on this one, then I'm up for it. You and Bish can join us while I have a word with her.'

'I just can't get away from you, can I?'

'No danger of that, Pen. I'm the ghost of the past, the present, and your future.'

Chandler shuddered. 'What did I do in a past life to deserve this?'

He laughed. 'You got yourself knocked up, realised you needed some stability in your life, and joined the police force.'

'It was rhetorical,' she called out after he'd turned to head back to his vehicle. She cupped both hands around her mouth. 'Rhetorical!'

SEVEN

BLISS DIDN'T THINK HE'D ever be overjoyed to see the inside of a Major Incident Room again, but he found himself buoyed as he stood front and centre, his stomach fluttering in anticipation of conducting another investigation. The awful truth was that it had taken the murder of two young boys to create the opportunity, but when people were killed, somebody must step up. So why not him?

'Thank you all for being punctual,' he said, pleased to see eager and familiar faces. 'Especially Lydia Keene, our crime scene specialist, who had to shoot back from Huntingdon to join us. This is not the first time I've stood up here before you, and hopefully it won't be the last. I've even done so before as SIO. The difference this time is whereas I previously had someone else – latterly DCI Warburton – to do the donkey work for me, that's no longer the case. Diane has graciously offered to help me out as much as possible, and has accepted the role of deputy SIO, but I'll be taking on more of the burden of admin and paperwork and enduring leadership meetings this time. Please bear with me, because if I'm making notes as the case progresses, then inevitably it'll slow me down. Any questions?'

Chandler's hand shot up. 'Yes. Tell us, what's it like to day release from the nursing home?'

Bliss laughed along with everyone else. He pointed at his old partner. 'Just for that, the next round of snacks is on you. Anyone else want to push their luck and get gobby with me? No. Good. Because Penny here would have to double her IQ just to be a halfwit, and I sincerely hope the rest of you are better than that.'

More laughter. With a smile on his face he let it fade away before continuing. 'Okay, so our random operation name is Scarecrow. I've classified these murders as category A, with the real possibility of being elevated to A+. That's an indicator of how seriously this is being treated in terms of potential threats to the wider community.'

'What if it's confined to just the gangs?' DC Gratton asked.

'A drugs war over territory affects everyone who lives in or close to that territory. We can't have that. And if we're looking at organised crime as opposed to a piddly little wannabe drugs outfit, then things can turn nasty in a heartbeat.'

'We don't even know that it is drugs related yet, do we?'

'No,' Bliss conceded. 'Not for certain. But it's walking, swimming, and quacking like a duck right now, so that's our initial hypothesis. If we're proven wrong, we'll deal with it. But for the time being, that is our focus. The usual suspects have established a gold group, this one headed by DCS Fletcher and including DSI Edwards, DCI Warburton, and myself. I requested both DS Chandler and DS Bishop be included at bronze level, which was accepted. Clearly, the murders and our investigation into them will draw a great deal of media scrutiny. Gold and silver officers will handle that side of things. As SIO, I may have to make an appearance at some stage, but we all know my lack of tact can be a risk in that area.'

Bliss waited for the chuckling and general mirth to subside before moving on. His disputes with reporters were legendary, and he paid no attention to the relevant jokes made at his expense. 'Family and community liaison are an urgent priority the moment we identify our two lads. DSI Edwards is urgently assessing the relevant impact statement, due to the inevitable need to fight fires when news of what happened is released to the public. Any questions so far?'

Heads shook. No one raised a hand. Bliss continued. 'I'm satisfied with the securing of the scene, the victims, and the evidence. I assessed all actions taken prior to my arrival at the crime scene earlier this afternoon, and in my opinion, everything that should have been done was done. Again, I'm happy with that element of this Op. I've opened up a policy book, so from this point on I will log all decisions and their justifications. You all know the drill, but as this is my first SIO job as a civilian, I want to make sure I'm ticking all the boxes.'

'First time for everything,' Bishop said, prompting more laughter.

Bliss stared him down. 'I did warn you. Bish, you are sharing snack duty with Pen. Now, then, I think we can all agree that our golden hour opportunities are long gone and out of the window. Identifying our two victims is still the top priority. Once we've done so, we shift into fast-track mode. If these two lads were involved as runners as we currently believe, then we clearly have a starting point when it comes to finding possible offenders. Whichever gang the boys belong to, we look hard at the opposition.'

'Could this not be the work of their own people?' DC Virgil asked, hand in the air.

Bliss found him with his gaze and nodded. 'It could, Alan. And we won't rule out the possibility. As I mentioned earlier, I believe the overkill was designed to send a message, and yes that message would be as effective if aimed internally as a warning to other runners. But at this early stage, I think we're right to look at opposing gangs first.'

'What intelligence can we rely on?' DS Bishop asked.

'My own small command team will be speaking with CID, intel, and our drugs teams to obtain a list of names and the most likely offender candidates. You'll be involved in that. If this is the work of a recognised organised gang, we'll also reach out to ROCU. In theory, the Regional Organised Crime Unit ought to be liaising with local drugs teams when it comes to intel, but delays causing time lags are inevitable, and things can slip between the cracks.'

'What's the thinking on location?' DC Ansari asked.

Bliss shrugged. 'Indeed. Why there? But then, why not there? It's as good a place as any, and better than most. What we have to ask ourselves is how the victims and the offenders travelled there, and did the offenders use the same mode of transport when they left? How significant is the location in terms of its proximity to local townships, the parkway, even the A+ which is not far away by vehicle? What degree of planning might that have entailed? Were the boys lured there, ambushed there, or taken there by the offenders? All questions we need to provide answers to.'

He let that sink in, then added, 'There's an awful lot to do, so many questions to answer, and as soon as we have IDs we can really ratchet things up. Our initial hypothesis is based on the sheer brutality of the violence used in carrying out the murders, coupled with the discovery of the two burner phones. If we had a single victim, I might be looking at alternative motives and perhaps even a random attack, but given we have two at the same time, in the same way, and in the same location, I suspect we're on the right trail in looking at them as runners and their deaths therefore relating in some way to the drugs trade. Knowing who they are and potentially being able to connect them to an OCG opens the door for us to step inside and turn our focus to the offenders.'

'The media are going to ramp up the angst factor when they learn the ages of these young lads,' DCI Warburton said. 'Undoubtedly, that will generate a certain amount of fear. We walk a fine line in, on the one hand trying to pacify the public by pointing to the murders being drug related, and on the other looking as if we're not taking them seriously for the same reason. As Jimmy indicated earlier, let me, Alicia, and Marion handle that side of things. I don't want anybody second-guessing themselves or being second-guessed. When it comes to our victims, you go about your business as usual.'

'With respect, boss,' DC Gratton said. 'This is far from being usual. My concern is we may have other bodies on our hands before we've even been able to identify the two from this morning.'

'I take your point, Phil. However, I suggest you keep your focus on what we have and what we know, and also in finding answers to unanswered questions. Speculating and also concerning ourselves with inevitable speculation won't do us any favours.'

Bliss stepped forward, hands raised. 'Look, we all realise we're dealing with something new and violently aggressive here. Whoever is responsible and whoever these victims prove to be, this is a major step up in terms of hostility. We can't discount the possibility of having additional victims on our hands, especially if there are reprisals. But Diane is right when she says now is the time to stick to the job in hand. Let's not forget, we don't yet know for sure that these lads are locals. We just have to hope prints and/or their mobile phones point us in the right direction asap. Lydia's team have released the two devices, which our tech specialists in Huntingdon are currently looking at.' His gaze alighted on Keene, who got to her feet.

A confident person, the CSI manager surveyed the entire group before speaking. 'Knowing the phones were likely to be critical in providing early intelligence, we concentrated our initial efforts on both those devices. My team taped, printed, and swabbed them. They are being analysed as I speak for fibres, blood, prints, and DNA. I can reveal that both phones had prints and blood smears on them. We also took prints from the bodies, of course. The ages of the victims may work against us in terms of identification, but it's certainly possible that either or both have recently been arrested and perhaps even charged. Let's keep everything crossed and hope for a break, because I doubt if their own mothers could recognise them at the moment.'

Bliss thanked the crime scene deputy manager and took a deep breath. He'd played this part on numerous previous occasions, but there was no doubt that it felt peculiar this time. Partly because of the nature of the crimes, but also because he felt different inside. No longer being a police officer meant he was no longer one of them. He liked to think that he had previously treated non-officer staff as part of the team, but the difference a warrant card made was marked.

He cleared his throat and said, 'I don't anticipate changing your usual roles. You each have favoured specialities, and I can see no reason why we would approach this any differently to the hundreds of cases we've worked together in the past. Identifying the victims will be the game changer. Until then, let's look at what we can be doing. In terms of the crime scene, there's a decent chance of gathering CCTV footage from the car park and possibly the steam railway station. Bish and Gul, that's yours to be cracking on with. And Gul, when we get results back from those mobiles, you pick up and run with whatever intel Huntingdon provides us with. Any bright ideas as to what else we can get stuck into?'

'With no house-to-house available to us,' DCI Warburton said, 'we're a bit stuck when it comes to witnesses. I realise we have no time of death as yet, but I doubt this was done in broad daylight. I suspect that rules out boat users and anyone being out for a stroll, but we ought to consider an appeal.'

Bliss agreed. 'I'd normally prefer to have our victim IDs when we do that, but in this case we should go with what we have. Hold off on the specific details relating to how they were murdered but identify the location plus what they were wearing and ask for any information on missing mid-teen males. In fact, let's get photos of their clothing and make them available. We won't be in time for the early evening local news, but we can certainly make the late broadcast. We can also get the appeal on our own social media pages, and work with the *Peterborough Telegraph* to get it up online as soon as.'

Warburton nodded. 'I can get that moving the moment we're done here. What else?'

'It has to be worth checking recently reported mispers. It's likely those two lads went missing Saturday night. That's two nights they haven't come home. Kids their age tend to get missed. Or am I being naïve?'

'A little bit,' Chandler piped up. 'If these lads are what we think they are, their parents might be glad to have them out of sight and out of mind. But I'll take a look at reports logged today and yesterday.'

'What do you want me and Alan to do, boss?' Gratton asked.

Bliss glanced at Warburton, before realising the DC had been talking to him. Only a month out of the Job and already he was questioning his role as a leader. He smiled kindly and said, 'Best make it just Jimmy. Diane's the boss. As for assigning you a task, you can help out as and where you can. To start with, if we're checking mispers, then we need to be doing so nationally. Pen will need help with that.'

With his colleagues busy, Bliss started making notes and writing in the policy book. After referring to a specific detail, he checked his wristwatch and put a call in to the fingerprint bureau based in Huntingdon, which served the Cambridgeshire region of the tri-force Scientific Service Unit shared with both Bedfordshire and Hertfordshire. He reeled off the forensic case number provided by Lydia Keene and requested an update on the fingerprints taken from both victims.

After being put through to the correct extension, he was told that one set of prints had come back with a name on record but was awaiting expert verification. 'That's good work,' Bliss said, feeling the tug of excitement. He picked up his pen. 'What name do you have, please?'

After a moment of hesitation, the voice at the other end of the line said, 'I'm sorry, but you know I can't release that information until it's been verified.'

Bliss puffed out his cheeks and made sure his frustration could be heard. Delayed second checking was so incredibly frustrating, but sadly all too familiar. He had rarely dealt with the fingerprint bureau in recent years, but on this occasion he was able to express himself.

'You mean you won't, not that you can't,' he insisted.

'No. I mean that I'm not allowed to. The verification process is in place for a reason.'

'I understand that. You want to avoid making mistakes. So do we. Look, I have no intention of releasing details or contacting next of kin. But having even a preliminary ID will give us a jump start on gathering intelligence. What can I do to encourage you?'

'I... I really am sorry. But SIO or not, I can't just...'

'You can,' Bliss interrupted, voice raised. 'And you know you can, so don't hide behind bureaucratic bullshit! Just forget about covering your own arse for one moment and let me have the bloody name. Please.'

Whether it was his harsh tone or the final, softer-spoken appeal, Bliss didn't know. Either way, it did the trick.

EIGHT

J IMMY BLISS SAT AT a shaded table on the raised patio outside his favourite local pub. The evening sky remained bright and cloudless, and the air was still pleasantly warm, with just enough movement to make him feel comfortable as he reflected on news the team had earlier received from the Hinchingbrooke county HQ. A sixteen-year-old by the name of Christopher Barrie had been identified as one of the murder victims. Since his arrest for possession with intent to supply a class B drug only seven weeks ago, the police had access to the young man's prints and DNA. Bliss had immediately asked DC Virgil to follow up on the Police National Computer as well as liaising with the drugs squad and intelligence team to gather further intel on Barrie and his known associates.

The evening briefing with his new UCT colleagues had passed off without incident. Beth Greenhill had traced ex-DS Ed Battersby, who had worked the original shooting investigation and who now lived thirty minutes north of the city in Bourne. She'd also gathered contact details for both DC Thomas Kerrigan, the last officer to have reviewed the case, and Reverend Iain Houseman. Foley and Corry had been equally busy, with a number of positive leads to chase up the following day. That suited Bliss, as he wanted to spend more time in his SIO role in the coming twenty-four hours.

Bliss had polished off his dinner and was enjoying a second pint of Guinness when a woman he immediately recognised pulled out a chair and plumped herself down opposite him. Max, who had been curled up by his feet, unwound himself and quickly became agitated. He reached down to fuss with the dog's head, soothing with stroking fingers.

'It's okay, boy,' he whispered. 'She's more friend than foe.'

'I thought I might find you here, you old reprobate,' Sandra Bannister said to him. She nodded at the glass in his hand. 'How many's that you've had?'

'You mean tonight or in my entire lifetime?'

'I don't think you can count that high, Jimmy.'

'Well, either way, it's none of your business.'

'What about the public's right to know?'

He grinned. 'As a reporter, it's your job to ask questions. As a… police employee, my role is to fob you off. But what exactly are you doing here?'

Bannister appraised him silently for a few moments. Eventually, she tilted sideways to peer down beneath the table. 'And who is this?' she asked, eyeing the still wary animal.

'Max is my rescue dog. He's a bit nervous with strangers, because of the abuse he endured at the hands of his previous owner. Don't worry about him. He'll settle back down.'

'He looks comfortable enough with you. I imagine you're good for each other.'

'I think you're probably right. Though I reckon I need him more than he needs me. But we're doing okay, which is all we can ask for.'

Bannister smiled and opened up her shoulder bag before withdrawing an envelope style folder from it. She slid it across the table towards him and tapped a finger on its flap. 'This is why I came. Most of the stuff we had on Justin Nolan is paper based only. And therein lies the problem, Jimmy. Typically, I resolve conflicts of conscience by reassuring myself that a good deal of the information I give you is online, or that it will eventually be made available online. That's not the case here. And there was sweet FA in our digital archives. I managed to dig out a folder, and it's all I have for you. Look at the contents or don't, but you might struggle to use what you find in there if you're unable to explain how you came by the information.'

Bliss knew the *PT* journalist was right. If he found something of value amongst the stack of documents she had provided, he'd have no way of detailing the source in any formal way. He nodded and said, 'We both know I'm going to look inside the folder. If there's anything in there that I can use, I'll have to work out a way to find an alternative source before I present it to my team.'

'And if you can't find another credible source?'

'Then I'll work through it logically and use what I'm able to explain away. Don't worry, I won't give up your name.'

Bannister leaned back but made no reply. She wore her usual smart-casual attire; a thin cardigan pulled over a multi-coloured ankle-length summer dress, flat shoes on dainty feet. Her cheeks glowed and her eyes sparkled. Bliss realised how fond of her he had grown. There was a point at which they might have had more together than this transactional relationship, but the moment was long in the past. He asked if she wanted a drink, but she shook her head.

'No, thanks. I have to get home. I have friends coming over later. I just thought I'd get this to you. I dropped by your house first, and when you weren't in, I thought I'd give this place a try before shooting off.'

'That's always a good bet.' Bliss nodded and smiled at her. 'And thank you, Sandra. I really appreciate it. Not that it's quid-pro-quo or anything, but regarding the incident over by Orton Mere, did you happen to pick up on the appeal for witnesses in addition to the initial statement?'

'Of course. I was going to speak to you about it tomorrow as soon as the second briefing came in.'

The statement he spoke of had merely indicated a 'serious incident' which police were treating with suspicion. Bliss knew DCS Fletcher wanted to hold back on any talk about murder until the identifications had been confirmed, so few further details had initially been provided. The decision to make an appeal had changed all that, and although they didn't provide the full facts, the discovery of two bodies was mentioned. He saw no reason not to alert this particular reporter to some of what they knew.

'You will be writing about murder,' he stated. 'Both of them. Bad. Vicious. I can't give you names because we don't yet have both confirmed. Neither can I give you any further information because we still have a great deal to verify and clarify before we're able to say who they are and why we think they were murdered. But I think that's enough for you to get started on a piece. You can fill in the blanks tomorrow.'

Bannister was grateful for the tip. 'Any theories?' she asked, prompting for something else he might be able to share with her.

'At this stage we suspect drugs involvement. But right now it's all supposition.'

She nodded. 'Thanks. I can write something up and use it or not. You look concerned, Jimmy. I can see you're troubled by this one.'

'I am. But more on that another time.'

'And the shooting from 1999?' she asked, eyeing the folder. 'Will there be anything in it for me?'

'If we solve it, yes.'

'You think you will?'

'Hard to say. It's been reviewed three times since it went cold, but this is complete reinvestigation will hopefully yield additional evidence. We also now have the missing murder weapon, so we're looking to make progress.'

'Okay, well keep me posted.' Bannister eased herself up out of the chair, then paused. 'How's that girl of yours?' she asked.

Bliss frowned, puzzled for a moment before realising who she was referring to. By his feet, Max stirred and huffed, disturbed once again by the reporter's movement. 'Oh, you mean Molly. Yeah, she's doing good, thanks. If her exam results go the right way, she'll be attending Bedford Uni studying forensic science.'

'Wow! Good for her. And not too far away, either. Will she stay with you and travel there and back?'

'I wish she would. I don't like the idea of her having to live in Luton.'

'And you can't persuade her otherwise?'

'No chance. Not in her first year, anyway. She wants the full immersive Uni experience.'

'Can't say I blame her. She can get all that debauchery out of the way before knuckling down to some proper study in her second and third years.'

'Not too much debauchery I hope,' he said uneasily.

Laughing, Bannister said, 'Are you sure you're not her father? You're certainly acting like it.'

Bliss arched his eyebrows momentarily, then let them fall back into place again. He'd rescued Molly from a sodden rooftop as the girl then just fifteen sought to end her life. Subsequent interactions had forged a bond between them that bordered on the familial. 'She has a perfectly good one of those back home in Torquay,' he said. 'He might not have a biological connection with Molly, but I can tell he loves her every bit as much as he does his own kid.'

'Fair play. It's great that she has that. But then she also has you in her corner. Not every teen has that second level of protection. That's one lucky girl, if you ask me.'

'I wouldn't go that far,' he said. 'Not with what she's been through. But, yes, things have turned her way now, and the life she's making for herself promises to be a good one.'

'Well, that's good to hear. I'm pleased for you both.'

'Cheers. By the way, how's Callum these days?' Bliss had rescued Callum Oliver, another *PT* journalist, from a disused fenland pumping station after the reporter had been abducted and left for dead.

Bannister sucked on her teeth. 'It didn't work out for him. He was off sick for six weeks or so following his ordeal. He started to phase back in gradually, tried some days working from home, but I think the mental and emotional trauma eventually became too much to bear. He left the paper and the city. As far as I know, he moved up to Nottingham.'

Bliss gave a grim nod. 'The poor sod came close to death. That's difficult enough to cope with, but the entire process will have stayed with him. Traumatic is probably an understatement. I know you never liked him much, but I'm sorry it ended up that way.'

'Believe it or not, so am I. We clashed when I realised he was after my job, and were not at all close, but I wouldn't wish that kind of torment on anybody. I can't begin to imagine how he must have felt being chained up in that awful old building, believing he was going to die from dehydration.' She shuddered and briefly rubbed her arms.

'Yeah, I know. Doesn't bear thinking about.'

Bannister shook her head abruptly. 'Right. I'm off,' she said. 'Bye Jimmy. Bye, Max.'

The dog huffed once more. Bliss smiled. 'He says goodbye.'

'I'm sure he does.'

'And thanks for asking about Molly,' he said before she left.

'Of course. I know how much she's come to mean to you.'

After she had gone, Bliss quickly polished off his drink and began the short walk back home. With Molly on his mind and Max by his side, he smiled all the way.

NINE

T HE FOLLOWING MORNING, AN invitation to attend a hastily convened joint task force meeting took Bliss by surprise. DCI Diane Warburton had notified him about it as he arrived at Thorpe Wood. When she asked if he wanted to be involved, he reminded himself that the 'civilian' tag associated with his new role was almost irrelevant at this stage. He was staff rather than an officer, but he was also the SIO for Operation Scarecrow, earning him a place in the room. Before heading upstairs, he'd left a message for his UCT colleagues informing them he would be late for their briefing.

The Assistant Chief Constable's presence confirmed the important nature of the meeting and how seriously it was being taken. However, it was the newly appointed Chief Superintendent Marion Fletcher who chaired the proceedings, her demeanour solemn throughout. The joint task force group comprised senior officers from the drugs team, CID, and the SCU, all from Thorpe Wood. Bliss and Intelligence Officer, Sophie Ballantyne, represented the staff side. And while he rightly kept his focus on the horrific murder of two young lads, he was also enthusiastic about addressing the wider-ranging possibilities.

He sat back quietly as others in the room said their piece. Fletcher's introduction included the goal of the JTF, to which Bliss gave a quiet nod of approval. Information that had come in overnight and first thing that morning confirmed they were on the right track in believing the two murders to be related to drugs gangs. Ballantyne took over the reins when asked to provide a more specific explanation.

'Essentially,' the intelligence officer said, 'the situation our city finds itself in has been coming for some time. We've witnessed disorganised chaos on the streets since DI Bliss – as he was at the time – and his team took Eric McManus and his crew off the map. Smaller gangs have since come and gone, working with little imagination or efficiency. That was always going to change, and gradually it did. Sad to say, there are now three OCGs all vying to fill the void. As we've already seen, this will only ever lead to a crimewave, resulting in increased levels of violence as the gangs jockey for position. They can see big money being made here, and none of them want to share that cash around.'

Bliss had felt the cut of a double-edged sword when he and his team disrupted Eric 'the eyeball' McManus's organised crime gang, which had left dozens of street dealers and five principal players behind bars. Nature might abhor a vacuum, but drug dealers will react swiftly to fill it because the rewards on offer can be vast. It might never have happened at all had it not been for his encounter with Molly, a county lines drug mule at the time. But now the proverbial chickens were coming home to roost. Sometimes good deeds ended up with poor outcomes.

DCI Brian Stanley, who ran Thorpe Wood's drugs squad, stood beside the projector screen to talk the group through a Power-Point presentation entitled Peterborough OCGs and County Lines. Its subtitles were 'Soke', 'Foxes', and 'City-Wide'. Bliss knew these were the names of drugs lines under investigation, the names originating from the gangs themselves as emphasised in various elements of intelligence. The Soke of Peterborough was a historical reference to an area surrounding the city, the use of the somewhat archaic term in this context was a surprise to Bliss. Foxes was the nickname of Leicester's local professional football team, which explained that one, and he speculated that the remaining line was named after its greater intended reach.

'Not too long ago,' Stanley began, 'Peterborough was either a way station for or on the receiving end of the county lines class A and B drugs business. Lines from London, Birmingham, and to a lesser extent Cambridge brought drugs into the city. We knew McManus was heavily connected to the London line known to us as Mayor. The emergence of the Soke line here resulted in drugs going out of Peterborough into surrounding towns and villages and even into places like Huntingdon, Wisbech, Grantham, and Northampton. The Foxes line from Leicester then muscled in, ferrying its drugs here in taxis. Now we have a third, who I'll come to presently. Any questions at this stage before I proceed?'

The ACC, Christopher Jackson, perhaps keen to have something on record, asked about overlapping line territories. The response he received gave the entire room a moment of consternation as it became clear that the city of Peterborough was up for grabs.

'As has already been pointed out,' DCI Stanley continued, 'we currently have three major gangs operating locally, each looking to become the top dogs in our city. The most entrenched is the Soke line run by Samantha Phillips. Its USP is local knowledge, support, and contacts. Saad Ali moved in from Leicester a while back and brought the weight of the Foxes line with him as an extension of his long-running county lines trade. We regarded it as a significant move at the time, and Phillips has been hard pushed to resist it. Soke has lost a few neighbourhoods, and there was rumour of pushback and counter pushback. Finally, our most recent intel tells us the latest move and the brand-new City-Wide line has come from Hector Karagiannis. It's a surprise shift if true.'

'The man has recently come to our attention,' DCS Fletcher said. 'He attempted to build a large casino in the city but ran into difficulties with his business partners over a side deal. Jimmy's team worked that Op.'

Bliss nodded, his gaze wandering. He wore an open-neck shirt today and was glad of it as the room was stifling. 'Never met the man himself. However, I do think we encountered one of his fixers. Karagiannis is clearly a shrewd operator and rarely raises his head above the parapet.'

'He was evidently looking to gain a foothold in this city,' Fletcher observed. 'And with the casino move on hold, he may have regarded drugs as his best way in.'

'Possibly,' Bliss allowed. 'But if we're saying this City-Wide line is already established, then he must have been setting it up at the same time as he intended to create the casino. Given the latter is a popular way to wash illegal cash, perhaps he deemed the two as essential to his plans.'

'You might be onto something there, Jimmy.'

'And by the way, if Samantha Phillips is the daughter of Sam, then I had a run-in with him a few years ago. He was shifting only cannabis at the time, and I wasn't aware of his kid branching out.'

'You're right about who she is,' Stanley confirmed. 'Her father stepped back after being diagnosed and treated for bowel cancer. Evidently, he's not long for this world. Against his advice and wishes, Samantha moved the business into the wider market.'

'What about his son?' Bliss asked. 'If I remember correctly he was the older of the two.'

'Passed over, according to our intel. Not the brightest bulb, by all accounts. He still works for the organisation, but his sister is the one running things. We were keeping a close eye on the Soke and Foxes lines, which was starting to get a bit tasty. The introduction of Karagiannis to the area appears to have thrown a large spanner into the works. We were already considering forming a JTF, and the murder of what we now know to be two young gang members convinced us to crack on with it even if we've not quite got all our ducks in a row. Peterborough has seen plenty of threats and attempted murders in the recent past, but these two victims have brought about a sharp focus – especially given their ages. Major Crime obviously has the lead on Operation Scarecrow, and rather than us trampling over each other's toes, we felt it best if we all came together as one to complete the bigger picture. Sophie, as our intel officer, will act as a central filter point.'

'Are we speaking to the NCA?' ACC Jackson wanted to know.

'Not at present, sir. We do intend having a word with ROCU to see what additional intel they can offer, but we wouldn't expect to involve them fully at this stage.'

Bliss nodded once more, approving of the decision. He had worked with the Regional Organised Crime Unit in Bedford, and they were a good first step. The National Crime Agency might yet have a role to play, but this was still early doors.

DCS Fletcher stood. She thanked the drugs team Chief Inspector, who retook his seat. Looking around the room, Fletcher's grave nod was one of foreboding. 'The challenge we face is potentially the greatest I've encountered during my time here at Thorpe Wood. We live with drugs-related criminal activity every single day, and we tackle it robustly as best we can. Various operations have helped enormously to remove a significant number of players and product from the game. But as we all know, for every one we manage to put away, another crawls out from beneath its rock. I'm sure you all appreciate how much harder the job has just become now that we have open warfare between organised gangs, even if you've never faced it before.'

She paused to rest her gaze upon DCI Warburton.

'Diane. Please let everybody know what the latest is on these murders.'

Warburton offered a tentative look of concern as she rose to her feet. 'It took longer than we would have liked to identify both victims. Even now we are still waiting for a second fingerprints expert to verify the identity of the slightly older victim, but we're confident. As you are all aware, they were both terribly disfigured in the attack. Neither had any ID on them, which is obviously standard protocol for these kids. Two basic mobiles were left at the scene – deliberately placed on the bodies, actually – and while they've been useful in gathering information, they initially provided few clues as to their owners. We eventually lucked out with one of the lads, whose prints we'd taken earlier in the year shortly after his sixteenth birthday. We were later able to ID his younger mate from information gathered, in particular a thread of messages between the two in which the younger victim's street name was used. Chris Barrie, street name "Rimmer", turned sixteen at the start of the year. His running mate was Jamie Ure, who went by "Midge". He was not quite fifteen.'

'Thank you. And how do you feel about negotiating your way through this JTF in addition to running a murder case?' Fletcher asked. 'DCI Stanley spoke about not stepping on toes, but that's bound to happen as priorities diverge.'

'Surely catching killers is always a priority,' Bliss said bluntly. 'No matter how much the bigger picture changes as the JTF makes progress, those two kids are at the forefront.'

The DCS peered at him. 'I understand where you're coming from, Jimmy. However, there may be occasions when that bigger picture you mentioned demands a response that doesn't quite fit in with Operation Scarecrow. So yes, catching whoever murdered the two boys is currently a major consideration, but avoiding further bloodshed is paramount.'

He thought about it for a moment, then nodded. The lads were gone and nothing he or the team did now could bring them back. Ensuring nobody else lost their lives was the goal for everyone in the room. 'Apologies,' he said. 'Preventing further loss of life is obviously essential. As SIO, I'm happy to work with others for the greater good.'

It was time for the most senior officer in the room to talk about steering the task force. Bliss knew ACC Jackson to be in his early sixties, but he looked lean and fit in his pristine white shirt without so much as a bulge at the stomach or waistline. 'For your information, I have informed the office of the Police and Crime Commissioner of recent developments and I have also promised to keep the PCC himself in the loop. It will not come as a surprise to any of you that bubbling beneath the murders and the potential for further violence are concerns about how this will play out in the media. I've been asked to communicate that any further statements and briefings must be cleared by either the PCC, CC, or myself. I will liaise closely with Chief Superintendent Fletcher and the Chief Constable in this regard.

'Now, to the investigation itself. The area drugs squad already has operations running in the city. The forming of this wider JTF and the subsequent larger remit can, we think, be considered an extension of that existing Op. So, while the MCU has the sole responsibility for Operation Scarecrow, it will also be part of the larger Operation Cuttlefish. Any questions?'

When there was none forthcoming, the ACC went on. 'Speaking to DCS Fletcher and DCI Stanley earlier, it became clear to me that our intel on the Soke line is good and current. When it comes to Foxes, it's a little more sketchy but still decent enough to know the names and roles of most of their people operating here in Peterborough, and many of those connected to the line source in Leicester. It's with City-Wide that we're coming up short. Clearly, improving that situation is one of our priorities. While the MCU continues with their investigation into the two murders, the rest of the JTF will put together a plan of action to prevent further bloodshed.' Jackson glanced across at DCI Stanley. 'Am I right in thinking our two victims worked for the Soke line?'

'That's correct, sir.'

'But what we don't yet know with any degree of certainty is whether it was Foxes or City-Wide OCG members who took them out.'

'Correct again. Our best guess at this stage is an escalation from Foxes, given they've been ramping things up of late.'

'Could it not just as easily have been a pre-emptive strike from City-Wide?'

'It could, yes. But they are still a very much unknown factor in all this, whereas our Leicestershire counterparts tell us that Saad Ali and his crew are suspected of several drugs-related murders, stabbings, shootings, and beatings. They have muscle who are tooled up and willing to use them.'

The ACC nodded. 'Very well. Are you and DCS Fletcher happy to work on gathering intel on City-Wide, the OCG behind the line, and confirming as best you can who carried out these vile murders?'

'Yes, sir. Together with both Diane and Jimmy from the MCU, of course. But before we can draw up a plan of attack, we have to first be sure who did what and when. We also need to be aware of reprisals. If Soke confirms before we do who took out their runners, I think we can be sure of a reaction.'

'I expect that's the case.'

Bliss raised a hand to interrupt the exchange, feeling as if the pair were talking around him. 'With respect, while I don't actually think it's the case, we still can't rule out some form of internal punishment on these lads from their own gang. It's a line of inquiry we can't afford to overlook.'

He received nods of agreement as his arm came back down by his side.

Sophie Ballantyne was next to raise a hand, index finger extended. 'One thing I'd like to know before we go much further,' she said, 'is what our end goal is here. My team and I can gather, research, evaluate information, and identify patterns, but it would help us enormously if I knew what the expected or intended outcome was. How do we measure the success or failure of this task force?'

It was a great question and one the ACC backed away from by lowering his head rather than meet the gaze of others. Detective Superintendent Fletcher accepted the responsibility to respond. 'I think there are several outcomes we'd regard as successful. Preventing the widespread outbreak of a drugs war would be one. Keeping the body count down to two would be another. But ultimately, what I think we'd most like to achieve here is removing the county lines drugs business from our streets. Like every other town and city in the country, we can't expect to remove the trade itself. But I want these gangs to know they are not welcome in Peterborough. That our intention is to drive them out and keep them out. Also, if Operation Scarecrow is now a part of Operation Cuttlefish, then another success will be identifying, locating, arresting, and charging whoever is responsible for the murder of those two lads.'

'I agree,' Bliss said, though nobody had asked for his opinion. 'And I think we should all also keep in mind that our two murder victims might also have been victims in other ways. Yes, they sell – or sold – drugs, but we don't yet know how or why. We don't know if someone applied pressure on them, or how much coercion they used, if any. They may turn out to have been mindless thugs looking to gain a street reputation. But they could just as easily have been exploited, so as SIO I will ensure the Major Crime Unit's officers and staff always keep that in the back of their minds.'

Bliss eased back in his chair and took in the exchanges that followed. From what he could tell, they were making all the right noises. Easy to do at this early stage, but once the media went at them, that might all change. Media priorities sometimes became Force priorities, but he felt the ACC had all the angles covered. And if he buckled, Marion Fletcher was unlikely to follow suit. Identifying the victims had represented a major step forward, but knowing precisely who murdered them was essential when attempting to form an appropriate response. He thought about his own SIO decision-making process. Unfortunately, that would involve visiting parents devastated by the news they would receive shortly after verifying the fingerprint.

TEN

UNUSUALLY FOR BLISS, HE didn't have much to say at the following briefing in the major incident room. So far there had been no related misper hits, and while the previous night's appeal for witnesses had resulted in several calls, upon closer inspection none of them were relevant to the investigation. The media showed a huge amount of interest and pushed hard for further updates, but through various channels he had let it be known that none would be forthcoming until after the two families were informed and formal identification had been made.

Compared to the vast spreadsheets she typically interrogated, the mobile phone data DC Ansari had received from digital forensics didn't amount to much. However, after noting a few names and their links to the victims, she entered them into the crime log. Meanwhile, intelligence on the two boys continued to seep in, much of it informative. The drugs squad were aware of their street names, but didn't consider either as real players. As surmised at the outset, they were little more than runners, earning a pittance selling for others on street corners.

'Were they pushed into the life or were they led?' Bliss wondered aloud. 'Let's dig into their backgrounds, Gul. Are these two kids who somehow and reluctantly fell foul of a gang making threats or were they up for it?'

'They wouldn't be the first to be forced into that way of life,' Ansari said.

The gathering and analysis of CCTV was proving to be a laborious task. The key problem proved to be the wide time window, currently set from an arbitrary 8.00pm on Saturday night to the time the canoeist discovered the bodies the following evening. DS Bishop hoped to narrow the window considerably after the postmortem, but he knew it could also grow wider.

'The one thing in our favour is we know the two boys were killed at the scene,' he told Bliss. 'CSI are confident that the volume of blood loss and the lividity created by pooling inside the bodies is consistent with them having been murdered where they were found. They definitely weren't topped elsewhere and then dumped beneath the flyover. Once we have an estimated time of death, we'll narrow our CCTV focus.'

'How about bus, taxi, and general dashcams?' Bliss asked. 'Orton Mere is the closest spot to the scene that you can drive to, and by some distance. At some point that night, at least one vehicle turned towards it from Oundle Road, and it also had to have returned. There's only one way in and out of that spot. With no cameras mounted at the traffic lights, we have to rely on whatever vehicles might have been passing that way at the time.'

'Yeah. Understood. But until we can narrow down the TOD we're stuffed.'

'I know, I know. It's asking a bit much with the information available to us at the moment. But it's something to pursue just as soon as you can, Bish.'

Bliss turned to Gratton and Virgil. 'I have a task for you to organise. I got caught up along with everyone else at there being no doors to knock on because of the crime scene location. But

I completely forgot about the mooring docks where I tie up my own boat. My fellow owners occasionally spend a night on board, so it'll be worth questioning them.'

Before he left to take the briefing with his new colleagues, he asked Chandler to request a record of their victims' known associates and to start drawing up a chart pinpointing which of them were most likely to be able to provide current information on both Chris Barrie and Jamie Ure.

'Going to be a long list,' she said. 'But I'll get it done. I also thought it might be worth asking the drugs squad to push their informants for recent intel. And didn't they have an undercover officer working the Millfield area?'

'They did, but I happen to know his handler pulled him out a couple of weeks back. As far as I know, he was mixing with smaller crews only, not OCGs. Nice idea about the informants, though. If a crew snatched Barrie and Ure up off the street, it'd be good to know precisely where from.'

Bliss paused to look around the room and consider his involvement to date. He couldn't think of anything else the team could be doing. Learning the identities of their victims had allowed them to make great strides, but the investigation wouldn't truly get going until they had notified and questioned the parents. Which reminded him to arrange for a member of the team to prepare the family liaison officers ahead of those notifications being made. He remained uneasy by what had happened, anxious to move the operation forward before things got worse. But from experience, he knew that each op had its own pace, its own beat that it marched to, seemingly unaffected by his team's efforts.

Smiling to himself, Bliss considered the thought. His team. Were they still his team, despite him no longer being a serving police officer? He pondered the question as he left the major inquiry room. When he walked into the Unsolved Crimes Unit office, he detected no frost in the air emanating from his colleagues. In fact, they appeared pleased to see him.

'Rumour has it you've caught a double murder,' Beth Greenhill said to him pleasantly. 'Grisly, by all accounts.'

Bliss quickly ran through the broader strokes, emphasising his priorities. 'But I'm here now,' he said. 'So, let's focus on our cold case. Ben and Guy, what do you have so far?'

Foley crossed over to the solitary wall-mounted whiteboard and used a black marker pen to indicate a bullet-pointed list. 'We began with the witnesses; the people who claimed to have heard the gunshots that night. We spent most of the afternoon tracing their current whereabouts, working through each one individually until we either had contact details or were able to draw a line through them.'

Nodding, Bliss said, 'I see three lines. What's the story there?'

'All three have passed away. Of the remaining four, only two still reside where they were living back in February 1999. I've arranged for me and Ben to interview them later this morning. As for the other two, we've already spoken to them. One had emigrated to South Africa, the other now lives in Kent. Neither had anything to add to their original statements, and when prompted could still recall the night in question and were confident they had correctly described what they heard at the time.'

'I'd have been shocked if you'd told me otherwise. I'm not expecting much from these interviews, but they have to be done. Good work on the tracing, you two.' He turned to Greenhill. 'How about you, Beth? Any progress on Reverend Houseman?'

Her response was enthusiastic. 'Yes. The church came up with the goods. I haven't made contact because I thought I'd wait for you to confirm if you wanted a face-to-face with him or not.'

'I think I'll leave him to you. I don't do well with religion. Plus, I'm more interested in chatting with our victim's wife and his work colleagues.'

'That's fine by me. I have their details, so it's just a matter of fitting them around your SIO work. Thankfully, none of them live too far away. Mrs Nolan has a place in Fotheringhay. Mr Nolan's ex-manager, Jeff Smalling, still lives in Werrington, while the assistant, Carrie Lott, is just down the road from us in Oundle.'

Bliss gave a satisfied nod. 'Perfect. Perhaps we can fit them all in during a single session.'

'I can try to arrange that. Ahead of those, you wanted conversations with somebody from the original case plus the last person to review it. I took a punt and guessed you'd be content with a phone call to the most recent case review officer, who is a DC Thomas Kerrigan, based in Cambridge. Ed Battersby was a DS on the 1999 investigation team, and I know you'll want to speak to him in person.'

'I do. I'll leave you to call DC Kerrigan, but I want you with me when I have a word with Battersby. As for the other three, let's spread the load. We'll both do Mrs Nolan and then divide and conquer with Nolan's manager and assistant.'

Nodding, Greenhill said, 'I'll get cracking on the arrangements right now.'

'Before you all pick up where you left off,' Bliss said. 'I want updates on actions we discussed at our last meeting. Specifically, enquiries made at the Post Office and Cuckoo pub in Alwalton, NABIS results, plus case records and exhibits.'

Corry informed him that NABIS had yet to examine the shell casing but had promised to fit it in that day. Foley had spoken with the current landlord at the pub, who quashed any hopes of a breakthrough by insisting nobody at the pub had worked there in 1999. Finally, Greenhill said she'd driven back to the village and had chatted with the elderly Postmistress who was working in the same branch at the time of the murder but had neither seen nor heard anything of value to the case.

Despite these minor setbacks, Bliss felt his pulse racing in a familiar way, invigorated by little squirts of adrenaline. He had fretted over how the two new roles he had taken on would mesh. An active case often took on a life of its own, with information and evidence coming in thick and fast in the early stages. With the unsolved shooting, they were going over old ground, albeit new to them. The SIO role was all-consuming, but previous experience told him there was always some down time, lulls in the investigation he hoped to take advantage of. And while he might have to limit his physical presence in this office, all three new colleagues were clearly more than competent and able to get the job done without being micro-managed. The arrangement was working well so far, though the new relationships were in their infancy. He couldn't deny how relieved he felt by the progress made and was already looking forward to the day ahead.

ELEVEN

THEY DROVE TO BOURNE in separate cars. That way, when they had finished interviewing ex-Detective Sergeant Ed Battersby, Greenhill could stop off at Werrington to speak with Justin Nolan's old manager Jeff Smalling while Bliss headed down to Oundle to interview Carrie Lott, the assistant. They would then meet up in Fotheringhay for the most difficult task of all in going over the victim's murder with his widow.

Battersby's large but unspectacular home was situated in a tidy close to the west of Bourne town centre, a short walk from the Forestry Commission. Decorated in neutral colours, the curtains and upholstery were a floral riot in stark contrast. A neat house, with everything in its place, Bliss almost felt uncomfortable accepting the offered seat on one of the lounge's two armchairs, with Greenhill taking the other. Battersby's wife made them hot drinks while the three ex-detectives made idle chit-chat about the Job and its many changes down the years. As soon as they had settled down with teas and coffees, their host was happy to get right into the Nolan case.

'One of the biggest of my career,' he said, eyes hooded as he reflected back. 'Not that the investigation amounted to much in the end.'

'Oh, why was that?' Bliss asked, as if he had only a vague notion of the case.

'Mainly because it lacked everything we needed for it to be successful. Nobody saw the shooting, nor the shooter, and not even the poor victim until it was too late according to our reading of the crime scene. Of those who admitted to hearing the shots, I think there were only three who bothered to look out their windows afterwards, and none of them saw a thing because of course by then it was already over. As for forensics, I think they got some footprint moulds which never amounted to anything. The killer clearly didn't get close to his victim, so we had no contact fibres, prints, or DNA to go on. We had no security footage, minimal phone data, none of which took us any further. All we really had was the bullet lodged into the fencepost, which was useless without the weapon to match it against. And try as we might, we found nothing in the backgrounds of either the victim or his wife to point us in the right direction. In short, we had bugger-all and it killed the op before it had even really started.'

Bliss was both pleased and distressed to see how much the case still affected the retired police officer. Pleased because it suggested the man had an affinity for seeing justice served but upset at the same time because the investigation clearly lingered in the man's thoughts after more than two decades, indicative of a mind refusing to let go.

'You obviously still have powerful emotions about this old case,' he said to Battersby. 'You think that's because you feel it never really got going or because you believe more could have been done?'

'Both, I suppose. When I look back, I'm so frustrated that we couldn't solve this one. Here was a decent man with a loving family, and we could find no reason at all why anybody might want him dead. So, yes, I wanted more. But it wasn't there. It just wasn't.'

Bliss looked hard at him. 'I'm sensing there's something else you want to say.'

'Not really. I mean, we did all that we possibly could have done. I was in the centre of the mix and believe me when I say we held nothing back.'

'But…?'

'But it always bothered me. Probably more than it should have.'

'Why, exactly?' Greenhill asked.

Battersby dropped his open gaze her way. 'Because none of it felt right, and that left behind lingering doubts. The consensus by the time we moved on was that Nolan just happened to be in the wrong place at the wrong time. That he was either shot at random by someone who had no idea who he was, or fell victim to a case of mistaken identity.'

'And neither reasoning did it for you, I take it?'

'No. No, it didn't. If this was some passing oddball looking to get his jollies by taking pot shots at a stranger, then why didn't we have more such cases? Oddballs like that don't satisfy their urges after one successful attempt. Yet nothing before or afterwards came anywhere close to having even a similar MO. But if it was mistaken identity, the moment the gunman realised their error they would surely have remedied it by taking out the person they were supposed to murder. Again, we had no such incident in the weeks or months following.'

'Leaves a nasty feeling in the pit of your stomach, doesn't it?' Bliss said. 'That sickening sense that you might have missed something.'

'Bloody right it does.'

'So, what do you think might have happened?' Bliss asked. 'Gut reaction?'

'Why not? It's sometimes the best reaction of all.'

'All right. Then and now, I believe someone intentionally targeted Mr Nolan and murdered him. We just never discovered by who or for what reason.'

'You're suggesting it was a hit of some kind.'

'I am. Not that it helps.'

Bliss nodded, then frowned as a thought occurred to him. 'This question might seem odd, Mr Battersby, but was much attention paid to the dog?'

'The… you mean Mr Nolan's dog? The one he was walking when he got shot?'

'Yes. There's no mention of the animal at all in the crime file.'

The ex-cop appeared puzzled. 'I'm not quite sure what you're getting at. How should the dog have featured exactly?'

'I can think of two things off the top of my head,' Bliss said, pleasantly, as if they were of little concern. 'First of all, seven people heard the gunshots, yet nobody reported hearing a dog barking.'

'They were reporting possible gunshots. I think they might have overlooked or disregarded a barking dog. That's if it even did bark.'

'Perhaps. And you could well be right. But a stranger approached Mr Nolan, got close enough to shoot him twice in the chest and then closer still to make the shot to the head. Then he had it away on his toes. All that, its master slumped to the floor in obvious distress, and the dog doesn't go even a little bit berserk? I've not had my Max for long, but I reckon he'd go off on one if the same thing happened to me.'

Battersby continued to stare at Bliss, but said nothing.

'What was the second thing?' Greenhill asked. 'You said you could think of two off the top of your head.'

'I saw no report of the dog being checked out by SOCO. I would have regarded it as potential evidence. For all we know, the animal might have taken a chunk out of our offender's leg.'

Battersby nodded, perturbed by the implication. 'I do recall something about that now that you mention it. If I'm remembering this right, the dog made its way back home after the shooting. Most likely did so the moment Nolan released its lead as he died. I can't be sure, but in replaying that night over in my head I don't think anybody in the team asked for the dog to be checked over.'

'It's probably nothing,' Bliss said with a deep sigh. 'But equally, it could have been everything at the time. If that dog had the shooter's blood on it…'

'Don't hold me to my memory,' Battersby pleaded. 'The SIO could have actioned it without me ever knowing.'

'I'll be checking into it,' Bliss assured him.

'I gather you've revived the case because of additional evidence. The discovery of the gun. Anything further with that?'

Bliss and Greenhill exchanged glances. Ed Battersby had worked the investigation as a Detective Sergeant, but he was no longer a police officer. After a moment, Bliss nodded and Greenhill said, 'The weapon will prove evidentially crucial at a later date. We're exploring the potential of other cases where the weapon might have been used, but so far there's no history attached to it. We have asked for the casings found inside the gun, a revolver, to be printed. You never know your luck.'

'I hope you get more of that than we did. The good kind, that is. What about Mrs Nolan? Sarah, I think her name was. Have you spoken with her?'

'We will be later on today,' Bliss replied. 'I wanted to have a chat with you first, to get a feel for the original investigation.'

'I'm surprised you didn't choose to speak to Matty Cleland. It was his investigation.'

'Like you, we work cases,' Bliss explained. 'We know the sergeants are usually all over it from top to bottom. Speaking of which, when you say everything that could have been done was done, is that a genuine statement or something you say out of loyalty to your old MIT?'

For the first time, Battersby raised a smile. 'I can see why you'd ask. Nobody likes to fail, and that one does feel like a failure. But no. I'm sure you went through the case file before visiting me, and I imagine you couldn't find any gaping holes in our investigation. Other than the dog, perhaps.'

'You're right. On both counts. But not everything ends up making the case file, does it?'

'If it didn't, then it didn't belong. There were no screw ups. Nothing we failed to explore. It just wasn't there, unfortunately.'

'I'm inclined to agree with you,' Bliss said. 'However, that does leave us with a problem. Because unless your consensus at the time was bang on, Justin Nolan was deliberately gunned down that night back in February 1999, and we still don't know why or by whom.'

*

Carrie Lott provided no additional information. She had worked as Nolan's assistant for over three years, and still regarded him as one of the best and brightest. As per her original statement, she was as certain as she could be that her boss had been his usual self up to and including the day he was shot dead. Greenhill reported having a similar conversation with Nolan's manager, Jeff Smalling. He recalled being stunned by the news, and described Nolan as the last person anyone would imagine losing his life in such a way. Neither of the murdered man's colleagues could think of anything that hadn't occurred to them at the time.

Bliss and his new colleague discussed their separate interviews at a quiet table inside the Falcon Inn, a house-sized pub and restaurant with a huge conservatory dining area to the rear in the tiny village of Fotheringhay. The only thing Bliss knew about the village was that its castle, razed almost four-hundred years ago, was where Mary Queen of Scots was tried and subsequently beheaded before being buried some fourteen miles away in Peterborough Cathedral.

The pair managed to squeeze in a quick drink and a sandwich before arriving on time for their appointment with Sarah Nolan at her home just on the northern side of the Nene. The widow had never remarried, and neither had she changed her name. Now in her late fifties, she shared her home with a partner who had retired earlier in the year and who studiously kept out of their way when discussing the murder.

'It was a normal evening in every way to begin with,' Nolan told them as they sat around a sturdy wooden table on the patio in the back garden. 'Justin came home from work, changed into more comfortable clothing, before pulling on his heavy winter coat and boots and taking Beano for his usual evening walk. My husband was a popular figure in the community, which meant the same walk could take him ten or fifteen minutes longer to complete depending on who he met along the way. In truth, I hadn't even had time to puzzle over his lateness when I was told about the shooting. I had a neighbour watch over our children while I rushed to Justin's side. To my eternal regret, I was too late. By the time I reached the cemetery, he was already gone.'

'I'm so sorry,' Beth Greenhill said gently. 'I can't imagine going through such an ordeal.'

'I barely recall much else about that evening,' the woman admitted. 'Being told about it is clear to me. So too my rising panic and fear and dread, I suppose, as I ran towards the church.

After that it all gets hazy, the specific details lost to me all these years on. The next thing I can clearly remember is having to break the news to our two children. And I think that only sticks because it's the hardest thing I've ever had to do in my entire life.'

'Tell us what you remember about the investigation,' Bliss said, moving them on to what he hoped was safer ground.

Nolan met his even gaze. 'The fact is, I don't know how to respond to your question. I mean, how much should the next of kin be involved? You see things on TV shows, you read things in books, but you don't really have a clue what's happening. After being interviewed, I had access to a family liaison person, but as for the man running the investigation I think I probably spoke with him only on two or three further occasions.'

'Each officer has their own way of working with families,' Bliss acknowledged. 'I wouldn't draw any conclusions from that. Can I assume that he updated you during at least one of those conversations, informing you that the investigation had led to no suspects and therefore no arrests?'

'Yes. He assured me the case wouldn't be closed, but that as the police had explored all avenues they would subsequently prioritise other investigations and put my husband's on the back burner.'

'That must have been hard to accept. All I can say, as somebody new to the case, is that from our initial findings, the team did their job perfectly well but simply had no worthwhile evidence with which to build a viable case. But in terms of when you were spoken to, Mrs Nolan, is there anything, anything at all, that you can think of now that wasn't apparent to you at the time? Something that has occurred to you since that may not have seemed significant enough to report, but is simply different or additional to what you originally told the investigators?'

The woman shook her head with some vigour. 'Nothing,' she said. 'Nothing at all. My husband was a good man. He had no issues at work, and even if he had, his job was not important enough for anyone to wish to kill him over it. He and I had a loving relationship and a strong marriage. I was asked about fidelity at the time and can assure you as I did the officer who asked me back then that we were both faithful. I know for a fact I was, and I've never questioned Justin's commitment to me and his children.'

Bliss thought back to the case file and the documented interview with Sarah Nolan. His mind lingered on one particular segment. 'There was mention of a Mr Trimley,' he said, watching her eyes.

She blinked and shook her head. 'Oh, that. What I can tell you about him is precisely what I said at the time. His name came up more as a joke than anything else in our house. David Trimley was an odd-job man we came to rely on. Justin joked he had to be my fancy man given how much work he did for us and how often he'd come home to find David working on something in the house or garden. No, the fact was, Justin was too busy and, I have to confess, not great when it came to DIY. So yes, we employed David to do many a small job. But that's all he was.'

'Your neighbours were less convinced of that, according to what we've read,' Beth Greenhill interjected. 'A couple of them mentioned his name in connection with you. They suspected there might be more between you two than you've told us.'

Nolan snorted. 'They were ones to talk. I know exactly who you mean and believe me if David was having relations with someone outside of their marriage, it was one of them hideous gossips. Perhaps even both. Look, there's no point in my denying that he was an attractive man. He had the gift of the gab, too. And yes, I freely admit he tried it on once or twice with me. But I knocked him back and he accepted it.'

'So, we're not talking about an unrequited love? One Mr Trimley thought he might do something about by removing Justin from the equation?'

The question impressed Bliss. They had not discussed Trimley ahead of the interview, considering him to be a false and unpromising lead. But Greenhill had followed his line of questioning unrehearsed just as smoothy as if the two had practiced in the car only minutes earlier.

This time, Nolan came close to laughing. 'Not at all. It was nothing like that. He fancied himself as a ladies' man, enjoyed a bit of flirting, and when he got nowhere with me, he moved on to the next.'

'Did you two keep in touch afterwards?' Bliss asked.

'You mean after I put him in his place or after my husband was murdered?'

'Both.'

'Yes. To both. In fact, he continued to do odd jobs for me. We kept in touch until I moved out of the area. But it was purely a platonic customer and business operator relationship. What's more, David was only ever sympathetic about what had happened and never again made a play for me.'

It was as Bliss had suspected. Even so, he made a mental note to locate and interview David Trimley. The original investigators had spoken to him informally, dismissing him from their thoughts at the conclusion of their conversation. It was a lead he thought would go nowhere, but was perhaps worthy of at least a follow-up.

Bliss asked Nolan how her children were, wondering how they had coped with the loss of their father. He was pleased to learn that both were content and happy with their lot, and that, although affected by Justin's murder, neither had allowed his absence to dictate their own futures. It showed a strength of character Bliss suspected came from their mother. He looked across at Greenhill and raised his eyebrows. She shook her head, telling him she had no further question of her own.

'One last thing before we shoot off,' he said to Nolan. 'It's just an itch I'd like to scratch. Your husband was walking the dog when he was murdered, yet in the case notes there's no mention of the animal itself. A DS who worked the investigation had it in his head that the dog ran off and headed straight back home. Does that sound about right as far as you can recall?'

She gave a faint smile as she nodded. 'It's weird how you react. I have this awful memory of worrying about Beano even as I hurried to be with my husband. I later found out that he'd found his own way home shortly after I'd left.'

'So not straight home, then?'

'Sorry?'

'Whoever told you your husband had been shot reached you before the dog did, suggesting he took his time.'

'I suppose that must be right. I just assumed...'

Bliss shook his head reassuringly. 'I'm sure it's of no consequence. The person who found your husband arrived within a couple of minutes of the shooting, and it would have taken only a couple more to reach your house if they ran all the way. According to our timeline, they were using the back way into their property as they arrived home from work, spotted your husband on the ground, saw what was wrong and instantly headed over. I realise it's more than twenty years ago, but does that sound about right?'

'Yes. As far as I'm able to recall. That was Wade Deacon. I didn't know the family well, but he and Justin had enjoyed a pint or two together in the Cuckoo.'

'Yes, I believe he was named in our crime logs. He made a full statement later that same night. Going back to your dog, Beano, do you happen to recall if the crime scene people checked him over?'

'Not to my knowledge, no.'

Bliss decided he didn't know if it was important or not. Presumably, if the scene investigators had taken swabs from the dog and had found something of use, they would have made entries in the crime book. Their absence suggested the animal had been overlooked, and as it was now impossible to know if that was a critical error, he decided to follow it up but not lose any sleep over it. He'd mention it in his report, but he wasn't going to make a big deal of it.

'I don't know if it means anything, but I did just remember something,' Nolan said, her features suddenly twisted with anxiety. 'I… I didn't mention this at the time. I'm pretty sure I wasn't functioning properly, and either I forgot or didn't think it was worth mentioning. But actually, Justin did have a change of mood not long before he was killed.'

'Tell us about that,' Bliss said, looking up. 'We can then decide if it's useful or not.'

'It was the December. Shortly before our last Christmas together. He was a bit gloomy, which was unusual for Justin, as he loved everything about Christmas. When I asked, he said it was nothing. Just a bit of bother with a contract. Somebody had made a complaint about him, which he'd found upsetting. But then when he came home on Christmas Eve, his mood was much improved. Back to normal. He told me his situation at work had been resolved, that the applicant had dropped the complaint. That was it. I really never thought about it again until just now.'

'Thanks for telling us about it. We'll give the matter some thought. I can't say if it'll be useful or not at this stage, but it's an anomaly which I'm always interested in.'

They left the house no closer to solving the case, but no more despondent for it as neither had expected to discover a smoking gun or a silver bullet. So far, they were only demonstrating just how difficult a case the original team had been given. Bliss could only imagine little would improve in the coming days.

TWELVE

FOLEY AND CORRY WERE out of the office conducting their own interviews, so when Bliss left Beth Greenhill to it back at the UCT, he asked her to ensure the three of them updated the review file and produced written reports on their findings to date.

'If you don't mind my bringing it up, how do you think it's going so far, Jimmy?' she asked him as he was heading out.

'Pretty much as expected,' he admitted, a little glum at the admission. He leaned against the frame of the door. 'Having fresh evidence available to us looked promising at the start, but unless they come back with prints on the casings we're still grasping at straws as far as I can tell.'

'I think you could be right. How about our esteemed colleagues? What do you make of them?'

Bliss smiled, unwilling to get drawn in at this early stage. He sensed that nothing he said to Greenhill would go any further, but he couldn't be certain. 'Both seem personable enough. And all three of you are clearly still very much able to do the job. We're doing everything right, but I'm just not convinced we'll improve on previous reviews.'

'I don't know about that. From what I can tell, they were cursory at best. I think this team is already doing more than that. The dog angle was a good spot. I think the original investigators missed that.'

'Me, too. Not that it helps us now.'

'Ben was looking into the casing prints, but as he's not around would you rather I chased them up again?'

He shook his head. 'They'll be as quick as they can be. Active cases will take precedence, but we'll get our opportunity.'

'Let's hope it turns that frown upside down.'

Bliss laughed. 'You have kids, I take it?'

Greenhill chuckled, rolling her eyes. He noticed a flush creep across her cheeks. 'I'm so embarrassed. That was such a mum thing to say. And yes, I have two. No longer kids, of course, but my children all the same. Actually, the last time I used that expression was with my granddaughter.'

'You're a grandmother?' Bliss blurted out before he could stop himself.

'Is that so strange? My daughter is in her early thirties.'

'Sorry. You just don't look… like a grandma. I know that's such an old-fashioned thing to say, but you don't.'

'I'll take that as the compliment you meant it to be.'

Bliss nodded. He thought the colour in her cheeks deepened. 'Some might say it was a crass remark, but thanks for taking it in good spirit. So, you'll write everything up, update the review file?'

'I will. Oh, and I'll chase up Reverend Houseman just to complete the set. I'll also make sure Corry and Foley do as you ask. We'll see you again when?'

He sensed she was now keen to have him leave, mortified by their clumsy exchange. He apologised once more, but she flapped it away and insisted it was not a problem. Before leaving her to it, they agreed he'd be back to run a briefing the following morning.

The major inquiry room was its usual hive of activity when he stepped inside just a few minutes later. Chandler was the first to provide an update. She had looked into all known associates of their two victims, logging their details together with street identities and adding the records of any who had passed through the system. She had also spoken with the drugs team regarding their informants and had run through the KAs with them. Nothing jumped out at anyone, but they did agree to apply pressure to their eyes and ears on the streets.

Between them, DS Bishop and DC Ansari had made decent ground. Although CCTV and other variations of video footage were still coming in, the pair were making short work of what they had. But nothing they had seen was significant in respect of the investigation.

'Mind you,' Bishop said, 'we've barely scratched the surface so far. I think we can all agree these murders are most likely to have taken place in darkness, so watch this space as we've only just about reached sunset. I've been in touch with the bus and taxi companies to warn them, and I'm just waiting to give them a more accurate time window. As soon as we obtain those timings from the pathologist, I'll make a further request for public help.'

'And the victims themselves?' Bliss asked, looking at Ansari.

'What I'm seeing and hearing is pretty routine,' she said. 'The more I dig into their backgrounds the more I see two boys who happened to be born and raised in the wrong area. They seem to have avoided trouble and resisted being pulled in to the gang culture for as long as they could, but eventually caved. To me it looks as if older lads began to exploit them, conceivably holding threats to their families over their heads until they complied. The usual shit we see in similar cases. Once they were in it, however, they appear to be looking to stay in. Typical one-parent families, low or no income, social housing, street gangs and drugs all around them. Neither did well academically, and basically, they lost interest in schooling and the education system seems happy about that.'

Bliss puffed out his cheeks. 'And so it goes. A vicious cycle. More like a hamster wheel; once they're on it, it's hard to stop. Any word on our PMs?'

'Postmortems are scheduled for this afternoon,' Ansari confirmed. 'Which will be a relief, especially if they nail down an approximate time of death.'

From Gratton and Virgil, he learned that the floating house-to-house of the vessels moored either side of his own boat had provided them with no additional information. As for the ongoing appeal for witnesses, someone unwilling to leave their name and contact details had called to say they had seen the lads working corners in the Fletton district. When a follow-up traffic vehicle drove around the area, an elderly woman waved them down to say she had spotted two bicycles propped up against a garden wall in a nearby alley on Sunday morning, but by lunchtime they were already gone.

'Was she able to describe the bikes?' Bliss asked.

Gratton checked notes on his screen. 'Only in terms of colour. One dark red, the other green.'

'Okay. Cheers.' When he enquired about family notifications and formal identifications, it was Chandler who responded first.

'All dealt with. If you're up to it, I have meetings arranged for this afternoon.'

'Did you attend the identification process?'

'Yes. It was as brutal as ever. Chris Barrie's mother and older sister came in to ID him. Both were completely broken by the time they left. Jamie Ure's mother was there with a bloke she's been seeing. Neither fell apart, though the boy's mum did seem in a state of shock. I reckon she might have been out of it but perhaps her GP prescribed something to calm her down.'

Bliss gave it some thought before agreeing to accompany Chandler. Meeting recently bereaved parents was never a straight-forward task, but in this case the victims were drug dealers most likely murdered by other drug dealers. He imagined extracting information from the family would be akin to pulling teeth, but irrespective of who and what the boys were, those they had left behind to mourn deserved respect and sympathy at a time like this. It wasn't always easy to deliver, but it was always necessary to attempt.

THIRTEEN

B OTH RESIDENTIAL AND INDUSTRIAL, the Woodston district had once been a key hub of the city. Major companies such as British Sugar and Pedigree Pet Foods all had large factories and office complexes located there at one point. The legendary stench emanating from both sugar beet and pet food manufacturing, combined with the landfill waste areas upon which much of the Hampton township would eventually be built, was something older inhabitants still talked about. Another major employer, Hotpoint, also finally gave up manufacturing white goods on their large site, and currently existed only as an outlet.

The area was familiar to Bliss. In the 1950s and 60s, thousands of Italian men were brought in by the London Brick company to work in the city's brick pits. Many of those who settled in Peterborough afterwards, did so in Fletton and Woodston. The neighbourhood's narrow streets mostly comprised two-up, two-down terraced housing, each in varying states of decay, brick walls heavy with grime accrued across many decades. Parking was an increasing nightmare, as was the case in Silver Street where Pamela Barrie lived with her daughter, Josie. Bliss and Chandler had to leave the Volvo a hundred yards away on another road entirely, the walk back allowing them to take in their surroundings.

Christopher Barrie's mother came as somewhat of a surprise to Bliss. His mind had conjured up an archetypal mother of a teenage drugs runner, but the woman who welcomed him and Chandler into her home was petite and unfussy, dressed well, clean and tidy, her hair neatly styled. With time not being in their favour, they turned down the offer of a drink and took their place in a stylish and uncluttered living room. Bliss cursed his own presumptions about this family before offering his sincere condolences.

'I am the Senior Investigating Officer in charge of the investigation into your son's murder,' he said. 'Sadly, I've done this sort of thing far too many times before, so believe me when I say I know how tough this must be for you. I expect the last thing you want to be doing right now is answering questions, but equally I'm sure you realise it's something we have to do.'

'I understand,' Mrs Barrie said, nodding. She was pale and it was clear that she had recently shed tears, but Bliss could tell by the way she clutched her hands together in a tight ball that she was doing her best to keep her emotions in check. The woman had only recently learned of her son's murder, so he knew how vulnerable she was and would make allowances for it.

'Good,' he said. 'Thank you for that. First off, how have things been going with Constable Linnell? I trust that she is keeping you informed and has been able to answer your own questions?'

Bliss had spoken with PC Gaynor Linnell before leaving Thorpe Wood. Her role as family liaison officer was a hugely demanding job, requiring an understanding and compassionate nature, often in the face of bitterness and misdirected anger. According to the constable, both the mother and sister were stoical and coping as well as could be expected. Her impression was that neither had known the lad was still involved in selling drugs. Mrs Barrie swiftly confirmed everything he already knew, including how the PC had interceded during an unexpected phone call.

'Tell me more about that,' Bliss said encouragingly. 'Was it a male or female voice?'

'Male. Young.' Mrs Barrie blinked and swallowed once. 'For just a second, I thought it sounded like... like Chris. My son.'

'Tell me what they said. As precise as you can be, please.'

The balled hands separated for a moment, fingers spreading. She wiped away a stray tear. 'He said if I didn't want the same thing to happen to Josie, I'd better keep my mouth shut about what Chris got up to and who his friends were.'

Bliss glanced at Chandler. When he was first told about the phone call, he had assumed it was the killer making contact. Now it sounded more as if it might have been somebody inside the gang the boy worked for.

'They used your daughter's name. They didn't refer to her as his sister or your daughter?'

'Yes. They mentioned her by name. I think Gaynor must have noticed my reaction even before I started to sob while I was still standing there holding the phone but unable to respond. She took it from me and asked who was speaking and what they wanted, but by then they'd rung off.'

Bliss momentarily closed his eyes. Drug dealers were invariably ruthless, relying on threats to keep people silent and in their own lanes. He took a breath and looked across the room at PC Linnell. 'Did you make a note of the incoming number?' he asked.

The nod he got back was a confident one. 'I did, boss. I immediately passed it on to DC Ansari who said she would look into it.'

'It'll be a burner, but it might still be active.' He turned back to Mrs Barrie. 'I'm sorry I have to ask this, but were you aware of what your son was involved in prior to his recent arrest?'

Another blink. Another tear squeezed out. This time both hands curled into separate fists. 'I knew and I didn't know. I suppose it would be more accurate to say I suspected and hoped it was a minor issue and nothing more than a phase he was going through. You'll probably think me stupid, but I genuinely had no idea he was still involved in that awful business.'

Bliss shook his head. 'I don't think you're stupid at all, Mrs Barrie. Just a mother who wanted to think the best of her boy. Tell me, had Chris and Jamie Ure been friends for a while, or was theirs a more recent relationship?'

'Oh, no, they'd been close mates for some time. Many years.'

'And what kind of lad was Jamie?'

'A sweet boy. But troubled. I was concerned about his home life, and I noticed a change in him. He became surlier and more distant and reluctant to chat, but then he was a teen, so that's what you expect of teens.'

'Going back to Chris, what made you first suspect his involvement in the drugs business?'

The grieving woman took a moment to answer, her eyes looking everywhere and nowhere. 'It wasn't so much one specific thing. He started going out at odd hours. He took and made calls he clearly didn't want me to overhear, and I didn't recognise the phone he used at times. When he and Jamie were together, they occasionally dropped a name or two I hadn't heard before. Also, Chris had extra cash. Money I'd not given him, I'm certain.'

'At any point did you try to intervene?' Chandler asked.

This drew a scowl from Barrie. 'Of course. What kind of mother do you think I am?'

With a wince of regret, Chandler apologised. 'I'm so sorry. That came out the wrong way. I meant no offence. What I ought to have asked was what response did you get when you challenged him?'

'I'm sorry, too. For jumping down your throat. I'm a bit…
fragile right now, as you might imagine. As for what happened
when I raised my fears with Chris, he denied it of course, and
the more I pushed the more he pushed back. You didn't ever
know my son in life, Sergeant Chandler, but when I looked at
him and spoke to him, all I saw was my lovely boy. My darling
Christopher. When we fought over it, he sobbed his little heart
out. He told me nothing was going on and that I had nothing
to worry about.'

'And after his arrest?'

'We had a heart to heart. No raised voices. No blaming or
shaming. He told me a bunch of older kids had forced him into
it, but that he was strictly small time and would find a way out
as soon as he could. He said he was frightened of what the main
dealers would do to him and perhaps even me and his sister, but
that he'd talk to them and in exchange for him not giving up any
names after his arrest, they'd let him off the hook.'

'Mrs Barrie,' Bliss said, drawing her attention back to him.
'Have you spoken with your daughter about this? Does she know
any more about it than you do? And if so, is she likely to talk to us?'

'Josie is not involved in any of this,' the woman said hurriedly.
For a second, her gaze flickered to the bedroom above before
coming to rest on him once more. 'Like me, she had her suspicions. But she never spoke about them with me. Or Chris, as I
discovered only yesterday.'

Something occurred to Bliss. 'Does Josie live here with you,
Mrs Barrie?'

'Yes. Where else would she be living?'

'I apologise. It's just that I know these houses quite well, and
I think I'm right in saying you have just the two bedrooms. I
wondered what the sleeping arrangements were with two teens
in the house.'

Seemingly puzzled, Barrie nevertheless responded. 'The room at the front upstairs was just about big enough to restructure into two smaller bedrooms. I have the one at the back of the house. Why do you ask?'

'Only because I thought that if the pair were crammed in together, Josie might know more than she thought she did. By that I mean snatches of overheard conversations, that sort of thing.'

'I see. But no, they had separate rooms. Only a partition wall between them, so quite thin, but believe me, Mr Bliss, if Josie knew anything she would have mentioned it to me at some point since we were told about Chris.'

Throughout his long career as a police officer, Bliss had come to understand just how little most parents knew about their own children. But he had a sense she was right about this; if ever there was a time for a young girl to open up to her mother, it was at a time of great sorrow and loss. He also got the impression they would learn nothing here that might advance the investigation, but had one last stab at it.

'Does the name Sam Phillips mean anything to you?' he asked.

Barrie thought about it for a moment before shaking her head. 'No. Sorry. Who is he?'

Bliss detected zero deception, no intention of fooling him by referring to Phillips as a male. It was perhaps a natural assumption to make when hearing the name, though a rather old-fashioned one. One he would have made. 'It doesn't matter,' he assured her. 'Just a name that came up during our checks. Oh, one last thing before we leave you in peace. Did Chris have a bicycle?'

'Yes. In fact, he took it with him when he went out on Saturday night.'

'What colour was it?'

'It was green. Olive green, I'd say. Is it important?'

'I doubt it. It's just that a woman reported two bikes had been left leaning up against a garden wall but later went missing. One was red, the other green.'

'Jamie's bike was maroon.'

Bliss grimaced. 'I imagine the bikes were stolen having been spotted just sitting there in an alleyway. This was in Old Fletton. But thinking about it now does lead me to ask another question you might not approve of, Mrs Barrie. You say Chris went out on his bike on Saturday night, but by the time you were informed of his death on Monday afternoon, you'd not reported him missing. Can you tell me why that was?'

Wiping her eyes, Barrie said falteringly, 'It was nothing unusual. He and Jamie spent a lot of time together. There was no room for Jamie to stay over here, but Chris would often doss down on Jamie's bedroom floor using an old sleeping bag. He wouldn't always tell me, and I suppose I just got used to it. Something else I'd change if I could go back in time.'

'I was young once,' Bliss told her casually. 'As hard as that might be to believe. I put my parents through the very same thing. They didn't think anything of it, either. And my dad was a copper. Besides, you couldn't have done anything about it. We're as certain as we can be that whatever happened to Chris happened on Saturday night or in the early hours of Sunday morning.'

Managing a weak smile, Barrie said, 'Thank you for that. I don't think it will stop me blaming myself, though.'

'Most good parents would. Blame themselves, I mean. That doesn't mean they or you would be right to do so. I'm not a parent, but I guarantee I've spent more time in the company of teenagers than you have over the years. And their parents or guardians. The simple fact is teens will be teens and those who want only to protect them can't do so twenty-four hours a day, seven days a week. It's impossible.'

After a moment or two of silence, Mrs Barrie said, 'Is it all right if I ask a question now?'

He nodded. 'Of course.'

'Do you know who murdered my son?'

Bliss was unsurprised by the question. 'Not specifically, no. We are, however, working on a hypothesis that the entire team agrees upon. For obvious reasons, I can't go into detail with you, but we believe another drugs gang murdered Chris and Jamie. One looking to send a message.'

'I see. And do you suppose that was who called my number and warned me off?'

Pausing this time, Bliss looked at Chandler. She nodded, and he agreed; there was no good reason to keep his suspicions from this woman. 'Quite the opposite,' he told her. 'I'm confident that call was made by somebody working for the gang Chris and Jamie ran drugs for. It's the only logical conclusion based on their precise warning.'

Mrs Barrie hugged herself, lips quivering as she rubbed her arms. 'Such a terrible business,' she said in a soft voice edged with regret. 'And I still can't help but blame myself.'

'Don't force yourself down that rabbit hole,' Bliss warned her with a shake of the head. 'Nothing good can come of it. Nothing. Besides, from my experience, you're wrong to think that way.'

'How can I be? I heard what you said just now, but Chris was my son. My responsibility. I could have done more. Should have done more.'

Bliss leaned forward, narrowing the distance between them. 'Believe me, Mrs Barrie, I know about taking on the full weight of blame. From everything I've seen and heard, nothing short of locking your boy in his bedroom could have kept him from doing what he did. That's how this drugs gang culture works. These people prey on the vulnerable. And even if Chris had ended up enjoying being a runner, that still didn't mean he deserved what happened to him. That's why my team and I will do everything in our power to find the people who did this, to charge them, and then bang them up where they belong.'

Not least because if we don't, then your son and his friend may not be the last to be found on open wasteland, he thought but didn't say.

'I know I'm supposed to ask for details,' Mrs Barrie said. 'You know the sort of thing: how did he die? Was it over quickly? Did he feel any pain? But I won't. I can't bring myself to. I can imagine, you see, and that's bad enough. To know might be more than I can handle right now.'

'I think that's wise,' Bliss said. 'But please don't dwell on it. That's another path that can only ever lead to more pain.'

Afterwards, as he drove the short distance towards Stanground, Bliss turned to Chandler with a smile and said, 'Look at us two. Back in the saddle again. Butch and Sundance, partners in crime.'

She rolled her eyes. 'It's as if you've never been away.'

'Four weeks is the longest we've been apart since I came back to Peterborough,' he reminded her.

Looking straight ahead she said, 'I know. Four whole, glorious weeks without a certain numpty doing my head in.'

'Yeah, right? You know you missed me. So how does it feel having me back as a member of staff? I bet that's weird.'

This time she did turn to him. 'It does feel a bit strange. You're there and running things the same way you always have, but at the same time it feels… different somehow. I can't really explain it. I mean, you were brilliant with Mrs Barrie just now and it felt like the good old days. But you're the boss and yet at the same time you're not.'

'For this investigation, I am. Why not look at it that way?'

'I'm trying. And for the most part, I don't even think about it. But when I do, I can't help but be conscious of the fact that you're not my DI anymore.'

He nodded. 'Yeah, I can understand that. Believe me, I feel that same awkwardness. But this arrangement is new to us all. A few cases down the line and it'll all be second nature.'

And although Chandler nodded and said no more about it, Bliss couldn't help but feel a certain distance between them that had never existed before. It was small, perhaps even minuscule. But not as insignificant as he would have liked.

FOURTEEN

B IG MOFO WAS A man who enjoyed his work. Not quite as much as his smaller, rounder friend, perhaps, but there wasn't much in it. He thought of himself as more of a stylist, preferring brute force using natural weapons such as his limbs and forehead, whereas Li'l Mofo was the creative one who took an almost erotic pleasure from terrorising and inflicting agony, not merely pain, with man-made tools. So, it had pleased him no end when his pal approved of his choice of location for their next job.

The big man's uncle had run a printing firm for over twenty years, and upon his passing from Covid two years earlier the keys and deeds were handed over to Big. Running a company was not Big Mofo's speciality, so he allowed the incumbent manager to take more of a lead. The slide in production began at the outset of the pandemic, and the downward slope had only become more slippery since. With the print shop eventually reduced to just two part-time members of staff, Big looked to sell the place as a going concern but following many months of no interest whatsoever he ultimately had to admit defeat and in 2022 closed the doors to business for the final time.

He often wondered what his uncle thought about that – wherever he was now. He'd probably have shrugged it off as one of those things, a fatalistic response typical of the man. Unlike Big's father, who would have weighed in with words dripping with contempt and spite before doling out punishment with his belt. Big still felt disappointed at his failure to keep the print shop viable, but meanwhile, he had a little enterprise of his own to take care of inside the lock-up style unit in Werrington.

He had to admit, the interior arrangement still gave him a bit of a kick, prompting happy memories of better days spent with his father's brother. Over time, the business had grudgingly moved forward with technological advances, except that it was always a decade or more out of date. Part of the shop floor was like a museum, and that happened to be Big's favourite part of all.

Tucked away in one corner stood an old cylindrical letterpress machine, with a bank of wooden drawers beside it containing metal blocks and moveable type characters. A desk-mounted curved blade guillotine squatted menacingly by its side. To the left was an old Itek two-colour workhorse dating back to the 1980s. The unit had been fastidiously maintained and was currently thumping away in the background with a grinding, heavy growl punctuated by sharp punches as it churned out a short run of leaflets listing equipment he'd shortly be putting up for sale. Ranged along much of the opposite wall stood a Heidelberg Speedmaster, capable of handling 11,000 sheets per hour. A beautiful piece of technology the business sadly no longer had cause to use. Big could almost still hear it thundering away, him and his uncle wearing ear plugs to deaden the noise.

Printing required cleanliness, and both his uncle and the manager had always ensured the place was in pristine condition. So, there was no debris to wade through, no grime or errant streaks of oil or grease to stain clothes and skin. The smell of ink hung in the air, an odd mixture of chemicals with a sweet undertone. By now, it was so deeply embedded in the walls and fabrics that it would be impossible to shift. Big breathed it all in and gave a loud sigh of satisfaction.

Until, that is, his gaze fell upon the bedraggled and battered figure handcuffed to a corrugated cast-iron radiator pockmarked by blemishes of rust. The man had remained in the same spot for several days, and whatever fluids or solids his body had naturally excreted remained with him, seeping through his clothes and attaching itself to his flesh.

'What d'you think?' Big asked his friend, gesturing as if to say *'here's one I made earlier'*.

Li'l Mofo switched his gaze from the hapless figure whose eyes appeared shrunken into his skull. 'I think he's cooked. I think it's time.'

'You sure? I mean, I know he's ripe, but man…'

'It's now or never. We're pushed for time, and so is he. Let's do this.'

Nose pinched, Big Mofo strode across the floor, grabbed at a length of tape secured over the man's mouth, and ripped it off in a single blur of motion.

'How's it going, man?' Big asked. 'Now that you've had some time to think about the situation you find yourself in, you got something you want to tell me?'

'H… Huh hugh!'

Big and Li'l exchanged puzzled glances. 'What he say?' the latter asked.

'I ain't sure, bro.' He turned to the man once more, kicked him in the thigh and asked the same question. He got the exact same reply.

This time, Li'l Mofo chuckled and said, 'I think he's telling you to fuck off.'

Big's lips formed a loose curl as he scowled. He stared back down at the stinking wretch with the shattered face. 'That right? You telling me to fuck off, bro?'

Spittle flecked with blood and slivers of enamel flew from the man's ruined mouth as he nodded and grunted unintelligibly. That he was currently unable to speak owed much to Li'l having smashed a heavy claw hammer into his face a couple of hours earlier. Riled by the man's silence and feeling the need to punish, the portly little brute hadn't held back. He'd wielded the heavy tool three times. With substantial force. Most of the man's front teeth were now jagged shards lying in a pool of dried blood and puke on the floor, though one incisor seemed to have taken up precarious residence on the shoulder of his hooded sweatshirt.

'I don't think he's going to tell us what we want to know,' Big said to his friend and partner.

'I make you right, cuz. I don't think he understands how serious we are. But we could try to persuade him one last time. I can fetch some of that caustic shit. Maybe a drill?'

The figure furiously tried to wriggle further away from the violent pair but got caught up in the rattling cuffs and ended up merely gasping like a landed fish. The big man gave him a look of contempt and one final opportunity. 'You gonna tell me shit, my friend? You down with that or you looking to be a dumb fucking hero.'

'Huh hugh!'

Big Mofo pulled back a leg, raised his knee, and stomped down on the side of the struggling captive's mangled jaw. His scream was loud and keening, but lost against the background of a printing press in full flow. Big threw his arms up in exasperation. 'Now look what you made me do!' he cried out, looming over the still-screeching man. 'I got blood on my new Vans, you fucking twat.'

Big gave the man one last kick for good measure.

Nipping forward like a bullish dog, Li'l said, 'Let's just send the message and get this fucker out of here.'

His friend gave him a sidelong glance and nodded. He picked up a piece of cloth and started wiping at his trainers. The smaller man walked away for a few seconds and then brought back something he'd taken from a cupboard that leaned against the far wall. He stood over the handcuffed man and bent forward as far as possible given the circumference of his stomach and the complete lack of a waistline. The man's eyes bulged when they spotted the item Li'l held in his hand. A butane torch tends to elicit such a response in the right circumstances. He started thrashing again, trying vainly to thrust himself away, flapping from side to side and splashing fresh ribbons of blood everywhere.

'Mnuh!' he shrieked. 'Mnuh!'

Li'l frowned and then laughed. 'Oh, what's this?' he said, indicating the gas bottle in his hand. 'You think I'm going to use this to hurt you? Nah, you got it all wrong, bruv. This here is your friend. Least, it's gonna be. You're gonna want me to use this, believe me. You're gonna be so fucking overjoyed when I eventually use this on you that you'll be puckering up to kiss my ringpiece, bro.'

The man stopped squirming and looked up at him, weeping through eyes that were no more than crusty slits and shaking his head despite the agonising pain it must have caused him.

'My friend is telling you the truth,' Big assured him. Then he pointed to a machine standing in its own area of the floor beside a long wooden bench. 'Because when that fucker is done with you, the flame of that burner is going to be the difference between you living and dying in a bloody mess on my floor.'

The figure slowly turned his head. He gave the device a long, hard stare before letting his chin slump to his chest and quietly sobbing in defeat.

'That beast over there,' said Big, 'is a Perfecta guillotine. It can slice through two reams of paper at a time. In a minute or two, my bro here is going to feed one of your arms into it. That blade will make mincemeat of your flesh and bone, believe me. It'll be quick, but it'll also be painful. Hey, at least it'll take your mind off your jaw and mouth. Result, right? The butane is for cauterising your bloody stump afterwards. So, happy days, you feel me? You get to live. Which leaves just one more important question. One you might want to answer this time.'

The man looked up at him hopelessly, blood, snot, and tear stains masking his features. He said nothing, but his eyes were less defiant this time.

Li'l leaned forward again and took over. 'Which hand do you toss yourself off with, Vic? You choose.'

FIFTEEN

K IRSTY URE PROVED TO be everything her fellow grieving mother
was not. Including grieving, as far as Bliss could tell. She had
refused to have an FLO, so he and Chandler were completely
unprepared, and the pair had needed to gain impressions and
form opinions on the fly. None were favourable.

This was a woman who neglected herself and clearly didn't
give a damn what others thought of her. Three kids, none of
whom looked older than twelve nor younger than five, ran about
shouting and screaming at the top of their voices, paying no heed
to their mother's threats of punishment in several vivid forms.
The family lived within sight of the parkway flyover just over
the boundary of Stanground. The house was as unkempt as the
clothing the kids wore and the hair that curled around Ure's neck
like rats' tails. It was the kind of home where you wiped your
feet when you left. Even if he and his partner had been offered
a drink Bliss would have politely declined.

'She had nothing useful to tell us,' he told the team upon their
return to Thorpe Wood. 'In fact, I don't think I'm being overly
harsh when I say it seemed to me, she might actually be happy

at having one less mouth to feed and could even have been revelling in her new role as victim.'

Chandler hissed through her teeth. 'I wouldn't disagree. She already has more than enough on her hands, and it's easy to see how her oldest son slipped under the radar. Poor sod. He was probably willing to do anything so long as it kept him away from that woman.'

DCI Warburton sat on a swivel chair, effortlessly using her feet to ease herself first one way and then the other. 'Sounds like a real charmer. And a complete waste of time.'

'The only thing of substance she was able to tell us is that the boy didn't own a bike – so I'm guessing the one he had was either borrowed or stolen. When we asked about any possible drugs connection, she flew into a rage and then clammed up tighter than Jimmy's wallet. It wouldn't surprise me if her own supply came from her son.'

Warburton sighed. 'Let's forget about her for the time being. Jimmy, you want to be brought up to speed now or wait for the evening briefing?'

Bliss eased himself into a nearby chair. He drew both hands down his cheeks. 'No, quick updates now, please. Where's Bish, by the way?'

'I asked him to attend the postmortems. He was thrilled, as you might imagine. I sent Alan with him.'

Bliss had been about to query DC Virgil's absence, too. 'Okay. At least we'll hopefully get a tighter window on time of death. Any progress with CCTV?'

'None so far,' DC Ansari told him. 'It's a bit of a slog and we've pulled in more people. I'm sure we'll get movement on this tomorrow once we know TOD. Also, after checking into the backgrounds of our two boys I'm pretty sure they were the small fry we assumed them to be. Neither were hardened villains, nor did they know any as far as I can tell.'

'Okay. Cheers.' Bliss got to his feet. 'Listen up. I'm going to finish up the day over at the mortuary. I've yet to see our victims and I'm sure Bish will welcome me sitting in on the second PM in his place. I'll send Alan back with him. Unless we get a major break, let's skip evening briefing and pick it up in the morning.'

A postmortem wasn't something any officer looked forward to or enjoyed at the time. It was, however, a necessary part of the job. It had been a while since he had attended one, and while he had to steel himself, he knew it was the right thing to do.

Nancy Drinkwater, the previous pathologist, had moved on to pastures new. Bliss felt bad that he hadn't had a chance to say goodbye and to wish her well. Dr Matt Wheeler had replaced her, and this was the first time the two men had met. The doctor's firm handshake and forthright manner impressed Bliss as they introduced themselves.

'I hope you have a strong stomach,' he said. 'Detective Sergeant Bishop didn't look at all well during the previous PM.'

'I haven't thrown up at a post mortem in almost four decades, so I think I'll make it,' Bliss told him.

'I actually think it was the sight of the body before I went to work on it that affected him more. And I can't say I blame him.'

'And that was his second sight of them. This is my first. I know what to expect, but I can't promise it won't turn my stomach.'

Dr Wheeler pulled back the sheet to fully reveal the body of Jamie Ure. 'Are you familiar with the skin's reaction to strong corrosive acid?' he asked.

Bliss had to fight himself not to look away. He swallowed thickly and nodded. When not treated, acid continues to work its way through the epidermis, dermis, and hypodermis, leaving ugly and deep burns. It was obvious, judging by the horrific patterns etched into the flesh, that someone had sprayed the liquid all over the boy's face. But then a monster had gone to work with a blade, the depth of the slashes and stabbings clearly demonstrating intent to inflict pain and terror before the fatal wounds were made. The attacker had left the victim's face looking like a shredded latex mask, swollen, ugly, and inhuman.

What followed was quite tame by comparison. Even so, Bliss had never once stood through a postmortem without feeling uneasy. He knew all about the incisions, the removal and weighing of organs, the examination of the brain, and had no desire to dwell on any of it. Observing the procedure like a voyeur at a macabre ritual dissection, he became restless and keen for Dr Wheeler to snap off his gloves and call it a day. When the moment finally came, Bliss heaved a heavy sigh of relief. The pathologist had performed the functions while talking into an overhead microphone for the benefit of a recording, and so had already revealed his findings.

'I'll send you a copy of everything, naturally,' Wheeler said. 'But this poor boy died in the exact same way his friend did. Sadly, before his organs started to shut down due to haemorrhaging leaving him to slip into unconsciousness, the pain from those burns and knife wounds would have been agonising.'

'Same type of blade as with the other victim?' Bliss asked.

'I'd need to compare the measurements I took and examine the casts I made before you arrived before confirming, but yes, I'd say so. Long, thin blade with a gradual but pronounced curvature.'

'Like a hook?'

'Yes.'

'So, a zombie knife.'

'That would be my initial assessment.'

'Time of death as per previous estimate?'

Wheeler nodded. Bliss had all he needed. There was nothing more to be learned. He thanked the pathologist and shook the man's hand as he said goodbye. By the time he walked out of the building back into bright sunshine, he felt as if a cloud of gloom had enveloped him, preventing the heat and light from touching his flesh. Nobody deserved to die the way Chris Barrie and Jamie Ure had. And nobody capable of inflicting such devastation upon another human being deserved to walk free among their own kind.

SIXTEEN

Bliss was sitting outside the Lakeside Kitchen & Bar at Ferry Meadows, sipping from a bottle of Doom Bar amber ale with Gunwade Lake lapping to shore under the boardwalk beneath his feet. He'd brought the beer from home, its partner standing on the table waiting for him to polish off the first. When the restaurant was closed, as it was now, he liked to take advantage of the tranquil setting and relax alone with his thoughts.

Though not any longer.

Not with the shadow that had just fallen over him. *For fuck's sake*, he thought, *why can't I have just a little bit of time to enjoy a beer in peace?*

'Good evening, Jimmy,' a woman said, a smile teasing her thin lips as she slid onto a chair opposite. 'It's nice to see you again.'

Bliss set his drink down before carefully appraising his uninvited guest. She had changed the colour of her hair from blonde to a vibrant and silky copper, while still keeping it resting on her shoulders. She wore a knee-length maroon skirt, into which she had tucked her pale lemon sleeveless T-shirt. A pair of grey ankle boots completed the look. Effortlessly stylish, Bliss thought. But potentially deadly with it.

He responded with a casualness that belied his concern at her unexpected appearance. 'Good evening, Danielle. I wish I could say the same about seeing you again.'

'Ah, so you know my name,' she said, her face betraying no trace of shock. 'You have been a busy drone.'

He shook his head indifferently. 'I had a word in passing with my old DCI about you, that's all. She tasked a couple of people to develop intel. No big deal. We couldn't keep referring to you as Range Rover woman.'

The two had encountered each other during Bliss's final few days as a DI. The woman carried a threat, though he sensed the delivery was meted out by others doing her bidding.

'A convoluted way of saying the same thing, surely?' she insisted.

'Not really. I was simply the messenger.'

She smiled at him. 'Of course. And as you're no longer a Detective Inspector, what exactly are you these days – if anything?'

'A civilian SIO and unsolved case investigator.'

'Hmm. Sounds impressive. But at the end of the day, you're no longer a real policeman, are you?'

'Civilian. Just like I said. But, please, spare me the small talk. What do you want? What are you doing here? Or did you just drop by to get on my tits?'

Danielle Halford crossed one bare, tanned leg over the other. Her eyes flashed. 'Not at all. I wouldn't dream of it. In fact, the reason I'm here is because I thought we might do each other a favour.'

The sun was starting to set directly behind her chair, forcing Bliss to squint. He took another pull from the bottle but gave no response.

She smiled once more before continuing. 'First of all, Jimmy, you need to know we were not responsible for those two boys you found murdered beneath the flyover. My boss was adamant that I assure you of that right from the off. He feels it's important for you to know that and to trust me on his behalf.'

'Your boss being…?'

Halford's smile broadened. 'If you know who I am then I'm sure I don't actually have to mention him by name.'

'Humour me,' Bliss insisted.

'All right. I work for Hector Karagiannis. Satisfied?'

'Are you?'

'I am, thank you. He's a good boss to work for.'

'A crook who, from what you just told me, is now making inroads into the drugs trade. Sounds delightful.'

Feigning astonishment and with a hand clamped to her chest, Halford said, 'What? Oh, I'm sure there must be some kind of misunderstanding. Mr Karagiannis is a hotelier and casino operator. A family business you can trace back generations.'

Bliss raised a hand, palm out. He looked around, but there was no need to lower his voice because they were alone. 'Please. Enough of all this old cobblers. It does my nut in and it's beneath both of us. I understand why you might not want to discuss his or your operations in detail, but don't elaborate the other way and mug me off. I know who and what he is. You know who and what he is. And I know that you know. So, please, tell me why you're here and then leave me in peace to finish my beer.'

Again, Halford seemed unimpressed with his outburst. He both admired and detested her fortitude. 'Okay. If you say so. Me, I'm a conversationalist. I do enjoy a good old chinwag. But I'll come straight to the point if that's what you prefer. You ought to know that Mr Karagiannis is extremely concerned by these recent developments. The tragic murder of two young boys is unnecessary and also terribly bad for business. He has no desire to see further bloodshed in the coming days, weeks, or months.

My boss prefers to make deals. To offer compromises the majority can accept.'

'What kind of concessions are we talking about?'

'On that subject, he is open to negotiation. As he sees it, this current three-way enterprise split could get extremely messy for all concerned. And I'm sure you don't want blood running down your city gutters. So, he is willing to work with the Soke line to remove the Foxes from the equation. Not with force, but with… persuasion. A solution they can live with. When it is just the two of us, we discuss matters like civilised business people. He believes their needs can be accommodated.'

'Really?' Bliss scoffed. 'I get the distinct impression your boss would like it all to himself.'

She gestured with one hand, her long fingers splayed. 'Perhaps that will be the accommodation. Anyhow, this is where he can be of some assistance to you. Because if you will consent to allowing him some latitude, he will ensure the takeover of existing lines becomes a smooth transition. No further escalation. No bodies. No battles. No war.'

'What kind of latitude?' Bliss asked, though he wasn't about to consider any such proposition.

'The mutually beneficial kind in which you allow him to carry out his business and look the other way while he does so. If you agree, before long there will be a single line and no daily carnage on your lovely city streets.'

His natural inclination was to decline impolitely and send her away with a flea in her ear. But Bliss recognised an opportunity and elected not to dismiss the offer out of hand. 'Are you proposing peace in exchange for immunity?'

'As close to peace as you're ever likely to see and as close to immunity as you're ever willing to offer. Your two recent victims won't be the last otherwise. Not, I insist, by our hand. It's just that

I happen to know the gang operating the Foxes line is readying itself for a swift and bloody conflict. Nobody wants that, least of all the police.'

'No, least of all our innocent citizens.'

Halford gave a nod of acknowledgement. 'Between you, me, and the gatepost, let's admit that drugs and the people who supply and deal them are not going away. It's a huge and expanding market, with vast sums of money to be made. One way or another business is going to continue. This city can have stability during that time, or it can have unpredictability. Perhaps even an unhealthy dose of anarchy. I'm here to discuss with you a potential arrangement to ensure the former.'

Bliss drained the bottle in his hand, set it down, picked up the other and took a swig before saying, 'The only reason I've not already told you to fuck the fuck off, Danielle, is because I acknowledge the point you make. But unless you're an awful lot denser than you look, you must realise the police can't be seen to be doing deals with criminals.'

'Then make sure you are not seen. A nod and a wink may be sufficient, provided the eventual outcome is as expected.'

Bliss pretended to give the notion some credence. He wondered if keeping an open dialogue going might be of some value to DCI Warburton and his old team. Eventually, he nodded. 'If I decide to bring this to senior officers, and if they agree to further discussions, I can guarantee they will not accept any deal while your boss continues to hide behind your skirts.'

'Really? Why not? I have such pretty skirts. Louis Vuiton, Ralph Lauren.'

Ignoring her smug manner, he said with emphasis, 'One of the people at the table will have to be Hector Karagiannis himself.'

Halford immediately shook her head and crossed her arms. 'That's not going to happen.'

'And yet here I am I'm telling you it has to.'

'My boss will never agree to that particular demand.'

'Then we have a stalemate here because neither will my more senior colleagues if he's not in the room with them. It's not open for discussion. If we're in, then so is he. And let's not pretend this is all about you doing us a favour. In return, your boss gets to rule the roost. He also avoids getting his hands dirty in a turf war with two other OCGs. Any mutual arrangement requires mutual trust. Or at the very least, a healthy mistrust. That works both ways, so if we talk, he talks. By that stage his... mouthpiece simply won't do.'

She paused to draw in a deep breath. Her eyes glimmered in a way that captured his attention. 'Oh, but I have such a beautiful mouth, don't you think? We both know you haven't stopped wondering what delights my lips might deliver since I joined you at the table.'

'Yes or no to your boss attending,' Bliss snapped.

'I can ask. But I already know what the answer will be.'

'In which case I can only say the same. Sorry for your wasted visit.'

A moment later, Halford narrowed her gaze. 'How's your delightful pooch?' she asked.

The question appeared not to carry an undercurrent, but Bliss still bristled. 'He's fine. Why do you ask?'

'Just taking an interest. It got a little bit intense there for a moment. And the girl?'

During their first encounter, Halford had observed him on his boat with Max and Molly. She had mentioned them both at the time, which Bliss had taken as an implied threat. 'The girl is out of bounds,' he said, adding a hard edge to his voice. 'Both her and my dog, in fact. You want something more than an agreement, you come at me. You look elsewhere and you and I will be having an entirely different conversation.'

Danielle Halford raised her eyebrows. 'My, aren't we the touchy ex-detective? I meant nothing by it, Jimmy.'

Bliss took another swig of his beer. 'I don't believe you. And I don't believe you because I don't trust you. You may not physically harm people yourself, but you know people who do, and I suspect they obey your every command. Even so, it would be a mistake on your part to ignore my warning.'

Seeking to appear puzzled by his outburst, she said, 'If I'm really as ruthless as you suggest, Jimmy, why are you being so confrontational?'

He set the bottle back down on the table and leaned forward. 'Because I'm speaking the only language people like you understand. I know gangs, I know the kind of people who work for gangs. I just want you to realise, understand, and accept that I won't be intimidated by any of you. I'm not as quick to anger as I once was, Danielle, which is the only reason you're still sitting there unharmed. But I won't stray from my lane, provided you keep your focus on me and my colleagues. And if you want to regard that as a threat, just know it's not a hollow one.'

Halford nodded once and stood. Smoothed out a crease in her skirt, openly inviting his glance. 'See what I mean about the quality? The fabric clings to every contour, doesn't it?'

When he failed to react she gave an exaggerated sigh and said, 'Understood. You have a word with your people, Jimmy, and I'll have a word with mine. I'll be in touch again soon.'

'I can't wait,' he said, finishing off his ale in two long swallows.

Again the smile. 'Oh, come on,' she said, pursing her lips. 'I'm sure you and I will eventually become the best of friends.'

'Don't hold your breath.'

'Be seeing you, Jimmy. I look forward to it.'

With a sly wink, she turned and walked away, leaving Bliss to wonder and worry in equal measure. Her hips swayed provocatively. Before she was out of earshot, he called Halford back. She turned, took a couple of steps in his direction before standing with her back arched in a seductive pose.

'Well? What is it?'

'Did you follow me here or did you lump my car?'

He couldn't decide which was worse: the fact that he hadn't spotted her trailing him or that she, or more likely one of her cohorts, had secreted a tracking device on the Volvo.

'Is that it?' she asked with a pout. 'Is that really all you want from me, Jimmy. I think you can see I have a whole lot more to offer.'

'What I see is a tease,' he said. 'So, did you lump my motor or follow me here?'

'Neither,' she called out. 'You spotted me and my Range Rover following you once before, so I had someone do the dirty work for me this time. They told me where to find you.'

'I'm still going to check for a lump.'

'You do that. I hear it's the healthy thing for men your age to do,' she said, turning once more and striding back towards the car park.

Oh, I will, Bliss thought to himself. He hadn't been looking for a following vehicle, so it was entirely possible that one of her flunkies had managed to trail him here from home. On the other hand, he'd put nothing past her. She was devious, and probably barely recognised her own lies she told them so often. He thought about her mentioning both Max and Molly, only this time he wasn't feeling threatened.

Danielle Halford had been playing him. And her offer, while absurd, was something he couldn't ignore and would bring to the attention of senior officers the following day.

SEVENTEEN

A FTER TAKING MAX OUT for his final walk of the day, Bliss sat in his usual recliner with the dog sprawled across his lap. He'd propped a new delivery of vinyl against the wall while the sounds of Supertramp's *Breakfast in America* leaked from the speakers. An album choc-full of hits, it was easy background listening while he considered the two investigations he was running.

Just two days in and his mind was pretty much made up about the death of Justin Nolan. If ballistics failed to come up with a print or prints on the bullet casings obtained from the revolver, he could see nowhere for the reinvestigation to go. Memories had faded, some witnesses were deceased, while others had nothing to offer. Like those before him, he felt there was more to the murder than a mindless shooting, but there was no evidence to substantiate that theory. He sensed purpose and meaning behind the murder, but could see no clear way to proceed.

The appearance of Danielle Halford earlier that evening had certainly put a different slant on their double murder case. He wasn't entirely sure why, but he had believed her when she told him her boss was not responsible. While he was undoubtedly looking to take over the supply of drugs in the city, the Foxes line came with a heavy reputation and were the more likely culprits. The offer of collusion was almost laughable. And yet, not an unreasonable approach for Hector Karagiannis to have suggested. As a strategy it made complete sense, effectively killing two birds with one stone by removing the competition while ensuring an easy ride if not outright cooperation from the police.

Not that anybody in the force would countenance such a deal. But Bliss wondered if there might be some mileage in stringing the man along. In having him show all his cards without the police ever having to dirty their own hands.

When his phone rang and he glanced down at the screen to see who the caller was, creased edges gathered around his eyes. For a second, he considered not answering, but curiosity got the better of him. 'Munday from Five,' he said calmly. 'This can't be good.'

'Don't be like that, Mr Bliss. My ego bruises easily. Tell me, do you happen to be at home right now?'

The even, cultured voice was instantly recognisable. 'No,' he replied. 'I'm not. I'll be out for the rest of the night as it goes.'

'Are you quite sure about that? Could you possibly check?'

'What do you mean? I know where I am, Munday.'

'How peculiar. So that's not you sitting in a reclining armchair in your own living room?'

Bliss swore. Turned his head to look out into the back garden. Raised a weak finger in the air. 'Sorry, I blanked for a moment, there,' he said. 'Could have sworn you asked me if I was in the office.'

He set Max on the floor, then stood to slide the French doors across and stepped outside to open the back gate to allow his MI5 contact in. As Bliss walked back to the house, Munday marched across the garden looking mightily pleased with himself. 'I was in the area and thought I'd pop by to see how things were going,' he said amiably.

As the pair each took a seat inside, Bliss narrowed his gaze. 'In the area? Pop by? I don't think so, somehow. Besides, most people tend to use the front door when they visit.'

Munday's eyes crinkled around the edges. 'Ah. You saw through my elaborate ruse. I can't say I'm overly surprised. It won't go down as a classic, by any means. Not one they'll be teaching at Spy School anytime soon.'

'It was a pretty feeble attempt,' Bliss concurred, enjoying the man's amusement.

'And who is this?' Munday asked, peering down at the dog who lay between Bliss's feet warily eyeing the stranger.

'Max. My rescue dog.'

'But not a guard dog, that's for sure. But a fine specimen nonetheless.'

Bliss nodded. 'So, what can a humble citizen do for an agent from the Security Services, Mr Munday?'

'Ah, yes. Of course. Your situation has changed since last we met. How is life without a badge?'

'Ticking along just nicely, thank you. Or it was until you showed up. I take it you want something from me?'

Munday didn't skip a beat. 'That is perceptive of you. I wonder, do you happen to recall that favour I did for you a few years ago?'

He did. All too well. The two had first met during a murder case that initially appeared to have been the work of a terrorist cell. In addition to counter-terrorism, MI5 had helped steer the debate by providing their own agent. At the conclusion of the case, Bliss had asked Munday to intervene in a stressful custody battle on behalf of Chandler, who at the time was striving to get her daughter back from the child's Turkish father who'd snatched the girl and taken her to his homeland. The MI5 man had made it happen, and Bliss had never forgotten Munday's act of generosity.

Bliss nodded. 'Of course.'

'Splendid. Then I take it you also recall what you told me at the time.'

'I said I owed you.' Bliss admitted. Then nodded. 'And I'm assuming this is you calling in that favour.'

Munday offered an apologetic shrug. 'I'm afraid so. I had hoped never to have the need.'

'We all imagine such promises never catching up with us. Let's hear it, then. I find the best way is to rip that plaster right off in one swift action.'

'As you wish. Tell me, then, how loyal to quests for justice are you now that you are no longer a police officer?' Munday asked.

Bliss stared at him. The man from MI5 had a quality about him that was hard to put your finger on. Undeniably sophisticated, with a sharp wit and a keen eye. Tall and upright, he was a man perfectly at home either taking command of a situation or melting into the background. Even his age was indeterminable.

'Nothing's changed,' he answered. 'Why do you ask?'

'Please understand that at this time, my interest is merely cursory. It may yet become more fundamental, but that decision is very much out of my hands.'

Bliss frowned. 'All right. Your interest in what, exactly?'

'I'm unable to provide a reasonable answer to that question. Secrets and all that sort of hush-hush nonsense. You understand, I'm sure.'

'I do. But then I think you'll agree it's a bit difficult for me to grant you a favour if I don't know precisely what you're asking for. Or why.'

Munday nodded, taking it all in. He pressed a finger to his lips for a moment. 'I remember you to be a diligent worker, Bliss.

A grafter. A chap who, once he has a foot on the throat, is disinclined to ease off. However, in respect of the cold case you're looking into, I'm wondering if I might be able to persuade you otherwise.'

Alarmed, Bliss said, 'You mean hamper my own investigation?'

'No, not at all. Not quite. At this stage we'd settle for you taking a longer pause than absolutely necessary to analyse the information you have acquired thus far.'

A few seconds of silence passed. Then Bliss coughed and said, 'Whatever the main favour is I'd hate to be around when it lands. Mr Munday, please correct me if I'm wrong, but what I think you're suggesting is that His Majesty's Security Services wishes me to slow the pace at which I and my team investigate the murder of Justin Nolan. Is that about the size of it?'

Munday mulled his statement over for a few seconds before replying. 'Not quite, but close enough to be getting on with. That said, I can't tell you any more about this than I already have.'

Bliss regarded him with barely suppressed annoyance. 'You've told me little, but you've also already said more than enough. Let me ask you one thing: who stands to gain the most from this delay you're asking for?'

'That pretty much depends.'

'On what?'

'On the outcome of the things I can't go deeper into without authorisation.'

'Then let me seek some form of clarity. What's the worst result? Both of the delay and of not delaying.'

Munday gave that some thought. 'Let me put it to you another way, Mr Bliss. If you choose not to drag your heels, you may well end up being ordered to do so. From your perspective, I imagine that's probably worse. If you delay long enough, however, there is every chance of there being no further interference. Indeed, we may even be able to assist you.'

'I see. But you can't tell me why, and clearly, you're not going to point me in the right direction here and now.'

'Obviously not. I'm sorry, Bliss, but my hands are tied. The truth of the matter is that my visit might turn out to have been unnecessary. On the other hand, it could prove to be crucial. At this stage we have no way of knowing, but it was felt that taking this approach at the outset might be the way to tackle a, shall we say, thorny issue.'

Bliss regarded him shrewdly. 'You come to me asking for a favour, yet already it's beginning to sound like much more. What's that about?'

Looking genuinely pained, Munday said, 'A genuine request, I assure you. But in this particular instance, I don't have a great deal of skin in the game. I'm very much the good cop, while the bad have their own rules and methods.'

'I see. And all you want from me at the moment is some time?'

'Correct.'

Bliss met the taller man's gaze. 'You know who our killer is, don't you?'

'I do not.'

The denial seemed sincere. 'Then your superiors do.'

'I rather doubt it.'

Bliss felt himself relax. 'Okay. Then you know something about it. You know why our victim was killed, at the very least.'

Munday shrugged, purse-lipped.

'You're an infuriating and insufferable old twat at times,' Bliss snapped at him.

'So I've been told. Many times. Often by members of my own family.'

Bliss shook his head. 'I'm going to have to give this one some thought.'

'At least that's not an outright refusal.'

'Not yet, no. If you're coming to me like this, I know there's a good reason.' He felt justified thinking of it that way, mainly because he considered Munday to be a fundamentally decent man. They shared a certain cynicism about the world in general, and Bliss liked to think they also shared similar values.

'Please take all the time you need,' Munday told him.

'One final question,' Bliss said. 'Whatever I decide to do, am I being asked for the right reasons?'

'To be perfectly honest with you, old bean, I doubt you would think so from your current vantage point. But in the long run, and in being able to see the much wider picture, I believe so, yes.'

Bliss stood. Held out his hand. At his feet, Max stirred and raised his head. 'Good seeing you again, Munday.'

The man smiled as they shook on it. 'Oh, I very much doubt that is true, Mr Bliss. But it's a decent enough way to leave things for the time being.'

'How long do I have to think things through?'

Munday shifted from foot to foot. 'When do you next meet with your fellow investigators?'

'Tomorrow morning.'

'Then that's how long you have. There is one more elephant in the room I'm afraid, Jimmy.'

Bliss's eyes narrowed. Munday had never used his first name before. 'Go on,' he said, still somewhat taken aback. 'Spill it.'

'Look, old chap, I meant it when I described myself as the good cop. I also meant it when I reminded you the bad cops are waiting in the shadows. But there's one more aspect you seem either ignorant of, unwilling to accept, or you've plain forgotten.'

'And what might that be?' Bliss asked him.

'Well, no offence, but you seem to have neglected your unsolved crime's single biggest factor.'

'Which is?'

'The crime was not solved, which means the gunman remains at large. If he is still above ground and remains in the same line of business, he could learn of your investigation and decide to return.'

'You think I could be in trouble?' Bliss asked him.

'Yes,' Munday admitted. 'I believe I do. And potentially from more than a single source.'

EIGHTEEN

S HADOWS DANCED UPON THE carefully landscaped boulders and plants surrounding the outdoor swimming pool to the rear of Hector Karagiannis's Hertfordshire Grade II listed Georgian manor house. Pale blue light reflecting off the water's surface provided the source of this serene animation. The man himself lay back on a reclining chair, stripped to the waist and dripping all over the striped fabric following a quick dip.

Sitting across from him, Danielle Halford regarded her boss with a lot more distaste than she had alluded to earlier when talking with Bliss. If she spoke about her feelings with any degree of depth and honesty, she might be accused of 'fat shaming', but she found Hector Karagiannis grotesquely obese. Behind closed doors, she had overheard others refer to him as the 'suited toad' and she could see why. His thick black hair and beard always looked greasy, his flesh slick and shiny – the man was forever mopping his brow with a white monogrammed handkerchief. True, the suits he wore came from Savile Row, but Halford constantly marvelled at how the stitching held together when encountering the man's vast bulk. Karagiannis was still relatively young at forty-five, yet he was already on his second set of hips.

She declined the drink he offered as he began to towel himself dry. It was a Remy Martin Centaure de Diamant in a sculpted circular bottle and she was aware of its fine quality, but she nonetheless resisted. Karagiannis gave her the kind of look that suggested she had no idea what she was missing, before gesturing for her to tell him what she driven down from Peterborough to say.

'I have baited the line,' she told him.

Her boss frowned heavily. 'Forgive me, Danielle,' he said. 'But that sounds very much as if you're telling me you do not also have this man on the hook.'

'That's an impossibility at such an early stage.' She stared back at him unblinking. 'He does not have the authority to make such a decision.'

'Then why settle for a sprat when you could have approached the mackerel?'

'Because what he lacks in authority, he more than makes up for in his ability to persuade and drive forward what he believes in. I light a fire beneath him, I know he will do whatever it takes. That fire is lit.'

'And how about you?' Karagiannis asked, pausing with a glass to his plump lips. 'Were you persuasive, Danielle?'

With a curt nod, she said, 'When am I ever less than? Believe me, ex-Detective Inspector Bliss is our way in. My offer intrigued him. I won't pretend he won't wriggle and fight once he bites into that hook, but we have his interest and the way his mind works I feel certain he'll allow himself to be reeled in.'

'I do hope so. You… you should do more than hope. You've yet to let me down, Danielle. The casino play could have been better handled, but I accept partial responsibility for its failure. I made some bad decisions, particularly when it came to person-nel. Which is another reason why I am relying on you to deliver this for me. You understand?'

Halford did. Hector Karagiannis could make mistakes and get away with it because the man wasn't about to punish himself. But she… she was expendable. He had made up his mind what he wanted, and no matter how difficult the task, her job was to deliver.

'Hector,' she said. 'I will get this done for you. But understand, there must be compromises. This is the police we're talking about. They won't simply capitulate. We need to be smart if we are to be daring. We're asking a lot. Let's not kid ourselves that they will agree to it all. We must be flexible in our thinking. Now, I have managed to persuade Bliss to take this to more senior officers. Inevitably, they will want to meet so that we might negotiate – it's too good an opportunity to pass up on. But only under one specific condition.'

The pig of a man actually grunted as he looked up. He did not take kindly to conditions being applied by others. He regarded it as an affront to both his manhood and his public standing. He waggled his fingers. 'Tell me,' he said. 'What precisely do these upstarts propose?'

'If there is to be a meeting at which our offer is discussed, they will send their most senior officers. But only if you also attend.'

Halford had feared informing him of this, but rather than react with anger he put back his head and laughed. After a moment, he smiled and said, 'But this is why I have you, Danielle. If you are no longer sufficient, why would I retain your services? That makes no sense. No, you must handle this. I will arrange legal representation, and you may bring with you whomever you please. But this is your job. You act on my behalf. You made the offer, now seal the deal.'

'Hector,' she said, leaning forward and meeting his gaze. 'This is not some other gang we are dealing with here. These people do not react to intimidation or threats of violence.'

'Of course they do. They are human, are they not? In which case, they have human weaknesses. This Bliss person will have weaknesses for you to exploit.'

'He does. And I already know what they are. But Hector, as I just told you, he lacks the authority. And if you're about to suggest I find out who does have the authority and exploit their weaknesses instead, what I'm trying to tell you is that these methods are no good to us when it comes to the police. Yes, they are organised in pyramid fashion, but no one person can make this work the way we want it to. They work by committee and should one person step out of line their decisions and actions are open to question.'

The harsh lines spreading across his features told Halford her boss did not appreciate being spoken to this way. But while she feared him – his reach at least – she could not afford for him to fall back upon the weight of his arrogance. One of her jobs was to offer advice, to explain situations to him as they arose. She calmed her nerves by telling herself that was all she was doing.

But had she stepped out of line in doing so?

'I can't say I am happy to hear such things,' he said. 'This is not the way I am used to doing business. I expect more from you, Danielle. It makes me question the wisdom of using you to conclude this matter.'

'That is entirely your decision, of course. But Hector, I found our way in. The hard work is already done. This meeting will happen. When it does, I can sell them your proposition. I know I can. But not if you don't agree to attend.'

'Out of the question.'

Halford sighed. 'Then I don't know what to tell you. If they agree to meet, they will set the terms. I guarantee that if I walk in there without you, they will walk away from this potential deal.'

'Then you will have failed me,' Karagiannis said bluntly.

But Halford shook her head. 'No, Hector.' She swallowed thickly, drawing moisture into her throat. 'You will have failed yourself.'

NINETEEN

SEEING SUPERINTENDENT EDWARDS BEHIND the desk for the first time in what was until recently Marion Fletcher's office, felt a little surreal. The two women were not only physically dissimilar, they also enjoyed different tastes and styles when it came to personal and professional displays within their working areas. Edwards had already decorated hers with family photos and framed certificates, items Fletcher had, for the most part, eschewed. But she looked at home as she greeted him and DCI Warburton, and despite their past differences, Bliss knew she would honour the position she now held.

'Thanks for taking the meeting,' he said. 'This will eventually need gold command approval if it's to go anywhere, but I felt I needed to run it by you both as soon as possible.'

Bliss went on to outline the essential components of his conversation the previous evening with Danielle Halford. As he spoke, he remained conscious of the later discussion with Munday, one he was inclined not to mention. Saying nothing about it bothered him enormously, leaving him to wonder if the mere act of not bringing it to their attention was a display of disloyalty. On the other hand, despite a sleepless night, he hadn't yet decided how he was going to address the request made of him by the old spy.

DSI Edwards was the first to respond to his news. Puffing out her cheeks, she said, 'When you asked to meet to discuss Hector Karagiannis, I had no idea it would lead us here. His offer is preposterous, of course.'

'Of course,' Bliss agreed.

'And yet I get a sense you're about to find a way to persuade me otherwise.'

'Not quite. But I do wonder if we might be able to use the situation to our advantage.'

Edwards leaned forward. 'This ought to be interesting.'

Bliss took a beat before making his play. 'Of course, there's no way we'd actually go along with this proposal. On the other hand, I think it could work in our favour. If we look at it dispassionately, whatever approach we take, the City-Wide line is now part of the fabric of Peterborough. Yes, there's some stern competition, but Karagiannis has a lot of clout on his side. To put it bluntly, his gang is bigger than their gangs combined. He's confident of the outcome of any drugs war on our manor, and we shouldn't take our eye off that. What's more, he knows we can't afford to ignore it. Therefore, the offer makes complete sense on his part.'

Edwards nodded. 'Absolutely. But when does it start making sense for us, Jimmy?'

'I'm not saying we go along with his nonsense. I'm just suggesting we get him into a room and listen to what he has to say. His organisation has dipped its toes in the water inside our city and clearly he's finding it comfortable here. That's boosted his already sizeable ego. Enough for him to put this offer to us as an act of hubris. As for it making sense for us, ask yourself how often we get the opportunity to have a sensible and open conversation with a drugs kingpin.'

'But it won't *be* sensible,' Diane Warburton warned. 'You just admitted the whole thing is nonsense.'

'And it is. But why not string him along for a while? Why not make him think we're actually considering it? He's bound to have a lawyer with him if he turns up at all, but even so, we could learn things from him during even a single meeting that we might otherwise never discover under our own steam. We'd demand some assurances over any little scheme he put to us, which means we might get an insight into his long-term plans. And... this is where it gets a bit fuzzy, we might also consider allowing him to demonstrate his clout to us by him persuading his competition to back off.'

Warburton's wide gaze narrowed, creating deep ridges above her nose. 'But then we'd *actually* be working with him, Jimmy. We'd be in an agreement with him one way or another.'

'A verbal one at worst. One that could end up helping us at a difficult time. If he can stop what we believe is an escalation from the Foxes line, then that has to be to our advantage. If we screw him over afterwards, then he'll have no option but to swallow it.'

Edwards blew out a long sigh. 'I don't know. He's no dummy, so wouldn't he think that far ahead? He's bound to at least consider it. And he must have advisors. Which makes me wonder why he'd even bother in the first place.'

'Don't you think I've wondered the exact same thing?' Bliss said. 'But in the early hours of the morning, I think it came to me. His problems are twofold: first, the competition, and second, the police. Even if he thinks we might end up backing out of a verbal deal, it's clearly worth him asking us the question. Why? Because at the moment our attention is divided between three separate main organisations and the usual array of piddly small fry. That's problematic for us in terms of resources and intelligence and could easily get much worse in a short period of time.

He might just be clever enough to have considered how much more effective we might be if he wins the war and we only have the City-Wide line to focus on. In that scenario, our gang is bigger than his. To combat that, he comes to us with a proposal. Provided he doesn't expose himself too much, it's a no-lose gambit on his part. He'll rid himself of the opposition eventually, and he'd still rather do that cleanly than go to war. If he doesn't succeed with us, he's lost nothing. On the other hand, if we stick to the agreement, then he comes out on top.'

Warburton was nodding. 'Okay. I get it now. I see what you're saying. And you're right, he stands to lose nothing but potentially gain everything. But what are the legal ramifications of us meeting with him and agreeing to his takeover? Come to that, what are the policing implications?'

'I don't think there are any,' Bliss said, studying the faces of both women. 'Whatever we say or agree to in a private meeting is in no way legally binding. Morally... well, I suppose you could argue a case against it. But we'd be doing so for all the right reasons. And if gold command plus his side are the only ones present, with all communication devices left outside the room, no one could know what was agreed upon other than those inside the room at the time.'

'Gold command plus you,' Superintendent Edwards said.

'I don't think so.' He shook his head. 'That's way out of my league.'

'But they approached you, Jimmy. And I'm guessing they did so for a reason. They might not even go ahead without you there.'

'I'm not sure. It's not as if I'll be part of the decision-making process.'

'No, but you are the operational SIO,' Warburton reminded him. 'This is your case. As Senior Investigating Officer, you ought to be demanding to be involved. The old Jimmy Bliss would have been.'

He stifled a mocking laugh. 'You mean the old Jimmy Bliss from just over a month ago?'

'Yes, that's the one. Jimmy, if you don't mind my saying so, you seem to have had a dip in confidence since you retired. You shouldn't need telling, but you no longer having a warrant card is simply irrelevant to this investigation and your role leading it. This is your op. It runs the way you decide you want it to be run – albeit with the usual oversight from Alicia and Marion. Forget your retirement, is what I'm saying. Ignore the fact you're not a cop anymore. You're the SIO, for fuck's sake. Make that count.'

Ten minutes later he left the office with those words still ringing in his ears. They had reached an agreement, and Edwards would alert Chief Superintendent Fletcher and the ACC to the proposal. At that point, Bliss realised he had no way to contact Danielle Halford and could only hope he had an answer by the time she got back to him. But for the time being he had to focus on the two cases. First up, briefing time with the SCU. That bought him some extra breathing space before he had to take the lead on the Justin Nolan murder reinvestigation once again. Time he needed to use wisely while Munday's voice continued to echo inside his head.

TWENTY

THE TEAM WAS BOTH shocked and galvanised by the results of the two postmortems. The most fascinating revelation came when they learned that, in addition to their facial acid burns and multiple sharp force wounds, both boys had also been attacked with a stun gun.

Bliss read from a copy of the report he'd been sent from pathology. 'Doctor Wheeler discovered skin lesions described as hypopigmented macules approximately 0.5 centimetres in diameter on the back of their necks. He noted several pairings, roughly 5 centimetres apart, which tells us both victims were stunned a number of times each. The wounds were slightly raised and erythemateous.'

'And in plain English?' Chandler asked to a gentle ripple of laughter.

'What, you think I understood any of that? The gist I gathered from our new pathologist is we're looking at peculiar pairings of red marks. Think welts and you won't go far wrong. The wounds indicate the use of a stun gun, so I reckon that would have been the first attack, and given the position of the marks, the boys were attacked from behind. According to the doc, their muscles would have gone into spasm, which resulted in them both going to ground. Then came the squirts of acid – and yes, it was squirted on, probably from a small plastic container. Finally, the boys were mutilated in a frenzied assault. It's probable, more than merely likely, that there was a minimum of two assailants. I don't think that comes as news to us.'

What spurred the team on, however, was being given the time of death window.

'As Bish is already aware from having attended the first PM, the lads died approximately between the hours of 10.00pm on Saturday night and 2.00am the following morning. Your eager DS immediately gathered intel updates, from which he was able to ascertain that the last sighting of these two boys on their Fletton street corner – if their bikes are anything to go by, that is – was around 11.30, narrowing the CCTV window even more.'

'Gul and I will get a move on with that as soon as we're done here,' Bishop said. 'It's the information we've been waiting for, so hopefully we can obtain something useful in finding the bastards who carried out this atrocity.'

Bliss nodded. 'Absolutely. It doesn't hurt to keep in mind that our two victims, although acting as runners for a drugs gang, were mid-teen children when push comes to shove. I suspect older gang members groomed these boys to sell, so we treat them like any other young victims of murder.'

'Any other actions?' Chandler asked.

'I think Bish and Gul could do with all the help we can spare. I don't know to what degree I'll be involved with my cold case today, but I do have to spend some time with it. However, if we consider the actions so far, I think we've covered some decent ground here. There's nothing more to learn from the parents or wider families of our victims. I think we can safely say we know well enough without actually knowing for certain that Barrie and

Ure worked the Soke line on the ground floor. We know how this goes: the runners at their level sell small quantities of cannabis, which helps fund the Class A gear, which is sold by foot soldiers one or two rungs further up the ladder... and so on. It might be worth having a word with Samantha Phillips, given she's the Soke boss. Pen, would you please have a word with intelligence and see if you can get an address on her? Maybe we can pay her a visit later today. I'd be interested to see how she feels about losing two of her boys.'

'Will do,' Chandler said. 'And Foxes? I was thinking of maybe having a chat with the Leicester OCG intel team to see if they have any idea who might have done this on behalf of Saad Ali.'

Bliss was all for it and happy to see his partner on the ball. 'Good idea. We might be able to organise some surveillance at a later date. Gather what you can, but sit on it until we have a chance to speak again. If the CCTV and dashcam searches come up with a vehicle or even faces, then we can see if it ties in with what you learn from the Leicester teams.'

*

Bliss entered the Unsolved Crimes Team office having composed himself barely seconds earlier. He had resolved not to follow Munday's lead. All talk of doing right for the greater good was in the abstract without details as far as he was concerned. Instead, he was going to weigh every scrap of evidence with a jaundiced eye, because the MI5 approach had convinced him there was something unnatural and potentially clandestine about the murder of a seemingly innocent man. If he could discover what that was before Munday contacted him again, as he undoubtedly would, the leverage would be nice to have in his back pocket.

Predictably, the mood inside the room was one of despondency. Guy Foley and Ben Corry had interviewed Trimley, the

Nolan's charmer of a handyman, and both investigators agreed on the man's innocence. At this point, the overall impression of the case was one of frustration and regret.

'We all have the overwhelming sense that there's something we're not seeing,' Beth Greenhill said. 'But also, that we could work this case for the rest of our lives and get nowhere with it.'

'We still have the result of the fingerprint search on the bullet casings to come,' Bliss reminded them, their glum faces making him feel more guilty. 'It just takes one break.'

'Ah. About that,' Foley said, shaking his head. 'Sorry. I forgot you weren't here when the report came in from ballistics. That's a no go, I'm afraid. Not even a partial to go on.'

That was not the news Bliss had hoped to hear. It literally was their last chance to gain a fresh lead. The unearthing of the weapon had provided them with impetus, but not a single scrap of new evidence. The initial investigation had failed. Now this one was going the same way. He had no need to heed Munday's advice, because the new team were faring no better than their predecessors. They weren't just easing off the accelerator, they were applying the handbrake and about to switch off the engine.

'I'm open to ideas,' he said, hoping to spark a moment of inspiration. 'Anything at all, no matter how ridiculous. We've spent less than three days on this and we're already staring defeat in the face. I'm not happy about that, and I don't expect any of you are, either. Look, so far, we've followed the logical order of things. We've worked the case by following all the steps taken by the first investigation team. But there are four new minds on the task now, so surely between us we can come up with an alternative approach to take.'

'You were the one who thought of something new,' Greenhill said. 'Asking about the dog might not have got us anywhere, but it was a good thought. For all we know, little Beano might well have had a quick nibble on the gunman as you suggested. And before you ask, yes I did look back through the case file and nobody thought to check the dog for blood.'

'A decent idea that gets us nowhere,' Bliss muttered. 'Which is about as much use as an ashtray on a motorbike. What we need is something we can genuinely get our teeth into. Something completely different to anything the original investigation did. Any suggestions at all? Please?'

The silence in the room was palpable. Bliss rubbed his forehead, which ached above both eyes. He wanted this. He needed this. Nothing was as it seemed, and for justice to be served Justin Nolan's killer had to be found. There was a good chance of Munday providing a crucial lead if only Bliss could persuade the MI5 man that their case had legs. All they needed was one fresh lead and a set of actions.

'What about Nolan's actual job?' Greenhill ventured. 'I mean, the original team spoke with his boss and his assistant, as you might expect. We've done the same. Neither of them was able to come up with any good reason why their colleague might have been murdered. But did anybody physically go through his workload, job by job, contract by contract?'

'What are you thinking, Beth?' Bliss asked, sensing a shift in emphasis.

'Nolan was a contracts manager. When you're talking about an organisation the size of the county council, you must be discussing some big money deals. In the millions, surely. Some he will have signed off on, some he would have rejected. Where there are large sums of money in play, there are often temptations. Temptations regularly matched by offers.'

'You think our victim might have been on the take?' Corry asked.

'Not necessarily,' Greenhill replied. 'In fact, more likely to be the very opposite. Maybe he refused to be bought just when somebody wanted to buy him.'

Bliss gave an excited nod. 'The original investigation did look into that. They discussed tenders and contracts with Nolan's boss. Having also sifted through his finances they concluded he wasn't being bought off, but neither were they able to spot any records offering the potential to warrant murder. You're right about the value of some contracts, Beth. We're looking at hundreds of millions of pounds overall. The issue I think the team faced was searching for the proverbial needle in a stack of needles. There were so many valuable contracts and even more tenders it was impossible to investigate all of them. We're talking about hundreds every year with a mountain of paperwork and legalese to decipher. It was simply too great a task. The SIO made the call, deciding the volume of work couldn't be justified as the team didn't think it would ever lead them to Nolan's killer.'

'Which is fair enough,' Foley said. 'But we have the advantage of hindsight. Plus, they focussed on signed deals for which Nolan might have accepted a backhander, whereas as Beth pointed out he could just as easily have upset somebody whose bid he rejected. Without digging too deep at the outset, we could put together a list of companies and assess which failed tenders badly affected the owners or shareholders. I mean, it's unlikely that a successful contract is going to lead to somebody wanting Nolan dead, so we set our sights on rejected tenders only.'

It wasn't exciting work – in fact Bliss saw only hard slog over paperwork and databases ahead – but it was something to pursue. In looking to name a killer, they were attempting to find a motive, and if Nolan had rejected an offer that resulted in a company going bust or perhaps left with land or property they couldn't sell, then the motive might become obvious. That was still a long way from identifying their killer, but it was a start. What's more, it was a way of prompting Munday to provide more details and perhaps throw them the bone they'd been searching for.

TWENTY-ONE

THE RESIDENTIAL AND COMMERCIAL settlement of Alconbury Weald stood upon the old RAF Alconbury airfield. Bliss had always found it odd that, despite the base being used largely by the United States Airforce since the early 1940s, it had retained the Royal Airforce name. Many American citizens had opted to remain in the surrounding area when the flights stopped coming in and out, but he guessed few of them would recognise their old place of work these days.

In the enterprise campus adjoining the one housing the county council's New Shire Hall building, a separate unit leased by the council was home to paper-based records dating back many years. It was here that Beth Greenhill had arranged for her and Bliss to meet with one of the administrative members of staff employed to manage the preservation and security of and access to the documentation.

Polly Abbott looked to be barely out of her teens, acne continuing to play havoc with her forehead and cheeks. When she greeted them, Bliss noticed the braces she wore to correct her teeth alignment. The smile dazzled, and the young woman's mood was enthusiastic as she led the investigators through to an area she had organised and prepared ahead of their visit. She had a bouncy gait, and her ponytail bobbed from side to side like a metronome.

The administrator ushered them into a square room measuring something like 24ft by 24ft, a good third of which was stacked high with cardboard boxes. The first sight of the multiple towers of paperwork caused Bliss to curse beneath his breath. He'd known they were in for some hard graft but hadn't anticipated it being a mammoth task with no possibility of completion.

'It looks daunting, I know,' Abbott said brightly, most likely having clocked the expression on their faces as they followed her inside the room. 'But don't worry, it's a much simpler system than it first appears. The white boxes contain signed contracts together with their tenders and associated documentation. The brown boxes are for rejected tenders. To make them easier to recognise, we've labelled each with coloured stickers indicating which decade they belong to, and by that we refer to the beginning of the process not the end. According to our records, Mr Nolan's work spanned two decades, between 1983 and 1999. The boxes are in date order stacked left to right, so you should have no trouble finding your way through them.'

'Many thanks for that,' Bliss said, somewhat relieved. 'You're extremely efficient and organised.'

Flushing a little, Abbott said, 'It's mainly the system. I just know my way around it. I've also drawn two tables together for you to sit at while you go over the materials. All we ask is that everything that comes out goes back in the exact same order.'

'You mean you're not staying to ensure that we behave?' Bliss asked, a half-smile on his face.

'Not enough staff around to allow that, not with the number of requests we get daily. As it is, we had to bump someone else down the ladder to get this arranged.'

'And we appreciate your efforts, Polly. If we find anything of interest, we'd like to be able to copy it. Do you have a copier close by?'

'We do, but it's for staff use only. I'd be happy to do them for you before you leave.'

'Thanks. How about related documents? I'm thinking of finances, blueprints, ground plans, maybe even lists of sub-contractors. Oh, and definitely things like inspection certificates if we're looking into new developments or even building refurbishments.'

The young woman nodded. 'I wish I could offer you reassurances, Mr Bliss. But as you might imagine, some people are more orderly than others. In theory, every single scrap of related documentation ought to be indicated by a specific code, but in reality, that didn't always happen. All I can promise you is if we have it and I can find it, I'll make you copies.'

Eventually left to their own devices, Bliss and Greenhill got stuck in. They had agreed during the short drive down from Peterborough to attack the task in reverse order, starting with Justin Nolan's last contract and working backwards. The relevant boxes were as easy to locate as Polly Abbott had indicated.

'Did you notice her getting all overheated?' Greenhill said to him as they removed the lid from the first brown box marked 1999-JAN-MAR. 'I reckon you made quite an impression.'

'I rather doubt it,' he scoffed. 'Probably saw me as some kind of father figure she was seeking approval from.'

'You think? If that is the case, then looking at her and looking at you, I'd say more like a grandfather figure.'

Bliss laughed, shooting her a sidelong glance. 'I thought I'd left all the ribbing behind in the Major Crime Unit. DS Chandler is usually the one giving me grief.'

'I'm perfectly happy to have stepped into her shoes.'

As they removed the lid and pulled wallet envelopes from the box, the pair chatted amiably.

'You have family, Jimmy?' she asked him.

'Nope. I lost my mum only a short while ago, but my dad died quite a few years back. I was married once, but she… well, she was murdered.'

He heard his colleague suck in her breath. 'Oh, shit! Me and my big mouth. I'm so sorry to hear that, Jimmy.'

Bliss nodded. 'It was a long time ago. Her name was Hazel. We were married for eight years and had known each other for twelve in all. A fellow copper stalked her for a short period before stabbing her to death in our home.'

'Oh, my God!'

'Naturally, I was the original prime suspect. He got away with it at the time, but I managed to get him banged up a few years ago. And before you ask and feel even more embarrassed than you already do, no, we never had any kids. How about you, Beth?'

She nodded. 'Married… for now. Two children, two grandchildren.'

'For now?' His eyes scanned a sheet of paper in front of him, but he was all ears.

'We're about to divorce. In reality the marriage was over a long time ago, but we stayed together for the kids. That was fine by both of us. It was worth it to keep their lives stable, and we seldom fought, so I'm pretty sure our children never knew a thing. They're long out of the nest, of course. Simon and I rubbed along together okay afterwards, and I thought we were both comfortable enough with our arrangement.'

'I take it that proved not to be the case,' Bliss said.

'You could say that. He went and found himself another woman.'

He winced. 'Ouch. Sorry.'

'I'm not. I'm okay about it. We had nothing going on as a couple, so why not?'

He kept his gaze on the documents in his hand, but his mind strayed. Beth Greenhill certainly wasn't old and looked younger than her age. She was attractive, too. He wondered if she was looking to move forward. He didn't want to make things awkward between them by inviting her to lunch, but immediately realised that was precisely what he had done the previous day in Fotheringhay. Then it had been perfectly innocent, but he wasn't at all sure it would be the next time he mentioned it. They had exchanged personal information. And both knew the other was free to do as they pleased. Having never been entirely certain how to react to such situations, Bliss erred on the side of caution and focussed on the job at hand.

'Look at this bloody lot,' he said, eyeing the columns of boxes with increasing despondency. 'And we don't even know what we're looking for.'

'Me and my bright ideas,' Greenhill said with a dour nod.

'No, it was a good shout. I'd go as far as to say the answer we're searching for might well be here. But when the reality exceeds what you imagine to this degree, you realise what an uphill task it is. I don't think our little team was designed to function under these circumstances.'

Realising how negative he sounded, Bliss took a breather. Eventually he took stock of the situation and made a decision. 'There's not a great deal in this first batch. Which stands to reason, because I'd guess most tenders aren't lodged and rejected so quickly. Now that I've seen what we're dealing with, we clearly can't justify spending so much time on something that might not even contain a lead.'

'What are you suggesting we do?'

'I was thinking about what Sarah Nolan told us. About her husband's work issue just before Christmas. If he rejected the tender in December 1998, then I'm guessing it was submitted much earlier, but probably in the same year. I say we begin with the first quarter and work our way forwards. It's a long shot, but I don't want to give up on this task without at least taking a look. How do you feel about that?'

Greenhill surveyed the room. Hands on hips, she said, 'I'm with you. We can spare some time now that we're here. But you're right when you say we haven't got a clue what we're even looking to achieve.'

'Tell you what,' Bliss said. 'If you find a gun in one of the boxes and it's still smoking, that might be worth putting to one side for later inspection.'

She rolled her eyes. 'Okay, smart…' Her words tailed off and she let her chin drop.

'You were going to call me a smartarse.'

'I was not.'

'You were. And that would've started up that whole conversation about arses all over again.'

Greenhill attempted to appear prim and proper. 'It would not. And even if it had, it'd be yours this time and we could leave mine alone.'

Bliss wasn't about to take that any further. He merely chuckled and turned his attention back to the piles of boxes.

TWENTY-TWO

H E SWIFTLY DISCOVERED A set of boxes marked 1998-JAN-MAR. There were three altogether. He opened one and slid it across to his colleague. 'Let's get cracking,' he said. 'This place is cold and sterile, and I don't like it here very much.'

'Sounds like a plan. Before we do, can you help settle an argument for me?'

'If I can.'

'Let's give it a go. Tell me, do you know what a GILF is?'

He almost did a cartoon double-take. 'A GILF? Are you sure you mean a GILF?' When his new partner nodded, he cleared his throat, then continued. 'Okay. So do you know what a MILF is?'

'I do. I'm not that naïve, Jimmy. The thing is, I have it in my head that the G stands for Girlfriend. I asked Ben and Guy and they just poked fun at me. They refused to say what they thought it was.'

Trying not to laugh, Bliss said, 'Well, you know how the M in MILF stands for Mother? In the case of a GILF, think more… the mother's mother.'

Greenhill's frown became wide-eyed astonishment, then a look of revulsion, followed by a glimmer of amusement. 'That little bastard,' she said.

Bliss just looked at her, waiting for her to explain.

'My youngest son told me his friends thought I was a bit of a GILF. He made it seem like a good thing.'

This time Bliss couldn't help himself. He barked out a laugh before managing to stifle it. 'Well, you told me you're a grand-mother, so technically speaking he's not wrong.'

'No. But he is a bastard.' Greenhill was also chuckling, but she still seemed to be in shock.

'Funny though,' Bliss said. 'Full marks on raising a son capable of having a joke with you about something like that. I'm guessing you'd rather be the MILF?'

'Of the two? Absolutely.'

'I'm sure you are in some young man's eyes. Or is that an inap-propriate thing to say?'

'To tell the truth, I'm not sure these days.' Greenhill shook her head as she perused another file. 'All I can tell you is I'm not offended by it. Plus, I raised the subject in the first place.'

'I'm glad to hear it. And to move on from a potentially embar-rassing faux pas on my behalf, let's get on with this lot.'

Blushing, his partner readily agreed.

They were on the third brown box from March 1998 when something started to nag at Bliss. He flipped back and forth between pages contained in one particular wallet envelope, believing he was missing something obvious. Eventually it clicked into place and he rooted around to see if there were associated folders, but there was just the one splayed open on the table he was sitting at.

'I might have something here,' he said, unable not to think of Munday. When Greenhill shuffled over to sit alongside him, he thought about how to shape what he was about to say. 'I think we generally agree we're clutching at straws here, so if I see a hat

I'm going to check to see if there's a rabbit inside. This folder could be that hat.'

'Go on,' she said. 'Frankly, I'd be grateful for any bone right now, no matter how small.'

Bliss smiled. 'You think we're mixing enough metaphors, Beth?'

She laughed and nudged his arm with her hand. 'You started it. So, come on, then, Sherlock. Spill.'

'Okay. When I saw the company name, it meant nothing to me, but the owner's name did. Even then I brushed it aside but found myself coming back to it and giving it more thought. Each time I did that the more I convinced myself I had something we might be able to work with. Does the name Callum Davey mean anything to you?'

Greenhill shook her head. 'No. Why, who is he?'

'I admit I'd probably never have heard of him either if it hadn't been for the fact that he and his company earned a massive contract to develop some software for an education system in the greater London area when I was still living there. I know he's since gone on to create a multi-billion-pound enterprise. And even though back in 1998 he was just starting to make a big name for himself, when I saw this rejection report my first thought was to wonder why somebody like him had his application turned down.'

'Okay. I get that. What was it for?'

'Without going deeper, I'm not quite sure what the overall plan would have been, but from what I can make out, Callum Davey's company bid to supply and install software by the name of Bug Zapper. And this was county-wide.'

'Some kind of anti-virus thing, you think?' Greenhill asked.

'That's precisely what I thought. But in fact, it has something to do with Y2K.'

'The Millennium Bug. Given the year we're talking about I suppose that makes sense.'

Bliss knew they might eventually be able to find the relevant successful bidder package in one of the white boxes, but the thought of rifling through them filled him with dread. Also, it was entirely possible that the winning bid hadn't been decided on by the time of Nolan's murder. Instead of kicking off another lengthy task, he took out his mobile and placed a call. Sandra Bannister answered on the third ring.

'I can't give you anything right now,' he explained, 'but I do want something from you.'

'Colour me surprised. So, what's new?'

'I'm sorry, Sandra. I'll get back to you before today's media briefing, I promise. What I'm after is something I hope you can find the answer to quicker than I can. I'm sure you remember Y2K and all that shit. Thing is, everybody was trying to protect themselves at the time, including the county council. I'd like to know who won the contract to fix our systems in Cambridgeshire.'

'Is that all?'

'What do you mean? That's a walk in the park for someone of your talents.'

She grunted and asked for thirty minutes. He asked her to make it ten. They agreed on twenty.

'You really think there's something here?' Greenhill asked, nodding at the open file. 'A connection to the murder of Justin Nolan?'

'I have no idea,' Bliss admitted. 'What I do know is this is the first document I've seen today to ignite anything inside my tiny brain. If you have a better idea, I'm happy to hear it. It just struck me as odd, that's all. I can't imagine Callum Davey being rejected over any bid, but it's probably just one of those things. For all I know, it happens all the time. Not my area of expertise.'

'You mean software?'

'Software, hardware, any kind of ware when it comes to computers. I'm much better at using them these days because I've had to be, but I always think I'm going to do something wrong. Besides, I have the others for that sort of thing. DC Gul Ansari mainly.'

Less than ten minutes later, the reporter was back on the phone with him. 'A company called Solution Providers Techsperts won the bid,' Bannister told him. 'Does that help?'

Bliss felt himself go cold. Hairs stood erect on the back of his neck. 'Are you certain, Sandra?'

'You think I'd provide you with bad information, Jimmy?'

'No. It's not that. Sorry. Just a name I didn't expect to hear.'

He thanked Bannister and again promised to get back to her later in the day. He fell into contemplative silence, and it was Greenhill who had to break it.

'What's wrong?' she asked. 'I heard what she told you. Is it bad news? Do you know this company?'

Bliss nodded. 'I do. It was the name of Callum Davey's first business. It's the name on the rejected application.'

'But your friend just told you that company won the bid.'

'I realise that. Call me a cynic, Beth, but you have to know what I'm thinking right now.'

'Yes, I believe I do. You're wondering if Justin Nolan stood between failure and success for Davey when it came to that bid.'

Biting into his bottom lip, Bliss said, 'That's precisely what's going through my head. I do believe in coincidence, but not in this case. What I'm reading in this file is that the bid was unsuccessful. What I just learned from Sandra was that Davey's company somehow still ended up with the contract. And somewhere in between, somebody shot and killed the one person standing in the way.'

TWENTY-THREE

WHILE GREENHILL SPOKE WITH Polly Abbott about obtaining copies of the documents in the file they had pulled, and having all related documentation scanned and sent to her in an email, Bliss called Munday as he waited out by the car. He suspected the old spy would have remained in or close to the area and his suspicion turned out to be spot on. They agreed to meet for a quick lunch. After dropping his colleague back at Thorpe Wood and asking her to work with the others to compile an intelligence report package on Callum Davey and his business empire, Bliss headed directly to the arranged meeting point.

From the outside, Badger's Café in Fengate looked weary and downtrodden like an itinerant at the end of a back-breaking day picking fruit in the blazing sunshine. The interior was not much of an improvement, but the staff were cheerful and friendly and the food plentiful. Sometimes it was more than half decent. Bliss had chosen the place mainly because he was hungry, but he also thought there was little chance of him being seen with the MI5 man by anyone he knew.

'What is so important you had me come here?' Munday asked. He regarded the tea he'd just been served up with disdain.

'I needed to speak to you. Isn't that enough?'

'You might have chosen more salubrious surroundings.'

Bliss smiled. 'What's the matter, Munday? You don't enjoy spending time with the common man?'

'Oh, I have no problem with the common man, Bliss. Only with where they choose to dine. Now, before I'm reduced to tasting the oily bilgewater in this suspiciously discoloured mug, please tell me why I am here.'

'Solution Provider Techsperts,' Bliss said, sitting back in his hard plastic chair to observe the reaction. As anticipated, Munday was his usual stoical self, though his left eye twitched more than once.

'That is unfortunate,' the spy said in a low, deep voice. 'And now you have successfully discouraged me from what I'm certain would have been a terrible lunch. You've been busy, Bliss. Even after I asked you to back off as a favour to me.'

'The case takes us where the case goes. Besides, as you well know I'm not the only one working it. One of my new colleagues made a suggestion and we followed it up. I had no idea where it would lead. Before I tell you how we got there, how about you explain yourself.'

Munday drew in a deep breath and then exhaled just as deeply. 'Before I do so, I need to know something. If I were to ask you to drop this reinvestigation into the murder of Justin Nolan altogether, what would be your response?'

Bliss raised his eyebrows. It was all the answer he felt necessary to give.

'As I presumed. In which case, I'm going to tell you a story.'

'Oh, here we go. This going to be some *Jackanory* bollocks?'

'You really ought to update your popular culture references, Bliss. But your point is well made, though mine is not a tall tale. It's merely pertinent.'

After Bliss had placed his order for a bacon and egg sandwich, he gestured for the MI5 spy to continue.

'First of all, I tip my hat. You found the scattered dots and then you joined them. But thus far you have less than half the full story. You've done exceptionally well to identify Callum Davey and his company. But you do not have his partner in crime. In fact, I'd wager you were unaware until I just mentioned it that there even *was* a partner in crime.'

'Of course we knew,' Bliss scoffed. 'A man like Davey doesn't get his hands dirty by pulling the trigger himself.'

Mundy shook his head. The movements were stiff. 'Oh, no. I'm not talking about the triggerman, Bliss. And, in part, that's one of the reasons we'd like you to back off. The way we see it, if you had plenty of time and even more resources, you might eventually discover the other man involved in this. That said, I don't see you and your three colleagues – as capable as they may be – being allowed to spend the rest of your days working this one unsolved murder. Moreover, nothing you find along the way will amount to more than speculation and circumstantial evidence at best. And what it definitely won't do is give you the gunman.'

'How can you possibly know that?' Bliss forced the matter with some verve.

'It all begins somewhere in the middle of 1998 and runs through to the early stages of the following year. This, as you may recall, was at a time when there was a great deal of panic concerning the year 2000 problem, more commonly referred to as the Millennium Bug.'

'Yes. I think I might have heard something about that.' Bliss teased. 'Wasn't it all just a big scam?'

'A view endorsed by many, but I will return to your question in a moment. The fact is, the problem was big business for some, and a great deal of physical and financial outlay for others. In retrospect, the original designers and programmers made such a terrible error. You see, when servers and computers were being manufactured, those who designed the systems never gave a moment's thought to the year 2000. And to save time when setting calendar dates, in many programs they identified the year with only the final two digits, omitting the one and the nine altogether. The problem being that by the time the year 2000 eventually clicked around, the systems using the software and hardware might find the zero-zero indistinguishable from 1900. Nobody quite knew what would happen if that occurred, but early testing suggested the results might be calamitous.'

Nodding, Bliss said, 'That much I managed to grasp at the time. People were claiming everything would stop working, that planes might fall from the sky, ships crash into each other, satellites fail altogether.'

'That's the gist of it, yes. So, by the late nineties, a campaign to respond to the problem was well under way. The task was immense. Essentially, every suspected system needed to be tested and, if found susceptible, upgraded with a software patch. A daunting proposition, and one nobody ever truly believed could be fully rectified. Hence the concentration on the systems presenting the most danger to life and limb.'

'And finance, I imagine,' Bliss said with a jaundiced edge.

Munday smiled. 'Of course.'

'And all this has what to do with Justin Nolan?'

'I think by now you must have already worked that out for yourself.'

'To a certain extent, yes. But I want to hear it from you.'

Munday ran a thumb and a finger over his thin moustache. 'At that time, Mr Nolan, as you're well aware, had a responsible position as head of procurement for the Cambridgeshire County Council. The decision as to who provided the county-wide response to the Y2K bug fell upon his shoulders. Records tell us he spoke to three companies. One of those came in with a solution that was three times more expensive to purchase as its nearest competitor but was supposedly far cheaper to implement, as it required fewer people to apply the fix. But when delivering the formal presentation, the company owner miscalculated when he mentioned his long and binding friendship with the then deputy leader of the county council. We are led to believe that at this merest hint of impropriety, Nolan dropped them like a red-hot coal.'

Bliss found himself seduced by the story. When his sandwich arrived, he pushed the plate to one side. He leaned in, listening intently. 'We're fast heading towards a case of corruption here, right?' he said.

Munday gave a single nod. 'You'll find no record of this, but we have it on good authority that the deputy leader and Nolan subsequently exchanged words. When Nolan stood his ground, the deputy leader had a meeting behind closed doors with Nolan's boss, Jeff Smalling. No minutes of that meeting were taken, but from what we've been able to ascertain, Smalling evidently offered some sympathy but claimed to have his hands tied. Nolan was the man responsible for procurement, and whilst his decisions were open to debate after the event, making them was his sole responsibility.'

Bliss stared hard at him. 'You're essentially confirming Nolan was murdered to ensure the bid went through.'

Munday spread his hands. 'That's not for me to say. What I can tell you, however, is that due to the urgency following Nolan's untimely demise, the procurement went ahead without further delay. It made the man who owned the company providing the fix a fortune, which in turn became considerably vaster.'

'Yes, I'd already reached that conclusion,' Bliss said. 'There is one thing I still don't understand, though.'

'And that is?'

'What your interest might be. That of MI5, I mean.'

'Hmm. Here's where it starts to get complex,' Munday said.

'That's fine by me,' Bliss said. 'I'll order another cup of this café's finest, and you can tell me all about it.'

TWENTY-FOUR

O FFERING A SUBTLE SMILE, Munday said, 'First, my dear chap, let me tell you how important it all was. Earlier, you referred to it as a scam. You're not alone in that belief. Many people questioned why the world did not fall apart in those early hours of January 2000. They said it was outrageous that so much money – estimated to be around £20 billion in the UK alone – was wasted on what turned out to be a non-event. Others argued this was to miss the point; that it was indeed a non-event purely because nations *did* spend a fortune on correcting the fault.

'But within that supposed non-event, examples of failure were discovered and admitted to. The safety systems of 10 nuclear power stations around the world failed simultaneously, electrocardiograph machines stopped working, and the US's critical defence intelligence satellites were out of action for hours. The banking system might have collapsed, as testing revealed that calculations would have thrown interest rates back by a hundred years. The US coastguard uncovered errors that would have caused the loss of steering control and fire detection. Many credit card systems actually did prevent access in the first days of the new millennium. Here in the UK, newborns received birth certificates for the year 1900. In fact, many date-related systems across the world that had not been Y2K prepared either failed or glitched.'

'I get the picture,' Bliss said. 'It was a big deal.'

'Massive,' Munday argued. 'More widespread than anybody ever imagined. Now, what we do know is that the software and hardware fixes to your county's systems worked a treat. Delivered and executed as promised. However, the predicted labour cost savings were not as advertised, and the total outlay was considerable. All of which made one man very happy, at least.'

'Callum Davey.'

'Naturally. But as I mentioned earlier, he wasn't alone. Given the deputy leader of the council at the time was vocal in his support for fixing the problem and ensuring stability, his star was on the rise. And so, to your question, Bliss. Five's interest began a number of years ago simply because of who these people are and what they represent. Because, you see, that deputy leader went on to run the council. He later became this city's MP. To this day he remains firm friends with Davey, the man who continues to pump money into a pal's campaigns and buys political support and influence for him along the way.'

'And your interest is what?' Bliss asked. 'Is Five looking to bring these men down or support them?'

'Neither. Our interest is undecided. I'm not personally a part of that evaluation, but we want to know if he can be of use to us. The thing is it just happens that one of the biggest secrets in politics today centres around this particular MP. He has largely remained under the political radar as a member of the shadow back benches. But here's where we have a distinct interest. You see, where there are secrets there are also usually rumours. It has come to our attention that he is being groomed as the next leader of the party. With the intention that he eventually becomes PM.'

Bliss puffed out his cheeks. 'No wonder he's captured your attention. And this candidate for future Prime Minister and all that entails is our man? The man who is currently MP for this city. You're talking about Robert Clay.'

'Precisely.'

'You think he and Callum Davey have skeletons in their own closets. You think these two high-powered men were responsible for creating a conspiracy to remove Justin Nolan as an obstacle in February 1999.'

Munday nodded. 'Absolutely we do.'

Bliss frowned. 'But why would MI5 not want these men to be arrested and charged?'

'Because we can't have an MP accused of such a horrendous act before we've decided if he can be of use to us. Besides, whilst at no time would such a crime ever be acceptable, exposing him now would be calamitous. Don't forget, Bliss, although he appears to be a minor figure, he is the party's biggest hope for the future in decades.'

Glancing forlornly at his now cold sandwich, Bliss said, 'I get the political implications, Munday. I'm more concerned with the legal ones. You'd rather this man walked free? Unpunished? Perhaps even gaining that PM job in the process?'

'As matters stand, Five would rather sweep the whole sorry mess under the carpet until such a time as the man responsible is no longer part of the political system.'

'At which time he'll probably be fitted for some ermine.'

'A cynical observation, but almost certainly true. The Lords house is every bit as important to Five as the government chambers, Bliss. Politics has survived a great deal in recent years, but having a declared murderer, or even one who sanctioned the act, would, it is felt, be a step too far. The public is sick and tired of politics and politicians. This would be the final nail.'

'Which is their right,' Bliss said. 'But what you're asking me to do is outrageous. And to be honest, you disappoint me.'

Munday offered a resigned sigh. 'I'm not saying I agree with the thinking. But you must admit, with politics in its current state this could provoke anarchy of a kind we have seldom witnessed before. Have you looked out there, Bliss? Have you gauged the mood of the nation? It's febrile. It's waiting for one more spark to ignite the fire inside the bellies of malcontents and spur them into action. No, my friend, irrespective of your beliefs or mine, the notion of exposing Robert Clay's deeds all those years ago is something too awful to contemplate.'

'Sounds to me as if you lot have already made up your minds about him, despite what you said to me earlier.'

'To be perfectly frank with you, Bliss, I don't see how he would possibly ever be a friend to us in the security services. A man of his background is much more likely to be an enemy or seek to have complete control. But even if he should become an irritant, having knowledge of who and what he is would afford us a certain amount of leverage.'

'You mean you could blackmail him as necessary?'

Munday's smile was almost imperceptible. Almost. 'I mean we could bend him to our will. Make him more malleable. I'm not saying it's right, but I am asking you to look at it in the round.'

Incensed, Bliss glared at his companion, but managed to lower his voice. 'You have to know what my answer will be. If not, then clearly, I made no impression on you at all.'

For the first time, Munday began to shuffle uncomfortably in his seat. 'I fear I do. But I must caution you, Bliss, to remember at all times that I am the good cop. The one they send ahead to, shall we say, smooth the waters. As for the bad cops of whom I've previously spoken, well, they can be very bad indeed. Ruthless, even. Believe me when I say you do not want to cross them.'

Bliss could barely comprehend what he was hearing. 'Are you threatening me, Munday?'

The spy straightened, chin out. 'I don't make threats, old chap. I leave distasteful tasks of that nature to others. I would not usually be so forthright, but you have obviously unearthed information we'd rather you hadn't. Plus, I like you. And I implore you to understand that in your twilight years you do not want to be on the wrong side of these people.'

'And I've already given you my answer,' Bliss shot back. He opted not to reveal Beth Greenhill being with him when he discovered the Callum Davey connection, though he feared having MI5 crawling all over the backgrounds of his new colleagues simply because they were all part of the same team.

With a shrug, Munday said, 'I understand. How about a compromise of sorts? At the very least, allow me to report back favourably. If I tell them you're considering your position, that will soothe their fevered brows for the time being. It would buy us both some thinking time.'

Bliss was willing to listen. 'Let's say I do that. Let's say I agree to listen further. And then let's be absolutely blunt about what you're ultimately asking me to do. You want me not to discover Mr Nolan's killer. Moreover, now that I have this information, I'm to ensure this cold case investigation steers clear of it. Is that about right?'

'It is. For the time being. And hopefully for the greater good.'

'I'll believe that when I see it,' Bliss scoffed.

Munday's sigh was lengthy and sounded regretful. 'You regard my employers unkindly, and so be it. You think you have Callum Davey and his company thus far. But you will not find any evidence to tie him to the murder. Nor any wrongdoing, for that matter. You might speculate, but I don't think you will get much further. As for Robert Clay, you will never connect him to the shooting of your victim. Not without the intel we have. And more importantly, neither will you have the shooter, who was quite possibly a foreign national brought in to carry out a single execution and who has since vanished back to whence he came. So, how about this? Follow your Callum Davey lead. Meanwhile, I'll report back and propose we speed up our own decision-making process. If we decide to feed Clay to the wolves after all, I will personally hand over everything we have on him. To you, if that wasn't clear.'

Bliss regarded him sullenly. 'So first the threat, and then the bribe. I didn't have you down as a stick and carrot man.'

Munday at least had the decency to appear wounded. 'Not forgetting the favour you owe me,' he reminded Bliss, despite his obvious discomfort. 'You don't strike me as the kind of man to ignore that.'

Bliss stared ruefully into the distance. 'I guess we're both about to find that out.'

TWENTY-FIVE

BLISS CALLED AHEAD TO ask Chandler if anyone had managed to get a location on Samantha Phillips. According to her, she'd had to dig deep but had eventually come up with some answers. The intelligence team's most recent information suggested the young woman had moved out of the family home in Newborough and now resided in one of the Fletton Quays apartments overlooking the river.

'Which means she and I are neighbours,' Chandler said, interrupting herself. 'Separated only by a narrow stretch of water. We could probably wave at each other from our balconies.'

'Lowers the tone of the place I reckon,' Bliss responded. 'Bloody riff-raff.'

'I know, right? Having drug dealers as neighbours is never acceptable.'

'No, I meant you, Pen. Property prices must have plummeted since you moved in.'

'Oh, comedian now, is it? Don't give up your day job, Jimmy.'

Bliss was happy with himself for having poked the bear. 'Is that where we'll find her now?' he asked.

'Tonight, maybe. Today she's more likely to be putting in an appearance at the family business. It looks as if her managerial job there pays a legit salary while also acting as suitable cover for her little drugs empire.'

Bliss knew where that was located and asked Chandler to meet him in the police station car park in ten minutes. He was uneasy at feeling trapped inside a mental and moral bind. And as he so often did at such times, he turned to the person he trusted most of all. As they made their way to the premises in Crowland, he let go of what was troubling him.

'I'm so sorry,' she said the moment he had finished talking.

'What for?' he queried. It wasn't the response he had expected.

'For putting you in this position. If you'd never asked Munday to do that favour for me, you wouldn't find yourself in this fix now.'

Bliss shook his head. 'No, I'm not having that. You didn't ask me to approach him in the first place. That was all me. I thought of it, I did it. It's my debt to owe, and now I'm being asked to honour it.'

'But you only did it to help me.'

'That's beside the point, Pen. You have nothing to be sorry about. This is on me, and I'm sharing it with you because I need to tell somebody. Somebody who understands and won't judge me.'

Chandler sniggered. 'I wouldn't go that far. I judge you all the time. Your poor taste in music, your awful taste in football teams, your hideous taste in clothes... I could go on.'

He screwed up his face as if he'd tasted something bitter. 'That's just hurtful. What's wrong with my clobber, anyway?'

'It's all so *Man at C&A*.'

'You're showing your age now, Pen. I can't remember how long ago they closed all their shops, but it was bloody donkey's years ago.'

'My point exactly. Old man clothes for an old man.'

'Has anyone ever told you to your face that you can be a bit of a cow bag?'

'Yes. You.'

'I rest my case. Anyway, back to me and my problem, if it's all the same to you.'

Chandler bowed her head, then turned to him. 'You know you can easily buy some time if you genuinely need to, Jimmy. And would that be so terrible? After all, you're not talking about back peddling on an active case. It's already been more than twenty years. Will another few days make any difference?'

'It's not just about pulling back on the reins of the case itself,' he said with a shrug. 'It's having to mislead my new colleagues that bothers me most. This is the cold case I chose, and they followed me down this rabbit hole. Yet here I am already betraying their trust after only three days in the job. The problem is, Pen, I'm conflicted. On the one hand, I owe Munday a favour. On the other, they're deserving of my loyalty and respect.'

'Oh, come on,' she chided him. 'It's a delay we're talking about, that's all. And from what you've told me, your new team might even learn the truth all by themselves if you allow them to.'

Bliss gave her a sidelong glance as he turned off the A47 and onto the A16. 'Isn't that the point? Allowing them to eventually discover the truth for themselves means I'm not telling them what that truth is now. I'm misleading them. Deliberately. In more ways than one. And whatever I owe Munday for having a word in the right ear on your behalf, how can I look these people in the eye knowing I'm betraying them?'

Chandler was silent for a few moments. Eventually she shifted in her seat to face him and said, 'I understand what you're saying. And of course you're conflicted. I also know how dreadful you must feel about the quandary you're in. But, Jimmy, what's your alternative? Munday has asked you to consider the bigger picture. Solving Justin Nolan's murder can wait. And you can swallow your pride or whatever it is and give yourself a break. Like I said before, you're only postponing things. It's not as if you're going to turn your back on it altogether and walk away.'

'And what if that's Munday's next request? What if his MI5 bosses decide they want to keep Robert Clay in place?'

'Then that's a different problem. One you face when it arises. It's not the issue confronting you today. Don't look ahead and worry about what to do then, look at resolving what's bothering you right now.'

Bliss sighed. 'Well, you're a big, fat help. When did you become so wise?'

'I've had a month without you dragging me down to your level.'

Her smile made him find one of his own. He missed this. The banter, the deeper discussions. The honesty. He mulled her words over while he found his way to the site of *S. Phillips Builders* on Greenbank Drain just outside the village of Crowland. He nosed the Volvo off the road and onto the site then parked up alongside a Jaguar SUV on the gravel outside a surprisingly smart-looking Portakabin.

When the pair entered the portable building being used as a site office, a man who had been sitting on a small sofa to their left next to a kitchenette literally jumped to attention. He sprang to his feet like a scalded cat, which was quite a sight given his considerable height and build. Either his blue suit was a size too small, or his muscles a size too large, but either way he was a unit. His face was unblemished, and his fair hair stood stiff and spiky with product.

'At ease,' Bliss said playfully, weighing up a potential foe before turning his attention to the woman seated behind a cheap grey laminate desk at the far end of the cabin. She was in her early twenties, with long, blonde wavy hair cascading over her shoulders. She wore plenty of makeup, including long false eyelashes. He knew her colourfully patterned dress came with a designer brand label; no knock-offs for this young woman. Amidst the tension of their intrusion, he held out his ID card and introduced himself. Chandler did the same.

'The old boy is no longer running the show,' were the first words out of Samantha Phillips's mouth. 'He's not well, so don't go bothering him at home, either.'

Her voice was pure Fenland, though it sounded as if she'd attempted to soften the edges.

'Funny,' Bliss said. 'I heard you two had fallen out.'

'You heard right. Don't mean I don't care about him anymore, does it?' Her voice rose at the end, challenging him to disagree.

'You want me to get rid of them, boss?' the big man said from the spot by the sofa where he had marked his territory.

'You can try,' Bliss muttered.

Samantha Phillips seemed to consider the suggestion for a second or two before shaking her head. 'No, it's all good, Ade. I don't see these two jokers being a problem.'

Just like her old man, Bliss thought. Arrogant and dismissive. 'You might want to ask your Ken doll here to wait outside,' he suggested, gesturing with a thumb. 'We need a private conversation.'

With a rapid shake of the head, Phillips said, 'No. Ade stays. Ask what you came to ask or say what you came to say. I don't have long, mind. We've got a lot on at the moment.'

'I bet you have,' Bliss said casually. 'I mean, those drugs don't sell themselves. And what with you being two runners short since the weekend...'

He was looking for a reaction but didn't get the one he'd hoped for. Phillips gave the sweetest smile. It was intended to disarm, and would have if you didn't know she sold poison, misery, and death for a living. 'I'm sorry, I have no idea what you mean. We run a building company here.'

'Superficially, yes. After all, you still need the appearance of earning an honest crust. But let's be adult about this, Ms Phillips. You also run the Soke drugs line, and two of your pawns were taken off the board over the weekend. We're here to have a word with you about that.'

'And yet still I don't have a clue what you're banging on about. You must have me confused with somebody else. Now, if you don't mind...' She gestured towards the doorway.

Bliss stood his ground. 'If you want to play games that's up to you, Samantha. But you'll hear us out. Our intelligence tells us you took over your dad's cannabis dealing business at the same time as you started managing the building side. The legit part. You quickly put your own stamp on things by moving into the dangerous world of selling class A drugs. Much against your old man's wishes as I understand it. Not content with that, you decided to set up a county line and start moving your wares around, buying, selling, redistributing, the whole shebang. You took your old man's tidy little business that ticked over unnoticed, turned it around, and made a name for yourself as the boss of a genuinely organised criminal gang. But in your haste and your greed, you trod on a few toes, one of which belonged to Saad Ali and his Foxes line. By way of a reprisal, Foxes moved into Peterborough. This prompted a few skirmishes between your two gangs, and now that has escalated, and it looks as if the Foxes want to run you out of your own city. To complicate matters, there's also a new OCG looking to become the one and only Peterborough-based county lines drugs firm. How am I doing so far?'

Phillips nodded and frowned at the same time. 'Sounds like a... modern-day fairy tale. One of those myths we hear so much about. But even if it is real, it still has fuck all to do with me. Like I said before, I'm not the one you need to be talking to. I know nothing about any of this.'

'It's just us here,' Chandler said, squaring her stance. 'You can speak freely.'

'Sure. Because the police are so trustworthy. Not.'

'Okay, then how about we look at the whole thing slightly differently? What if we think of it as purely hypothetical? How does that sound?'

'Will it get you out of here quicker if I agree?'

'I imagine so.'

'Well, crack on then, darling.'

Chandler smirked. 'Hypothetically, then, Samantha, if you were the boss of the Soke drugs line, you'd probably be furious about having two of your runners murdered. Of course, it's highly unlikely that you give a shit about the boys themselves, more a question of being disrespected. You might be so upset that you were considering a revenge attack of your own. If that were the case, the point of us being here would be to talk some sense into you. Because if you react to their escalation, life is going to get very messy very quickly. I mean, you understand the cycle you'd be perpetuating, right?'

After taking a beat to consider, Phillips said, 'If, hypothetically speaking, I *am* the gang boss in this story of yours, it sounds to me as if I'd be justified in responding to an attack on *my* people and *my* business. If I'm understanding you properly, it seems to me as if you ought to be having a word in this Saad Ali person's shell-like.'

'He's being spoken to by detectives from his own area force,' Chandler confirmed. 'Believe me, nobody is being left out of this discussion. Our job, Samantha, is to prevent more bloodshed. The loss of two lives this past weekend is two lives too many.

Reaction tends to provoke further escalation, which leads to a greater reaction… and so on. I don't see how that benefits any of you. Especially you. In theory, that is.'

This time, Phillips showed some genuine interest by cocking her head. 'Why especially me?'

Chandler regarded her pointedly. 'Because you'll lose what you already have, right down to what you began with.'

'The fuck I will.'

'Oh, but you will. Because the Foxes line is so much bigger and more established. It's already started to apply the pressure, which suggests Ali means business. You poked the bear by trying to slip into his territory, so now he wants yours. And if he wants it, he'll have it. Don't let your pride or ego tell you otherwise. And it's got nothing to do with you being a woman. He'd just as easily take it off your old man if push came to shove.'

The young woman glared at him. 'Maybe you don't know how determined I can be. If I am this gang boss, that is. Which of course I'm not.'

'Then don't allow that determination to rule what you surely must know deep down,' Bliss told her. What he saw in her scowling features was a fierce resolve. What he heard in her voice was fear. 'If this becomes a war, Samantha, you'll lose it. And you'll lose badly. It could cost you everything. And I don't just mean your money and your businesses. You might be willing enough and demented enough to put yourself in the firing line, but people like Saad Ali won't stop with you and your thugs. They'll make you suffer first, starting with hurting your family. Risking your own life is one thing, but risking theirs is a step too far. I hope you're capable of understanding that.'

This time she made no reply. Her eyes fell to her hands which were clasped on the desk, the knuckles white. Bliss recognised her doubt and risked one more push.

'Samantha, believe me when I tell you we're not here to save you or your family from all the strife you have coming your way. Personally, I couldn't give a toss about any of you. You're all scum as far as I'm concerned. Except perhaps for those two boys who were so brutally murdered. But the fact is, we're thinking of the damage such an outright war might cause if it spills over into the public domain. Which it inevitably will. But there is one more thing you ought to be aware of. Something I hope you'll consider before you act with aggression.'

'What's that then?' she asked, setting her jaw as she looked up at him.

'Our intel – and believe me I know it's accurate – suggests that the outcome of any battle you have with the Foxes line will be short-lived. City-Wide are bigger players than you can possibly imagine. You don't know who runs it, but we do. And I'm telling you now that they'll gobble Soke and Foxes up and spit you both out in bubbles. But if you play your cards right and sit tight, you might just find a solution dropping right into your lap.'

Her eyes drilled into his. 'What do you mean by that? What do you know?'

Bliss knew he had her interest and gave her a wink. 'I can't tell you that. But I know enough. There are things in play behind the scenes. We, the police, are not about to allow this squabble of yours to tear this city apart. We're interested in a more peaceful, viable solution. One you might even be happy to go along with at no cost to your reputation. So, do yourself a favour and be patient. Think about what we've said before you act irrationally.'

'Are you working for them?' Phillips asked, angling her head. 'This… this City-Wide mob. Is that what this is all about? Two bent cops earning a few quid on the side by working for my opposition.'

'Don't insult either of us,' Bliss told her sharply. 'And yes, comparing us to the likes of you *is* an insult. No, Samantha, this is not a shakedown. It's everything we just told you it was, and more. So, bide your time or it's going to come back to haunt you.'

The cabin was silent for no more than three seconds before a young man wearing a tracksuit and a baseball cap wrenched the door open. He entered in a hurry, swiftly followed by a stumbling figure who whimpered like a beaten dog. 'We can't wait any longer,' Baseball Cap blurted out. 'You have to let me get him to a hosp…'

He staggered to a halt and his voice trailed off when his gaze fell upon Bliss and Chandler. His mouth yawned open as he seemed to reflect on his error.

The man he had preceded into the hut began to wail and moan and weep through a heavily battered face while holding up what remained of his left arm.

TWENTY-SIX

'FUCK OUR ROTTEN LUCK!' Bliss said. He eyed the troops deject-edly. 'We had her. I'm convinced we had Samantha Phillips just where we wanted her. I kicked it off with some old flannel, Pen followed up with the "hypothetical" ploy, before I finished things off with as much sincerity as I could muster. Then Fre-drick-fucking-Sykes bursts in and puts the kybosh on the lot.'

'Fredrick Sykes? I don't think I have his name listed any-where,' DC Gratton said, thumbing through his notes. 'Who is he, Jimmy?'

Bliss looked at him sideways. 'Fredrick Sykes. The Fugitive.'

'Who? What?'

'The one-armed man, Phil. You've never seen the film? Never even heard of it? Harrison Ford, Tommy Lee Jones. Sykes *is* the one-armed man in the film. Ford is hunting him, while Tommy is hunting Ford. No? Nothing?' He threw his hands up in despair. 'Philistine.'

'To be fair,' Chandler said. 'Only a movie nerd like you would remember the name of the actual killer.'

'You think this fresh victim killed the play?' DCI Warburton asked, getting back on point.

Bliss oscillated a hand. 'I don't know. Your guess is as good as mine. It certainly wouldn't have improved Philipps' mood.'

While Chandler had busied herself summoning the duty inspector, a response unit, and an ambulance, with Bliss on his phone to the drugs squad, Samantha Phillips's finely coiffured muscle shepherded the wounded man back out of the cabin, trying to keep him calm and quiet and failing miserably on both counts. The man who had brought him to the office stood in the corner by the desk, exchanging harsh whispers with his boss. Fury etched itself into her every feature, and whenever her eyes drifted and found Bliss staring at her, she squinted and glared back. When their phone calls were over, he and Chandler waited for everyone to arrive at the scene, and as soon as they were through updating the newcomers, they left to drive back to Thorpe Wood.

'From the scraps of their conversation I was able to overhear,' Bliss said, 'our wounded man received his injuries yesterday. The bloke in the tracksuit had a go at treating the wounds as best he could. But the man's pain eventually became so bad they went to Phillips to beg her to let him go to hospital.'

'What I fail to understand,' Bishop said, 'is why they punished this bloke to such an extreme but then left him alive. If anything, that's a de-escalation from a double murder. What's the game there? Assuming this was Foxes acting up again.'

'Actually,' Bliss replied. 'I reckon it might be quite a clever move on their part. With a few beatings and minor stabbings, they first established their interest. Then, out of the blue, they step things up with murder, but targeting only of a couple of kids nobody's going to miss and who will be replaced in an afternoon. Then, instead of upping their game again, they grab somebody from higher up the ladder but toss him back into the pond. Albeit minus part of one arm and without much of a mouth and jaw left from what I could see.'

'And exactly how is that clever?' Warburton wanted to know.

'It's painting a picture for Samantha Phillips. It's telling her we can get to your two-bob runners without you knowing. We're proving we're willing and capable of going the whole way by topping them. Now we're not only showing you we can get to one of your more major players, but also that we can be merciful. We can't go as far as to give him back unharmed, but take the win.'

'What makes you think this one-armed bloke is a player?' DC Ansari asked.

'Because Jimmy had me take a photo of him and shoot it over to both the drugs squad and intelligence,' Chandler said. 'One of the druggies came through and recognised him. Put a name to the face. He's not top level, but respected and loyal.'

'And now he's gone and fucked up our pitch to Samantha Phillips,' Bliss complained.

'You think she'll respond badly?' Warburton asked.

'She was spitting feathers as it was. She might calm down once she realises he's going to make it, and she might even read into it the same thing I did. But right now, inside her head, I have no doubt she's plotting and scheming and none of it will be favourable. I can only hope she stops to consider everything we told her before she acts.'

Bliss had turned off his work phone's ringer for the meeting, but felt it vibrating in his trouser pocket. He was waiting for an update from the hospital concerning the condition of the most recent victim, subsequently identified as Vic Tolley. He was also still expecting to hear back from Danielle Halford. He stuck his hand in his pocket, took out the phone, and looked at the screen. He didn't know the number, and it wasn't one of the contacts he'd entered into the new phone. Puzzled, he answered without hesitation.

'Time's up,' Halford said. 'Do you have an answer for me?'

He, DCI Warburton, and DCS Fletcher had previously agreed on a strategy for when Halford or one of her minions made contact. It was time to see if he could pull it off.

'Seven o'clock tonight,' he said. 'Meeting room at the Holiday Inn. Room A.'

'The hotel at Thorpe Wood? I was thinking more of neutral territory.'

'Life's full of disappointments.'

Halford made no comment at first, then said, 'I do hope you're not one of them, Jimmy. Okay. I assume you'll be coming mob-handed, but there will be just the three of us. Myself, an associate, and a company lawyer.'

Bliss didn't miss a beat. 'That number had better rise to four, and the fourth better be Hector Karagiannis. If not, don't bother to turn up.'

'I did warn you about his reluctance.'

'And I warned you, Danielle. No him, no us. If you failed to emphasise our insistence on his presence that's on you. We'll be there for seven tonight. If you're not in the room by seven-thirty, we'll leave. And please don't test me on this. No Hector, no meeting.'

After a lengthy pause, she said, 'For him to even consider attending he will have to believe that you will meet his demands.'

'His demand not to be there wasn't.'

'Oh, you're in a tough guy mood now, are you? Don't overplay your hand, Jimmy.'

Bliss paused before responding, trying to get a feel for how it might all play out. 'I don't intend to,' he said. 'It really is very simple, Danielle. If we negotiate at all, it has to be with the man running the operation. Tell your boss if he has demands he should keep them to himself. We're not interested in them. Suggestions, particularly those we can work with, are welcome. A willingness to listen and cooperate, too.'

After a moment, Halford said, 'My boss is used to getting what he wants.'

'And I'm not saying that won't happen. Just don't count on it. Compromises might have to be made. The main thing is we get everybody at the table talking. I'm confident we can thrash out a deal if both sides are willing to give and take.'

'I'll see what I can do.'

'We're on,' Bliss told the others when he ended the call. 'Now it's just a question of whether they call our bluff.'

'What exactly are we trying to negotiate with them?' DC Virgil asked. 'I'm still a bit hazy about the details.'

DCI Warburton cleared her throat, indicating she'd be answering this one. 'For as much as we can get while giving as little as possible away.'

'What does that actually mean, boss?'

Bliss left her to talk the team through the proposed arrangements while he took the opportunity to step out onto the stairway landing to make a call to Sandra Bannister. 'Are you okay to talk?' he asked, knowing the blunt question would put her on alert.

'Absolutely. What do you have for me?'

'I read your online article. You've gone for a big push on the inevitability of a drugs war in the city.'

'That's how it's shaping up. My editors decided to go for the throat. What aren't you happy about, Jimmy? I can hear it in your voice.'

'I wasn't overly thrilled with the impression you gave that the police are powerless. But that's not the issue. I'm calling to suggest you take a breather. The piece implied there was more to come as you go ferreting around. I thought I should let you know you might actually be digging a hole for yourself and your newspaper.'

'Is that so? In what way?' Bannister sounded dubious.

Bliss had been considering his response since reading the item. There was much he couldn't tell Bannister, but suggesting she hold back wasn't a huge commitment on his part. He never had and never would provide her with operational information unless it was about to be broken in a media briefing, but her online section had taken a line he hoped might be shattered following the meeting with Karagiannis. A heads-up from him at this point might save the reporter from embarrassing herself and putting her credibility at risk.

'It's an ongoing operation,' he eventually said. 'Which means I can't reveal any details. But, Sandra, there is a great deal going on behind the scenes. I'm not telling you this so's you'll go sniffing around elsewhere. In fact, I'm warning you not to do precisely that. But the fact is, the landscape is liable to shift over the next few days and weeks. If it goes the way we hope, your prediction might prove to be nonsense.'

After a momentary silence, Bannister said, 'Are you brokering some kind of peace agreement?'

He smiled to himself. Her mind worked very much like his own, and she had grasped the logic immediately.

'That's more than I'm willing to admit. And it might not go the way we want. So, all I'm saying is, it's probably in your best interests not to follow-up that article with more of the same. Leave yourself a back door ready to be opened.'

The journalist thanked him, and he told her he'd be in touch. Before heading back to work, he made one more call, this time to the MI5 man, Munday. 'It's Bliss,' he said. 'I thought I owed you the courtesy of telling you what I decided. I'm sure you already knew there was no way I would turn my back on this case. I am, for the time being at least, not sharing the information we discussed with my new team. But I have to say they are looking hard at our money man, a lead they achieved purely from sound detective work. If there's an obvious connection to Clay, then I'm sure they'll find it. If it's hidden as well as those two men hope, then the lead may go nowhere.'

'All of which means what?' Munday asked. 'You are or are you not intending to allow them to search away oblivious to what you know?'

Bliss could almost taste the displeasure in his mouth. 'I'm going to look into it more myself. But the moment I become convinced we can not only find a connection but also prove it, I'll find a way to bring them into it.'

'I can live with that. As for those bad cops I mentioned, I can hopefully make sure they keep their distance for the time being. But that gunman may still be around, Bliss. If he so much as catches wind of your interest, he might well decide to act.'

'Are you and your colleagues actively looking for him, Munday?'

'No. Nor will we unless he somehow presents as an obstacle. Our concerns begin and end with Clay. I, however, have taken a personal interest. To a large degree my hands are tied, but I have my own reach, my own contacts. Whatever I learn I will share with you.'

'I appreciate that,' Bliss told him. 'I'll reciprocate if I can.'

'Then let's both get to it. And Bliss... please take great care. If we're right about these two men, then theirs is a long-buried secret. I suspect they will do anything and everything to keep it that way.'

TWENTY-SEVEN

I<small>T WAS HARD FOR</small> Callum Davey to be unobtrusive when he was sitting behind the wheel of a Bentayga Azure, but Robert Clay assumed his friend's arrogance was responsible for him bringing the huge SUV to what was supposed to be a clandestine meeting. He himself had borrowed his wife's Peugeot, which he pulled alongside the tech entrepreneur's hulking set of wheels.

The abandoned diner's car park lay behind the boarded-up premises, so the expensive machinery was unlikely to be seen by vehicles passing on the A47. Even so, as the two men shook hands, Clay couldn't quite mask his annoyance.

'The Bentley?' he said with a fierce shake of the head. 'Really?'

Davey's grin was wide and unafraid to reveal a perfect set of teeth. His Cartier sunglasses were equally polished and shiny. 'You'd rather I bought my red Bugatti, Robbo?'

'I would have preferred it if you'd brought your wife's car like I did.'

'The Aston or the Porsche?'

Clay rolled his eyes. 'How the other half lives. Okay, let's not hang around any longer than necessary. I asked for this meeting to discuss this bloody police investigation.'

'I've not heard anything about it. What investigation?'

'The Nolan murder. It's become a cold case.'

Davey snorted derisively. 'Oh, don't worry yourself about that. They have to review them every so often.'

'No, that's not what this is,' Clay said, shaking his head. 'It's a reinvestigation. The first to be selected by a new team in the city.'

Raking his neck with manicured fingernails, Davey said, 'Okay. Well, that's less than ideal. On the other hand, what are they going to find out now that they missed back then? It's not as if there was any DNA left behind. And even if there was, it can't lead back to us. You're worrying over nothing, Robbo.'

'On the contrary, Cal. I'm worrying the precise amount the situation demands. You seem to forget one significant factor. For us, there are two concerns. There's the murder itself, which could come back to haunt us. But then there's also the man who carried out the murder.'

'What about him?'

'He may still be around. If so, and he gets to hear about this, he might reflect and have some doubts of his own.'

'What kind of doubts?' Davey asked.

'About us. Judging by the fact they never caught him we should assume he did his job properly. In which case he might not be overly bothered about the shooting itself biting him on the arse. But when it comes to us, the people who hired him, he can't be quite so certain, can he? What if he decides he can't take a chance on us not being caught this time or, more to the point, keeping our lips sealed if we are?'

Davey took his time to consider the implications. Finally, he shook his head. 'He was a professional. If he'd wanted a peaceful life, he'd've done what you just suggested at the time rather than wait all these years. Besides, if you think about it, he doesn't have the full picture.'

'What do you mean?' Clay asked.

'I was his only point of contact. He knew there was someone else involved, but he didn't know who.'

'But he could have found out. You just said he was a pro. I doubt he'd take on a contract without knowing everything there was to know.'

Davey acknowledged this with a dour nod. 'Let's say he did. He still has no idea you were part of it. I don't see him reacting now after all this time just because of a reinvestigation. It's no different from the last one. But even if he's so inclined, he's not about to harm me without completing the puzzle. As long as he doesn't have you, he really doesn't have me, either.'

'But he can find his way to me through you.'

'As if I'm going to blab. Your anonymity is my leverage.'

'And if he forces it out of you?'

'Come on, Robbo. You're getting bent out of shape over nothing. Relax. I'm the one who hired him so if either of us has a right to be concerned it's me.'

'And you're not?'

'No. I'm not. Look, I agree it's likely he put a face to the name. But there can't be any new or different evidence for the police to investigate, so theirs is nothing more than a box-ticking exercise. That's all this will be.'

'That's not what I'm hearing.'

Davey pouted. 'Okay, so even if they go all out, there's still nothing for them to find. Probably a lot less after all this time. Besides, what if you're right? What if the shooter does get nervous and considers taking action? What are you going to do about it? What do you imagine *we* can do about it?'

Clay shrugged. 'I… I don't… I don't know,' he stammered. 'Nothing, I suppose. I just thought we needed to be aware. That way, we can take precautions. Maybe more than precautions, if you get my gist.'

'You're hardly being subtle, Robbo. Listen to me, you and I are safe. It's too great a risk to come looking for us now.'

'Can you not trace him, somehow? Warn him off?'

'And look over my shoulder every five minutes after rattling his cage?' Callum Davey shook his head. 'Uh-uh. No way. I'm not prepared to live like that. I didn't at the time, and I refuse to do so now. What you do is up to you, but I won't be a party to it.'

'So, we're just going to sit back and do nothing?'

Nodding, Davey said, 'That's what I'm doing, pal. You? You can keep an eye on this investigation if you like. From a distance, of course.'

Clay nodded. 'I can do that. Yes. And if they get a new lead, I'll find out as much about it as I possibly can.'

Davey patted him on the arm. 'You do that, Champ. Meanwhile, you prepare yourself for greater things. I didn't do all this for nothing.'

*

Bliss sensed the heightened expectation the moment he walked through the door into the Unsolved Cases Team office. Greenhill, Corry, and Foley were busy tapping away on their laptop keyboards as he entered, and as one they looked up at him.

'This County Council stuff is a terrific lead,' Corry said, his face beaming. 'I can't believe we've made progress on a cold case this old.'

'Just when we thought it was dying on its arse,' Foley added.

'It was,' Bliss agreed. 'And it still might.' He glanced over at Greenhill. 'I take it we got more from young Polly?'

'We did. Do you want the good news or the strange news?'

'Give me the good first, please, Beth.'

She flashed a broad smile. 'In March 1999 the council eventually accepted the bid put forward by Callum Davey's company. Polly confirmed this.'

'No more than a month after our victim was shot dead.'

'Precisely. And the strange thing is that Polly also told me there was no alternative submission. The decision to award the contract was based on the original tender. The exact same one Nolan turned down.'

Bliss mulled that over. He had to be careful here. He couldn't ignore any subsequent logical conclusions, but at the same time he was wary of where any speculation might lead. He waited for one of the others to make a suggestion, which Guy Foley did.

'Weren't you going to speak with Nolan's manager again?'

'Yes. Beth met with him on her own last time, but I thought we'd both go for a second interview.'

'You might want to devise an interview strategy ahead of turning up on his doorstep. It's his name on the agreed contract. But, if you remember, the original crime file suggests Jeff Smalling washed his hands of it when the submitting company complained about the tender being rejected. He told them he couldn't step in, that it was against regulations.'

'He told me much the same when I spoke with him,' Greenhill said. 'There were no acceptable grounds to overrule Nolan's decision.'

Foley nodded. 'So, the question is, how did we get from there to that same company being awarded the contract so soon afterwards? Did this Smalling fellow simply change his mind, or was pressure brought to bear?'

'By who?' Bliss asked tentatively, before adding, 'There is a third consideration. He could have been persuaded some other way. Perhaps some form of financial inducement. We looked into our victim's finances. Maybe now's the time to look at what

Jeff Smalling might have gained in those early months of the new millennium.'

Once again, he felt pangs of regret and guilt. He wasn't supposed to have the information Munday had provided concerning Robert Clay's influence and could think of no legitimate way to introduce it. That didn't prevent him from throwing out a leading suggestion, however.

'If Smalling wasn't bribed, then perhaps he bent beneath the weight of pressure from above just like Guy suggested. It might be worth looking at the management setup, see who he answered to. He clearly stepped up immediately after Nolan's death, and the council accepted the bid before employing the man's replacement. But I can't see him overruling one of Nolan's decisions without some hefty persuasion or authorisation.'

The others were in agreement. All three seemed buoyed by the progress they'd made, and Bliss was happy enough in having given them a decent steer in the right direction. He remained conflicted by the bind Munday's request had put him in, but if he and his colleagues could somehow reach the same conclusion without him having to back down on his pledge to the man from Five, all might not be lost.

TWENTY-EIGHT

B LISS POURED HIMSELF A glass of water from the jug in the centre of the large table. A second container of orange juice stood close by, alongside pots of tea and coffee. While he sipped the cold liquid, his mind drifted back to earlier in the day. As the late afternoon had bled into early evening, he and his unsolved case team had continued to work the investigation. Experience had taught him that what you knew and what you could prove were important stepping stones, but in the initial stages of many investigations it was the unknowns that slowed you down. It wasn't simply a matter of finding answers to questions, more the struggle to unravel the questions themselves.

Justin Nolan's manager, Jeff Smalling, looked clean. No obvious injections of cash, no suspicious gifts of money or property. Not even a promotion, or a more gilded position elsewhere. The man had seemingly not profited from finally accepting Callum Davey's bid, at least not as far as Guy Foley and Ben Corry were able to discern following their exhaustive dive into the man's background and finances. The existence of an offshore bank account could not be discounted, nor payment by way of stocks or bonds. But if such inducements had been offered, neither investigator uncovered any evidence to that effect.

After work and prior to the meeting at the Holiday Inn, Bliss had joined senior officers in the conference room to discuss the ground rules. Each of them understood precisely what was at stake, but Chief Constable Michael Wood-Lewis was at pains to point out the boundaries beyond which none of them should stray. The meeting, he insisted, was no more than a ruse to gain as much from Karagiannis as possible while at the same time making no promises of their own or giving anything of importance away. It was a strategy whose active component of deception he was happy to take part in, but he reminded everyone seated around the table just what kind of person they were dealing with.

Dragging himself back into the present, Bliss was happy for the preamble to be over and to be inside the hotel meeting room, but decidedly unhappy at one notable absence. He took another sip of his preferred drink before casting a withering gaze across the table.

'Your boss has five minutes,' he told Danielle Halford, who looked both professional and elegant in a back pinstripe trouser suit. 'If he's not here by seven-thirty, we're gone. And we won't be back.'

She offered only a hesitant shrug. 'What can I say? He's a free spirit. A man who knows his own mind.'

'In other words, he's either biding his time so's he can provide a grand entrance, or he's toying with us. You might want to call him, let him know I don't bluff.'

Halford looked around the table at the men and woman flanking Bliss. She flashed that secretive half-smile of hers and said, 'Something tells me there are more important voices than your own here tonight, Jimmy. You may not bluff, but do you speak for them?'

Two men sat on either side of her. The bulkier of the two she had neglected to introduce. The other, immaculately dressed in expensive attire, was a solicitor eminently capable of thrashing out a deal on behalf of their boss; or so Halford had insisted. He gave his name as Smith and left it at that. Bliss raked his irritated gaze over each of them before speaking once more, only louder this time.

'I'm the Senior Investigating Officer attached to the murder of two young teens. I have all the authority I need, lady. If I get up and walk, so do they.'

The 'they' Bliss spoke of were his CC, DCS, DSI, DCI, and a DI from the intelligence team. High-ranking top brass for the most part, but he had entered the hotel that evening knowing each of them supported his stance. They had all agreed to follow his lead without equivocation, provided he remained within the parameters outlined by the Chief Constable.

Halford studied him for a few seconds before nodding and pulling a phone from her jacket pocket. He realised that he had never seen her carrying a bag. She thumbed in a text and sent it. 'It's done,' she said. 'He'll either be here or he won't.'

'If he's wasting our time, he can pick up the bill for this room,' Bliss responded.

'You are spikier than usual this evening,' she said, her voice a playful tease. 'What's wrong, Jimmy? Time of the month? Or are you more anxious than usual?'

'The truth is I'm bored, Danielle. These small-minded games piss me off, if you must know. Tell your boss these antics don't prove he's a gangster. More like a toddler.'

Halford turned her head to face the room's only door as it opened, at which point her smile broadened. 'Tell him yourself,' she said.

All heads turned as Hector Karagiannis entered the room. More legend than flesh and bone, yet here for all to see. To say he was a large man would have been an understatement. A receding jet-black hairline gave way to a heavily wrinkled forehead, which owed a great deal to frequent exposure to the elements, Bliss thought. If the pronounced widow's peak wasn't quite an island, it was certainly a peninsula. The gangster leaned on a gnarled wooden walking stick as he made his way across the room to join them. Intel had described a botched hip-replacement, compelling him to use the support to alleviate pain.

'Somebody wishes to tell me something?' he said as he took his place alongside Danielle Halford. He hooked his stick over the back of his chair and appraised the assembled police officers. And Bliss. Who got the impression the man's gaze lingered on him in particular.

'Only to say we're not impressed by the late arrival,' Bliss insisted. 'The short time between Danielle's text and your entrance tells me you were already close by inside the hotel. If you were trying to make a point, it wasn't necessary.'

A handsome man behind the bulk, Karagiannis flashed a winning smile. 'You must be Bliss. Am I correct?'

'You are.'

'Danielle warned me to watch out for you.'

'Is that right?' Bliss allowed his gaze to briefly stray across to her face, which betrayed no emotion.

'She told me you had a touch of both the fox and the wolf about you. Cunning when you wish to be, volatile when required. Where I come from, Mr Bliss, we might refer to you as *atromitos*, which means *fearless* or *unflinching*.'

Bliss remained impassive. 'Her opinion of me means nothing. Neither does yours. Let's crack on, shall we? Now that you're finally here.'

The man spread his large hands. 'As you like. Before we begin, I hope my presence here tonight proves to you my desire and good intentions. I made my offer in earnest, and I am here to assure you all that ours can be a mutually beneficial arrangement.'

Bliss gestured with his hand to those seated around him. 'You wouldn't have men and women of this calibre on our side of the room if we weren't serious about hearing you out. Before we begin and I make introductions, I must insist on carrying out a number of security measures. If you don't agree to them all, we walk.'

Karagiannis grinned and his eyes sparkled, crinkling around the edges. 'I'm intrigued. Please, what are these measures you speak of?'

Bliss counted them off. First, he'd confiscate all phones which he'd place inside Faraday bags to ensure a complete lack of external access. Second, Karagiannis, his two colleagues, and his legal representative would submit to a search for further devices and weapons. Third, he'd sweep each of them for listening or recording equipment. The room was clean, but the police had to ensure nobody on the opposite side of the table had brought such a device into the meeting with them. Finally, he proffered an affidavit for both Karagiannis and the man's solicitor to sign. He explained without going into detail that the document was essentially an enforceable legal waiver should any word of the meeting leak from the gangster or his associates.

'I must be permitted to do the same,' the gang boss said smartly, as if he had expected nothing less. 'Nobody outside of our two organisations can know I met with you.'

Ten minutes later they were done and ready to continue. Karagiannis got to his feet, his eyes narrowed but not with suspicion. 'What I have proposed is perhaps unique, no? The first time the police have sat down with somebody of my status to work together on agreeing a deal between our two opposing sides. The mere fact that I stand before you now is evidence of my commitment to see this through. As for you? You are here, so you must be interested in what I have to say. Before I go into further detail, please tell me, is there one of you present who has the authority to make such an agreement between us?'

Wood-Lewis did not stand, but he cleared his throat to draw attention and gave a convincing nod. 'You have all you need here, Mr Karagiannis. But please let me make something quite clear. We will reach no final agreement here tonight. For us, this is a fact-finding mission. What we learn we will later discuss, including any and all of your undertakings and commitments. We understand in general what it is you're about to suggest. But, as ever, the devil is in the detail. And now, the specifics, sir, if you please?'

The gang boss retook his seat. 'Of course. And since none of us will disclose what is said inside this room, I will speak plainly. Our signed legal documentation allows me to feel free in what I am able to reveal. Let me begin, therefore, by demonstrating my trust. As you already suspect, but I can now confirm for you, it is I who runs the City-Wide drugs line in Peterborough. I have spent my time not only distributing and selling our wares on your streets but also in getting to know my opposition lines. The weaker of the two is Soke, who are starting to feel the pressure of their instability. Foxes, more powerful and far more determined and organised, have begun their move to take control. They believe doing so at this point will deter my own line.' He shrugged and smiled. 'This is only because they do not yet realise who is behind City-Wide. This, then, is where we are. Agreed?'

'Agreed,' Bliss told him. 'Though there is currently greater momentum behind Foxes, perhaps more than you know.'

A dismissive hand gesture told them the gangster thought nothing of it. 'Make no mistake, I want this city. I want the areas beyond this city. I want the City-Wide line to mean much more in terms of spread. But all great works have humble beginnings. Our business here has only just begun. As I believe Dannielle has previously indicated to you, Mr Bliss, we are fully prepared to fight our opponents over both territory and reach. Soke will crumble quickly in the face of the kind of onslaught we are capable of unleashing. Foxes will stand their ground to fight, but they will not prevail. However, the loss during such battles is incalculable. The more you commit the more you leave yourself exposed. I have no doubt as to our eventual victory, but what lies at the end of it all, of course, is you. The police. I doubt you will take any of this lying down?'

'It's not in our nature,' Bliss said. 'In addition, we owe our citizens more than rolling over.'

Karagiannis chuckled, deep from within his belly. 'Precisely. All of which I have calculated. And while I am unafraid to travel that particular path should it prove necessary, I believe I have a better, and significantly less problematic, solution. As Dannielle has already mentioned, I have an offer for you to consider. It is, perhaps, simplistic. But that is one of the reasons we are here tonight. I believe between us we have the solutions. I am convinced that I can persuade both the Soke and Foxes lines to back off. No, more than that, to be more specific. We can persuade them to pull out altogether. They will effectively kill their business here in this lovely cathedral city, walk away from it without so much as a glance back over their shoulders. And all with little or no further bloodshed.'

'As easy as that,' Bliss said, doubt obvious in his tone. Karagiannis spoke with purpose and seemed comfortable despite the presence of so many police officers, leaving Bliss quietly impressed with him.

The man's cheeks bulged. 'I did not say it would be easy. I have no doubt it will require a great deal of persuasion. But I genuinely believe I can provide the exact level of inducement and intimidation necessary for my efforts to be successful.'

'Inducement and intimidation?' Detective Chief Superintendent Fletcher repeated uneasily. She inclined her head. 'I'm not sure I like the sound of the latter, Mr Karagiannis.'

'Of course.' He smiled and blotted his brow with a handkerchief. 'But my plan is for the… the mere suggestion of the intimidation coupled with the inducement offered to be sufficient. I won't pretend that idle threats without having the passion and desire to back them up are worthless, so we intend to deliver a show of strength and intention wherever and whenever we need to. But I stress, we are looking to carry out a peaceful takeover. If they believe I will deliver on both my threats and promises, they will see sense. Of this I am certain.'

'And our role in all this?' the Chief Constable asked. 'I'm led to believe that you not only want us to turn a blind eye to each element of your appropriation bid, irrespective of what those entail, but also to tolerate a certain level of presence in Peterborough by way of payment for having you resolve our escalating drugs crisis.'

'Essentially, this is correct,' the gangster agreed. 'You are the police. People expect you to police your city streets. I am, of course, not anticipating you all standing idly by while we carry out our business unmolested. But, yes, in payment for a peaceful city with a well-organised and tolerable drugs presence, we will expect improved co-operation and some degree of leniency. Working with us to a certain degree, rather than wholly against us.'

'Preposterous,' Bliss said, adhering to the agreed strategy of initial opposition. 'Our own citizens will hang, draw, and quarter us. Making a deal with a county lines drugs organisation? You surely can't expect to get away with that.'

'But who will know?' Karagiannis demanded, gesticulating with his shoulders and arms. 'Outside of this gathering, who will know?'

'Our officers on the ground, for one thing. You think they won't notice the difference? You think that won't get out? You think people living in high crime areas won't see what's going on? I'm sorry, we said we'd hear you out, but this is a nonsense.'

'I understand, Mr Bliss. Believe me, I do. The notion seemed crazy to me when I first conceived of it. But please, I have had a great deal more time than you with this plan. I have analysed and assessed the positives and the negatives. But let me ask you this: when the ordinary person on the street sees less crime around them, is victim to fewer crimes themselves, when there is less violence and threat on the city streets, and ultimately your crime statistics begin to tumble, who do you imagine will be against this small miracle?'

This time, the Chief Constable did rise. He stood with both hands splayed on the table, staring down at the Greek. 'You must realise we cannot officially be party to any such agreement. I presume you have thought that far ahead?'

At this point, Karagiannis turned to his solicitor. The man leaned back in his chair and said, 'We understand and accept there will be no agreement in any way other than verbally. We are not so naïve as to expect a signed declaration. We also acknowledge that the police are free to say one thing now and do something else entirely at a later date. We have not been doing business for this length of time without having some awareness. The arrangement we are seeking, therefore, is wide-ranging and open to negotiation and, dare I say, interpretation. The ideal would, of course, be full co-operation. The minimum acceptable contribution on your part is to treat accordingly any ramifications surrounding our initial and peaceful objectives.'

'Specifically...?' Bliss asked.

'Let me put it this way for you. If members of, say, Soke or Foxes were to approach you with claims of persecution citing my clients as the aggressor, these allegations would be treated with disdain during any subsequent investigations. We do not expect you to turn a blind eye to acts of violence. However, the previously mentioned intimidation is something we feel you can choose to pursue or... not.'

'Let me get this straight,' Bliss said. 'If we get called out to the scene of a brutal beating, you'd expect nothing less than a full and vigorous investigation on our part. But if somebody reports being leaned on, we're to make little or no progress on looking into it.'

'I don't expect the earth or for you people to give up your ethos and integrity,' Karagiannis stated bluntly. 'And while your full compliance would be a bonus, we don't require it. We do, however, demand your full co-operation in other areas as compensation for my organisation's intention to handle any takeover as delicately and sensitively as possible.'

'And for acts that fall between the two?'

'Ground for further healthy debate, surely.' The man flashed his wholesome, toothy smile once more.

'With you?' Bliss asked.

'I don't expect so. Danielle enjoys my complete trust in such matters. She will liaise between us, Mr Bliss. Whatever unexpected complications arise, I would expect you two to be able to sort them out amicably. After all, ours will be a partnership in all but name.'

'No,' Bliss said, shaking his head firmly. 'It will be nothing of the sort. We may eventually agree to give you an inch, but you take a mile you will know all about it. Trust works both ways, in that neither of us trusts the other. That said, we're not unaware of how badly things might go if your proposed takeover becomes more hostile. We came here to listen. Now it's time for us to consider. Do you propose a timeline?'

'I believe the clock has already started. You have two bodies and a terrible disfigurement to attend to. I suspect more of the same, and I'm sure you are of a similar mind. Be quick about it is all I will say. Meanwhile, we will make our own plans and will put them into action if we do not hear from you within twenty-four hours.'

Bliss glanced across at the CC, who gave an almost imperceptible nod. He then looked at Danielle Halford. 'Send me a number – one you won't dispose of for at least the next day or so. I'll be in touch.'

Her self-assured demeanour did not alter. He couldn't help but wonder if there was more going on here than met the eye, but at the same time couldn't think of a single misstep either he or his colleagues had taken.

TWENTY-NINE

B LISS HAD PROMISED TO meet Chandler afterwards to bring
her up to date and found her in the Charters Bar barge on
the river just outside her apartment knocking back a cocktail
of some description judging by the fruit, multi-coloured straw,
and tiny umbrella sprouting from the glass. He bought himself
a pint of Green Devil, the strongest and tastiest of their Oakham
Ales, then joined his friend at her table. A cool wind blew in off
the river, which had customers reaching for jackets or cardigans.

'What on earth is that you're busy getting on the outside of?'
he asked after knocking back a good quarter of his own beer.

Chandler held her drink up for closer inspection. 'A Long
Island iced tea,' she revealed.

Bliss grunted. 'I'm betting the one thing it lacks is tea.'

'And you'd be right. It's tequila, triple sec, vodka, gin, rum,
lemon, and cola.'

'What the hell is triple sec when it's at home?'

'It's an orange liqueur.' She smacked her lips. 'Tasty.'

He turned away. 'Ugh. Sounds disgusting.'

'No more than that pint of chemicals and water you're putting
away, my cockney friend.'

'I'll have you know this is chock full of hops and wheat and various golden delights.' He belched as if to end the topic with a definite full stop.

They fell into a low conversation. Bliss fed her the basics on the meeting he'd just come from, explaining that the gold group had arranged to discuss it more fully first thing the following morning.

'What's the best either side can expect from all this?' Chandler asked.

He nodded pointedly. 'I've asked myself the same thing. I know what we want out of it, but I can't help but wonder why Karagiannis would expose himself to us at this critical juncture. But then again, will there ever be a better time? At the moment, he gets to stare us down without fear of repercussions. As a result, he's able to speak freely. Now that I've met him, I'm positive there's no way he's expecting to get much out of this other than his minimal demands. And I think that'll be enough. Basically, he's letting us know some tough negotiations will be going on in the background and if we're able to steer clear then we might yet avoid further outbreaks of violence.'

'In other words, he's suggesting police interference might jeopardise a peaceful transition.'

'That's about the gist of it, yeah. As for the stated inducements and intimidation, I can hazard a guess.'

Chandler nodded. 'I think we all can. Essentially, a bung to walk away. A one-off payment, or maybe a monthly premium to basically do nothing but stick money in a safe to top up the old pension pot. All backed by a show of power and threats to steamroller them if they don't step aside. Will that work do you think?'

'That will probably boil down to the kind of money he offers. It also depends on the level of intimidation he rises to or threatens. The way I see it, Samantha Phillips knows Soke is small fry.

She fancies herself as an empire builder, but I strongly suspect that Danielle Halford can persuade her to go back to pushing weed and leaving the City-Wide line all the class A business. In return for a good few quid, naturally. Saad Ali is a different proposition. He runs a long-established OCG, not some newcomer outfit like Soke. But you have to remember his presence here in Peterborough is in its early stages. If Ali can back down without losing face and earn a few bob in the process, then I think there's a chance this ruse might work out.'

'And what about our response?' Chandler asked, her quizzical look also blighted by concern. 'We can't have this tosser strolling around thinking he has us in his pocket.'

Bliss laughed, more than a little scornfully. 'There's no danger of that, Pen. The CC has agreed to stop, look, and listen when it comes to the drug lines. We'll do whatever we can to make it seem as if we're looking the other way. And if doing so for real doesn't hurt us at all, we might even go part of the way there. But what won't happen is us sitting back and letting Karagiannis rule the roost unchallenged. No, Wood-Lewis is adamant that we are the net gainers from all this.'

'And you? How do you feel about it? After all, you helped get these negotiations under way.'

Bliss took a long swallow from his glass. 'I don't want to see any more young kids tortured and murdered. I don't want any more arms chopped off. I'll also be happy to see fewer stabbings over territory. I'm not about to bend over and take it up the arris from anybody, but I am willing to concede a bit of ground if I can see the merit in other gains.'

Their conversation drifted on to the unsolved case. Not having to withhold information freed him up to talk openly, which he needed. It was frustrating and also a little unsettling having to watch his every word around his three new colleagues. There was much he knew that could easily slip out if he didn't take care when speaking. Despite these misgivings, their attitude and their desire to make inroads into the reinvestigation delighted him.

'Do you think they can get there on their own?' Chandler asked. 'Solving the previously unsolvable, I mean.'

Bliss gave that all the thought the question warranted. They seemed like a dogged bunch, and given it was the first case for the team they'd be busting a gut to succeed. He believed they would eventually get further than they were, but as for solving the case… When he and Munday were walking back to their vehicles following lunch, he had posed a similar question and Munday had responded with typical scepticism. The wily old spook pointed out that it was easier to work backwards to find the connections to Callum Davey, the County Council, and the Y2K software agreement once you had Robert Clay's name. It still required grunt work and one or two leaps of logic, but if you began with Davey, it became much more difficult to find yourself at Clay's doorstep. Knowing his name was the key, and Munday didn't think the Unsolved Cases Team had either the time or manpower to get there without it.

Chandler listened intently as Bliss relayed this to her. She took it all in and acknowledged her comprehension with a nod when he was done. 'Makes you wonder, then, doesn't it?'

'Wonder what?'

'Why Munday came to you in the first place? I mean, essentially what he's done is ask you to back off from an investigation he apparently doesn't believe you can solve. I ask again: why? Why bother? Why include you at all?'

Bliss regarded his friend closely. 'What are you saying, Pen? Just spit it out.'

'When he spoke to you about this the last time, he told you it was easier to work backwards once Robert Clay's name surfaced.

If you work the rest of it backwards, you can see that even when you do pair the two of them together there is still no hard evidence against either man. And perhaps more gut-wrenching is that none of it brings you closer to the man who pulled the trigger.'

'I agree. So, yes, you do have to question why Munday stepped forward at all. But I'm guessing you have a suggestion waiting at the end of all this.'

'I do.' Chandler took a suck on her straw before continuing. 'Tell me, Jimmy, what's your usual response when someone tells you not to do something?'

Bliss stared out along the river for a moment. 'I tend to do it anyway.'

'Exactly. Your five-year-old child's mind doesn't compute the instruction. It's like you seeing a wet paint sign and having to touch the painted item anyway. Munday knows this about you. He might not have spent an awful lot of time in your company, but he will have worked out what kind of character you are.'

Nodding, Bliss said, 'So you're suggesting Munday told me to steer clear with every expectation that I would do the very opposite?'

'Precisely.'

Bliss was silent for a few seconds. He had already asked himself the same question and arrived at the same conclusion, but he was still unable to establish a legitimate reason why Munday might take such a risk.

'But to what end?' he eventually asked. 'If MI5 hasn't been able to find hard evidence against either man, then four retired detectives aren't likely to discover anything they missed. Plus, you're forgetting one important factor. Our man from Five didn't instruct me not to work the case. In fact, the more I think about it, he was at pains to avoid doing so. He asked me to repay a favour. To tread water for a short while, not to kill the case entirely.'

'The difference being?'

'It doesn't prompt the same visceral reaction from me. It doesn't make me all gung-ho to traipse across the paths he's told me to steer clear of, because he didn't tell me anything of the sort. Instinctively, it's not the same thing at all.'

He could see Chandler wrestling with that. Eventually she said, 'Okay. Let's say I accept your argument. Can we at least agree that the reason he came to you, the reason he gave you Robert Clay, is not the same reason he told you it was?'

'I have no doubt you're right about that.'

'In which case, I think Munday had a completely different agenda. I don't think he is happy with the way his department is handling this sorry mess. I think he's torn between toeing the line and doing the right thing. He said backing off was the best way to go if you looked at the bigger picture. I reckon the picture he was talking about was not how useful Robert Clay might prove to be to MI5 in the future, but the one you and your new team are facing. He's slowing you down in order for your team to connect Clay to Davey if only you can find a way to lead them there without being obvious.'

Confused, Bliss felt his brow furrowing. An ache began to stir in his temples. 'You're saying just as *I* need to point *them* in the right direction without them knowing how I came by my information, Munday is having to do the same with *me*.'

Chandler took a final lengthy suck on her straw before saying, 'Yes. Why not? He has his orders, but also perhaps his own principles. And you can't suddenly know all about Robert Clay shortly after Munday's visit. No, no. I can see it now, Jimmy. He's told his people that he can use his relationship with you to persuade you to put the brakes on but without having to provide you with any relevant information. If you immediately focus on Robert Clay, then they'll know Munday said more than he ought to have.'

Bliss took his time to take it all in. 'Munday is not playing me, then. Not the way I suspected, at least. He wants what I want, and he's trying to help me get there in such a way that doesn't lead back to him.'

'I think so, yes. This might not entirely be about testing your loyalty after all,' Chandler said. 'Perhaps Munday is struggling with the same moral dilemma himself.'

THIRTY

THE MILK IN THE fridge was out of date, and Bliss wasn't willing to test it. He'd had a thing about spoilt milk since childhood, and the very thought of it on his lips made him feel queasy. He tossed the remains of the carton down the sink and ate his cereal dry; honey Cheerios were tasty either way. Max sat back on his haunches close to his bed, patiently watching the morning unfold. He was familiar with the rhythms and movements around the house, understanding that each one took him closer to the lead being popped off its hook by the front door. The moment Bliss loitered rather than heading upstairs, Max knew it was game time. He left his spot in the kitchen and began to turn circles huffing and moaning as he spun. Bliss crouched, stroked the dog's head, attached the lead to his collar and out they went.

For their first walk of the day, Bliss habitually took Max to the large playing field separated from the Bushfield Academy by tall and ragged undergrowth. Today was no exception, and with no other dog walkers in sight he let the animal off the lead to run around. The dog's initial bursts of unleashed energy were a joy to behold, and Bliss loved the sight of Max in full flow with the fur on his face peeled back. He looked on, calm settling over him to ease the ache of tense muscles, but moments later he became aware of a slight figure appearing alongside to his right.

'This is starting to feel like harassment,' he called across to Danielle Halford without so much as a sidelong glance in her direction.

'How do you know I'm not here for your body?' she replied smoothly, easing towards him.

'Fair point. But I'm guessing you'd prefer dead over alive.'

'You shouldn't sell yourself short, Jimmy. I reckon you have one final yawp in you at least. Though perhaps not as barbaric as it might once have been.'

This time he did turn to face her, surprised by the literary reference. 'You know Walt Whitman? Or did you just remember the line from *Dead Poets Society*?'

Her eyebrows rose and fell. 'I'm more learned than my choice of career might suggest.'

'You call working for a criminal thug a "career"?'

'Do you ever give a girl an even break, Jimmy?' Halford asked testily.

'Only if they deserve it.'

She folded her arms. 'Okay. My line of work and not my career. That better?' She smiled that smile of hers, and he felt her eyes draw him in.

Max came closer and Bliss sent the dog's chewed-up tennis ball high and far into the air with the aid of a launcher device. His gaze firmly on the animal once more he said, 'What do you want today, Danielle?'

'What if I want you?' she purred, sidling closer to him. He'd noticed her slender figure this morning, a white T-shirt tucked into pale denims leaving not a great deal to the imagination when it came to the shape beneath. The warm morning air suggested another hot one, and she had dressed for the occasion. But Bliss wasn't having any of it.

He snorted and shook his head. 'Don't fuck about. Get on with it or sling your hook. I don't have either the time or inclination to play mind games today.'

'You old spoil sport, you. Okay, business it is. I just came to ask you what you thought about the meeting last night.'

'Our gold team is due to gather shortly. They are the ones who will make the ultimate decision.'

'But with your input as SIO, right? You did say you had authority.'

'At the meeting, I did. Things have moved on. Besides, they already have my recommendation.'

Halford looked up with renewed interest. 'Care to share it with me?'

'No. I don't care to share anything with you. I don't know where you've been.'

She laughed. As he'd expected. She was hard to rattle, this one.

'So then tell me how you thought it went, Jimmy. Were you impressed by... no, clearly that's the wrong word and you'll pick me up on it, I'm sure. Were you *convinced* by the offer? How genuine it was.'

Bliss kept his eyes fixed on Max, who was happily jumping around tossing the ball to himself. 'It felt like a genuine proposal, yes. It came with its own agenda, of course. Your boss doesn't come across as an altruistic man. I'm pretty sure we know what he's looking for, what kind of agreement he will eventually accept, and what he stands to gain from it.'

'That all sounds positive.'

'Only if we're willing to go along with it and play our part. Like I say, I've made my feelings clear and now it's out of my hands.'

'Fair enough. For my part, Hector and I had a long conversation afterwards. We stopped at a service station for some appalling coffee. Believe it or not, he liked you. He told me you were a worthy adversary. So much so he'd rather you were on his team.'

'That's never gonna happen,' Bliss scoffed.

'I told him you'd say that. The thing is, he also trusted you. He thinks you're a man of honour, a man of your word. His impression was that you would do everything possible to bring his offer to fruition.'

Bliss grinned. 'Are you trying to get me to slip up and accidentally reveal what my recommendation was?'

'Possibly. Is it working?'

'Not a chance. You'll find out in due course.'

Halford slapped her hands on her thighs. 'You can't blame a girl for trying. But Jimmy, you do know that if it goes ahead, we'll need more of these meetings? I am your liaison, after all. There's no reason for you to be so combative with me all the time. I can be great company, even if I do say so myself, and I'm willing to show you how great. Perhaps we could share a meal and a nice bottle of wine next time.'

Bliss made no reply. Given their differences, he wanted to dislike her more than he did. She was bright and attractive, and he imagined under the right circumstances she would be good company. But there was no getting past who she worked for and what she did to earn a crust, though he doubted she ever actually got her hands dirty. In a different life and a different existence, he knew Danielle Halford was physically his type. But in this life, living this existence, what she represented repulsed him. Despite that, he wondered how loose lipped she might become in a wholly different setting.

'It'll have to be on your expense account,' he finally said. 'I don't have one anymore.'

THIRTY-ONE

JEFF SMALLING LIVED ALONE in his retirement and spent much of his time painting in the large conservatory at the rear of his house. From the open-plan kitchen and diner where Justin Nolan's ex-manager had them sitting on stools on one side of the central island, Bliss could see a few pieces of work in different stages of completion adorning easels. Still life and portraits seemed to be his forte.

'Not into landscapes?' Bliss asked.

'Occasionally,' Smalling acknowledged. 'I prefer seasons other than summer for those. But I don't suppose you came to talk about my art.'

Beth Greenhill had been happy for him to take the lead, so Bliss nodded and met the man's intrigued gaze. 'We needed to speak with you again, sir, because new information has come to light. Something Beth was unable to explore when she visited you the other day.'

'I'll help all I can. Happy to, in fact. I just don't see what else I might have to offer.'

'Perhaps nothing, Mr Smalling,' Bliss allowed. 'Either way, we have to follow up on the leads we have. Our visit today is in reference to one contract in particular. I realise that might feel like a reach after all these years, but we believe you'd remember this one.'

'Like I said, I'll do what I can.'

'I can guarantee this contract was unique. It arose from a need in 1998 for the authority to find a way to test and protect their computer equipment from the so-called Millennium Bug. Your department received and rejected many bids. And yet one of those rejections caused quite a stir. Do you recall the one I mean?'

Bliss had been watching the man closely, and with each word he grew more uncomfortable. He wasn't exactly squirming in his chair, but he was certainly shifting around, and his flesh tone had become ashen. Smalling shook his head slowly, as if with great reluctance.

'Naturally, I'm aware of the whole Y2K kerfuffle and the county requirements to implement a fix. As for the specifics, I really can't be sure.'

'It was a long time ago,' Bliss said. 'But let me try to remind you. A company owned by the IT software mogul, Callum Davey, made a bid for the contract. Their name at the time was Solution Providers Techsperts. Mr Nolan rejected the bid. Not only that, he also included in his explanation for doing so the suggestion of impropriety on Davey's part. Specifically, that he claimed to know somebody higher up the totem pole than Nolan and that whoever this person was they could and would use their influence if necessary.'

'I can assure you that influence was not me,' Smalling said, a little more forcefully than he had perhaps intended. He gathered himself before offering more. 'And now that you mention it, I do remember this contract. My own boss spoke to me about it, as happens whenever a company raises an objection. My recollection is that I stood by Justin's decision.'

Bliss nodded and said, 'Yes, that was our understanding. So, to clarify, the request for tenders went out, Callum Davey's company bid, Mr Nolan then rejected it, at which point Davey raised objections. At that stage, you were happy enough with the process to stand by Mr Nolan. Do I have that right?'

'Mostly. In point of fact, it really wasn't a case of my electing to stand by Justin. It was part of the process. It was his job to award contracts and reject bids. For me, that's where it began and ended. Procedure. It's there for a reason.'

'And I'm pleased to hear it,' Bliss said encouragingly. 'So, tell me, were you aware that Callum Davey's business was ultimately awarded that contract? I'm sure you must have been, given the nature of it in the run up to the millennium.'

Smalling began to fidget, his hands wringing as he became more anxious. 'I'm sorry,' he said. 'I don't mean to be evasive. But you should know that I signed a non-disclosure agreement. I'm unable to discuss contracts. And by that, I mean any contract.'

The existence of an NDA took Bliss by surprise. 'Is this something you had to agree to when you accepted a job with the county council?' he asked.

'No. Not at all. It was a requirement they introduced at a later date.'

'I see. Was that date before or after Justin Nolan's murder?'

Swallowing thickly, Smalling brushed the back of a hand across his mouth. He struggled to maintain eye contact. 'Now that you ask, it was afterwards. That doesn't mean the two things are connected.'

'I didn't suggest they were. But it's one hell of a coincidence. You say you can't discuss contracts. How about the tenders and bidding process? Are they covered by the document you signed?'

'They are. But I'm not a stupid man, Mr Bliss. I see what you're getting at. You're implying somebody bought favours to push that bid through after its initial rejection. All I am willing to say about that is I'm not your man. I was not high enough up the food chain.'

Bliss nodded. 'I understand. But I reckon you know who did step in to push Callum Davey's bid through. After all, you were filling in for Mr Nolan at the time it happened. You will have seen the paperwork, perhaps even been involved in other aspects of the process.'

'And again, none of which I'm able to talk about. Look, the fact that wealthy and influential men like Callum Davey tend to get their own way should come as no surprise to either of you. Men like him – and they most often are men – don't like to lose. You already know that Justin rejected the original bid because Davey had tried to influence him in an unacceptable way, so I am free to refer to it. But not everybody has the kind of integrity he had.'

'I sense you have more you'd like to say,' Greenhill said, leaning towards him. 'There's only us here, so why not?'

'Because I, too, have integrity,' Smalling said, pulling himself together. 'I accepted the non-disclosure document for what it was and I will abide by it. But I will tell you this, both of you. I don't have the information you're looking for. Were there rumours? Yes, naturally. But I'll have you know more than one name was mentioned at the time. A county local authority is a sizeable organisation, and people like to talk. I have my own opinion, but I have no facts for you. Besides, none of it will help Justin now, will it?'

Bliss accepted the statement with a shrug. 'That's true, but of course he wasn't the only one to suffer. He had a wife, a child. He had family and friends. None of us can bring him back, but if we can put his killer behind bars then some form of justice will have been done.'

'Then I wish you all the luck in the world,' Smalling said, standing to tell them the interview was over. 'I genuinely do. I liked Justin. We were not friends, but we got on well. His murder shocked me, and I'd like nothing more than to see the person responsible for his death locked up. I just can't help you find him, Mr Bliss. And I'm sorry about that.'

'Yeah, me too,' Bliss said. 'One thing before we go, Mr Smalling. I'm going to have that NDA of yours checked. I'm also going to have another look into your background. If I find you've been lying to us, I'll be back. And next time I won't be anywhere near as pleasant.'

THIRTY-TWO

B LISS LEFT THE COLD case team to continue looking into the contract agreement to see if they could find any evidence of who had eventually stepped in to ensure the business went to Callum Davey's company. Acutely aware of Munday's reasoning allied to his own common sense, he didn't think they would have much joy approaching it in the conventional way. He decided against offering up the name, but did suggest starting at the other end of the deal and working their way back to Davey in case they had overlooked any obvious connections.

Shortly afterwards, he opened the Operation Scarecrow briefing with an update on the previous evening's meeting, essentially providing the same information he had fed Chandler over their drink together. He went on to reveal Halford's presence earlier that morning on the field where he walked Max.

'She's not the type to let you see her anxiety,' he said. 'But her just showing up out of the blue suggests she is. Anxious, I mean. I suspect she is under a huge amount of pressure to get this deal over the line, and I don't think her boss is the kind of man who takes failure at face value. I also get the impression he needs our agreement to work more than I previously imagined.'

'Why do you suppose that is?' DCI Warburton asked.

'I'm only speculating, but I was thinking it might have something to do with timing. If they are able to go about their business without fear of us intervening and pulling their people in off the street, they'll reach their ultimate goal more quickly. Considerably so. That leaves me wondering if they have a major shipment due. That would explain a lot. They won't want to sit on it for any length of time, so the sooner they redistribute the better.'

'I get what you're saying,' DS Bishop said. 'If we've backed off while they negotiate a takeover, they can distribute virtually at the same time.'

Bliss nodded. 'Precisely. Like I say, it's speculative, but to me it makes sense. And it would explain their eagerness to reach this agreement with us as soon as possible.'

'What are you thinking, Jimmy?' Chandler asked him. 'I can see something churning over in that noggin of yours.'

'Let's say I'm right. It could be an ideal opportunity to kill two birds with one stone. On the one hand, we benefit from a change of the guard without a great deal more nastiness occurring on the streets. On the other, if we keep a close watch on the City-Wide line, we might be able to intercept their consignment before it gets cut, repackaged, and sent on its way.'

'Now that is an interesting idea,' Warburton responded eagerly. 'It would cause widespread disruption and slow everything down just enough for us all to take a beat.'

'Temporarily,' DC Ansari argued. 'We know Karagiannis has the resources to organise a replacement shipment and to change all his existing locations, so it won't put him out of the game entirely.'

'No, but it would knock him off his stride,' DC Gratton said. 'Especially if we can pull a few of his top people in along with the shipment.'

Chandler agreed. 'Karagiannis will not be a happy bunny.'

'Ah, bless him,' Bliss said with a crooked grin. 'The unhappier the better, as far as I'm concerned.'

'Do we know enough about his operation and his people to intercept a shipment?' Warburton asked.

'Probably not. But if we liaise with intel and the drugs squad, they might be able to give it a good go. Half the problem is knowing when shipments are due, so if we suspect it has to be soon, then we can narrow our focus. Or they can. Also, if we know that Soke and Foxes are out of the picture, we can throw everything at City-Wide instead.'

Warburton was nodding. 'I like it. It's worth piling in on it. If we don't make it work for us, then we're no worse off. But if we do, and can make a dent, I'm all for it. Is this something you want to commit to in the policy book, Jimmy?'

Bliss did not hesitate. 'Absolutely. Let's take it as far as we can. If Karagiannis is trying to pull a fast one behind our backs, there's no harm in us launching a covert op while he's busy looking elsewhere.'

'And if he isn't?'

'Then he'll be pissed off, but so what?'

The DCI grinned and said, 'Nice one. I'll have a word with drugs and intel as soon as we're finished here. Now, let's go back a step to your meeting with Samantha Phillips. What more do we know about this man who came in minus a hand and half his forearm?'

DC Virgil got to his feet. He moved across to the whiteboard and used a magnet to fix a photo to it. 'Meet Vic Tolley. Mid-level, as we were told, but influential for all that. Phil and I interviewed him yesterday evening, but as you might expect we got sweet FA out of him. We also contacted Samantha Phillips, but she was no more forthcoming.'

'What did the doctors have to say about the wound?' Bliss asked.

'Beneath the cauterisation, the cut was surprisingly smooth and straight. Initially, they assumed a single, clean strike with a very sharp weapon. However, there was a deep depression further up the arm, as well as some bone damage. They thought it looked like a crush-type wound. That implies something powerful held the arm in place at the time of the bladed wound.'

'Sounds like a heavy-duty guillotine to me,' Olly Bishop suggested. 'I've seen them in action and that would explain the crushing and the clean cut.'

Bliss jabbed a finger his way. 'Good thinking. Put together a list of local businesses that might use one and let's pay them a visit.' He looked around the room. 'Right, that's all from me. Anybody have an update?'

'I do,' Bishop said. 'We finally got CCTV footage from the steam railway station. Me and Gul stayed on last night to sift through it. We have our own view on what we saw, but I'm assuming you want to see it for yourself.'

Bliss did. Gul brought up the file on the laptop connected to the e-board projector and ran it. 'I've edited the source file to include only the relevant pieces of footage,' she said, appraising the faces turned her way. 'I warn you now, the quality is shite. There are no identifications to be made here, but Bish and I still think it's interesting.' She pointed to the screen with one hand and tapped the mousepad with the other. 'The timestamp, as you can see in the bottom right corner, says it's 11.27pm. The footage is grainy grey, but if you look dead centre, the darker horizontal strip is the footbridge across the river. Now, moments before the clock shifts over to 11.28pm you can just make out four figures moving from left to right across the bridge.'

'Reverse that and play it back will you, Gul?' Bliss said. He pulled out his reading glasses and put them on to watch it again.

'And one more time, please,' he said, removing the glasses and pocketing them once more.

'I know the detail is poor, but you can just about make them out,' Gul insisted.

'With your young eyes, I'm sure it's a doddle. But yes, I can see them if I squint hard enough.'

'What we found interesting,' Bishop said, 'is the way those figures travel over the bridge. They're unhurried, for one thing. As if they're out for a casual stroll. What's more, nobody is being dragged or shoved. They all appear to be moving freely. To me and Gul that suggests none of the four are being taken across against their will.'

DC Ansari nodded. 'We watched it countless times last night, Jimmy. It doesn't look any different this morning. Skipping on, the timestamp now says 11.51pm and once again we see movement across the bridge. Now they're walking right to left, and this time there are only two of them.'

Nodding, Bliss said, 'I'm satisfied this is them. I take it you have no corresponding footage from the car park itself?'

Bishop shook his head. 'There are too many blind spots. The worst thing is the one camera that might have clearly shown entry and exit is on the blink and has been waiting months for repairs. Sadly, then, this is as good as it gets. Gul itemised the relevant bus and taxi data, but no buses ran past the turning into the car park at that time. We are still checking through taxi dashcam data. To be honest, I'll be staggered if we get that lucky.'

Bliss could only agree. 'If we do, then great. If we don't, we're no worse off. But you're right about the footage from the railway station. Our two victims went willingly, which I find strange. If I hadn't seen Samantha Phillips's bloke climbing up the wall in pain after having half his arm chopped off, I might now be thinking this was Soke leadership punishing a couple of their own runners. But if I'm convinced the wounding incident was Foxes on Soke, then I have to stick to believing the murders were part of the same increased aggression.'

'So where does this leave us?' Warburton asked.

Bliss rubbed at the small scar on his forehead. 'Intelligence left an overnight note on file. Between them and their counterparts in Leicester, they've come up with four names for us to look into. Saad Ali employs a couple of thugs known to be up for the type of violence we've seen working for him in the Leicestershire area. Zack Gilney and Anil Shah are both from Leicester and have connections to the Foxes line going back four years. Information packs are being compiled as I speak for this pair, but we have them as IC1 and IC4. Now, shortly after moving his line into Peterborough, Ali acquired the services of a number of local lads, including an odd duo who go by Big Mofo and Li'l Mofo. Their real names are Jamar Jay Tapper – also known as JJ – and Ritchie Morrison. This dynamic duo have been identified as IC3 and IC1. Intel suggests some refer to them as the odd couple because Tapper is black, wears his hair in dreadlocks, and is built like a brick shithouse, while Ritchie is white, short, podgy, and bald as a billiard ball.'

'Are all four working together or is one pairing more likely than the other to be our suspects?' DCI Warburton asked.

'It's thought unlikely that they are working as a foursome. Intel has their money on the local lads being our prime suspects. I thought me and Pen might follow up on them. We'll limit ourselves to some covert observations at this time if we can run them down. We have no current addresses for either, and both appear to be off the grid and have been for some time. But they're known to us so we can check out their history and maybe find some local faces they might be hanging around with.'

'Okay. What else do we have to move on?'

Bliss scratched his chin and said, 'I think we're probably done with victimology. There's not a lot more to be learned about our two murder suspects, and what's left isn't going to provide us with anything of value. As I mentioned earlier, our man missing most of one arm refused to talk to us and didn't even give his name at the hospital. I can summarise the status if you like.'

'Yes, please,' Warburton said. 'I think that would be helpful at this stage.'

'Okay. So, let's start with what we know. Drugs are at the root of everything we're investigating. The murders and the amputation are down to an escalation in hostilities by the Foxes line on the Soke line, while City-Wide are keeping well out of it for the moment. Behind the scenes, we're attempting to negotiate with City-Wide. Our aim is for them to carry out a peaceful takeover of the drugs business in the city, while at the same time we're looking to scupper what we think might be an imminent major shipment coming their way. But that's neither here nor there when it comes to Operation Scarecrow. Our focus there is the murder of Chris Barrie and Jamie Ure. Finding their killers is our driving force, and everything else is secondary. Our usual digital methods have largely been unhelpful, but that's the way it goes sometimes. Leaning on good old-fashioned intelligence, then, I reckon our best approach right now is to follow up on the four names our colleagues in Leicester gave us.'

'Who do you want on the pair of thugs still working out of their city?' DS Bishop asked.

'You volunteering, Bish?' Bliss said with an easy grin.

'I've had enough of all the CCTV bollocks. I want to get out and about.'

'Good. Then let's keep others working on outstanding actions. You and Gul get your arses over to Leicester to see if you can get eyes on these Gilney and Shah characters. Firm up on them with the locals, just in case our Peterborough pairing aren't in the frame. Phil and Alan, I want you two here managing the office but keep on your toes in case either Bish and Gul or me and Pen need some backup.'

Bliss cut it there. He was pleased with both the summary of the op to date and the immediate actions aimed at identifying their suspects. He approached DCI Warburton to ask for an update on the gold team meeting which had taken place ahead of the operation briefing. She told him they had yet to make a decision, but that after everybody had aired their views, DCS Fletcher and the Chief Constable remained deep in conversation. Chandler was waiting for him when he was done, tapping her watch before holding it up to her ear.

'Come on, old man,' she said. 'Tick-tock. Time is wasting.'

'Tell me about it,' he grumbled.

'Where do we start looking for our odd couple?' she asked.

'We begin our journey with a cup of tea,' he said. 'Proper tea, not the crap you get here. Then we talk it over. Without a digital footprint available to us, I don't see many avenues to explore other than family and friends. If you think otherwise, keep it to yourself until I've had my cuppa. I'm bloody parched.'

THIRTY-THREE

B LISS HAD DRIVEN LESS than a hundred yards away from the nick when his phone rang. The Bluetooth in his Volvo allowed him to speak freely while driving. The caller was Detective Superintendent Edwards, with news from the gold team meeting. They had agreed to accept the offer from Karagiannis; or at least, for Bliss to let Danielle Halford know they had. He was to impose a number of restrictions and caveats, the main one of which was that if there were further outbreaks of violence, the police reserved the right to investigate each incident on its merits. If the police believed City-Wide line or any of Karagiannis's people to be the aggressors, all forms of cooperation would desist immediately. Meanwhile, Edwards informed him, a secondary team comprising officers from CID, Intelligence, and the drugs squad were about to be tasked with gathering intel in connection with the anticipated shipment of class A.

Chandler blew out her cheeks as the conversation ended. 'This is fast becoming a major operation, Jimmy. We'll need to keep an eye open for any overlap into Scarecrow.'

'Precisely what I was thinking,' he said. 'There's bound to be some. Especially if we're right about our potential suspects here in Peterborough.'

'Exactly. We don't want them scared off before we've had a chance to track them down.'

Something dawned on Bliss at that moment. 'They might not need to be scared off. If Karagiannis is as good as his word, then Saad Ali might end up calling them off. That's a positive, obviously, but our suspects might go deeper to ground if they're not out punishing for him.'

Before leaving Thorpe Wood, he'd asked DC Gratton to acquire as much intelligence as he was able to on either Ritchie Morrison or Jamar Tapper, though Bliss quite liked thinking of them as Big Mofo and Li'l Mofo. The nicknames seemed pertinent. When he heard the familiar ping of an email hitting his Inbox he was pleased to see a list of names from his colleague. He had Chandler read the message out loud while he nosed the big SUV in the direction of the city centre. Altogether, the list comprised seven names. Tapper's parents and brother, together with four shared known associates. The message ended with a note telling them Morrison had no living parents or siblings.

'Known associates first,' Bliss said. 'Get back to Phil. Thank him for the list. Ask him to go through the KA records while we have our tea break. I want to know which of them is local and likely to be available for a chat. Contact details, including work if relevant. He knows the score, so tell him to send over only the info we're interested in.'

They had their drinks in his favourite little café on the Mancetter Square industrial estate, Bliss also managing to force down a small forest fruits pastry. As they were preparing to leave, he received an update from Gratton. He read the message and shook his head as he turned to his partner.

'That list just became a lot more manageable. Of the four KAs, one is dead, two are in the shovel, leaving just the one still living here in the city. His name is Charlie Warden, aged forty-five. He also did a short stretch inside but has apparently gone legit upon his release just over a year ago. He runs his own decorating business. Phil gave them a bell and found out where he's working today. He has a contract just round the corner from here in Gunthorpe.'

Chandler mopped her lips with a paper napkin after polishing off some of the pastry before Bliss could. 'That's handy. I didn't fancy traipsing across the city.'

'Me neither. But it does mean we have less time to prepare an interview strategy.'

'Less time on the road,' she said. 'But more time in here, perhaps. Another cuppa?'

Bliss brightened. 'Of course.'

'Another pastry?'

'It'd be rude not to. You going to scoff down half of mine again?'

Chandler grinned and got up to go to the counter.

*

Warden had landed a nice earner by the look of it. A block of two-storey flats off Pennine Way owned by a housing association was a decent enough job. Warden's white van stood outside on the road, parked slightly up on the pavement. The planners had struck again by building homes for up to sixteen families, but leaving no room for parking bays, creating a nightmare knock-on effect for the neighbours.

The ex-prisoner proved to be a jovial bloke, carrying a lot of excess weight around his stomach and a set of prominent moobs under a huge T-shirt. Bliss remembered a time when painters wore white bib and brace overalls, but those days were long gone. The hot day meant Warden carried a thin film of sweat on him, with dark pit stains and a curved line of dampness beneath his chest.

'I haven't laid eyes on Big Mofo or Li'l Mofo since before I went inside,' Warden told them, necking water from a large bottle. The more he poured the more it looked as if it came straight back out of him from several leaky pores. 'I spent my time in prison doing a lot of thinking. Coming up, I had all these dreams of being a successful gangster riding around in a gold Roller, using twenty-pound notes to wipe my arse, with a bird in every neighbourhood across the city. By the time I got put away, I was single, in debt up to my eyeballs, and driving around in a clapped-out Ford Fiesta. Some big-time gangster, eh? I knew nothing would change if I went back to it when I got out, so I made up my mind to go straight. And that meant cutting ties with anybody living on the wrong side of the law.'

Bliss looked around them. They were standing in the stairwell which Warden had been prepping by filling cracks and sanding down. 'Looks as if you made the right decision,' he said. 'Do you feel some pride in earning an honest crust, Charlie?'

Warden slapped his belly. 'These days all I do is eat and drink away my dough, but yeah, I do it with some pride now. I'm not completely back on my feet, but if this contract goes well, I stand to get a few more decent earners on the back of it.'

'Good for you. I hope it works out.' He meant it. He wasn't a believer in prison reforming its inmates, but when it worked out that way, he was more than happy to have one less ex-con to worry about. 'Anyhow, getting back to your old mates, what can you tell us about them?'

For the first time, Warden appeared uncomfortable. 'Look,' he said. 'Being out of the game is one thing, ratting on the people I used to work with is something else altogether.'

'We're not asking you to finger them for anything, Charlie,' Chandler told him. 'Besides, if you haven't seen them for a while, then you won't know what they're doing now anyway. Right?'

'Right.' Another quaff of water.

'There you go, then. No, what we're after here, Charlie, is some background. Mates of theirs. Places they liked to hang around together. You know, pubs, cafes, clubs maybe.'

The big man nodded. 'None of that seems unreasonable. Not as if you couldn't find out all that from other people. Big – that's Big Mofo – likes to work on his body. He's one of those ripped blokes. You know he's black as the ace of spades, yeah?'

Chandler nodded.

'Right. Of course you do. Anyway, I can't remember which gym he uses, but he works out pretty much every day. And now that I think about it, as a pair, they do enjoy a frame or two every so often. The Mansfield on Lincoln Road is their snooker hall of choice. As it happens, that's where they meet up with a lot of similar-minded mates. I don't know many names, but if you strike out in the gyms, I dare say you'll find them or people who know them in the Mansfield.'

'What's your opinion of them?' Bliss asked. 'And it's not ratting, Charlie. But you've spent time with them. You know them well. Tell us about them.'

'Like what?' Warden asked with a slow shrug.

'Let's start with temperament. It's no secret they're prone to violence, so you won't be giving us anything we don't know already on that score. But are they both quick to turn, or is one more relaxed than the other?'

Warden's eyebrows arched. 'There's a difference there, that's for sure. Big is this massive fuck-off physical presence who'd scare the shit out of you just looking at him, but he's so laid back he's almost horizontal. Smokes a lot of Ganja that one, so he's pretty chill. And that's not a stereotype; he just does. I won't say he's one of the good guys or anything, but he's a nice bloke once you get to know him. And once he gets to know you. Yeah, I've seen him tear it up, and it's a fearsome old sight when he gets going. But it takes a fair bit for him to lose his rag. Li'l is the very opposite. His temper is on a hair trigger. Slightest little thing and he's off on one. He reminds me of that actor in Goodfellas. The little, podgy bloke.' He snapped his fingers. 'Joe Pesci. You ever see that film?'

Bliss had, and he knew precisely what Warden meant. 'Yeah. One of the greats. And I get what you're saying about the Pesci character. He played Tommy DeVito. He had little man syndrome coming out of his arse.'

'Yeah, that's the fella. Well, that's Li'l Mofo all over. He just flares up and strikes, but while his mate is happy enough to deck his opponents, Li'l badly wants to hurt them. We used to call him The Punisher. He bloody enjoyed it, too.'

The account cemented what they already knew. Only Warden had opened up a couple of doors for them to walk through. To Bliss, trying the gyms first seemed the sensible approach, especially if they wanted to get the big man on his own to begin with. Bowling up at the snooker hall might provoke Li'l Mofo to press the self-destruct button, so a bit of covert surveillance might be in order.

'You know what they drive around in?' Chandler asked Warden. Bliss winked at her for catching a question he'd forgotten to ask.

'If they're together it's usually Li'l who drives. He's a Bimmer man. Always goes for a convertible. As it happens, Big also likes his German wheels. He has one of those old BMWs that looks a bit like a shark?'

'Six series,' Bliss shot back. 'Nice motor. M635CSi I think it was.'

'Nerd,' Chandler whispered from the corner of her mouth.

'That's the one,' Warden said. 'His was silver. Don't know if he still has it, but if he does, he probably doesn't use it often because it's obviously a classic motor.'

Bliss nodded. 'Anything else you can tell us, Charlie?'

'Only that Li'l has a kid somewhere. Don't know the mother, or where they live. But he mentioned them one day, which came as a surprise to most of us as I recall.'

'That might be worth following up on,' Chandler said. 'Cheers, Charlie.'

'Yeah, well.' He looked down at his feet and then back up again. 'Maybe I said too much. It won't come back to bite me, will it?'

'Not from us it won't,' Bliss assured him.

'Good, because I don't want that maniac after me.'

'What you've given us is generic. Could have come from any-body. But thanks. It might prove useful. And Charlie... I was serious when I said I hope it all works out for you. Overall, I prefer people not to do the crime, but if they do and they also do the time, then I like to think of as many as possible finishing their stretch and going on to make a contribution outside.'

'Cheers,' Warden said, sticking out a hand he'd been wiping with a rag when he and Chandler first interrupted him at work.

The two men shook. Chandler did the same. Bliss felt better for meeting the man. It felt like a positive message. One of hope and potential. Something to keep in mind the longer the op went on.

THIRTY-FOUR

OR JIMMY BLISS, CHASING a lead was a visceral experience. Familiarity over time had taught him when to get excited and when to wind his neck in. While it was the logical next step, checking the gymnasiums got them nowhere. They found the club where Big Mofo was a member but were told their suspect had been and gone earlier in the morning. Bliss was okay with that, having decided that it might be better after all to eyeball Tapper and Ritchie Morrison when they were together. He and Chandler discussed their options and settled on locating the snooker hall.

The main problem they discovered with the Mansfield Snooker Club was the lack of covert observation points. They were able to access the club itself via a driveway between residential properties, but the moment they pulled into the narrow courtyard, Bliss knew they were about to encounter a surveillance nightmare. Weeds thrived within the enclosure, blowing through surface cracks weakened by years of neglect. Discarded rubbish now gathered in corners where it had been deposited by the wind. It looked both old and new, as if the council hadn't swept the cobbles in many weeks. The customer car park sat directly opposite the entrance to the building, which was only a few yards away and therefore useless to them for reconnaissance purposes; not that any were currently available. A couple of spaces to the left of the entrance had been marked 'private' to be used by club staff only. Bliss parked in one of them but left the engine idling in neutral.

'Well, that's plan B scuppered as well,' he said. He and Chandler had agreed to find a vantage point from which to keep a close eye on the club. They were not allowed to park on Lincoln Road, and it looked as if they were equally stymied off the main street.

'Do you happen to have a plan C?' Chandler asked.

'Do I have a plan C?' he echoed contemptuously.

'Well, do you?'

Bliss shook his head. 'Nope.'

Their only viable option at this stage and under these circumstances was to enter the club on an official basis, which wasn't something he was prepared to do. He no longer had the powers granted to him by his warrant card, which meant Chandler alone would have to arrest the two men should they be inside the building. If either suspect kicked off, Bliss could intervene as a citizen, but it made the whole proposition decidedly ill-advised. He did have an idea, though it was less than ideal.

'How about I go in alone while you shoot off and drive around until I'm done?'

'You can't go in there on your own,' Chandler shot back immediately. The shake of her head was firm. 'You know I can't let you do that, Jimmy.'

'Of course you can. I'm a civilian now. I can go inside and have a quick shufti. These two chancers will be easy to recognise. If I spot them, I'll call in some backup. If not, I'll maybe play a frame in case they show up. I'll have a word with the manager or owner, tell them I just moved into the area and have been looking for a club. You circle the area while I'm in there.'

'What are the chances they'll be inside?'

Bliss shrugged. 'What were the chances they'd show up while we had the place under observation? Look, we're here and we have some time. Let me go in, give the place the once over so's I'll at least have the lay of the land if we have to go in mob-handed at some point.'

Chandler conceded reluctantly. He winked at her as they both climbed out and she got back in behind the wheel this time. 'Don't scratch it,' he warned. 'You know how much I prize my motors.'

She flipped him two fingers, which meant all was well between them. He knew she'd still have clear memories of him writing off two vehicles in rapid succession while working cases.

The building was a single-storey L-shape, and Bliss found himself having to blink rapidly to adjust his vision to the gloom the moment he stepped across the threshold, the door squealing theatrically on rusty hinges as it closed behind him. He could see several tables and a bar in one corner with some bench seating opposite. The large room resounded to the clatter of ball on ball and indistinct conversation. The place was big enough to provide elbow room but not so large that he couldn't make out the features of everybody inside it. Nobody fit the description of either Morrison or Tapper. He wandered over to the payment counter that adjoined the bar. The young woman who stood behind it looked up expectantly. She wore black clothing to match her black lipstick, and an interesting array of earrings and other pieces of metal bracketed a narrow, almost gaunt face.

'Do you have a table open?' Bliss asked her.

'You a member?' Her tone wasn't openly hostile, but it wasn't exactly welcoming either.

He shook his head. 'I'm not, no.'

'Didn't think I recognised you. Sorry, but you need to be a member to book a table.'

He nodded. 'Okay. Am I able to join and play on the same day?'

'No reason why not.'

'Great. So, do you have a table open?'

'No. Won't be one for an hour, maybe.'

'Fair enough. I probably won't hang around.'

'If you take out membership, you can book your table in advance for next time.'

Bliss shook his head, an idea beginning to form. 'No, I'll leave it, thanks. I had some time to kill and fancied a few frames while I waited for Big Mofo and Li'l Mofo to show up.'

The woman's sudden rigidity told him he'd played it all wrong. She said nothing at first, staring hard at him. Then she shook her head, feigning ignorance. 'Big who and little what? Never heard of them.'

Cursing himself, Bliss nonetheless stood his ground. He gave a chagrined smile and said, 'I think we both overplayed our hands there, sweetheart. I shouldn't have mentioned them, and you shouldn't have been so bad at pretending you had no idea who I was talking about.'

Placing both hands firmly on her hips, she confronted him. 'What the fuck is wrong with you? Do I have to call for help? We have a lot of customers here today who'd like nothing more than to give one of you lot a good kicking.'

'My lot?' Bliss replied, unflustered.

'Stevie Wonder could see you were the Filth from a mile away.'

Bliss laughed. 'Then he'd be wrong. I'm not a copper.'

'Of course you're not. Now, do yourself a favour and fuck off. Before I raise my voice and people start looking sideways at us.'

'Okay. Calm down. I really am not a police officer, but I'll go quietly.'

'Best you do. And best you don't come back, either.'

'Oh, I don't know. The ambience is great and the staff completely disarming.'

The woman's hands moved from her hips, and she crossed her arms beneath her chest. 'I don't know if you have a death wish, mate, but this really is your last chance to walk out of here under your own steam.'

Bliss eyed her for a couple of seconds before turning to leave. He'd remember her face for next time, and he'd make sure one of his colleagues felt her collar for whatever reason he could make stick.

*

Bliss confessed his error of judgement as soon as he got back into the car. He'd called Chandler and asked her to meet him at the end of the driveway. He didn't think his misstep had been too costly, but he felt sure the woman behind the counter would inform Morrison and Tapper that someone had been in asking about them.

Chandler dismissed his annoyance and told him not to worry about it. 'They weren't there, so what have we lost?'

'They're going to know someone is looking for them. The mouthy sort behind the counter was confident I was a cop, so there's that.'

'Yeah, but she didn't know for sure. When she mentions it to our suspects they might wonder if you were somebody else entirely. Someone enquiring about them for entirely different reasons. Face it, you could pass for a villain just as readily as one of us.'

He nodded. 'Yeah, maybe. Don't suppose we'll ever know. We could get a couple of people in there as members, keep the place under observation from the inside. On the other hand, if that same woman is behind the counter she might be a bit suspicious of more new members showing up on the same day I fronted her.'

'It's still worth considering,' Chandler said. 'Especially if we don't get any additional intel on our pair of charmers. Then again, us two not spending time watching that club might prove to be a good thing. What were you thinking? What was I thinking?'

'How d'you mean?'

'Jimmy, you're the SIO. Coming out and doing interviews is one thing, but surveillance? You're supposed to be back at the ranch running things with a wider overview of everything. Instead, you want to sit in the car with me watching a bloody building. You shouldn't be doing that, and I shouldn't be letting you.'

'Oh, really? Since when have you held sway over my decision making?'

'It's *my* decision making that might soon be under scrutiny.'

'How come?'

Chandler smiled. Glanced across at him while also keeping an eye on the road ahead as she drove. 'I'm stepping up. Some bully of a bloke I know made me realise it was time for me to be all I can be. I'm in the programme and there's a chance I'll get an acting DI role with Major Crime.'

Bliss turned in his seat, grinning from ear to ear. 'You sly old bat,' he said. 'Kept me in the dark on that one, didn't you?'

Nodding and looking delighted with herself, she said, 'I talked it over with Anna. I'd just broken up with Graham, you'd retired, I was about to go on annual leave, and I must admit I was feeling at a loss and a bit sorry for myself. Anna reminded me that you were coming back, that me and Graham weren't close enough to have made it work. Somehow, she got me talking about the Job and, admittedly under the influence of alcohol, I realised I felt like I was in a bit of a rut. I put in my application the next morning.'

Chandler's daughter was a wise head on young shoulders. Bliss realised he ought to have approached Anna in the beginning to ask her to persuade her mother to go for promotion. 'I could not be more delighted for you, Pen,' he said. 'You'll make a wonderful DI. I've always told you that. And if I had to bully you, then so be it. Bish had his opportunity and didn't take it. You'll do it with bells on.'

'Me and Quasimodo.'

Bliss said, 'Yeah. Speaking of which, you better wear some slap the day you take your exam, just in case. Don't want them thinking you always look like that.'

This time the two raised fingers were accompanied by a verbal allegation that he pleasured himself.

'I'm doing this for me,' Chandler assured him. 'Me and Anna. Not for you. Understood?'

'Understood. And I don't give a flying fuck why or who you're doing it for. I'm just so pleased to hear you're finally taking that next step up the ladder. You dithered around at DC for too long, and you were starting to do the same at DS. Inspector is your natural role, Pen. Any higher up and the job won't suit you. You could go a lot further before you're done, but you wouldn't enjoy it. At DI, you'll have the team and those above you eating out of your hands.'

'Like you did, you mean?'

Bliss chuckled. 'Not at all. Nobody can do it the way I did it, Pen.'

'Something we're all thankful for. One Jimmy Bliss was enough. Which reminds me...'

'I know, I know.' He raised both hands in submission. 'Don't call you Pen.'

THIRTY-TWO

B LISS DROPPED CHANDLER OFF at Thorpe Wood before making a call to Danielle Halford. She seemed pleased to hear from him, and he suggested they meet at the Guildhall in the city centre. The 350-year-old columned historical landmark in Cathedral Square was built as a marketplace, later used as the town hall, and now served as a meeting place for locals and tourists alike. He picked his way around a bunch of squealing toddlers running in and out of the pavement water fountains, their parents probably wishing they could do the same beneath the fierce heat of the day.

Halford was waiting for him when he arrived, sitting on the stone steps sipping from a Costa 'to go' cup. She handed one to him, which he sipped from in silence before discussing the issue in hand. He revealed that the most senior officers in the area had reached a tentative offer, then went on to explain the conditions and caveats.

'I think I can swing most of that,' Halford said, as self-assured as ever. 'I do have one serious concern, however.'

Bliss arched his eyebrows. 'I thought you might.'

'This is no trifling matter, Jimmy. I understand why you insist there is no violence on our part. As I hope you realise by now, that is also our wish and our intention. But what if that violent behaviour you fear so much is directed at us? We must be able to defend ourselves. You can't expect us to sit idly by while our people are attacked… or worse.'

'I understand your unease,' Bliss said. 'But whatever the arrangement between us, we can't condone acts of violence even if they're retaliatory. If another gang attacks your people, report it and we'll respond accordingly. Just know that if you look for vengeance, we'll react as forcefully as we would if it were anyone else. That is non-negotiable. We can't be seen to take sides. The police will afford you the leeway as previously discussed, but only if you don't step out of line.'

'That rather ties our hands should the situation arise, wouldn't you say?'

He shook his head. 'No. As it happens, I wouldn't. We're willing to police a peaceful takeover by staying out of the way, but the moment it goes beyond that we'll take a different view entirely. And before you argue, it's not open to debate.'

Halford regarded him with obvious disappointment. He thought she looked a little pale and tired, and wondered if their dealings had given her a few sleepless nights. 'I thought we were bartering here, Jimmy,' she said coyly. 'You know, give a bit and take a bit? I rather enjoy giving a bit and taking a bit, don't you?'

Bliss took another sip from his cup, ignoring the affected flirting. 'We've given all we're willing to give. Those are the terms, Danielle. Accept them as they are or walk away.'

Using a hand to shield her eyes from the harsh sunlight, she appraised him for a few seconds before saying, 'I'm seeing a different side of you today. You're much more bullish. And a lot less friendly because of it.'

He hardened his gaze. 'I have two young lads sliced to shreds with half their faces missing lying in mortuary freezers. I have another man missing a hand and part of his arm. This shit is real, so I don't have time to piss around with the likes of you.'

Halford reared back. 'That's harsh.'

'Bollocks it is! You think your knowing smile and easy charm earn you my favour, but you're still one of them. One of the bad guys.'

This time she looked genuinely affronted. 'I'm disappointed to hear you say that. I thought you and I had an understanding. And I don't consider myself to be a bad person.'

'But you work for bad people, and you're happy to take their money no matter how they earned it. You also order bad people to do bad things. Maybe that doesn't make you a bad person in your eyes, but it sure as shit doesn't make you a good one.'

'You're being unfair. We didn't even have anything to do with the incidents you mentioned.'

'Not this time, no. But pound to a penny you work with and for people who have done some equally terrible things.'

Halford sat quietly sipping her drink for a few moments. Bliss realised he'd become unnecessarily heated, but the woman seemed to believe she was floating around somewhere above all the mess and the chaos and the ruined lives, living a squeaky-clean life. He'd deliberately tried to dissuade her of that notion, and if in doing so he had hurt her feelings, so be it. She was tough enough to get over it.

Eventually she turned to him and said, 'I've done my research on you, remember? When you first came to Peterborough you also worked for and with bad people. Just because they were also coppers doesn't make the killers and liars among them decent or good people, nor you a bad person because of your association with them. Yet you still work for the police.'

Bliss shook his head, unwilling to take lessons from someone he considered an enemy. 'That's completely different, and you know it. The fact that you think you and I are even remotely similar sickens me. And we're done here, Danielle. You have our response to your offer. It's down to you now.'

'I'll get back to my boss with the details,' she said, her tone clipped. 'I'll text you with his response.' Her eyes looked beyond him, taking in the columns when her lips twisted in distaste. 'Look at all the graffiti. What is wrong with people? When you suggested we meet here, I looked it up on Google. This remarkable structure has stood for hundreds of years, yet young people think nothing of defiling it. And for what reason?'

'Because they can,' Bliss muttered, equally appalled. 'Because nobody ever told them not to. Because nobody ever told them it was wrong. And probably because it *has* stood for hundreds of years. It's a remnant of the past, which is something they despise and are busy trying to eradicate.'

Halford looked at him and smiled. 'See. I knew we were the same beneath it all. You live and work on one side of the line, while I do the same on the other. But we're no different. We have standards. We know what's right and what's wrong.'

Bliss shook his head. 'And yet you clearly don't understand the meaning of irony. How can you talk about right and wrong when you conveniently ignore the difference between the two when it suits?'

'Just because I work for criminals doesn't make me one.'

'I say otherwise. That money you take from them is stained with the blood of others, and you know it.'

'Are we having a fight, Jimmy?' Halford said after a slight pause, her sly grin back in place. 'And if so, are you as turned on by it as I am?'

He finished the last of his coffee before replying. 'I don't usually have trouble working people out. But you… you're an enigma. On the one hand, I think you have the capacity to be a genuinely warm and enthusiastic, caring woman. But then I wonder if it's all show. Maybe you're a psychopath. Maybe the real you *is* the uncaring and vicious employee of a monster. You don't want to break one of your perfectly manicured and painted nails, so you have thugs to do the bone crunching for you. But deep down where it counts you can be just as dark-hearted as they are. Is that you, Danielle? Is that who you see in the mirror every morning? Do you slap on the smile along with the blusher and lipstick?'

Her eyes became slits. For the first time, she looked genuinely appalled. 'You really don't think much of me, do you, Jimmy?'

'The problem for me is, I don't know what to think of you.'

'And that worries you, doesn't it?'

Bliss nodded. 'It worries me more than I care to admit. It means I could underestimate you. And I get the feeling that's the point at which you'd slide a knife between my ribs.'

THIRTY-SIX

N THE UNSOLVED CASES Team office, Bliss found his colleagues clustered around the same laptop, with Beth Greenhill holding sway at the keyboard. They each looked up in turn as he entered the room, all three faces betraying immense frustration. Their displeasure sparked an inevitable sense of guilt inside him.

'You're just in time,' Foley said. 'The stress in this place is reaching fever pitch.'

Ben Corry agreed. 'I hope you have some ideas, Jimmy, because we're sorely in need of inspiration.'

Bliss walked around the desk to join the team. He gestured towards the laptop screen. 'Tell me what you're working on?' he said.

'We're still gathering information on this bloody bid acceptance deal,' Greenhill told him. 'County records sent over a shitload of scanned documents, but we can't make sense of what they're telling us. Or if they're telling us anything at all. If I was a betting person, I'd put my house on documents being missing. Either that or somebody previously doctored those we were given.'

Taking a slow breath, Bliss said, 'Okay. Explain it again in words even a moron like me can understand. What do you have and what are you missing?'

'We have the bid package. We have the rejection letter and the resulting report. Those are the files we had copied while you and I were at the records office. They all make perfect sense. We then have a resubmission of the bid. All three of us have read and digested it, but none of us can spot a single difference between it and the one that was rejected by our victim.'

Bliss shrugged. 'So far that tallies with our earlier intel. What else?'

'Following the chronological trail, we have a resubmission report written by Justin Nolan's boss, Jeff Smalling, and an email indicating that the report was sent up the chain to *his* boss, Len Wallis. That report offers no opinion, just a statement of facts. We then have an authorisation document signed by Wallis to accept the bid as it stands. Two days separate the report and the authorisation. But we know from various email and memo exchanges that overturning a rejection and accepting a resubmission with no substantial alterations requires higher approval than a departmental boss. So, what we are missing is evidence identifying the name of the person who gave the ultimate nod.'

'Logically, that could be this Len Wallis's boss, yes?'

'Right,' Greenhill confirmed. 'Except that he didn't have a single line manager. He reported to any or all of three staff members further up the food chain. Our problem being we don't have a single email, memo, report, or scanned document to point us in the right direction.'

Bliss understood their obvious annoyance. It was always the conclusive files that went astray when something unsavoury had taken place, with 'astray' often a loose term to mean shredded. 'Do we have the names of Wallis's trio of managers?'

Greenhill tapped the screen in front of her with a perfectly manicured and painted index fingernail. 'That's where we'd got to when you walked in. I was just showing Ben and Guy the page

I'd found online. It contains a PDF file that I think lists those names. I can't be certain, because the department is identified only by an internal code, but I'm pretty sure I'm on the right lines.'

'Good. If that's what you have, then go with your instincts,' Bliss said. 'What's your next move?'

'We hadn't had time to discuss it,' Corry told him. 'But the first thing we need to do is find out if any of those people still work there. If they do, then we can arrange to speak with them. If not, we try to track them down by other means.'

'You think they'll speak to you voluntarily?' Bliss asked. 'I mean, from what you've just told me we could have one, two, or all three of them involved in making sure Callum Davey's business was awarded that contract. Whoever did so is unlikely to confess.'

'What do you suggest, then?'

Bliss regarded Foley, who had asked the question. 'Keep working on the first stage. Confirm that these three people are who you think they are, and if so, then find them. After you have that information, do the necessary homework on them. Look particularly at their financials. Start with early 1999 but extend the parameters if you get no joy. Of course, it could be that they sold their souls for a bag of cash received only after Davey got paid. To that end, let's see how they're living, whether they moved into a more expensive home or bought a yacht or an island somewhere. Anything that looks remotely iffy.'

'And then?' Greenhill asked. 'Assuming we find something?'

'Then we get together and work out a plan of action. If any or all of them look good for this, we develop an interview strategy for whoever is involved.'

The jolt of guilt Bliss felt in that moment was like the deep and persistent ache of indigestion, coupled with the flare of heartburn. This was the slippery slope he had hoped to avoid for far longer and had wished never to encounter. There was another line of enquiry he ought to have suggested, but he was holding back. He had bided his time, wishing one of his colleagues would think of it, and it wasn't too late for that to happen. But the situation he found himself in was no longer ambiguous. He either did his job or he gave in to external pressure.

'I've had another thought,' Bliss said, reaching a decision. 'I must assume these three managers don't represent the very highest echelons of power at County Hall. Therefore, there's no reason to assume the final verdict came from one or all of these people. For all we know, they sent it further up the ladder and so on. Just because the paper trail ends with them doesn't mean the accountability did. What I suggest you do for now is carry on with what we just discussed. Get these three managers checked out and let's see if any of them are hiding something. But don't stop there. Dig deeper into the organisational structure. Find out how many additional levels this thing might have risen.'

'How far do we go?' Foley wanted to know. 'What level do we take it to?'

'As far and as high as necessary to discover the truth. After all, that's what we're here to learn. Delve into the organisation, find out who held those roles back then, and let's take a good look at them all.'

All three nodded in agreement. Then Greenhill turned to him, a crease of concern on her brow. 'I forgot to mention something. We finally heard back from records and exhibits. Given the volume of items associated with the case and the lack of space we have here, they're willing to loan us a room within their administration offices. I didn't know what to say as we're heading full steam into the county council records, so I said we'd get back to them before the close of play today.'

'Good thinking,' Bliss said. 'For my part, I reckon we chase this down as far as it will go, while we all still think of it as a hot lead. Those case files and exhibits will still be there if we need them, and I'm hoping we won't.'

'What shall I tell them?'

'Thank them. Let them know we're neck deep in something else, and we'll get back to them as soon as we can.' Which will be to say thanks but no thanks if I have my way, he thought. None of us are going to waste time with case records, not when I know what I do.

*

Satisfied that he had pushed his team closer to discovering what he already knew, Bliss made his way back to the major incident room. Since Gratton and Virgil were locked in a meeting with their counterparts in Leicester, he gathered DCI Warburton, Bishop and Chandler, and DC Ansari to inform them of his conversation with Danielle Halford.

'It's going to happen,' he concluded, then turned to DS Bishop. 'Bish, I want you and Gul to liaise with whoever is running the shipment Op. Pen and I were chatting about it earlier and our concern is overlap with our own murder investigation.'

'Of course,' Bishop said. 'We'll get onto it as soon as we're done here.'

'Cheers. I think Diane and I are going to meet with Superintendent Edwards to prepare for a further gold group meeting.'

Warburton nodded her confirmation.

'What do you want me working on?' Chandler asked.

Bliss considered the question for a few seconds. 'That largely depends on what Phil and Alan bring us back from their meeting.'

'We drew a blank when we visited the Leicester main nick,' Bishop said, indicating Ansari who sat alongside him. 'The best we were able to achieve was arranging for a small team to visit us. Hopefully Phil and Alan will learn something new and worthwhile from them.'

'If they obtain a location for these Big Mofo and Li'l Mofo characters, then I want you to take the lead on following them up. The way I see it, the county lines will hopefully now take care of themselves, leaving us with just City-Wide to contend with. But I don't want Foxes pulling back and throwing up the barricades if, as we believe, their blokes are our killers. I want those bastards, but I'd also like to know who gave them the job and that they are also finished giving out such orders.'

'You want me to sniff around Saad Ali himself?'

'No. Not unless he appears on our patch. But I do want you to push the Leicester team who are working on taking down Foxes to nail Ali if he was the one with a finger on the button.'

Bliss looked at Chandler. 'And in answer to your question, Pen, your job is to close in on our suspects, using every scrap of intelligence that comes our way.'

The team moved on to discuss various approaches. Bliss filled in parts of the policy book, but also made additional notes on a separate pad. He'd work the language a little more before entering the result into the book later that evening. After assigning actions, he and DCI Warburton attended their pre-gold team briefing with DSI Edwards. The meeting went well and there was no dissent regarding the plans as they stood.

'Just to clarify,' Edwards said when Bliss had finished speaking. 'Your team will have no input into the drugs shipment discussions and decisions, is that correct?'

'It is, yes.' Bliss nodded. 'We don't want to stretch ourselves to breaking point. However, if the crossover that we fear does occur, then DS Chandler and I might involve ourselves a little more. Timing is likely to be the thorny issue. We clearly want

Karagiannis to work his magic before we nip in and grab up the expected major shipment. The problem we might face is if the drugs are due prior to that happening.'

'I'll make sure the gold team is aware of that. I'm sure there will be differences of opinion on this, but in your view, Jimmy, which operation takes priority?'

'Scarecrow,' Bliss said adamantly, defending his own investigation. 'It's murder. If we can't intercept the consignment of drugs at the most ideal date and time, then we can always go after it when we're fully prepared. Our two murder victims demand our immediate attention.'

Edwards smiled. 'I thought you might say that. I happen to agree with you. In terms of the shipment, do you have any information from Intelligence concerning surveillance?'

'No. I've steered clear. It's not my Op, so I'm keeping well away until we're needed.'

'I'll keep Jimmy and his team informed at all stages,' Warburton told her boss. 'Hopefully, the gold team meeting will put together the missing pieces.'

'It all feels a little rushed for my liking, but the sense of urgency is palpable,' Edwards said. 'A successful outcome serves many purposes, but there's an awful lot that can go wrong.'

'If we get a lead on the whereabouts of our suspects I'm going to want immediate arrests,' Bliss insisted. 'These are dangerous men, and they need to be removed from the streets.'

'I take it you don't have enough to charge them with as things stand?'

'Absolutely nothing. Truth is we don't know with absolute certainty that these are our wrong'uns, but all the information coming in from our drugs team, their Leicestershire counterparts, and both pods of intelligence suggests they're good for it. Once we have them in custody and get access to their phone information and perhaps even vehicle SatNav data, we'll be able to see if they were in the area at the time.'

Warburton shook her head. 'I have my doubts about these two. If they are experienced pros, then tech might not give us what we want. If we don't have that, then we'll be relying on one or both of them coughing because there are no forensics to tie them to.'

'But the truth is we all know they aren't going to even comment after being arrested,' Bliss added. 'So, it's tech or nothing. Or...' He shrugged and looked pointedly at the two senior officers. 'Perhaps Danielle Halford knows some people capable of loosening their tongues.'

'I'll pretend I didn't hear that,' Edwards said.

'Hear what?' DCI Warburton muttered beneath her breath.

Bliss just smiled and decided to circle back to that particular idea.

THIRTY-SEVEN

To THE NORTH OF the city centre lay Frog Island, part of Leicester's vast industrial and commercial complex. Located between the River Soar and the Soar Navigation, its grim mills historically manufactured clothing, machinery, and materials essential for the local hosiery trade. After a period of deindustrialisation, the mills and factories became derelict, leaving the island largely neglected. Waterside regeneration saw new life reinvigorate the area, leading to rapid regrowth. It was a mix of the very old and the very new, seemingly at odds with itself.

On the bank of the Grand Union Canal sat the vast Foxes Cash & Carry Wholesaler site owned by Saad Ali. In the early evening, with the premises closed to the public, he held court in the market and auction plaza. Gathered before him stood his closest allies, together with their assorted fixers and muscle. They would not approve of what he was about to say, which was why his own array of hard men – each fully armed – stood close by should anyone choose to step out of line.

'My friends,' he said, spreading his hands wide in greeting. 'I've asked you all here today because I have some major news that affects us all. Some of you have been working hard to push the

Foxes line into Peterborough, with designs on eventually gaining a foothold throughout Cambridgeshire. You've all done a splendid job, and I have no issues with any of you on that score. As you're all aware, I recently ordered you to step things up, and you did so. Again, my congratulations to each of you. And with the Soke line crumbling and the City-Wide line still largely unknown to us, you might ask why I have made the decision to pull the plug on our operations in the county.'

His words initially provoked disgruntled mutterings, which swiftly became a low rumble of outright anger. Fists waved and heads shook. Ali waited for it to subside, knowing that nobody who took his shilling had the balls to openly confront or defy him on this matter. Not here. Not out in the open. Not with his protective detail close to hand.

'I understand why this move is not popular,' he said when the gathering was once again hushed. 'Many of you saw an opportunity to grow and establish yourselves, and your disappointment with my decision is not unreasonable. But hear me out, my friends. You will know then what I do now, and you will see that in steering away from the course we were on, I have in reality secured our futures.'

Naturally, he was not about to reveal the true reason behind this change of direction. The drugs business had always been a constant battle, leaving leaders like him to choose each of them wisely lest they all die on a hill not worth fighting for. Learning that Hector Karagiannis ran the City-Wide line had come as a severe blow to Ali's aspirations. The Greek himself was powerful enough, but with the full weight of his family behind him it was no contest. The man's emissary had offered a generous financial package, and when put together with the promise of a peaceful transition it made good business sense to step aside. There was no room for ego or pride in such matters. The way Ali saw it, a percentage of something significant with all of his people left intact and therefore capable of being utilised elsewhere, was preferable to nothing and the kind of carnage that would decimate everything he had built.

Ali clasped his hands before him as if in prayer before continuing with his lies. 'We had all but seen off the Soke line and eventually the upstart City-Wide line would, I have no doubt, gone the same way. Both gangs feared us and the war that was coming their way. Which is why they capitulated, begging me to come to the negotiation table with an offer. My friends, the offer I made them was simple. Soke goes back to the business of selling weed, while City-Wide continues to push whatever they like across that cursed county. Let them do all the hard work, the buying and selling, taking all the risks, and putting their people out on the streets to face all manner of danger. Because in exchange for my allowing them to continue, they have agreed to pay us a considerable sum of money each month. This leaves us all free to plough new furrows, seek new targets, and all the while earning on the back of another line's sweat and blood.' Saad Ali held his arms aloft. 'My friends, I have pulled off a mighty coup and we will all reap the benefits.'

The colossal cheer that went up and echoed off the walls was music to his ears. He had pulled it off. Only those closest to him knew the truth. Being driven out of Peterborough had crushed his spirit and felt like the worst of insults to his manhood. But to have had it all ripped away in an inevitable war without any financial reward whatsoever would have been so much worse. His disciples now believed he had honoured them in victory and would ultimately be all the more loyal as a result. In defeat, he saw victory, and took comfort from that.

But as he nodded and smiled and looked around at the joyous faces turned his way, he noticed one remained clouded and thundery, eyes blazing with fierce anger. Ali punched the sky, inviting a greater ovation. All the while he kept those enraged eyes on the periphery of his vision.

Your displeasure is of no consequence to me, he thought. *Hate me if you will. While you still can, my friend. While you still can.*

THIRTY-EIGHT

ONE OF THE THINGS Bliss most liked to do when his mind felt cluttered and incapable of stringing cohesive thoughts together was to drive. After taking Max for his final walk of the day, he jumped in the car and took off feeling more than a little out of sorts. He rarely had a destination in mind when he set out on a nighttime drive, preferring to point his vehicle in any direction and let the moment seize him. After twenty minutes he found himself on the quiet Hod Fen Drove travelling between the villages of Holme and Yaxley. He was familiar with the route as it was the one he usually took after spending an evening in the Admiral Wells pub.

The source of his disquiet that night lay in his new job. He felt a little better at having quietly steered his three new colleagues in the right direction. Whether they discovered the correct information and managed to piece together the resulting connection was out of his hands, but they were good enough to reach the right conclusions. Gathering evidence was by far the harder step.

In his SIO role, he had no such qualms when it came to his own input, despite the frustration levels being depressingly high. Locating their two prime suspects had so far proved more difficult than any of them had imagined. In fact, though the entire team had worked late, the result they so badly wanted continued to elude them. There were no further reports of murder, nor outbreaks of drug-related violence, for which Bliss was hugely grateful. The joint task force team had made excellent progress in identifying where and when to expect the handover of the City-Wide line's consignment. But having no intel on the whereabouts of Big Mofo and Li'l Mofo left a sour taste in the mouth. His job was not to change the working arrangements of various drug lines. It was to solve the murders of two minor runners, kids who'd barely had time to grow, and the only two suspects he and his team had were nowhere to be found.

Bliss was halfway between the two villages and had just crossed Caldecote Dyke when he looked up at the rearview mirror and spotted headlights approaching fast. At first, he thought it might be a youngster testing the limits of whatever tiny fartbox hatchback they'd souped up. But just at the point at which he thought the car would overtake, pulsing blue lights merged with the white LEDs in the mirror.

His first reaction was to smile, but that faded instantly when he remembered he no longer carried a warrant card to flash. Even so, he wasn't overly troubled. He'd not been speeding, and the SUV was in good condition, all lights working. He hadn't consumed any alcohol other than a single bottle of Peroni over the past couple of hours. Quite why the officers in an unmarked saloon behind wanted to pull him over he couldn't imagine, but he felt sure it wouldn't be a problem. His own headlights revealed a grain storage area on the nearside, so he slowed to pull off the road and into the wide entrance. As soon as his tyres found a patch of dirt and gravel, he stopped and slid the automatic gearbox into park. Moments later, a Jag came to a halt a few yards behind him.

No sooner had Bliss slipped out of his vehicle and two figures exited theirs than he instantly realised he'd been wrong. Neither the man who'd been behind the wheel nor his female passenger wore a uniform, and both looked intent on posing a huge problem for him. Bathed in the bright glow coming from both cars, the couple approached.

'Hello there, sir,' the woman said affably enough. 'And how are you tonight?'

'I was doing just fine until about thirty seconds ago,' Bliss replied as evenly as he could with his heart banging away beneath his ribs.

'That's good to hear. Would you mind telling us why you're out here on this road at this time of night?'

'I do mind,' Bliss said. 'But I'll tell you anyway. I do some of my best thinking when I'm driving, so on a whim I decided to take the car out for a spin. As far as I'm aware, I've done nothing wrong. Certainly, I've broken no laws.'

'And you've not been drinking?'

'No. Earlier, yes. Just a bottle of beer. I won't test positive if you breathalyse me.'

'Good. Then hopefully we won't delay you too long, Jimmy. I can call you Jimmy, yes?'

Bliss swallowed thickly. They knew his name. Either they had checked the Police National Computer system to retrieve his details prior to pulling him over or this was more than a chance encounter. And who exactly were they? Because he was beginning to get the impression that they were not police officers. He opted to front up to them and snapped back, 'No. You can't call me by my first name. It's DI... sorry, *Mr* Bliss to you.'

The man might as well have been mute. He stood a pace or so behind his colleague, eyes studious, happy to allow her to continue. 'No problem,' she said. 'Would you like to know why we have intercepted you tonight, Mr Bliss?'

'I insist you tell me why now that you have stopped me.'

She smiled. It contained little humour. 'We'll get to that. But the funny thing is, you haven't even asked who we are.'

'That's because I already know who you are. I misidentified you at first, thinking you were coppers. But not now. So, yes, I know who you are. Your kind, anyway. Intelligence agency of some description, I'm guessing. Not MI5, exactly, but one of the Special Branches, perhaps.'

The woman seemed impressed this time. 'Good. No need for introductions, then. Mr Bliss, you've recently been in contact with one of our colleagues from Five. We're here to inform you that matters have since moved beyond his involvement. Today you have us. Should you need to be detained in the future, it may well be us again. What I'm essentially saying is that our hope is to settle this issue once and for all. Here and now. How does that sound?'

Bliss's glare hardened. 'First of all, let me disabuse you of your own sense of authority and control of this situation. You have no power to detain me, let alone arrest me. I'm hearing you out as a courtesy.'

'I might say we are doing much the same. Where's your own authority these days, Mr Bliss? And without it, what are you exactly?'

'Okay. So, you know something about me. Big deal.'

'With the intelligence we have on you, Mr Bliss, we could certainly make it a very big deal by calling in your ex-colleagues to arrest you.'

His head shooting up in alarm, Bliss said, 'Intelligence? Arrest? What the fuck are you on about?'

'No need for the bad language, Mr Bliss. We're just doing our job.'

Bliss refused to be put off his stride. 'Fuck you and the horse you rode in on if you don't approve. I don't give a shit. Just tell me what's going on here.'

'Sir, we have it on good authority that you have recently been associating with a certain Mr Hector Karagiannis. The man, as I'm sure you're fully aware, happens to be a gang boss. One who is deeply involved in organised crime. Sadly, it seems you've been working with Karagiannis by helping him to take over as the sole county drugs line here in Peterborough.'

Bliss laughed at the absurdity. His anxiety diminished and he continued to laugh until his stomach ached. 'Oh, boy,' he said, shaking his head in disbelief. 'You couldn't have got this one more wrong if you tried. Lady, your intelligence is wrong. Double wrong. I'm not doing anything of the sort, and I'm not working with them on my own. My team and I are running a sting on the man, you bloody morons. With, I might add, the full approval of our Chief Constable.'

The woman's features did not alter in the slightest. 'We're well aware of the back story. But that's all it is. A story. A tall tale you've sold your bosses. We know there is no sting intended even if one is being planned. It's just you assisting a gangster in exchange for both cash and merchandise.'

Still shifting his head from left to right, Bliss said, 'Nope. Sorry. That's complete nonsense, and if you don't know that's the case, then you really are as stupid as you look.'

The pair looked at each other. The male nodded. The woman said, 'Consider yourself extremely fortunate that someone above our pay grade decided to give you one last chance. You can probably thank your pal Munday for that. But please be aware that we will overrule his objections if we have to come at you again.'

'Come at me for what?' Bliss said, perplexed by their outrageous move. 'As I told Munday, irrespective of what I do, I have three experienced colleagues working the same case. I can apply the handbrake all I like, but it's out of my hands if they find their way to the truth.'

'The way we hear it,' the man said, speaking for the first time, 'you have at least one hand on the tiller at all times. Steer them into the shallows if you must. All we're asking for is time.'

'And if you don't get it?'

'Then you'll find yourself arrested and interviewed by the police, after which they will charge you.'

Bliss scoffed. 'For what exactly? I've done nothing wrong.'

'Are you quite sure about that, Mr Bliss?' The woman had asked the question, and for the first time her smile was genuine.

'Yes. I'm positive.'

'In that case, you might want to give your vehicle a thorough search just to make sure you're not transporting anything incriminating. It's one thing to argue the toss over words and veiled threats, quite another to do so when the police stack evidence against you.'

Bliss glanced over his shoulder at his Volvo before meeting her gaze once more. 'What have you done?' he asked.

'No, sir… it's what you might have done that counts here.'

Seconds later the pair were back in their car and speeding off into the distance, Bliss staring after them until the red glow of their rear lights disappeared. He then walked behind his vehicle, opened up the boot, took a torch from his backpack, and proceeded to rummage around inside the rest of the boot and rifle through his backpack, eventually spilling its contents out onto the carpeted area. Having found nothing to concern him, he went front to back inside the cabin, checking the glovebox, the central storage compartment, and finally beneath the seats.

From the passenger side, he retrieved a bag of flour wrapped in plastic. Sellotaped to the top was a printed message that read: THIS COULD SO EASILY HAVE BEEN A KILO OF COCAINE. Beneath his own seat lay several small bundles of newspaper, again wrapped in plastic. Its note carried the same theme, only in place of a kilo of cocaine it suggested the contents could have been stacks of banknotes.

Bliss stared back along the dark, quiet road. A stiff breeze swept across the open ground, its bite chilling his exposed skin. His mind drew lines between Munday, the two spooks who had stopped him, and the concealed packages.

The meaning was obvious. At some point, they had managed to bypass his alarm and get inside the Volvo. What they left behind was harmless, but if they had wanted to this time or decided to in the future, they had the capability to fit him up in a way he'd find difficult to defend. Whichever agency the couple represented was telling him that the initial friendly warning had now moved on to become a clear threat. The next stage would be to ensure his arrest and detainment, derailing not only the cold case but in all probability seeing the end of his new civilian twin roles – if he was fortunate enough to avoid conviction and imprisonment.

Bliss collapsed back against his motor. He shivered despite the clement weather. Chilled by the encounter, he considered its deeper meaning. He took out his phone, located a contact number, and pressed the green icon. Seconds later a distinguished voice answered his call.

'Did you know they were going to do this to me?' Bliss demanded, almost shouting into the device jammed against his ear. 'Were you told ahead of time and just couldn't be arsed to warn me?'

'Jimmy?' Munday said. He sounded puzzled and a little alarmed. 'Calm down, lad, and tell me precisely what happened.'

Still seething, Bliss ceded to the demand. When he was finished, he asked the old spy the same question. The reply came with bitter undertones.

'Of course I didn't know. You truly believe they would make me aware of this beforehand and that I wouldn't have the decency to contact you?'

'Is that so fanciful? You work for them, Munday. You do their bidding. You owe me no loyalty.'

'All of which is true, old chap. But clearly, I hold myself in higher regard as a person than you do. And I realise this is going to sound ridiculous, but right now you ought to be grateful.'

'Grateful? Are you out of your tiny mind?'

'Thankful, then, at the very least.' Munday's tone was scathing. 'Jimmy, you do realise they could just as easily have decided to break into your vehicle to secrete the real thing, don't you? Stashed away drugs and cash inside your car and then followed up with an anonymous call to the police. If their intention was to destroy you, that's precisely what they would have done. The fact that they didn't do so, and instead allowed you the opportunity to redeem yourself in their eyes, is remarkable.'

Bliss recalled elements of the encounter. The woman had suggested he might have Munday to thank for the second chance, and he'd taken it the wrong way. The Five man wasn't complicit, he simply still carried a great deal of influence.

'If this is their heavy-handed way of getting me to drop the investigation then they don't know what they're doing,' he blurted unthinkingly. 'Because I can't do that. You know I can't.'

'I do. And so do they. Jimmy, they told you as much. If you were calmer and less emotional, you would understand more fully and accept this for what it was. These people do not make a single move without first calculating every step from every conceivable angle. They also understand your work benefits from a team effort. My guess is this is a colourful reminder to keep what you know to yourself, to allow the investigation to unfold naturally, in the hope that it takes your people nowhere until such time as the powers that be decide otherwise. As you and I discussed, my friend, it's a tough one to resolve without the missing piece of the jigsaw.'

Bliss took a deep breath then exhaled into the night air. 'Bloody hell, Munday. Do you know how I usually react to such intimidation?'

A gentle chuckle rattled down the line. 'I have a good idea. But I sense you're reading the tea leaves this time and realising there is no positive outcome for you if you react like the Bliss of old. My advice to you is to be patient. The fact that you are not currently under arrest tells me you are being given a final length of rope. Use it and use it intelligently. Let this play out naturally. Do not hang yourself with it.'

Somehow controlling his anger and his breathing, Bliss said, 'Okay, let's say I do. What if your people decide Robert Clay might be useful to them in the future? He gets away with murder and I'm supposed to just accept that?'

'We have to hope it doesn't come to that,' Munday said softly. 'But if that's how this pans out, please believe me when I tell you it's a war you cannot win. You won't make it past the first skirmish. These people fitting you up as being on the take is the very best you can hope for in terms of a way out should they turn against you.' The man from Five paused, and then with a sigh added, 'Believe me, Bliss, the worst is beyond your imagining.'

THIRTY-NINE

B LISS GROANED INTO HIS pillow when he heard the familiar
ringtone of an incoming call. He blinked a couple of times
but saw nothing but dense blackness, which meant it was still
extremely early in the morning. He'd snatched a little sleep, which
had been neither deep nor restful, but he knew it was over for
the night. He reached for his phone, which was charging on the
bedside cabinet, and noticed it had just turned 3.00am. The time
and Diane Warburton's name on the caller ID told him this was
important.

'Morning, sunshine,' she trilled when he answered with little
more than a grunt. 'Splash some cold water on that grumpy face
of yours, throw on some clothes and get your arse into work.'

Drawing his free hand down both cheeks, Bliss said, 'This
better not be some sort of prank, Diane. What could possibly
be so urgent but still have you sounding so chirpy at this ridiculous hour?'

'Oh, I don't know. How about an address for Jamar Tapper and
Ritchie Morrison?' Warburton said smoothly. 'That good enough
for you? I thought you might want to make an early arrest. Pull
them while they're still half asleep and groggy.'

'They won't be the only ones,' Bliss grumbled, stifling a yawn. He quickly gathered his wits, shifting sideways to perch on the edge of the bed. 'But yes. Absolutely. Thank you. Give me twenty minutes.'

Warburton's experience and foresight meant that by the time Bliss arrived at Thorpe Wood, she had already contacted all relevant operational departments, including firearms, the dog unit, and an area force tactical support team. When he walked through the incident room doors, she informed him that officers were on the road heading up to Peterborough from their Hinchingbrooke base. He grabbed them both a drink from the closest vending machine before they sat down to discuss strategy.

'I still can't believe we have their address,' Bliss said, excitement bubbling away inside his chest. 'Are you sure the source is reliable?'

'Impeccable. The tip-off came from Saad Ali himself.'

Bliss felt a warm glow of satisfaction slip around his entire body. The name of the informant had come as a surprise to him, but it also made sense. 'When I last spoke with Danielle Halford, I threw that in as a specific request attached to the main deal. I made it clear to her that for us to have faith in the arrangement, we needed the killers off the streets. I admit I didn't think either of them would go for it, but it seems it was worth a punt.'

Warburton congratulated him on his instincts. 'Good man. I confess I did have an inkling that you might have had something to do with it. And it paid off, so that was a great shout, Jimmy. The information we have indicates Tapper and Morrison are holed up with a friend and his wife just off Lincoln Road. The couple own the house and our two suspects are both staying there. Our people had eyeball on the property less than forty minutes after receiving that intel, so we're as certain as we can be that we'll find all four of them still safely tucked up inside.'

It was the best news the investigating team could have wished for. Certainly, one of the better reasons to be losing sleep. Over the following half an hour, the major inquiry room began to fill almost to overflowing as one by one the Major Crime Unit team and their fellow officers from Huntingdon joined Bliss and Warburton. With the target property highlighted in a GoogleMaps capture on the eboard screen, Bliss walked everybody through the plan he and Warburton had discussed. The order of entry was key to a successful raid, and Bliss was adamant that the dog handler release the animal into the house at the same time as the firearms team went in. He went back and forth on that with relevant officers for a while, before deciding to ease off and let the two teams arrange it between them. They were the specialists, after all.

'Whatever you decide, we need that property contained,' Bliss insisted. He felt tired and sluggish, half a mind still on his fraught encounter the previous night, but still he felt the need to reinforce the point. 'Has anyone carried out a close recce?' he asked, looking around the charged room.

'Yes,' Chandler replied immediately. 'A tactical support officer joined the team watching the house and filmed a walk by on his phone. A couple of us looked at the footage a few minutes ago. I can tell you that it doesn't have a reinforced front door, but it's a newish composite with multiple locking mechanisms. The dynamic entry team are going to need the hydraulic equipment, but it's still going to take time to get inside so we'll lose the element of surprise.'

Cursing beneath his breath, Bliss said, 'In that case we must assume they'll be prepared for us by the time we eventually breach. Prepared and possibly armed.'

'That's not a problem,' a specialist firearms officer said with evident confidence. 'We'll enter the premises as soon as the entry team has the door off. Mindful of your concerns regarding containment, the dog unit will follow close by so that if anybody tries to make a run for it, they won't make it too far.'

Bliss gave an appreciative nod. 'Inhibiting movement and containing all four targets inside the house is obviously favourable, but if one of them does skip out the back we have that covered. Behind the wall at the end of the property's back garden is a medical centre, and we'll have additional units waiting there should anyone try to escape that way. Oh, and we'll make sure a drone team are all set to launch the moment they get the word to go.'

'Any further questions?' DCI Warburton asked. 'Anything left to clarify? Speak up if you have concerns.'

Nobody did. It was time.

*

From the darkest shadow of St Mark's church, Bliss looked on as fingers of sunlight clawed at the sky and scratched away the darkness above nearby rooftops, gradually bringing light and warmth to the new morning. By the Volvo's dash clock, it was closing in on 5.00am. He stifled yet another yawn and stretched out his arms and legs, fed up with waiting in the church car park for everybody to take up their positions outside the relatively new and tidy-looking two-storey terraced house.

He heard someone wrench open the vehicle's nearside back door, and the SUV rocked as DS Bishop climbed aboard. 'All set, Jimmy,' he said, his voice surprisingly calm.

Bliss raised a thumb and filtered the plan through his mind one last time. They hadn't had a great deal of preparation time to pull this together, but they had left little to chance. Each team had plenty of experience with this type of raid, and they preferred going in early while the suspects were either still asleep or having recently woken. They had all mutually agreed that waiting a further twenty-four hours was too great a risk, leaving them good to go the moment Bliss gave the word.

He glanced to his left where Chandler sat, then in the rearview to check on Bishop and DC Ansari who was quietly on edge as usual ahead of a raid. 'The moment the door comes off its hinges we go. But none of you are to enter that property until firearms clear the entire house. You hear me?'

They did.

'I mean it,' he warned. 'No heroics. I want our suspects on the ground and cuffed with weapons pointing at them before you make the arrests. Firearms have all the ballistic protection they need. We've got stab vests. It's no contest. Understood?'

They understood.

Bliss changed the channel on the Airwave device clipped to the lapel of his soft leather jacket. 'Command, this is Bravo One. We're in position. Do we have your authority to enter the premises?'

He was taken by surprise when the Chief Constable himself answered, having expected to hear Detective Chief Superintendent Fletcher's voice. 'You're good to go. You have gold team full authority.'

Thumbing the communication device back to the operational channel, Bliss swallowed once and said, 'This is Bravo One. All teams are set. Dynamic entry team to strike, strike, strike!'

Before his final word had died in the still morning air, the four of them flew out of the car and rushed across the gravel surface of the car park. Upon their arrival under the safety blanket of darkness, DC Ansari had placed a small set of aluminium steps behind a churchyard wall. She quickly retrieved them from their hiding place, yanked them open and stood them by the black iron railing fence separating the church grounds from the narrow road beyond. Within seconds, they had each clambered over and were sprinting across the block-paved street towards the target property. A uniformed tactical support officer stood on the raised threshold between the path and the crumpled door yawning inwards. His considerable bulk made a formidable barrier. He had one hand on his Airwave, the other raised in their direction.

'Sorry,' he said. 'But it's not been cleared.'

It had been barely twenty seconds since their strike team colleagues had achieved entry, so Bliss was not unduly concerned. He heard indistinct commotion and raised voices emanating from inside the house. Again, nothing unusual in this, but he thought he detected an air of urgency in the tones being used. Airwave chatter was rapid and difficult to follow.

'Did I hear they have two in custody?' Bliss asked, glancing around at his team.

Chandler nodded. 'Yes. The married couple, as far as I could tell. I think I heard a few voices saying one suspect had done a runner out the back door.'

'Yeah,' Bishop said. 'And I'm pretty sure someone responded by telling them the dog handler went after the suspect along with firearms support.'

A second tactical support officer appeared in the open doorway. 'The suspect who bolted isn't coming easy,' he told them. 'We have him trapped, so he's not going anywhere, but he's waving a knife about and threatening to use it. Last I heard, we had tasers on him and as you can hear, the dog is kicking off big time.'

Bliss thought he might well have heard the animal's barking from his own bedroom back home. However, the next piece of chatter caused a sinking feeling in his stomach. If he had heard correctly, they now had three in custody. But as they were still hunting for the second suspect, they were unable to clear the house.

'This is Bravo One,' he said into the radio. 'Which of our suspects do we have in cuffs out in the back garden?'

There was a harsh squawk, followed by, 'Bravo One. This is Alpha Two. We have Tapper in custody by the wall at the far end. I repeat, Tapper in custody. Don't bother to come through, we're bringing him your way. No sign of Morrison at this time.'

Bliss licked his lips. Nervous energy heightened his emotions while he and his colleagues waited impatiently to enter the house, and you could cut the tension with a spoon. Firearms had cleared all rooms and cupboards and were now checking the loft via a hatch in the upper floor landing ceiling. Behind Bliss and his team, four transport vans rolled to a gentle halt outside the property. He couldn't help but wonder if they might not now require one of them.

Moments later, movement along the passageway inside the house caught his attention. A firearms officer barrelled his way through, closely followed by a huge man wearing only jogging bottoms. Big Mofo certainly lived up to his billing. The hulking brute was all bulging veins and a seething mass of fury as he struggled against the officers who held his cuffed wrists as they moved towards a waiting van. He snarled and spat and wriggled and heaved, but uttered not a single recognisable word. Not, that was, until he spotted the four detectives huddled together on the path. At that point, he forced a huge toothy grin and started to chuckle, a harsh grating sound from somewhere deep inside his huge chest. Shifting his head from side to side, he said, 'You got me for now, bro, but you ain't got my fam.'

Bliss ignored the statement, as did Chandler who formally arrested the man as he continued to strain against those who had captured him. Bliss waited until the officers began to lead the prisoner away before turning to those closest to him. 'They're not going to find Morrison up in that loft. If he was ever here, he was long gone before we turned up.'

'You can't know that, Jimmy,' Bishop said, his own impressively large frame shifting anxiously. 'He's probably tucked himself out of sight somewhere. We'll find him.'

But Bliss shook his head. 'I admire your positivity, Bish, but there's no chance. Did you clock the look on that cocky fucker's face just now?' he turned sideways to watch as the same pair of officers hauled Jamar Jay Tapper inside the first transport vehicle, whose suspension dipped and swayed alarmingly. When he switched his attention again, he realised his eyes were now hooded, shoulders sagging. 'He knew we wouldn't get everything we came here for. His mate is still out there somewhere. And we should assume he ain't going to be happy when he finds out we have his "fam" in a holding cell.'

FORTY

B LISS SPENT THE REST of the morning working Operation Scarecrow. Ritchie Morrison, aka Li'l Mofo, remained at large, having not been found inside the house. Everyone involved shared their disappointment, but for once, Bliss regarded his glass as half full. When he eventually spoke to the team, he was adamant about their next move.

'From everything we know, the houseowners Bobby and Tina Fleece are nothing more than friends of our two suspects. Predominantly, they are closest with Jamar Tapper, but they also socialise with Morrison through him. Neither Bobby nor Tina has a record, and they are not known to us as drug dealers or even users. Bobby Fleece works in car sales for Kia over at Boongate. Tina is a mobile hairdresser and nail stylist. They have all the appearances of a non-criminal, hard-working couple who happen to know our suspects. So far, they haven't asked for a solicitor, and I say we go at them hard to find out where our little motherfucker might be.'

'Do we suspect them of knowingly assisting an offender?' Ansari asked.

Bliss shrugged. 'I can't answer that at this time, Gul. Frankly, I'm not interested in their lives, and that's what we need them to understand from the outset of their interviews. As far as I'm concerned, they're immaterial at this stage. But drum it into them that if they have any idea where Morrison is and they don't tell us, their situation will change in an instant. And not in a good way.'

'Who do you want in the room with them?' Warburton asked. She sat poised to enter details into her notepad. Bliss knew they were his to crib from later when he updated the policy book.

He checked his watch, conscious that Jamar Tapper's custody clock was ticking down. He was confident of obtaining an extension if requested, and also didn't think they would need much time to interview the seemingly innocent couple.

'Bish and Alan to take Mr Fleece,' he decided. 'Gul and Phil can have the man's wife. Pen and I will observe. When we're done with them, I want Gul and Phil to then take Tapper.'

'What about strategy?' DC Ansari asked. 'Should I take the lead, you know, woman to woman? Phil can then jump in hard if she seems to be stalling or unwilling to talk.'

Nodding, Bliss said, 'Yes, I like that. In fact, if it comes to it and you think she might be about to go but is dithering because she's unsettled by Phil's presence in the room, throw him out on his ear. Make her feel comfortable again. If she's genuinely innocent, there's no reason for her not to tell you everything she knows.'

He gave different instructions to DS Bishop and DC Virgil. He told them to ask questions alternately to keep Bobby Fleece off balance, never allowing him to settle into the soothing rhythms of a single interviewer. With his encouragement ringing in their ears, the four detectives set off for the interview rooms on the ground floor.

DCI Warburton asked Bliss and Chandler to hold back before heading down to the monitoring room. She was keen to know how the new SIO role was going from both their perspectives. Bliss let his partner go first.

'From my point of view there's not a great deal of difference compared to when Jimmy was a DI,' Chandler said. 'Besides the fact that he now goes missing for hours on end when he's working with his other team, of course. But in some ways that might actually be helping the rest of us to keep our focus narrow. When you're on the case twenty-four-seven and things aren't coming together as you like, you tend to overreach and follow strands down blind alleyways just to rule them out. Because we don't have Jimmy with us all the time, we seem to manage it differently and keep a tighter rein on the investigation as a result.'

'Jimmy?' Warburton said, turning her attention to him.

'It's obviously different. But not bad different. Just different different. I completely get and accept Pen's point. I think it has helped us keep on the straight and narrow. In fact, in some ways we're forced to do so, but it seems to be working in our favour.'

'And the administrative SIO aspect? Let's not forget that's your role now.'

'I think I'm doing okay. I clocked you making notes for me, and I hope you know how grateful I am for that. I'm more hands-on than you were as SIO, but that's just my nature.'

'You mean you're a control freak?'

He laughed and heard Chandler chuckling beside him. 'You could say that. You know me, Diane, I can't stand to be cooped up. I'd rather spend my time out there than languishing in my office.'

A smile crept across Warburton's lips. 'Is that what you think I did when I was senior investigating officer?'

Bliss shook his head. 'No, I didn't mean that. Not at all. Let's face it, we all know I'm winging it. If you check my policy book right now, you'd find it lacking. I have bundles of notes and reminders which I'll add to yours, so before I go home tonight it will be bang on. You were organised and efficient. You *were* an SIO, whereas I'm still just playing at it.'

'Hmm. I might try to forget you said that when it comes to your evaluation.'

He shrugged. 'We both knew what we were getting when I took this job on. I don't think I've let anyone down so far.'

The DCI was quick to reassure him otherwise. 'Don't worry, Jimmy. At the point at which it doesn't work or gets in the way of an investigation, I'll let you know. As it happens, I think this Op has gone rather well so far. It's far from the easiest case to run, but I've yet to spot a misstep. And that's what I'll be telling the DSI and DCS.'

Bliss thanked Warburton, then jerked his head at Chandler. 'Come on,' he said. 'Let's see what's happening in those interview rooms.'

*

It was obvious after less than ten minutes of being lightly grilled that Tina Fleece knew nothing about the connection her husband's friends had with county lines drugs or organised crime. Still in shock following the dawn raid on her home, her surprise at learning of their involvement could not have been faked, her look of horror entirely genuine. Wearing the tracksuit the police had allowed her to pull on before being led out onto the street, the dishevelled woman hugged herself and gently rocked back and forth in her chair. Her cheeks were flushed, highlighting old acne pockmarks.

'You must think I'm such a clueless bitch,' she said. 'Typical blonde airhead. I never used to think of myself in that way, but now I'm wondering. How could I have missed it?'

'You say you never heard your husband and his two friends discussing criminal activity,' DC Ansari said. It was a statement based on Fleece's assertions so far.

'No, never. Bobby's no criminal. Not even close. If he ever knew what them two got up to, he never mentioned it to me and neither did he let anything slip while the four of us were together.'

'Moving back to that,' Ansari said. 'On how many occasions have Tapper and Morrison been to your home in, say, the past six months?'

She had to think about that, but nodded after a few seconds. 'JJ has popped over maybe three or four times. Ritchie was with him on two of those visits.'

'Just to be clear, JJ is Jamar Tapper, yes?'

'Sorry, yes. Jamar Jay Tapper, so we call him JJ.'

'Did you know him by any other name, Mrs Fleece?'

The young woman, just twenty-three, blushed. 'I've heard him called Big Mofo before. Ritchie is known as Li'l Mofo. But oddly enough, they only get called that when they're together.'

'Does your husband know them by those other names?'

'Well... yes. If I know, then of course he knows. They're *his* friends. But he never calls them that himself. Not once when I've been around.'

Ansari smiled and nodded. She read from a sheet of paper she'd withdrawn from a wallet folder. 'Tell me,' she said. 'How is it that Tapper and Morrison came to be staying at your home?'

For the first time, Tina Fleece appeared uncomfortable. DC Gratton must have noticed her hesitation, because he leaned across the table and snapped at her. 'It's a simple enough question, Mrs Fleece! Why were our two murder suspects staying in your home?'

Rattled, Fleece swayed backwards, eyes wide and fearful. 'I'm sorry, but it's not that easy. I don't know exactly why they were staying. All I do know is that Bobby called me last week and asked if the pair of them could stay for a few nights. He said he'd asked why when JJ spoke to him about it, but said Ritchie had got a bit lairy at being questioned. He's the volatile one, the one you have to watch what you say around, even though he's the smaller of the two. Bobby let it go, and I didn't press for answers.'

'Were you afraid to say no?'

'Not afraid as such. More uncomfortable.'

'When was this?' Ansari asked softly.

'Um, Friday afternoon. They rocked up later that night.' Fleece's voice was calmer now, her eyes aimed at the female seated directly opposite.

'And they both stayed with you over the weekend and through the week?'

'Well, we never saw them on Saturday night. Both were here the following morning when we woke up, but they went out on Saturday evening and must have stayed out late because they weren't back by the time we went to bed.'

'Which was at what time?'

'Around midnight, I think.'

'So how come Ritchie Morrison didn't stay with you last night?'

She shrugged. 'I have no idea. JJ said there'd been a few issues at work, and Ritchie had buggered off on his own. He wasn't there for dinner and still hadn't shown up by the time me and Bobby went to bed. JJ stayed up, and I think we assumed Ritchie would turn up when he felt like it.'

Nodding, Ansari carefully put away the slip of paper, then asked, 'Here's the big question, Mrs Fleece. Do you know where Morrison might have stayed last night, given we were unable to locate him at your home?'

Her face betrayed no outward sign of emotion. 'No. Honestly. I don't know why he was there in the first place, and I don't know why he wasn't last night. And as I've already told you, I had no idea he was a criminal or involved with criminals. Like I said before, maybe you think I had to be stupid not to know. Well, I'd rather you thought that of me than believe we'd mix with that sort if we knew what they were into.'

'But you just told us Ritchie Morrison was volatile,' Gratton reminded her. 'What did you make of that? Did you never wonder what that might mean?'

'Yeah. Of course. I'll go as far as to say he frightened me at times. But you don't go from there to wondering if he's involved with a drugs gang. I don't, at least.'

'Phil!' Ansari said curtly to her colleague. 'Tone it down, will you? Tina here is helping us, but you're not making it any easier for her. If you can't keep your attitude in check, I'm happy to continue without you.'

Gratton said nothing, so the young DC continued to smile at Fleece and said, 'Apologies. I know you're doing your best. As you must understand, we really need to speak to Morrison. So, let's approach it from a different direction, shall we?'

Fleece nodded, matching Ansari's kind smile.

'You had no idea why Morrison didn't come back to your house last night, and you have no idea where he might have been instead. Have a think about this, then, Tina. How about before he came to stay? Did Bobby or maybe JJ ever mention where Ritchie lived?'

Following a slight pause, Tina Fleece said, 'I'm really trying to help, so I'm thinking as hard as I can. JJ was born in Downham Market but raised here as far as I know, and Ritchie was originally from just outside Leicester. Market Harborough, I think. I know they both used to work mainly in and around the Leicester area, then JJ told us he was coming back to Peterborough for a while. That's when we met Ritchie for the first time.'

'Okay. This sounds promising. Do you know where they were living when they first moved back here?'

Fleece brightened. 'Maybe. I'm not certain. But maybe.'

'Just tell me what you do know, Tina,' Ansari said, nodding encouragement.

'JJ inherited his uncle's business. I'm pretty sure it was a printing firm. He also inherited a flat. I assumed he'd either rented it out or sold it, which meant they both needed a room while they were looking for somewhere else to live.'

'So, you're saying Morrison was staying with Tapper?'

'Yes. Yes, that sounds about right.'

'Tina, this is very important,' Ansari said, injecting severity into her voice. 'Do you have an address for us? If not, do you have the uncle's name?'

Fleece shook her head. 'I don't have an address, no. To be honest, I never paid much attention. I know it was somewhere in Orton Malborne, but not the road or number.'

'That's fine. You've narrowed it down for us, which will help. How about Tapper's uncle?'

'JJ called him Henry.' Her face brightened as a thought occurred. 'Oh, that's right. He sometimes called his uncle The Hammer. When I asked him why, JJ said it was because his uncle had the same name as some old boxer.'

'Henry Cooper,' Bliss said from the observation room. He glanced across at Chandler. 'That's enough for us to be getting on with, Pen. The name will give us the premises, and pound to a penny that's where we'll find Ritchie Morrison skulking.'

FORTY-ONE

THE INTERVIEW WITH BOBBY Fleece went pretty much along the same lines as his wife's. More reluctant to elaborate when he spoke, he nonetheless came across as an innocent man doing his best to be straight with the police. He remembered similar details, and while he also mentioned the uncle's name and nickname, he was less certain when it came to where the man lived. Leaving the pair in their respective rooms, Bliss met with the team and shifted the emphasis to Jamar Tapper.

'I don't expect him to give up the address of the flat he inherited from his uncle,' he said. 'We can look into that ourselves, so let's not touch on the subject during this interview. I don't want him to know more than we need him to at this stage, and if we don't manage to nail him for the murders and he walks out of here we can't have him warning his mate. If he thinks we don't have that information, he'll either leave Morrison where he is or he might even pay him a visit. Either works for us, because by then we'll hopefully have everything we need. Bish and Alan, I want you two digging into the uncle while Gul and Phil are in the room with JJ.'

'And if we locate the flat?' DC Virgil asked.

'We sit on it until we've strategised the fuck out of every scenario,' Bliss replied flatly. 'After all, let's think about what we know and what he might know. For one thing, we curtailed his little reign of terror just as he was getting warmed up. Saad Ali pulling the plug must be the work problem Tina Fleece referred to. I'm guessing Morrison didn't approve and went off in a huff, hopefully to cool down as opposed to taking it out on some poor unsuspecting sod. Since then, of course, their old boss gave us him and his partner in crime. Does he know? Has somebody managed to get that information to him? Is he aware we have his mate in custody? While we don't have answers to these questions, we can give them our best guess. I'm betting he does know, because these people always have a network ready and willing to blab in exchange for favours or money. If that's the case and he's holed up inside that flat, then he's keeping his head down, thinking he's safe because he trusts JJ to keep schtum. He can't possibly have a clue what information we have, so that works in our favour.'

'You want to leave him for a dawn raid in the morning?' Warburton asked.

Bliss nodded at his DCI. 'I think so. But that might change depending on how things go with his mate. We have him until at least 6.00am tomorrow, by which time his twenty-four hours will be up. Even if we don't have more on him by that stage, we'll apply for the additional time, and I can't see why a judge wouldn't grant us another twelve hours at the very least. Thing is, I'd really like to tug Morrison before we're forced to charge Tapper or let him walk.'

'Why not go earlier, then?' Virgil asked. 'Once we find the address and have all the respective teams on board for another dynamic entry, we can go whenever we like, surely.'

Bliss understood why the young DC had posed the question, but was inclined to disagree. 'There's a reason we prefer dawn raids, Alan,' he said. 'A fully awake Ritchie Morrison will be both vigilant and wary. If he's armed, then we must also consider him to be dangerous. It's by far the safer option to wait until his physical defences are at their lowest ebb. We'll get a surveillance team as close as possible once we know where he's likely to be, so we can make sure he doesn't leg it before we take the door off. If we do it right, we can even attempt to confirm he's inside, but planning for that will be part of the overall strategy.'

'So how do you want Tapper played in this interview?' Warburton asked.

Bliss was ready for the question. 'Nothing the Fleeces gave us affects our approach as far as I can see. We're not going to mention his uncle, so I think we stick to Saad Ali and the Foxes line. Press hard on the murders. Even if he thinks somebody gave him up, he can't know precisely who because he's not had contact with anyone other than his brief since he came in. I say at some point we inject that information into the interview and see if it changes his demeanour.'

'You think he'll cave if we tell him his boss gave him up?' Chandler asked.

'No. But I do think it might rattle him, which could be useful later on, especially once we have his mate in custody. So, pour it in and let it simmer. In terms of the interview itself, my guess is he'll offer no comment to every question.'

As things turned out, Bliss was wrong about that.

As he wound his way around the building to meet up with his cold case colleagues, he reflected on Tapper's refusal to utter a single word, not even to acknowledge his own name. After DC Ansari had discussed the potential charges and the evidence the police were working to, the suspect's solicitor informed them he had advised his client to provide a written statement, but Tapper had refused. Instead, the hulking man sat perfectly still in his chair, arms crossed throughout, staring at a point directly between the two officers sitting opposite. He remained unmoved, even when Ansari mentioned his role working for Saad Ali and how the Foxes line boss had given him up.

It was only the first of several conversations Ansari and Gratton intended to have with Tapper during the rest of the day and evening, but Bliss decided he'd seen enough. He told Chandler where he was going and to contact him if anything significant broke. As he entered the UCT room, his mind was heading into a dark tunnel, wondering how to tackle Ritchie Morrison should they locate him and what terrible acts of violence might unfold as a result.

FORTY-TWO

THE ATMOSPHERE WAS DIFFERENT this time. Bliss sensed it the moment he stepped inside the room. He saw it in their faces and their body language. Something had changed. Something significant. And for the better.

'What is it?' he asked. 'What have you got?'

Beth Greenhill was the first to react. She got to her feet, her eyes gleaming, a huge smile plastered over her face. 'It's all down to you and Guy. You suggested we look higher up the rank ladder, which was what we got to grips with the moment you left us. But it was Guy who took that suggestion and ran with it.' She broke off and turned to Foley, who gave a narrow grin accompanied by a humble shrug.

'I asked myself why not start at the very top,' he said. 'And once I'd decided there was no reason not to, I spoke with Beth and Ben about it, and they agreed with me. To be honest, we're not entirely sure what to do with what we've discovered. But it's something. It's definitely something.'

Bliss took a seat, unsure how he felt about the team making progress in his absence. Ordinarily, he'd be as excited as they were. But he had to temper that enthusiasm knowing how close they might be to steering the investigation in the one direction MI5 wanted them to avoid. 'Go on,' he said. 'Talk me through what you have.'

Foley obliged. 'Of course. The next thing we did was to check the records to see who led the county council in 1999. His name was Aaron Clarke, but we quickly lost interest in him because he died in a car accident only a few months later. However, when we came up with him, we also spotted who the deputy leader was at the time. I have to admit, Jimmy, we were all shocked. Not so much at learning the name, but at the inevitable conclusions we drew afterwards. I take it you know who Robert Clay is, yes?'

'I'm not a huge fan of politics,' Bliss said as casually as he was able. 'But I do know the man is our MP. By that I mean Peterborough's MP.'

Foley nodded. 'He is. He's a shadow backbencher, but one of the things we discovered is he's starting to make a bit of a name for himself. Rumour has it he could be in the first cabinet formed by a new government.'

'I had no idea he was a rising star,' Bliss lied.

'More importantly, the reason I'm talking about him at all is because Clay held the position of deputy leader of the county council at the time of Justin Nolan's murder. He later went on to become leader, before turning his attentions to parliament.'

'Okay. That's a great start. I'm guessing there's more to come.'

'Much more. Using him as a fresh starting point, we investigated any potential connection he might have with Callum Davey or any of Davey's businesses. What we discovered wasn't too hard to find once we had Clay's name. It was the break we needed. Thing is, Jimmy, Clay and Davey are close. Too close to ignore. First of all, they attended the same university at the same time, though we can't be certain they knew each other there. But fast-forward a few years and Davey is widely known to be a vocal and financial supporter of Robert Clay. Once we had that information to work with, we wondered if their relationship was in any way reciprocal. As you might expect, if there's evidence of collusion between them over contracts, we've yet to find it, but it's a logical and reasonable deduction. Davey wanted that Y2K contract and there was Clay sitting at the right hand of the head of table. If we read between the lines, their friendship was probably the reason Justin Nolan gave for turning down the bid in the first place. It's not hard to imagine Robert Clay being that influence.'

Bliss swallowed thickly. All manner of scenarios played out inside his head, but he knew what he had to say. 'That all sounds positive. The logical connections are all there. But why wouldn't Clay simply use his own influence as council deputy leader to overturn the decision?'

'There are two good reasons we reckon,' Ben Corry said, his cheeks flushed. 'First, Clay is unlikely to want his name officially associated with such a manoeuvre. Far too risky sticking his oar in to ensure a pal gets such a major contract. That's something a good newspaper reporter might sniff out. But then there's also a practical reason: the policies and procedures didn't allow for it. Still don't, evidently. That's why Nolan's boss could do nothing about it, either. They could only accept that same tender ahead of the one Nolan had chosen by removing him from the equation. Once that happened, Davey was free to resubmit the bid, allowing Clay to have a word in the right ear behind closed doors to make sure it went Davey's way.'

Bliss let that sit for a few seconds. He felt as if a fierce tidal wave was buffeting him against the rocks, that he might be swept beneath the raging surface no matter how much he fought against it. He desperately wanted this information out there, but he feared the potential repercussions. The friendly warning from

Munday and the less sociable version from two unnamed members of what he assumed was a version of some Special Branch agency were his own risks to take if he ignored them. But what if Greenhill, Foley, and Corry continued to make progress to the point where the next logical step was to confront the MP, Robert Clay, with questions? How might MI5 and Special Branch react? He'd been the more obvious target to approach up to this point, with Munday doing him a favour by volunteering to lead the way. But ally or not, he had found himself pushed to one side while others took up the challenge. Nothing good could come of them putting his cold case colleagues in their crosshairs.

'I think you're right,' he finally said. 'At the very least, you've discovered information we can't ignore. But we do have to take a couple of steps back to consider our next move. Robert Clay is not a nobody. He's not some gangster our top brass will be delighted to see under investigation. I'm not saying that as the Member of Parliament for this city he's out of bounds, but we will need to acknowledge and allow for his elevated position in society before we go in all guns blazing.'

'You think they might stand us down?' Foley asked.

Bliss shook his head. 'They won't want to go that far. Our Chief Constable is a sound bloke. And while you don't rise to his position without having political nous, he won't put that first. Detective Chief Inspector Marion Fletcher is as good a DCS as I've ever encountered, and she won't be putting up any barriers, either. On the other hand, both are savvy enough to demand concrete evidence or at a minimum sufficient circumstantial and corroborative evidence before they allow any of us to approach Clay in person. Depending on what we're able to show them, they might decide it's the right time to take it out of our hands. But that's how this cold case malarkey works.'

Corry sighed in frustration. 'So, what do you suggest we do?'

'At this stage, we do what we'd do if we were still carrying warrant cards. In our previous positions, there's no way we'd be storming the gates demanding to speak with Clay and Davey. We'd be drilling deeper to find a more comprehensive way in. We have an established and seemingly long-running connection between the two men, which is a terrific start. Given the circumstances of our cold case, that raises suspicion, but to my mind very little else. I say for the time being we focus on discovering as much as possible about their relationship, but at the same time we cannot overlook one critical issue.'

'And that is?' Greenhill asked sharply.

'Who pulled the trigger? Do any of us think Davey or Clay himself did that?'

The others shook their heads. As did Bliss. 'No. Then we still have the shooter out there. He is the vital missing link between our two men. Find him and we may just find more answers.'

'But how? It was almost a quarter of a century ago.'

'I didn't say it would be easy. But we have to start somewhere, so let's assume for the sake of argument that the gunman didn't do the job for free. If his payment was money rather than banking a favour he could use later on, then there could still be a trail. Hitmen don't come cheap.'

'And I doubt he took American Express,' Foley said. 'So, we're talking cash, and a decent amount of it, too.'

Bliss nodded. 'The person most likely to be able to find that down the back of the sofa is Callum Davey, so that's our first area of focus. We might even be able to borrow a forensic accountant from Hinchingbrooke if I ask nicely. That's where I'd begin. Plus, search for more connections between the two men.'

Corry agreed. 'The more often we can place them together the more likely we are to get others to believe in a conspiracy to murder.'

'Correct. I want Davey if he got richer on the back of having Mrs Nolan widowed. And if Clay was in on it, or even knew about it, I want him hung out to dry as well. But I'm not going to forget the man who pulled the trigger. The other two might be responsible, but somebody else did the deed. Whatever we do next has to include taking him down as well.'

FORTY-THREE

EEING AS IT WAS Friday and his fellow unsolved case team members were off shift for the weekend, Bliss invited all three to lunch. Enveloped by another scorching hot June day, he drove them to the Boathouse pub in Thorpe Meadows. They took a table outside overlooking the river. Taut canvas shields protected patrons from the damaging rays of the midday sun, leaving them able to enjoy the shade as well as an infrequent light breeze coming in off the Nene.

The four were relaxed and chatting companionably when Penny Chandler and Olly Bishop unexpectedly appeared. Bliss waved his friends over and dragged in two spare chairs from a nearby table. He then took the opportunity to nip to the bar to buy another round of drinks, including a pint of cask ale for himself. When he returned, he was intrigued by the general chatter punctuated by snorts of laughter.

'Just telling your new friends about some of your past exploits,' Chandler said as he retook his seat.

Bliss shook his head dismissively. 'Don't listen to a single word this soppy tart has to say. She's demented. She's also an inveterate liar.'

Beth Greenhill smiled at him. 'Really? So, you driving your car into a lake never happened? Getting knocked down while you were chasing an intruder in your jockey shorts never happened? How about falling arse over tit as you chased after a brutal killer and having your blushes spared by a diminutive female DC? As for being compromised by a masseuse...'

'Yeah, yeah, yeah,' Bliss said, holding up both hands in mock surrender. 'Tell me none of that same shit ever happened to you lot. You spend as long as I did in the Job, you either witness or are involved in every kind of debacle going. We all know we're only one step removed from the Keystone Cops at any given moment.'

This provoked only more laughter at his expense, but he took it as they had intended. He then added to their mirth by reminding Chandler about the time they'd had to strip down to their underwear when visiting the secure inner building at HMP Belmarsh. 'That is not a pretty sight at the best of times,' he said, jabbing a finger in her direction. 'But having her standing a few feet away while she's almost starkers is enough to make any man want to claw his own eyes out.'

'And you're knicker melting, are you?' Chandler shot back. 'With your hairy paunch, moobs, and vanishing hairline.'

The others cracked up at that one. Bliss gave her the finger, she gave him two, accompanied by a tongue. He chuckled along and felt some of the weight he'd been carrying slip from his shoulders.

'So, how's your cold case going?' Bishop asked, piling most of it back on again.

Greenhill, Corry, and Foley all looked to him.

'Oh, oh,' Bishop said, a knowing grin spreading across his face. 'What kind of minefield did I just wander into?'

'The awkward kind,' Bliss admitted.

'That's okay. You can tell us. We're police officers.'

Chandler nodded fiercely. 'Yeah, come on Jimmy. Cough, you cockney bastard.'

Despite the seriousness of the cold case, he couldn't help but shake his head and laugh at his friend. 'You can be such a cowbag at times, Pen.'

'I know. And don't call me Pen. So, what is it? What kind of mystery and intrigue have you got yourself into now? And please, tell me you don't have to flash your shorts this time.'

'There's not a great deal I *can* tell you,' he confessed. Chandler had played it just right. While she was aware of the details, she had to pretend to be in the dark while at the same time making light of it. 'It's operational and we're still figuring out our next moves. But we have made progress. More than the original investigating team did. We think there's a conspiracy to murder, and we believe we know two of the conspirators.'

'Now you really have to tell us more,' Bishop said, urging him on. 'You can't leave it there, Jimmy.'

Heaving a long sigh, Bliss said, 'For your own sakes, I'm forced to leave out the specifics. At least until we're more certain. But it does look as if our victim stood in the way of one man's lust for wealth, at which point another man suggested ways in which he might help.'

'But it needed your victim out of the way,' Chandler concluded for him. 'Sounds exciting.'

'I agree. And with a bit of luck, you might not have to wait too long before I fill you in on the details. Thing is, this new team can go a stage or two further, but there will come a time when we are obliged to hand it all over so that someone can put together an arrest package and then action it. As this is a murder case, with some corruption thrown in for good measure, I'm assuming it will go to Major Crime to finish off.'

'How much longer do you think you need with it?' Bishop asked.

Bliss regarded his three new colleagues. 'What d'you reckon? Another couple of days after today? Say, Tuesday evening or Wednesday morning?'

'Sounds about right,' Foley said after a brief pause.

'And what of your other case, Jimmy?' Beth Greenhill asked. She pushed aside her plate and took a sip of her lime and black-currant cordial.

'The usual ups and downs,' he replied. He told them about his little scheme to use one drugs gang to force out their two com-petitors. 'They've done everything we expected of them so far,' he added. 'Including arranging for the Foxes line from Leicester to give up the names of our two killers.'

'Risky move,' Foley said. 'Criminals make for bad bedfellows.'

'Yes, they do. And it's a bed they'll shove me out of after tonight when another team takes down a major drugs shipment of theirs.'

Foley chuckled, his initial look of concern extinguished. 'I see how it goes now. You get them to do the hard yards and then screw them while their backs are turned. I'll say this for you, Jimmy, you've got balls.'

'He certainly does,' Chandler said, glass raised to her lips. Then she gave a single snort. 'Dry and dusty ones, if I remem-ber correctly.'

Everybody looked at her as if she had lost her mind. Using both hands to wave their stares aside, she said, 'It's an inside joke. I cannot – I repeat – cannot confirm their dryness or dustiness from personal experience.' She paused to giggle behind her hand for a moment, then added, 'Please, take no notice of me.'

Bliss nodded. 'Yes, everybody please do that. This is what I had to work with for far too long. Anyway, my balls aside, there's always a risk when you tackle drug gangs. These county lines mobs are not so dissimilar to those who came before them, they just have a different way of working. Fact is, it's starting to look as if we might have two lines fewer to worry about. I'll take that, plus a major consignment off the market, in exchange for their ire. They won't be the first nor the last hard and nasty bastards to have a grudge against me.'

'Does that not concern you?' Foley asked.

'It makes me wary. It makes me careful. But it's been my life for forty years, so I can't allow myself to live in fear of reprisals.'

'Not even now that you're no longer a cop?'

'Did you have to bring that up?' Chandler said, giving Guy Foley the stink eye. 'We've all thought it, all wondered if Jimmy being a civilian now makes him fair game. We were just polite enough not to mention it.'

Foley raised a passive hand in surrender, though the half smile teasing his lips suggested he didn't give a damn.

'So, you have your suspects in custody?' Greenhill asked, shifting the group away from a potentially awkward silence.

Bishop was the first to reply. 'Not quite. We have one of the two. He's built like the proverbial brick shithouse and is about as communicative. He's not said a single word to us. Our interviewers are having another pop at him in an hour or so.'

'I must say, you've done a great job so far keeping the media at bay. This kind of double murder would normally have them frothing at the mouth.'

'We can thank the DCI and the DCS for that. The Chief Constable as well, I imagine. They're holding firm, sticking to press releases with no Q&A allowed. The pressure is building, and at the one week mark I suspect there will be a further concerted effort from the media.'

'Any lead on the other suspect?'

'His mate was supposed to be at the same address we raided first thing this morning, but for some reason he was elsewhere. We have a general idea where he might be now, so our colleagues are currently trying to narrow that down to a specific address. If he's not there, either, then we might have problems.'

'You think he's done a runner?' This from Corry.

'We think he originally became pissed off at his boss for being stood down part way through their mission here in Peterborough. By all accounts, he's a right vicious and violent bastard, and if he's responsible for what we've seen so far, then he's a force to be reckoned with.'

'Our hope is he'll lie low and cool down at the same time,' Bliss said. 'But if he's as unstable as his reputation suggests, he might just be simmering. If he comes to the boil, who knows what might happen?'

As he said the words, Bliss's eyes fell upon Chandler and Bishop on the other side of the table. The idea of either or both having to confront Ritchie Morrison in full flow chilled his blood. The man seemingly had no qualms about squirting acid in the faces of two young kids, no conscience when it came to finishing them off with a sharp weapon, and most likely hadn't thought twice about cleaving a man's arm off. Bliss understood that if a team burst into the flat in which Morrison was hiding away, a wall of armed officers would stand between the man himself and Bliss's friends. But if Morrison decided to act rather than wait to be hunted down, he might well aim his fury at any one of them.

Could be me as SIO, he thought. Equally, it could be anybody on my team. Saad Ali, the man who gave up Morrison and his mate, was bound to be one of the thug's ultimate targets. But who might he be prepared to move out of the way first? Bliss didn't like the answer he came up with and could not shake off the thought.

After lunch he drove Greenhill, Foley, and Corry back to Thorpe Wood but remained in his vehicle while they entered the building. From the car park, he made two phone calls. The first was to Sandra Bannister. After ensuring their conversation was off the record, he asked her to search the newspaper's archives for all articles and photographs featuring Callum Davey and Robert Clay together, irrespective of the subject matter. When she enquired what the information was for, he refused to say, only that it could help him, which in turn would help her secure a scoop. The intel he'd already fed her in addition to the details provided during media briefings had so far led to Bannister producing two exclusives, for which she was grateful and happy to repay in kind.

The second call he made was to Danielle Halford. He realised his bridges to her and the Hector Karagiannis organisation were scheduled to be burned later that night when the police intercepted the drugs shipment, so he decided to make use of their relationship while he could. He remained silently reflective during the expected initial teasing, letting her know his call had a serious purpose. When he told her what he wanted, he left her in no doubt just how significant it was.

FORTY-FOUR

COTTON END STOOD ON the southern outskirts of Bedford. And on the southern outskirts of the tiny village itself lay Swallow Farm. Due to the topography and boundary edges reinforced by dense foliage and trees, the police were forced to carry out surveillance of the farmland and its buildings by drone only. The monitoring team had swiftly established that there was only one way to reach the farmhouse and its largest barn, which came as a welcome relief. Looking at the property from above, it soon became obvious that once vehicles entered after first opening a tubular steel gate, they followed a single tree-lined track before it broke and curved around to the left, ending outside the house. The track gave way to a rectangular expanse of gravel that ran all the way to the end of the concrete-panelled grain storage barn.

The strike teams assembled in the Bedford Town Football Club car park, less than four miles away from their target. The drone unit had positioned themselves much closer, their vehicle tucked away off road inside a small thicket. Secure in the knowledge that they had concealed themselves from traffic passing through all roads around the target farm, they spent their time piloting two DJI Matrice devices in a constant rotation; bringing one back in while sending out its replacement, then swapping out the first unit's battery. Twenty-four-hour surveillance was difficult to maintain, but not impossible. However, it was not feasible to do so for days upon end, so the exhausted operators were delighted when they spotted a line of vehicles comprising three vans and three SUVs entering the property. While his colleague alerted the control team of the arrival, the current operator flew the airborne drone as high as he could to ensure it would not be seen or heard at that vital moment.

Less than fifteen minutes later the raid team sped into the farm. The size of the suspected haul was too significant not to have involved the National Crime Agency, and their presence alone amounted to a dozen people. Four officers from the UK Border Force also attended, their primary focus on customs and learning how the drugs had entered the country. The usual tactical, drugs, firearms, and dogs personnel meant that in excess of sixty law enforcement officers carried out the largest such raid in the county's history.

Colleagues like to joke about armed officers champing at the bit to fire their weapons, but the reality was that other than the odd over-adrenalised hothead, each of them entered the fray hoping they would not have to pull the trigger on anything more powerful than a Taser. The happy truth was that deciding whether to fire a shot was a choice few firearms officers ever had to face. For the most part, their mere presence was enough to convince people to do precisely what they were told and take a nicking rather than a bullet.

Everyone who took part was delighted to end the raid without a single weapon being discharged. The execution was perfect, the various teams using muscle memory and experience to reel in every gang member on the premises without a great deal of resistance other than the odd skirmish. The police made twenty-one arrests, including a dozen of Hector Karagiannis's associates. They then took ownership of vast quantities of heroin, cocaine, various opioids, ketamine, MDMA, and cannabis, plus a large sum of the Greek gangster's cash. Police across Bedfordshire and Cambridgeshire would put away more than a few sherbets in the days and weeks to come in celebration of such an amazing success.

All of which Chief Superintendent Fletcher relayed to DCI Warburton, who in turn passed on the news to overjoyed Major Crime Unit colleagues, including Jimmy Bliss. He received the update while wearing a huge grin, after which he settled down to negotiate the next stage of his own plan.

FORTY-FIVE

H E HAD SELECTED THE meeting point after consulting Goog-leMaps. For the sake of the feasible deception he had in mind, he'd sought a location as close to equidistant as possible between Peterborough and Leicester. Uppingham seemed to fit the bill. But as his eyes scanned the online map, he realised he didn't need to go into the market town itself. He spotted a commercial estate on the corner of the main A47 and the southbound Ayston Road, and deduced that, although it would be deserted in the early hours of the morning, the area would still be sufficiently illuminated.

Much later, as Bliss entered the car park, he noted a half-hearted attempt to prevent travellers from accessing the adjoining large field, albeit two concrete blocks and three small posts planted some distance apart were unlikely to offer any genuine protection against a more determined trespasser. He swung the car around and backed into a space that offered a couple of exits close by, along with an excellent view of any other vehicle driving into the complex. He put the Volvo in park but kept the engine idling. Then he settled back into his seat and considered the events that had led him there that night.

Although his team had been unable to track a mobile phone to either JJ Tapper or Ritchie Morrison, it was obvious to them that both had been using unknown burners. They had collectively felt a building excitement after the crime scene investigators discovered an old Nokia in the bedroom Tapper had been occupying in Bobby and Tina Fleece's home. The device held a lot of numbers, though each had been assigned a code rather than a name. Still, it was reasonable to assume that one of them must connect to Morrison's own burner, with perhaps several others relating to older phones long disposed of.

While the data was being copied across to the system, the team continued to work on uncovering details for Tapper's uncle's business and home addresses. They found nothing in either the Company's House records or the electoral register, suggesting the man had intentionally kept a low profile. At that point, Bliss had called time on the day and sent everyone home. Shortly afterwards, the gamble of calling Danielle Halford paid off. He'd asked her to contact Saad Ali to obtain a list of phone numbers that were still in use, and as he sat in the office updating the policy book, he received his answer via a text. When he checked the list of numbers obtained from Tapper's phone, it was buried in there.

His eyes now fixed on the commercial estate's car park entrance, Bliss smiled at the thought. He felt no guilt whatsoever in using Halford one last time. She had complied with his request because at that precise moment she believed theirs was still a two-way exchange of information. By now she would know otherwise, and he could only imagine her reaction.

While his mind was still preoccupied with the raid and its widespread effects, he felt astonished when his mobile rang and displayed Halford's name. He had expected never to hear from her again, especially now that the interception of Hector Karagiannis's drugs consignment had played out in textbook fashion.

He imagined she was calling to bend his ear about it. He briefly considered ignoring the call, but then took a deep breath before answering.

'I thought you were the honourable sort,' she said without hesitation. 'I had you down as a man who understood the way the world worked better than most people did. We had an agreement, Jimmy Bliss. With you, with the police. We played our part. We oversaw the immediate withdrawal of the Soke and Foxes lines from your city. We did precisely what we said we would do. And this is what you do to repay our good faith. You even had the audacity to ask a favour of me earlier and I fucking well did it like the twat I am.'

Without the slightest hint of remorse, Bliss said, 'Tell me, Danielle, is the air rarified up there on your high horse? Or is it a pedestal you're calling from? Is there any danger of you coming back down to earth to engage in an honest and open conversation?'

She snorted. 'That's rich coming from you. What do you know about honesty?'

'Tell me how I've been dishonest.'

'You know very well. You were supposed to allow us to go about our business without police interference. I would call seizing our money and shipment a significant interference, wouldn't you?'

Her voice was acidic, the tone harsh. Bliss understood her anger. But that didn't mean she wasn't wrong. 'You were all too eager, Danielle,' he explained. 'I realise you're furious right now, but take a deep breath and a step back. Just a moment ago, you said you'd done everything you told us you would do. You'd driven out your competition, which meant it was all now under your sole control. Did we intervene during that specific period? No. We steered clear. As we said we would. As per our agreement. But by the time of the raid, your line was already running things in my city. That meant our deal was over and you were fair game once more.'

'What?! You have to be fucking with me.'

'Danielle, I hate to break it to you, but the Devil is in the details as always. So, no, I didn't lie to you. The police didn't lie to you. We kept to our side of the bargain just as you did. But your protection expired the moment you drove Soke and Foxes out of the city.'

'You mealy-mouthed prick!' Halford snapped. 'Taking down that shipment was part of the plan all along, wasn't it?'

'Not all along, but for much of it, yes, it was.'

'You took the piss.'

'I did nothing of the sort. The fact that our arrangement didn't go as per your own plans is neither here nor there. I always said that post-takeover we'd be treating you like any other villains. Again, I was true to my word.'

'We barely had time to breathe before your lot acted,' she said with real venom.

'Timing is everything,' he replied coolly. 'You can have no complaints.'

'Oh, I've got complaints coming out of my arse. And you are the target of every single one of them.'

'As it should be. You're the criminals, I'm on the side of good. Remember that.'

After a moment of silence, Halford said in a softer, yet edgier tone. 'If you think for one moment that we're going to let this stand, you are very much mistaken. I was all that stood between you and the worst kind of villains you can possibly imagine. But you and I are done, Bliss. The gloves are off, and it won't be my hands that end up wrapping around your throat.'

'If I didn't know better, I'd say that was a threat,' Bliss said without inflection.

'Call it what you like,' she said. 'Me, I'm completely embarrassed by what happened tonight and fucking riled about it. As for my boss, he's apoplectic. Tonight's raid has cost him an absolute fortune, and he's not about to turn his back on that without resolving the matter with some kind of reaction.'

'I'd pretend to be surprised, but I think you'd see through it. Or maybe you wouldn't. You know, if you stop to think about it, although you've lost this one you can regroup and start the winning process all over again. We caught wind of this shipment because your boss got greedy. It was too large, too vast a quantity of drugs and cash involved. Somebody was bound to talk, and we were bound to hear.'

'And? What are you saying?'

'I'm saying that if you go back to usual volumes and change your locations we'll be lagging behind as usual. Ours is a cat-and-mouse relationship, Danielle. Sometimes we're Tom and sometimes we're Jerry. What your boss ought to be focussing on is that while we won this battle, he still won the war. He has Peterborough free and clear now to run as he sees fit. Of course, we'll be coming after him, and yes we'll make arrests and take people and money and stashes down, but drugs kingpins stay in business if they're clever and determined enough. They don't allow the odd failure to get in the way of that.'

'I'm sure Hector will realise all of that as soon as he has calmed down. But do you really think anything is going to save your neck?' she asked.

He exhaled in a long sigh. 'Danielle, I was in the Job for forty years. You're not the first to threaten me, and if I continue to do my job well, you won't be the last. But let me just say this before I go… if you think life in the drugs game is tough tonight, imagine what it will be like if you take the life of an ex-copper and current SIO. You, your army, your boss, you'll all face being hounded out just as you did to the Soke and Foxes lines. Only it won't be quiet, and it won't be pretty. Chew on that and discuss it with the Bubble. Bye for now.'

'Be seeing you, Jimmy,' Danielle said with all the menace she could muster.

'I look forward to it,' he shot back.

After ending the call, Bliss sat quietly for a few seconds, tapping the phone against his lips. For a man in his vulnerable position, he ought to be buckling beneath the weight of anxiety, yet in many ways he felt better than he had in quite some time. He remained largely unbothered that danger lurked in every corner no matter which way he turned. MI5 and/or Special Branch were unhappy with him, and the spooks had a way of dealing with people that generally went unheralded. If the man who had shot and killed Justin Nolan got wind of Bliss and his new team being hot on the gunman's trail, he might well be active and willing to end more lives to remain unknown. And now there was also a mob boss apparently determined to put him in the ground. But far from causing him concern, it made Bliss feel relevant.

All that potential for danger, and then there was the meeting he was about to have.

Earlier in the day he'd called the number Halford had texted him. It went straight to voicemail. He was about to try again when he decided to leave a message instead. 'You don't know me,' he said. 'But I know you, Ritchie. Or Li'l Mofo, whichever you prefer. I know of you and Big Mofo because I work for the same organisation you do. Or should I say *worked*? Thing is, my friend, I'm as angry as I think you are at the way we lost respect in fucking Peterborough, of all places. But there are also a few things you might not be aware of. If you've seen the news, then you'll know the police arrested Big Mofo. You would have been, too, if you'd been there. What you won't know, mate, is that somebody gave you up. And I know who that somebody is. If you're interested in finding out the name of the person who fucked you over, meet me and I'll tell you. I'll also let you know how and where to find him when he least suspects it. If you think I might be the Filth trying it on, you're wrong. Ask yourself how I would have this number if I wasn't on the inside. And if I was a copper, wouldn't I just track your phone and find you that way? Wouldn't I be hammering on your door right now? Like I say, you don't know me from Adam, but I'm doing you a favour because I don't like the way they're handling things. And I don't want to see you banged up like JJ.'

Bliss had then given the meeting point and time. He imagined Morrison was bound to be there at least thirty minutes early, which is why he'd got there half an hour before that. He knew that others might regard this course of action as a further example of his irrational, potentially self-destructive behaviour. But to him, it was completely reasonable. Forget MI5 and their stealth tactics, forget the hitman determined to remain free, forget the aggressive gangster and his hired thugs. A man who used acid and blades on people without a second thought was by far the greater threat and to be feared more. Bliss had made up his mind not to expose any of his colleagues to the proximity of this vicious bastard unless he was already in cuffs.

Ask forgiveness, not permission.

That approach had worked for him in the past. Which was not to say it always would. But he was prepared for any eventuality. And at 1.37am precisely, he was in good spirits when a soft top BMW pulled into the car park.

FORTY-SIX

A S INSTRUCTED, RITCHIE MORRISON guided his wheels to the parking space furthest away from the entrance. Seconds later, Bliss called the same burner phone number and this time the man answered it immediately.

'You sit there as long as it takes to feel comfortable,' Bliss said. 'When you're confident I'm not stitching you up and that there are no ARVs circling the area ready to swoop in, kill your lights, switch off your engine, get out of your car, and then walk slowly across the car park towards me. As soon as I see you on your way over, I'll also get out and I'll tell you when to stop.'

'Now, just you hold on one fucking minute,' Morrison barked. 'Before I do any of that, you tell me who the fuck you think you are to be giving me orders.'

Li'l Mofo was too far away to see him clearly, so Bliss allowed himself a wry smile. 'I'm the man willing and ready to help you, Ritchie. I'm the man who wants to give you a way to pay back the fucking rat who turned you in.'

If anything, Morrison's voice became louder and more strident. 'I get that, otherwise I wouldn't be here. But you don't tell me what to do, you feel me? I don't know you, and I don't take fucking orders from you. I'll get out, you get out. I'll stop wherever the fuck I like, and then you say what you've got to say.'

Keeping his cool, Bliss said, 'Okay, I hear you. But the thing is, while we may not know each other, I do know your reputation. No way am I going to stand toe-to-toe with you when I give you the information I have. I'd rather drive away now, but if I do, then you have fuck all. Think about that. Look, Ritchie, tell you what, you see the green telecoms box surrounded by the low wooden fence in the centre of the car park?'

'Yeah, I see it. What about it?'

'You come over and stand on your side of it, and I'll stand on mine. I'm gonna leave my engine running, so if you go off on one, I'll nip back to my motor and fuck off out of here before you get a chance to lay a hand on me.'

'What makes you think I'd do something like that? You're here to give me information I want, right?'

'Right. Only once I've done that, you might decide I'm of no further use to you. And I've heard all about what happens to people who get on the wrong side of you, Ritchie. Believe me when I say I'm just keeping all my options open, that's all.'

'What the fuck do you take me for?' Morrison said heatedly.

'See, you're already getting narky with me,' Bliss said sharply. 'I'm telling you, we do things my way or I drive out of here now.'

'Yeah? And what if I chase you down, run you off the road, and beat the information out of you? How about that?'

Bliss put some heavy frustration into his reply. 'All right, pal. That's me done. I tried to do you a favour, so now good luck finding the answers you want without me.'

'No, no, no. Don't go. I'll do as you ask. But I'm telling you, if you're faking me out and you're really Five-Oh, there ain't nothing ever going to prevent me from causing you the most pain you've ever felt in your life. You feel me?'

Almost before he'd finished speaking, Morrison extinguished the BMW's headlights. The low rumble and crackle of the exhaust died. Bliss looked on as the man heaved himself up out of the car. Short, stocky, bald. He looked like half the crowd in the Matthew Harding stand at Stamford Bridge where Chelsea played. Only this man was truly dangerous, and not with fist, boot, or forehead. Ritchie Morrison played for keeps and took lives.

Perhaps, he reminded himself.

For all they knew, it had been Jamar Tapper who'd squirted the corrosive liquid onto those young faces. Morrison might then have gone on to use a sharp blade to slice tender skin apart. Or maybe Tapper was responsible for both. Yet intelligence suggested otherwise. Big Mofo was very much a punch and choke kind of thug, a man who enjoyed using his strength and brute force to overwhelm his opposition. No, it was Morrison who enjoyed the darker side of violence, the one who got a kick out of inflicting pain and misery.

Satisfied, Bliss nodded to himself and exited the Volvo, knowing he was about to involve himself with a malignant creature lacking any kind of empathy for his victims. A man who regarded him as perhaps the next on what might well be a lengthy list of targets for his particular brand of brutality. Bliss could only hope he was good enough and quick enough for Morrison, because the closer the two drew together the more Bliss questioned his own sanity.

Within mere seconds, he faced his suspect across a few yards of gravel corralled by a flimsy three-bar wooden fence. Rarely had Bliss encountered such an unmemorable physical presence who nonetheless carried with him so much raw energy and malice. Undiluted malevolence oozed from the man's every pore, so much so that Bliss could almost smell the fetid odour of evil escaping into the dense, humid night air.

The two men weighed each other up before Morrison shrugged his large, rounded shoulders and said, 'Come on then, bruv. You got me out here. Now, tell me who gave me and JJ up to the Feds.'

Bliss came close to giving himself away by laughing. Did this thug's entire vocabulary originate from watching episodes of some lame American cop show or movie? Just a few seconds ago he'd been speaking like a regular bloke, but now he was coming over all gangsta and sounding pathetic.

'That's why we're here, Ritchie,' Bliss said, setting aside his disdain. 'I'm going to give you the name you want. But before I do, I need to know I can trust you, yeah? Because if his people find out it was me who gave him up, then it's me who dies next.'

'Fuck that!' Morrison turned to spit on the ground. 'There's no chance of that happening. I ain't saying nothing, and who's he going to tell once he's dead? You give me the name and where I can find him. That's what you promised me. I find him and I kill him. That's my promise to you. Yeah, I'll take my time with whoever this slimebag is, so it'll be slow and righteous because he vex me. But he be gone when I'm done. Nobody to tell, nobody to hear.'

With the conversation having gone much the way he had anticipated, Bliss feigned a more urgent concern. 'See, that's kind of what bothers me, Ritchie. It's why I'm being so cautious. I give you the name, you go and do whatever it is you're gonna do to him. But then I know what you did, so maybe then you come at me and want to shut me up as well.'

'Why, you ain't going to rat on me are you, bruv?'

'No.'

'Well then? You came to me, remember? I don't hurt who don't need hurting.'

This was close enough to the kind of opening Bliss had been working towards. 'That's not what I hear, Ritchie,' he said. 'Word has it you and Big Mofo hit those two Soke kids. Did them up proper for no reason at all.'

Morrison shook his head and Bliss noticed him making fists of his hands. 'Then whoever told you that shit don't know fuck all. Me and JJ hit them 'cause killing them was part of the Foxes plan. Me and him got the contract.'

'But they say it went down nasty, man. That you both went too far.'

'Our job was to fuck them up, so we did. As it goes, JJ really didn't do a lot. We both hit them with stun guns first. You know, to put them down, like. I had a small backpack with me, told them it was their new stash. But really, it was for my gear. It was me who brought the acid. I squirted it on them but didn't have enough to finish the job. That's when I pulled my Zombie and sliced them up good. We were told to hit them and make it look bad, so we did. How we went about it makes no fucking difference.'

He sounded pleased with himself, almost to the point of being proud of his filthy night's work. Bliss was nodding along, though his mouth had dried up. 'Fair play. That makes sense. We both work for Foxes so if the boss tells you to do something you do it. I know how that goes.'

As he spoke, Bliss moved his body as if he was becoming animated by the conversation, but in truth his eyes took in everything happening opposite. Morrison had a habit of bouncing from one foot to the other, swaying as if to a back beat. But every few times he completed the movement he inched slightly to his right, which had gradually taken him from his starting position towards the corner of the wooden pen. He was being casual about it, but definitely making his way to the angle, which would eventually leave no barrier in front of him if he decided to kick off. To Bliss this meant only one thing: the man had no intention of allowing him to leave. He was coming for Bliss no matter what, and it was just a matter of time.

As Bliss stood his ground working out how to play things, Morrison's hands clenched and unclenched, his breathing increasingly erratic. Then the tubby man snapped his head around, alerted by the slow crawl of tyres over gravel. Bliss had already caught the vehicle's stealthy approach in his peripheral vision, and his first thought was that Munday, or some other spook had ordered Special Branch to follow and intercept. But he could hardly have been more shocked when he recognised the car as it passed beneath a streetlight.

'Who the fuck is this now?' Morrison demanded angrily, his eyes mere slits as he stood there like a risen Buddha with those sloping shoulders swelling. He turned the furious glare back on Bliss. 'This your doing, whoever the fuck you are?'

'No,' Bliss answered, his thoughts swirling, turning over all the possible scenarios. 'And believe me when I tell you these people are no fans of mine.'

FORTY-SEVEN

RUNNING LIGHTS NOW EXTINGUISHED, the large SUV crawled around to the fenced section. Its engine sounded well-tuned and virtually silent, and its brakes didn't squeal at all as it came to a halt. Barely a second later, Danielle Halford climbed out of the passenger side, while her familiar minder exited from the other.

Morrison turned their way but left one hand resting on the upper horizontal strip of wooden fence. 'I don't know who you wankers are,' he said with a menacing growl. 'And neither do I give a fuck. But you ain't got no dog in this fight, so do yourselves a favour and fuck off before I lose my nut.'

'That's an awful lot of rage in such a small package,' Halford said, not helping matters. 'But, see, I know all about you, Li'l Mofo. And what I hear is that you're well handy. But as you can see, I've brought my own handyman with me.'

'So? Am I supposed to be impressed or something?'

'Well… yes. Not only is he bigger than you, and better than you, and quicker than you, and brighter than you, he's also more vicious and sicker than you can possibly imagine.'

'Is that right?'

'It is. He'd suck your eyeballs out and spit them back down your throat if I asked him to. We call him Hagar. Not because it's his name, and not because he's a Viking, but because he's fucking horrible.'

At this point the smaller man became puffed up, inflating himself with only his reputation to fall back on. 'You two wankstains want a ruck you've got one. But it'll have to wait because I'm taking care of business right now. So please, just fuck off and come find me another day.'

Bliss noticed he'd left all pretence at street patois behind.

'Ah, you see, now we're at the crux of this little problem,' Halford said. 'The thing is, your business also happens to be my business. And as of recently, my business has taken over yours. My boss wanted it done quickly and quietly, sweeping up behind us as we went. This tends to make the odd enemy or two, and an angry man like you is clearly looking for some kind of revenge. So, what is it? What was this man here about to tell you?'

Unmoved, Morrison continued to stare her down. 'Fuck all to do with you is what it was.'

Halford sniffed the air in a show of dismissal. 'Fair enough. But you do know he's with the police, yes? Please tell me you had the good sense not to come out here alone without first weighing up your opponent.'

Morrison swung his head around, his chest heaving as if he'd run a hundred-yard sprint. 'What's she talking about? She better not be right about you being a copper. I told you what I'd do if you was.'

'She's not,' Bliss said. 'And I'm not.'

'Listen, you got me here on the promise that you had information for me, but so far, you've given me fuck all. So how am I to know who the fuck you really are?'

'You don't. But I'm not a copper. I'm an ex-copper. Though I confess I do still happen to work for them.'

'You what?! You fucking lied to me.'

Bliss frowned, steadying his stance in case he had to make a run for it. 'Woah, why is everybody calling me a liar tonight? I didn't lie. I told you I wasn't a cop, and I'm not. I'm a citizen just like you, Ritchie. The difference being, you're a criminal and I still work for the police.'

Morrison jabbed a meaty finger his way. 'You told me you worked for Foxes.'

'Okay. You got me there. But that's it.'

'You said you were going to tell me who fucked us over and where I could find them.'

'Which I was just about to when they turned up. That I didn't lie about. I just wanted to make sure I'd wrung you dry of information first.'

The man's large head seemed to swell two sizes. He rounded fully on Bliss, ignoring the two new arrivals. 'You taking the piss, you fucking maggot? You think you can treat me like a clown and get away with it?'

'Now, hold on there, Li'l Mofo,' Halford said hastily. 'Let's not get over excited, because you're going to have to wait your turn. I haven't decided what I want to do about this prick yet. He fucked me over as well. And I think we were the first in the queue, so step back and get in line.'

'You want him, you can have him,' Morrison called out over his shoulder. 'Do whatever the fuck you like with him. But not before he gives me what I came here for.'

'I'm guessing that's the name of the man who hung you out to dry, right?'

This time Morrison did spin around to face Halford. She smiled before continuing. 'All you had to do was ask the right person. You don't need this sorry excuse for an ex-copper, Li'l Mofo. Because I also know who did that to you. And I'm sorry to tell you this, but it was Saad Ali who gave you up. To us and to the police.'

'Ali? That fucker!'

'I know, right? Who can you trust these days? What's more, it was my boss who insisted he did.'

'And who the fuck might your boss be?'

'Hector Karagiannis.'

The name clearly meant something to Morrison. Tension left his body, and his colour began to return to normal. His chest still rose and fell more than was good for him, but he was calming himself down. 'You're the reason we were ordered to stand down in the first place. Now you're telling me Ali turned us in because of you, too?'

Halford nodded. 'That's about the size of it. But rather than make you angrier still, I can see you've settled right down. As well you might if you know what's good for you. It's one thing losing your rag with some nonentity of an ex-copper, but an entirely new ball game showing the same kind of anger towards me and my boss.'

'Yeah. I get it.' Morrison seemed resigned, his bravado punctured like a balloon. 'Me and JJ got shafted. That's the way it goes.'

'But not before you took lives.'

'And a fair bit of another bloke's arm,' Bliss reminded them.

His plan coming into this had been to put Morrison off balance with the news about Ali and to then overpower him. Section 24 of PACE allowed him to make an arrest without warrant of anybody in the act of committing an indictable offence. He'd intended to goad the man into action, to take the first swing. At which point Bliss would have been justified in defending himself and making a citizen's arrest. He'd made allowances for Morrison being a psychopath, but also knew the villain's best mate was the one handy with his fists. With Danielle Halford and her hench-man having arrived on the scene, he now had to make decisions on the hoof, and they rarely stood up to the first response.

'Whichever way you look at it he's a wrong'un, Jimmy,' Halford said. 'Bit like you in that way. But he didn't work alone.'

'We pulled his mate, JJ,' Bliss told her. 'He's already in the nick.'

'But for how long?' Halford was now addressing him directly for the first time since her arrival. 'If you can't get the CPS on board, then you won't be charging him. And I don't see what you have against him.'

What she'd said momentarily shook him to the core. She shouldn't have that level of information, but she wasn't wrong. None of the evidence discovered during the investigation so far placed either Tapper or Morrison at the crime scene. They had no forensics, there were no living witnesses other than the two suspects, and despite everything he'd admitted to tonight, the police wouldn't be able to use a single word against him.

He cocked his head. 'You think you can do any better?' he asked her.

Halford flashed her wide, toothy grin. 'Oh, I can absolutely guarantee it. Because unlike you, Jimmy, we're not limited by the rules of PACE. Or by conscience, for that matter. I gather Jamar is telling you nothing. Not a single word so far. But we don't have him here, we have his mate instead. And I reckon this tub of lard will cooperate.'

'What, this bloke?' Bliss said, indicating Morrison. The man stood mute, perhaps trying to keep up with the conversation going on around him.

'Sure. Why not? Let me put it this way: if you fancy going on one of those drives you like so much, me and my friend Hagar will stick around and take care of your suspect. I guarantee we'll not only get him to give himself up, but to throw us the bone of his mate as well.'

Glancing over at Morrison, Bliss noticed the man starting to look edgy, shuffling from foot to foot, clearly shaken but frightened enough to keep from trying to make a break for it. 'What do you say, Ritchie?' he asked. 'These people here want you and JJ behind bars almost as much as I do. They don't want to leave you out here harbouring grudges. They'd like me to disappear for half an hour or so while they persuade you to confess to the police and tell us precisely what your mate Tapper did while you're at it.'

The man's head was by now on a swivel. 'Persuade me how?'

'You were listening. Did you hear her specify? See, now I'd be perfectly happy to detain you here until backup arrives with warrant cards and handcuffs. They'll place you under arrest and you can tell your story – and JJ's, of course – once we're safely tucked up inside our nick back at Thorpe Wood. How does that sound?'

Morrison caught on immediately. 'How about we get the first bit over and done with and then when you ask about JJ I'll tell you to go fuck yourself?'

Bliss puffed out some air. 'Yeah, I get the impression that's precisely what Danielle and her tame gorilla are looking to avoid. They want you squealing so hard you give up everything, and they don't mind how they go about their business.'

'And you'd let them do that?'

'Now you're beginning to catch on,' Bliss said. 'See, Ritchie, it's simple enough. One way is really easy, and one way is much tougher. For you, that is. The tough way sees you... well, I wouldn't want to speculate about the work of a third party, but I imagine it involves sharp and heavy tools, plus a lot of screaming and bleeding on your part. You can avoid all that by surrendering yourself to me, but it's your call.'

Morrison bit into his bottom lip, shook his head, then said, 'I've got two words for you, bruv. Fuck and you.'

'You sure? Last chance.'

'You won't do it. You won't hand me over to them. You ain't got it in you.'

Baring his teeth, Bliss uttered a low growl of fury and took a step towards Morrison. 'You think? Why, because I was a cop and so I must have standards? That might even be true, but I saw the results of your handiwork, you barbaric prick. They were just kids, for fuck's sake. Why did you have to do that to the poor little buggers?'

Morrison blew hard, lips flapping. 'It was a job. And I enjoy my work.'

With an ache deep inside, Bliss gave Halford a nod. 'He's all yours. Just a word in his shell-like for now. If that doesn't do the trick, then you can have his sorry carcass.'

He didn't drive away, but he did go for a short walk while Halford spoke with the man, Hagar moving close enough to intervene should the conversation get out of hand. Ten minutes later when Bliss made his way back, Morrison approached him, looking visibly shaken.

'You made up your mind, Ritchie?' Bliss asked. 'Tell me, are you going out with a lion's roar or down with the squeak of a mouse?'

'I'm being stitched up either way,' the man said on a sigh of submission. 'Might as well make it easier on myself.'

For all Morrison's notoriety and earlier bluster, Bliss had thought all along that he'd be the one to crumble if it meant saving his own skin. Not that he'd had any intention of leaving the gangster in the hands of Halford and Hagar. A thought occurred to him, and he couldn't pass up the opportunity to mention it. 'As things turned out, you don't amount to much without your muscular sidekick around. You are one sick and depraved individual once you have the drop on a victim, Morrison, but you need someone else to do the grunt work for you. On your own, you're nothing.'

He turned to Halford. 'Are we okay?'

She straightened her back. Gave a single nod. 'For now. For tonight. You get this piece of shit banged up and I'll sleep on your future.'

'Fair enough. But before we wind things up, what exactly are you doing here? Were you following me or following Morrison?' It had been bugging Bliss ever since the pair had shown up.

She took a couple of strides across the car park, stopping just a few feet away from him. 'You, of course.'

'How? I know there's no tracker on my car.'

'But it does have GPS. And we pay good money to have hackers work their magic.'

Bliss gave a rueful shake of the head. 'Care to tell me why?'

'I don't see why not. Like I told you before, my boss was not happy about the loss of his shipment. I told him a number of different teams were involved, but not yours. Despite that, he reckons you had to have been behind it.'

'So, what? You were looking to take me out?'

'Not necessarily, Jimmy. But I won't lie, it was one consideration. My boss is okay with whatever I decide. Me, I haven't quite made up my mind. Like I said, I'll sleep on it.'

'Yeah, you do that. Just remember that if you come for me, I'll see it from a mile off.'

'And what of it?'

'Well, then you'll have to take your chances.'

Halford smiled. 'Noted. But just so's you know, I tend not to play fair.'

Bliss winked. 'Me, neither Danielle. Me neither.'

FORTY-EIGHT

UNLIKE HIS 'FAM' IN the room three doors along, who steadfastly refused to so much as acknowledge that he had a partner in crime, Ritchie Morrison gave up his mate within a few minutes of his first interview getting under way.

Bliss put it down to earworms.

Sometimes he only had to hear a phrase from a certain song or phrase for it to play on a continuous loop inside his head. For Morrison, that worm had manifested itself after Danielle Halford informed him that if he didn't cough to everything and throw his partner under the bus at the same time, his remand period in HMP Peterborough would be short-lived. And yet, the pain and suffering inflicted upon him every single day would make his stay there feel like an eternity.

And if that wasn't enough to convince him, Halford also made Morrison aware that she knew exactly how and where to find his son. On that understanding, from the moment he handed over the squat and sturdy thug to the uniformed backup he had summoned, Bliss was confident of a win. In addition, the man's fresh hostility towards Saad Ali and the Foxes line was the icing on the cake that meant his team was about to have the gang leader lifted and hopefully charged with soliciting murder.

Bliss had been observing the interview for twenty-five minutes when he took a call from DCI Warburton requesting his presence in Detective Superintendent Edwards's office for a debriefing. Since Morrison's arrest, he'd spent a fair bit of time considering how to explain the circumstances that had led to the man's eventual detention. Having decided there was no way he could emerge with credit, he opted for a combination of the unvarnished truth and the omission of certain conversations and events, hoping for the best possible outcome.

He did not attempt to defend his decision making and subsequent actions, but he was keen to explain them. 'In my estimation, Ritchie Morrison would have reverted to type if cornered like a wild animal and confronted by overwhelming numbers. The man is a psychopathic brute who enjoys being violent, and I didn't like the idea of him getting in even a single early shot. Neither did I want his likely death on the conscience of one of our firearms officers if I could prevent it. I genuinely believed that if we kept it one-on-one, I could handle that situation with minimal fuss.'

One significant earlier consideration was whether to mention the presence of Danielle Halford and her burly companion, Hagar. They had played a substantial role in Morrison coming in as willingly as he had, but Bliss saw no reason for the suspect to bring them up, and many why he'd be better off keeping his trap shut about their involvement. He decided to risk leaving them out of his account.

Edwards and Warburton exchanged glances before the more senior officer said, 'How exactly did you manage to do that, Jimmy? As you mentioned before, Morrison is an avid devotee of raw violence. Yet you somehow managed to persuade him to give himself up to you and you alone without a single blow being struck. That's quite a trick, even for you.'

'I put it down to my usual cordial manner, boss,' Bliss said. 'That and my reputation for diplomacy. You know me.'

'I do indeed. Which is why I'm not convinced.'

'Perhaps we'd all be better off focussing on the positives,' he suggested. 'Morrison is coughing up a lung in that interview room and is doing a splendid job of dropping Tapper into the same mire he finds himself drowning in. We're also going to get a crack at Saad Ali out of this, which is a real Brucey Bonus. If I were you, I'd call that a win and wouldn't waste my time looking for answers that make no difference to the eventual outcome.'

'And if Ritchie Morrison screams coercion?'

'He won't. He's too busy telling us everything he knows.'

'For whatever the word of an animal like that is worth. After all, we only have his say-so where Tapper and Ali are concerned,' Warburton reminded him. 'It's going to take a great deal more before we can move on to the charging stage.'

'Understandably. But that's far from unusual. Gathering the evidence and putting a case together for the courts is always the most demanding, time-consuming, and challenging part of the job. Fingering Saad Ali might be a push, but we could still get enough out of Morrison for the CPS to agree to charges. Then it's down to us and them to make the case against him.'

'I hope that's true. Now, getting back to your own actions,' Edwards said, 'I suspect DCS Fletcher will want a word or two about your performance in that regard. Arranging an encounter with a violent suspect on your own without informing your colleagues might not fall under the remit of a civilian SIO.'

'Hopefully results will count more than procedure.'

Edwards's eyebrows arched. 'Nothing really changes, does it, Jimmy? I seem to have been having the same conversation with you since the day we first met.'

'That's entirely possible,' he admitted. 'But I get the impression you understand me a great deal better these days.'

She continued to look less than convinced. 'If things go the way we all hope they will based on Morrison's statement, I expect any wrinkles where you are concerned to be ironed out at worst, overlooked at best. But if we ignore for the moment the merits or otherwise of you making that arrangement to meet with our suspect, explain to me how you managed to obtain a number for him in the first place. Last I knew we had no knowledge of him having a mobile.'

Bliss had been mentally compiling a list of explanations, and once again erred on the side of frankness. 'I made one final use of our temporary relationship with Hector Karagiannis and his people. They'd recently applied pressure and offered inducements to Saad Ali, who had to be able to contact his man should he need to do so. I asked for a favour, and they delivered.'

Warburton fixed him with a look of utter shock. 'They obtained Morrison's mobile number from Ali and fed it to you?'

'They did.'

'Which means you had a way for us to trace his whereabouts so that we could organise a raid, and instead you lured him out into the night under some pretence that put you two together alone.'

'I already explained that. And I can be persuasive when I need to be.'

'And slippery always.'

Bliss remained impassive. 'Like I said, I didn't want anyone else getting hurt. You might think it was irresponsible, an act of recklessness, but to me it was the right thing to do. The only thing to do. So, I did it.'

'Unapologetic as usual,' Edwards said without rancour. 'But then when it's your MO I imagine it's difficult not to be... yourself.'

'Virtually impossible,' Bliss said.

The look she gave him was a puzzler. He couldn't tell if she was irritated or impressed. Given their history, he doubted it was the latter, but he thought by now she had grown to admire his dogged determination.

'You do realise Karagiannis will be furious with you, Jimmy?' Warburton pointed out. 'You might as well have pinned a target on your own back.'

Bliss dismissed the notion with a shake of the head. 'No, I don't see that happening. It wouldn't be a smart move on their part, and they know that as well as I do.'

'Why so?'

'They face a stark choice between putting me six feet under or leaving me be in the hope that I'd be more useful to them alive than dead. They're savvy enough to realise that there's no coming back from the former, but it remains an option further down the road if they go with the latter.'

'So, get rid of you or make the most of you while they can.'

'Exactly.'

'I often have the same conundrum.' Warburton immediately raised an apologetic hand while Edwards did her best to conceal a snigger. 'I'm sorry. That just slipped out. You get results, after all. But if those were genuinely their considerations, then count yourself lucky to still be with us. You do like to live life on the edge, Jimmy.'

'Actually,' he said. 'That's not entirely true. I don't *like* to. I don't enjoy it or get some kind of kick out of it. It's just the way things are. I have a habit of ending up in the thick of things. Believe me, it's not by design. Anyway, Karagiannis won't relish going to war with the police, which is what will happen if he takes me out.'

'That's what you're banking on? A criminal showing common sense?'

Bliss shrugged, but made no comment.

After a moment, the DSI spoke. 'All right, I think that will do us for the time being. Get it all written up. Statements, reports, and I hope your policy book reflects every single one of those decisions and how you arrived at them.'

Bliss inclined his head. 'It will.'

'I'm sure. Let's have one final briefing on Monday morning, at which point we can probably bring to an end your first SIO Op as a civilian.'

'What about our two suspects? Morrison's as good as toast, but Tapper is maybe a bit iffy. All we have on him is his mate's statement. What if the CPS decide not to charge?'

'Then you stay on until we find enough evidence to change their minds. Is that going to fit in with your cold case role?' Edwards leaned forward, as if challenging him.

'Whether I'm working with the team to find suspects or helping them compile evidence for prosecution, it's all part of the same SIO job. We've all juggled with heavy caseloads before, so I'm not facing anything unfamiliar here. In fact, having only two investigations on the go is a bit of a luxury.'

Edwards relented with a nod. 'Fair enough. But if they are both charged and remanded, the team can put the rest of it to bed. Your primary job was to find out who murdered those two young lads and to make sure they were held accountable. I have a good feeling about this one, Jimmy, so make sure your paperwork is thorough and ready to hand over. And come to think of it, I really ought to have congratulated you earlier. This one has not been easy to navigate, so bloody well done.'

Wonders will never cease, Bliss thought. But he had to admit, it felt good.

FORTY-NINE

JIMMY BLISS WAS THINKING about the past, and for the first time in as long as he could remember, he didn't feel the gentle sting of melancholy as he did so. He felt neither regret nor any indulgent self-flagellation, just logical and open-minded rumination.

Following the murder of DS Mia Short several years ago, he and his team had undertaken mandatory sessions with an area force therapist. She questioned whether he had genuinely accepted the tragedy. Bliss responded by insisting he had moved beyond the acceptance stage, refusing to wallow in misery, when in fact the very opposite was true. He did admit that he could sit and weep every minute of every day for the rest of his life and still not run out of tears. Not solely over the death of his friend and colleague, but also for the incremental sadness attached to the loss of his father and wife, plus the forfeiture of the life he and Hazel had planned together. But he had also acknowledged that was not the way forward, no way to live out his days. He didn't agree with her observation that he was mentally wilting as some might have believed, but he was perfectly okay with some reflection and even introspection. In his view, both told a person a lot about themselves, and he considered it entirely healthy.

How much of that was true at the time, Bliss could barely recall. Perhaps the intent had been there, though he doubted he had ever achieved the right balance in those early months of therapy. But that was then, and this was now.

It was perfectly fine for him to reflect on the past. More specifically, he had been thinking about home. Whatever that might mean. Was home the bricks and mortar he was delighted to have paid the mortgage on? Was it the city in which he lived at any given time? Was home wherever he happened to have his boots under the table? Or the house he had shared with his late wife, Hazel?

No. It was none of these. To Bliss, home was the house in which he had grown up; a baby to a toddler, toddler to a child, child to youth, and finally the youth becoming a man. The house in which his parents had raised him beneath the secure, comforting blanket of warmth, safety, and love, planting the seeds so that he might grow to become the person he now was. Home was soot-stained brickwork, narrow cobbled streets, dim lighting, the call of the rag and bone man and the clip-clop of his horse, the smell of fish and chips on a Friday night and the rustle of the paper it came in, pub fights spilling out onto the cracked and broken pavements, the sound of rasping coughs, much laughter, and sirens. Lots of sirens. Home was the east end of London. And it always would be, though Bliss could never live there again.

His thoughts turned full circle, leaving him to contemplate the future. His future home. He'd recently considered moving, to find a more solitary place for him and Max nestling by the river. Yet whenever he stretched his mind to look ahead in the longer term, he didn't see himself remaining in the city. Not even close. He knew that if he stayed in Peterborough when the time eventually came to stop working, he'd always find a reason to revisit old haunts, drive by Thorpe Wood, pop in to have a natter with

Chandler and the others… and so on. He'd linger like the foulest of smells because he wouldn't be able to help himself. Over time, the city had grown on him, but he was aware of its weaknesses and its dark underbelly.

He puffed out a gentle sigh. Soon enough, you'll be nothing more than a memory to others, he told himself. It was too late to get on with your life by the time you reached that stage, which meant it was already long past the hour to start making plans for what came next. No longer looking ahead to the autumn of his life, more the bleakest winter.

The sight of Chandler carrying two drinks across the raised decking outside his favourite boozer shook Bliss from his musing. He reflected on how he was always at his happiest in the company of his closest friend.

'Here you go,' she said, handing him a pint of Guinness before joining him at the shaded table. 'Aren't you glad I rescued you from a boring afternoon of listening to some crappy music and glazing over as your fish do whatever fish do?'

His hand already wrapped around the glass, he frowned. 'First of all, my collection of albums, CDs, and MP3s contains no crappy music. And secondly, you diss my fish one more time and you're dead to me.'

Squeals of delight and the laughter of children playing wafted over from the playground at the far end of the property behind the car park, and the gentle bubble of chatter came from nearby tables. Chandler's own chuckles drifted off into the warm afternoon air.

'Whatever you say, old man. But at least this way you get to spend more time with little old me.'

'That's true enough. And I suppose that's not such a bad thing. There are worse ways to spend a Sunday afternoon.'

'Agreed. And did you spend yesterday celebrating a great job well done?'

Bliss took a couple of swallows of Guinness before replying. 'Not exactly. I didn't get away from the factory until mid-afternoon. By then the old spins had crept up on me so I pretty much just laid on the sofa watching old films and feeling sorry for myself.'

Chandler's smile became a look of concern. 'Oh, no. Bad one?'

'Not the worst, but not the best.' At one point he'd felt as if he had been caught up in a maelstrom of vertigo phases coming at him one after the other, each arriving just as he started to recuperate from the last. No throwing up this time, which was always a bonus with Meniere's. But as usual, in the wake of a bad spell, he now felt hugely fatigued and lethargic. He'd probably have spent another entire day lying down if his friend hadn't called to ask him out for a drink.

'Have you heard from Edwards or Fletcher today?' she asked.

'Nope. Not sure if that's a good, bad, or indifferent sign.'

'How about Diane?'

'Again, not a peep. I would have expected her to have at least messaged me if there was any news, so I'm banking on the custody clocks being extended for both suspects.'

'Hmm. I wonder what that means for Saad Ali.'

After taking another swallow of his drink, Bliss looked up and said, 'Oh, so you know all about that? Who filled you in on the details?'

'I spoke to Diane yesterday afternoon,' Chandler told him. 'I went online to check on the case file and saw a number of notes had been added. I was curious, so I called her for an update.'

'Yeah, I was watching Morrison's interview when I had to give my debriefing. I'm hoping everything has gone the way we expected, but although I'd anticipated showing my face at the station sometime today, I just wasn't feeling up to it. Not that it matters. Shit happens whether you're there or not.'

Chandler smiled and raised her glass. 'Just as well, or you'd be missing out on this. Anyway, you can't change what the CPS are going to do at this stage, so you're probably better off here with me than sweating it out back at Thorpe Wood. Forget about it for now. Instead, tell me how your new team is shaping up.'

'Nicely,' he said, nodding in agreement with himself. 'They're all very good at what they do, and none of the three seem to be there just for the additional finances. They're there to do a job, and to a certain extent they've surprised me.'

'And your issue with Five?'

'I'm really not sure. I'm guessing I'll find out more tomorrow.'

'Why, what's happening then?'

'I'm pretty sure we'll be looking to have words with both Callum Davey and Robert Clay.'

Chandler gaped. 'Really? Your new team managed to get there without your help after all, then?'

'They would have. I gave them a slight steer, but nothing more than a nudge in the right direction. A day longer on their own and it would have come to them, anyway.'

'You gave them a steer, knowing full well that was precisely what you'd been told not to do.'

'I did. I had to. My conscience got the better of me. But I could have given them the name and all the accompanying details, so I did still hold back a little.'

'Either way, Five are not going to like that, Jimmy.'

'I don't suppose they will. But it's where we are now.'

'Any hard evidence against either of them?'

Bliss shook his head. 'With what we have now we'd be hard pressed to prove Davey even buys favours. If we hand over everything we have to the fraud unit, they might eventually make a case, but that depends on how well both men covered their tracks. Assuming they did so wisely, I'm not sure how much further we can go. It's a long way from where we are to where we need to be, but we're going to proceed to the interview stage in the hope one of them cocks up. For me, I just need to see it in their eyes or in their body language. That'll be enough to make a case for continuing.'

'You really think they're both guilty?'

'I do, Pen. My gut tells me Clay was just happy enough to pull the right strings as soon as they'd removed the barrier, but I'm convinced he knew precisely what took place to secure Davey that contract.'

'In other words, he was at least complicit. But like you say, how are you going to get him for it?'

Bliss finished taking another pull of his drink before shrugging. 'I'm really not sure. All I know is we have to try.'

FIFTY

For the first time in a month, Bliss woke to a leaden sky and light rainfall. The break in the weather didn't feel as if it had affected the temperature a great deal, so after walking Max, Bliss took a shower to wash off the stickiness. Despite the unexpected gloom and flurries of rain, he arrived at the UCT office that Monday morning in a fine mood.

His weekend had started out eventfully and had ended on a genuine high, having received a call from DCI Warburton at almost spot on 8.00pm the previous evening. He heard both relief and delight in her voice as she informed him that both Jamar Tapper and Ritchie Morrison were being charged with the murders of Chris Barrie and Jamie Ure.

They had not been as fortunate with Saad Ali, who had attended Thorpe Wood voluntarily for his interview under caution. He was later allowed to leave pending further investigation. According to Warburton, who had observed the entire interrogation, it became obvious that they had insufficient evidence to detain him further. Though the Foxes line boss had almost certainly ordered the hits and Bliss hated to see him walk, he was confident the man's day would come before long. For the time being, it was enough to have two murderers behind bars.

'Rumour has it you had a busy weekend,' Beth Greenhill said as he walked into the room. She held an open box of pastries under his nose, from which he selected a forest fruits Danish.

Bliss thanked her and gave a hesitant nod. 'Partially. Friday night and Saturday morning were interesting to say the least.'

'I reckon that may be the understatement of the year. This place was buzzing when I came in a few minutes ago. I don't know all the facts, but it's definitely put a smile on everyone's faces.'

Bliss added his own. 'Taking a couple of killers off the street always provides that kind of lift,' he said. 'You know that as well as I do. A win in such a high-profile case is good news for everyone. Now my team just has to make it count.'

'I'm sure they'll do you proud,' Corry said. 'Cracking job, Jimmy. Does that mean you're free to work full time with us this week?'

'It does. For now, at least.'

'Good to know. Have you decided how you want to play this?'

'Yes. I gave it a fair bit of thought as it happens. I want you and Guy to take Callum Davey. With as little forewarning as possible, please. I know that can sometimes be awkward when tracking down a suspect, but find out where he is and pay him a visit as soon as you can. If he or any of his people try to fob you off by saying he's tied up in business meetings all day, brush them aside and get in their faces. Insist on the interview and let them know you'll make a public arrest if necessary.'

Foley looked up from the chocolate croissant he'd been nibbling on while also muttering about the flakes of pastry falling across his desk. 'Are you and Beth approaching Clay with the same mindset?'

'Yep.'

'No political sparring?'

'He's the politician, not me. I'm not even a police officer anymore.'

'Which is kind of my point. How do we back up our threats of arrest?'

Bliss had expected the question. 'Boldly. First, they're unlikely to know you're not allowed to make an arrest. Second, if they do, simply reinforce the public aspect by emphasising how bad it will look if uniforms in a marked car are called in to drag Davey outside in cuffs.'

'You mean bluff them?'

'No. Believe me, Guy, if I ask for arrests to be made, they will be. Superintendent Edwards won't like it, but she will back whatever move I make.'

'Even with the city's Member of Parliament in your sights?' Greenhill asked dubiously.

'That's an irritant we could do without,' Bliss agreed. 'But this is a new team's first case, and it won't be a good look if a senior rank hinders our progress, no matter who our suspect is.'

They spent the following thirty minutes discussing interview strategies. Bliss explained his thinking. Instinct told him the two teams should use the same building blocks wherever possible, but with one eye on the different roles the two men likely played in what eventually took place.

'Robert Clay is a political animal allegedly destined for great things,' he said. 'He might think he can survive this if he plays his cards right. Beth and I can feed him just enough to convince him that he will fare much better if he dissociates himself from Callum Davey. And the more he does that the greater his chance of survival.'

Greenhill turned to Bliss and said, 'I take it we're not actually going to make him a deal along those lines.'

Bliss shook his head. 'Of course not. But if he thinks we might, Clay could go for it. All he has to do is lay it at Davey's doorstep. Provided he didn't know what might happen prior to the murder, or suspect anything afterwards, he could emerge clean. Albeit not squeakily so and looking a little naïve and tainted by the faint odour of nepotism, if not outright corruption.'

'And he'll arrive at that conclusion how?' Ben Corry asked.

'Jimmy's going to lead him there,' Greenhill said confidently.

'But our tactics need to be different,' Foley sought to clarify.

'They do,' Bliss agreed. 'Unlike Clay, Davey is primarily driven by financial greed. Greed and the kind of control and power that comes with money. Also, if we're right about him being the man who organised the hit on Justin Nolan, then it's much harder to convince him he can walk away relatively unscathed. No, I think the approach with him is to dole out in small chunks what we know and what we believe. Let him sit with those thoughts circling inside his head before adding further elements. Then perhaps suggest that a problem shared is a problem halved.'

'You mean if he gives us Clay?'

'I'm pretty sure he won't, but it's worth a shot if you think you can draw him out.'

'And the gunman?'

At this point, Bliss felt torn. He badly wanted all those responsible for the murder, but if it was a choice between Clay and the shooter, he'd rather have the man who pulled the trigger. He told the team precisely what he regarded as the best result, but also what he'd settle for. There were no dissenters.

His spirits elevated by the arrests made in the murder case, Bliss was in a positive frame of mind as he and Beth Greenhill left the building a short while later having tracked down Robert Clay's precise location. MPs frequently held their surgeries on Fridays after returning from their duties in Westminster, but

Clay had been unwell ahead of the weekend and had postponed his. They set out to speak to him at this morning's hastily rearranged venue inside an empty ground floor unit at Queensgate Shopping Centre.

Arriving earlier than anticipated, the two investigators bided their time until Clay had spoken with the last of his constituents. As Bliss and Greenhill finally stepped forward, they found their way barred by a rugged-looking man who introduced himself as Brendan O'Callaghan, Robert Clay's personal secretary. He told them the surgery was over and that his boss had an important event to attend. He asked if they would like to schedule an appointment for later in the week, but Bliss and Greenhill showed their credentials and insisted they have a few words with Clay no matter what. O'Callaghan curtly told them to wait where they were before turning on his heels and striding purposefully across the room to speak to the MP.

Moments later the politician was all smiles and humble manner when he introduced himself, making sure to tell them just how supportive he was of the police. Neither dissuaded him of the notion they were serving officers.

'Is there any chance we can delay this until a later date?' Clay asked, checking his wristwatch twice just to make sure they noted the gesture. 'I do have something I really need to get to.'

'That rather depends,' Bliss told him bluntly. 'Personally, I think talking to us here and now is more important than any other conversation you might have arranged for the rest of the day. Week, month, or year, come to that.'

With a sigh, Clay asked what it was about. Bliss was happy to respond. 'Briefly, it concerns a member of the local county council staff. He was murdered in February 1999. We have a few questions for you about that crime, including the role a friend of yours might have played in it.'

The MP was good at deflecting as all politicians are, but even he could not hide the cloud of trepidation that scudded across his eyes. It was precisely what Bliss had expected to see, and now he knew for sure that Clay was involved. To what degree he had no idea, but the man was carrying guilt. Of that he was certain.

Following an anxious conversation with O'Callaghan, Clay had his personal secretary step outside the store and lock the door behind them. He instructed his staff member to grab a cup of coffee and wait for a text notification to say when he was finished. When it was just the three of them, the MP invited Bliss and Greenhill to draw up a couple of chairs so that they could have a quiet chat with their backs to the store window which, although plastered with posters, nonetheless afforded shoppers a view of the interior.

'Please don't take the dismissal of my aide as a sign that I have any idea what this is about,' Clay said at the outset. 'I simply chose to devote my undivided attention to you and the subject matter, as it sounded quite serious.'

'It doesn't get a lot more serious than murder, Mr Clay,' Greenhill said.

'Of course. And please, do call me Robert.'

'Robert it is,' Bliss said, keeping his tone even but his features stern. 'Do you happen to recall the murder I mentioned, Robert?'

Clay nodded. 'Actually, I do. Though you'll have to forgive me, as the victim's name eludes me for now.'

'Nolan. Mr Justin Nolan. Ring a bell, does it?'

'Now that you mention it, yes. I apologise for being a bit slow on the uptake. A lot of water under the bridge since then.'

'True enough. After all, during that time you've risen from the deputy leader of the county council to becoming this city's Member of Parliament. I'm told you're a shoo-in for a government role. You've managed to take significant steps in the almost twenty-five years that have passed.'

The MP's response was to pout and brusquely shake his head. 'Hardly meteoric. I'd been deputy leader of the council for quite a while when the poor man lost his life. It was tragic for all concerned.'

'Hardly put you off your stride, though,' Bliss pointed out. 'Someone gunned down a colleague of yours shortly before your rise to the summit began. Some might have choked on that terrible tragedy, let it affect them negatively. Not you, it seems.'

For the first time, Clay dug his heels in. 'I get the sense you're trying to suggest something, so let me put a lid on it now. It's clearly devastating for the family and friends of the poor man who was murdered. I'm sure he was a great loss to the council. But I personally never met him, so if you are trying to suggest my cold-hearted ambition got the better of my morality, you could not be more wrong.'

Bliss gave that some thought. Greenhill, however, had other ideas. 'Mr Clay, what role – if any – did you have in authorising county council contracts in the early weeks and months following Mr Nolan's death?'

'I'm not sure what you mean? Why would I have any role in that side of things?'

'I'm sure you wouldn't under normal circumstances. But the man responsible for awarding and rejecting contracts had recently been murdered, and it is our understanding that his boss required the seniority of others to make decisions about specific issues, including complaints about rejected bids.'

'I suspect several levels of seniority exist between that specific role and mine. I can't imagine I had any influence, let alone gave authorisation.'

'It would surprise you, then, if we had found evidence to the contrary.'

Clay's features became rigid. He checked his watch for a third time. 'Look, you're asking questions about the events of more than two decades ago. Was it my job to authorise or reject contract bids? No. Is it possible that one or two of the larger or more complex bids came across my desk? Yes, it's possible. Do I remember the specifics? No. And…' He stood and buttoned his suit jacket, brushing away the odd crease. 'I'm afraid I've given you all the time I have available this morning. If you need to talk to me again, do please arrange an appointment next time.'

'We have only a few questions left,' Bliss said.

'That's as maybe, but I'm already in danger of being late for my next function. Please, call my staff if you want to continue this conversation and they will make time in my diary. But only if you have specific and relevant questions. No fishing, please. I'm a very busy man, as you might imagine.'

Bliss said nothing, but Beth Greenhill stood to shake his hand. 'Thank you for sparing some of your precious time. I'm sure we'll speak again.'

The look on Clay's face suggested he'd do whatever it took to make sure that didn't happen.

FIFTY-ONE

EN CORRY AND GUY Foley fared less well than their colleagues. They arrived shortly before 11.00am at the Techsperts (formerly Solution Providers Techsperts) headquarters situated in the Cambridge Business Park to the north of the city, only to be informed that Callum Davey was working from home that day. After flashing their ID cards, they persuaded the receptionist to provide them with Davey's home address. A quick jaunt along the A14, then northbound on the M11 and twenty minutes after leaving the business park they were pulling up outside Davey's fabulous home in Oakington.

The turning circle at the end of a wide gravel driveway led first to a triple garage followed by the main house built in red brick. Its imposing four-column porchway with a huge, burnished oak front door stood squarely between a series of six bay windows. Foley rang the bell and made a bet with his colleague that a member of staff would answer, but both men were surprised when a woman opened the door and identified herself as the entrepreneur's wife, Mrs Barbara Davey. Furthermore, she informed them that her husband had left the house at his usual time of 7.30am to drive to his office at the company HQ.

Corry had the presence of mind to ask what vehicle he was using. Armed with that information, the two bemused men headed back to the car where they sat for a few minutes discussing their next move.

'What are our choices?' Corry asked. 'Now that we're in the area I'd really like to get this interview over and done with. But he's not here, and he's not at work either, so where does that leave us?'

Equally uncertain, Foley said, 'Don't you find it all rather too convenient and highly suspicious? On the very morning we drive down to speak to him, Callum Davey happens to be unavailable with neither his wife nor his staff knowing where he is?'

'Of course, but perhaps it's just coincidence. After all, who could possibly...?' He caught Foley's pointed gaze. 'Robert Clay. But no, that doesn't make sense, either. Davey's wife told us he went to work as usual, and I have to say I believed her. Yet they were under the impression he was working from home, which means he notified them after he'd already left his house. He deviated from the norm while we were all discussing the actions back at the office, at which time Clay was oblivious to all this.'

'That's true. But if both his wife and his company think he's with the other, then technically he's missing. For all we know, he's caught on to the reinvestigation and has scarpered. I say we get his vehicle flagged on ANPR then find ourselves a place to have a cup of coffee and see if he pops up anywhere.'

Corry agreed. They stopped at the Bar Hill Tesco Extra just a few minutes further along the M11, ordered their drinks, and sat back to wait. Neither felt particularly hopeful, but with their lattes barely touched, Foley took a call. His eyes darted back and forth as he listened then spoke, asking the caller to repeat a piece of information before ending the call and turning his attention to his companion.

'That was a uniformed sergeant attached to a response car. Earlier this morning a farmer looking to gain entry to his field found the gate blocked by a Mercedes. The farmer got out to have words with the driver only to find the man dead behind the wheel. Police were called, discovered the victim had been shot once in the head. Up close, apparently. It's our car. The police were just about to send a unit to his home. Callum Davey has been murdered.'

*

They drove to the scene in New Road, Oakington, a few miles from Davey's home. An appropriate paramedic had pronounced life extinct, but the body remained in situ, still awaiting examination by the crime scene crew. The investigators were greeted by the same officer Foley had spoken to on the phone.

'Can you tell me why you had an ANPR alert flagged to Mr Davey's vehicle?' Sergeant Adam Tambling asked.

'We were looking to interview him as part of a cold case investigation,' Corry explained. 'We visited his place of work but were told he was working from home. But his wife told us he'd left for work at the usual time this morning. We weren't sure if that was suspicious or not, but decided not to take a chance.'

Tambling raised both eyebrows. 'Then I imagine him getting shot in the head is even more suspicious.'

Foley nodded. 'Yeah, you could say that. Anything you can tell us, or is it early days still?'

'At this stage, there really isn't much I can share with you. As you can see, there are no CCTV cameras around, no properties, no pedestrians, so we're going to have to rely on cyclists and other motorists for information. We might get lucky with some dashcam footage, but it could be days before we hear anything in response to an appeal.'

'And you found him sitting in his car exactly as he is now?'

'That's correct. Window down, shot at very close range. Looks as if he pulled off the road and stopped to talk to somebody. As you can see, the grassless patch between the verge and the gate leading to the field is substantial, so definitely room for two vehicles. We've laid down some markers for CSI to check out where we found what look like fresh tyre imprints in the baked dirt.'

'They might be useful,' Corry said. 'But nothing to get our teeth into immediately.'

'No. Sorry. Not that helpful a scene for the most part. You need to see the victim?'

The two investigators exchanged glances. Foley shrugged and said, 'I suppose we'd better had.'

'I can't let you get too close to the vehicle itself,' Tambling warned them. 'But from behind the cordon we've strung out you can still get a clear view.'

It wasn't a pretty sight, but then it never was. Both men had seen far worse in their time. The entry point was usually far less destructive than the exit, which was larger and took more flesh, bone, and tissue with it. His head slumped back against the leather seat rest, there was a hole just above Callum Davey's left eye, missing the socket itself by the smallest of margins. Other than a thin line of blood trailing down from the wound, the trauma was unremarkable. The back of his head would be a different matter altogether, and neither felt like hanging around to see that mess.

The pair thanked Tambling, then made their way back to their own car. Once again, they sat quite still for several minutes, discussing the shooting and what it might mean. Only then did it occur to them both almost at the same time what this murder might also mean for Davey's friend, Robert Clay.

FIFTY-TWO

B LISS AND GREENHILL HAD grabbed breakfast and were circling the Queensgate multi-storey car park, heading towards the exit when his phone rang. He reacted to Ben Corry's excitable voice by telling the man to calm down and repeat himself slowly. His mind raced at the shocking news, but then his instincts quickly kicked in.

'Okay,' he said. 'This is what I need you to do. Contact the fire-arms team. If they don't have an ARV in the city, tell them to get one here now. If there is one close by, have them put on standby awaiting imminent deployment. We'll find out where Clay is due next and then call back with the location. Do it now, Ben.'

By this time, they had reached the barrier, which rose to let them out into Bourges Boulevard. Bliss remained in the slip lane, pulling up onto the pavement to make room for other vehicles before braking and flicking on the Volvo's hazard lights.

'Call Clay's office,' he told his colleague. 'We need to know pre-cisely where he is this minute and for how long he's due to remain.'

Bliss's fingers drummed anxiously on the steering wheel. Callum Davey's murder surely meant only one thing: hiring a hitman to eliminate the lone stumbling block to his early empire

building ambitions had come back to bite him in the most conclusive way possible. The unknown shooter might be unaware of
Robert Clay's involvement, but Bliss was not willing to take that
chance. And if the gunman did know, then he couldn't dither,
either. There was one final thorn to remove, and the police had
to reach him first.

He listened to his partner's side of her phone conversation.
When she ended the call, Greenhill turned to him and said, 'Clay
is the main attraction at a breaking new ground ceremony. It's at
a place called Hampton, which I presume you know, and the new
development is beside Beeby's East Lake, close to the railway line.'

Bliss killed the hazards, thumbed the handbrake off and put
the gearbox in drive. He stamped down on the accelerator, ignoring the horn and flashing headlights of the car he'd cut off. 'I
know where it is,' he said. 'Beth, call Ben and have him relay the
location to firearms. I want an ARV there as soon as possible
and plenty of backup, as well as an ambulance. Make them aware
that the suspect we're after is currently unknown to us, but they
should consider him armed and dangerous, since he's probably
already taken one life today.'

He pushed the car hard across Crescent Bridge that traversed
the railway line, and continued on along Thorpe Road, onto
Longthorpe Parkway, before turning left to join the Nene Parkway heading towards the Serpentine junction and on into the
Hamptons. Throughout the drive he remained silent and pensive,
while Beth Greenhill appeared to recognise his need to concen-
trate by saying nothing to deflect his attention.

To Bliss's mind, the logic of summoning a firearms unit was
sound. His team had no evidence of Robert Clay's complicity in
the slaying of Justin Nolan, and therefore no proof the MP was
in danger of being shot and killed. They lacked anything that
might convict him in a court of law, but perhaps just enough to

save his life. Inaction was the wrong move here, and if he had to apologise after requesting various teams respond to what might result in a non-event, then he could live with that.

At the same time, he sought desperately to fathom a way to make the armed response work in his favour. Despite the rebuff back at the Queensgate centre, he remained hopeful of eventually breaking through Clay's relatively calm exterior. Perhaps this was the moment to turn things to the cold case team's advantage. A whisper in Clay's ear, coupled with the horror of Callum Davey's murder, might just be enough to push the politician over the edge. Bliss realised his aims would be called into question, but with the death of Clay's accomplice earlier in the day, this opportunity might never arise again.

By now the scattered showers and slate sky had given way to a pale sun and warmth. As he pushed the Volvo on oil-slick roads, Bliss wondered what turnout there might be for the event. The first thing he noticed when they arrived at the development site was the size of the crowd. He estimated there were between forty and fifty people standing close to the small group of smartly attired men and women alongside Robert Clay, who currently posed with one foot on the neck of the obviously ceremonial golden spade biting into baked soil softened by the morning's showers. As the MP had officially broken ground, Bliss assumed the initial speeches were also over. If something was going to happen it would surely be either now or shortly after the crowd had dispersed. Shooting while the area was busy might create the kind of confusion and chaos a skilled hitman could make use of in his bid for escape. Alternatively, he might prefer to carry out the hit when there were fewer people around to intervene or later identify him.

As Bliss observed Clay being ushered away by his private secretary towards the MP's official car, his phone rang. He saw

Guy Foley's name on the screen and realised he hadn't updated his colleagues on the latest situation. But before he could tell the full story, Foley interrupted him.

'Sorry, Jimmy, but I think you need to hear what Ben and I discovered.'

Intrigued, Bliss allowed him to continue.

'Quite by chance, we ended up speaking with a member of Clay's staff. They're all clearly concerned, and I happened to voice my surprise that MPs didn't have their own security detail. The woman I spoke to agreed, but added that their boss was safer than most because his personal secretary was the man's shadow. When I asked what she meant by that, she told me Brendan O'Callaghan came with a fearsome and sterling reputation. Evidently, he's ex-Regiment and also worked as a CPO.'

Bliss let that sink in. The 'Regiment' was the Special Air Service's nickname, which meant O'Callaghan had once been an elite member of the armed forces. In addition, his experience working as a Close Protection Officer implied he also had the necessary skills to keep his client safe under more extreme circumstances. As he gave it more thought, he let his gaze drift, spotting Clay and his secretary disappearing into the distance towards their gleaming black Jaguar.

'Guy,' he said in a hushed tone. 'Did this woman happen to mention how long O'Callaghan had worked for Clay?'

'Not exactly, Jimmy. But that does lead me to the part I thought you'd be equally interested in. According to her, the two men have been friends since their university days.'

'Just like Clay and Davey were.'

'Precisely. Notable, I thought.'

Bliss allowed his mind to wander free, clutching at associations. Close friend. Close protection. A man familiar with weapons and unafraid to use them. Perhaps the kind of man who would do anything to help a friend. And potentially the kind of man who knew exactly when to cut those bonds of friendship.

'Okay,' he said, reeling it all back in. 'Guy, get hold of that same woman. Find out what time Clay had his first appointment this morning and whether O'Callaghan was with him for that. Get back to me as soon as you have an answer.'

Bliss kept his mobile in one hand. He felt Greenhill's eyes on him. He swallowed and nodded. 'Yes, I am thinking what you're thinking,' he said.

'You don't know what I'm thinking.'

'If you're half the investigator I reckon you are, then you're at least considering the possibility.'

His colleague straightened and said, 'You might be right. But what now?'

'Now we find a way to prevent them from leaving.'

FIFTY-THREE

'WE HAVE TO GET close to them without causing O'Callaghan to become suspicious,' Bliss said. 'But we need to come up with a viable reason to keep them here.'

He began walking towards the Jag, Greenhill quickly by his side, and after only a handful of strides the pair broke out into a gentle trot. Clay and O'Callaghan were approximately a hundred yards away, but less than twenty from their car. 'Call out,' Bliss suggested, hearing a familiar siren in the distance. 'Wave your hands around. Get their attention. Tell them to wait.'

Greenhill did as he said. At first her shrill cries seemed to go unheard, but then Clay stopped and turned, searching for the source. He was too far away for Bliss to clock his reaction, but he at least remained in place rather than continuing on to the waiting vehicle.

As the pair moved closer to their quarry, they slowed to a brisk walk. 'Any ideas?' he asked beneath his breath. 'What excuse are we going to give him?'

'Maybe we break the news about Davey.'

'If we're right about O'Callaghan that might just make the man nervous.'

'Then we take the chance, because I can't think of any other reason why we'd be holding them up for a second time today.'

By the time they'd caught up with the MP and his secretary, Bliss had reached a decision. 'I'm sorry, Mr Clay,' he gasped, wasting additional time to gather his breath. 'We just received some bad news, and I thought you needed to be made aware of it as soon as possible.'

Although visibly irritated by the interruption, Clay nevertheless nodded and waited. After sucking in a deep lungful of air, Bliss said, 'I'm sorry to be the bearer of such awful news. But earlier this morning a farmer discovered the body of your friend, Callum Davey, inside his car on a road not far from his home. He'd been murdered, I'm afraid.'

While making their way across the open stretch of land, Bliss had been running the likely story through his head. By the time they caught up, he was convinced that Clay had instructed his secretary to kill Davey. Yet the first thing the MP did when hearing the news was to shoot a narrow sidelong glance at O'Callaghan.

He didn't know, Bliss realised, stunned by the revelation. *He didn't know, which means he couldn't have ordered the hit.* And as the penny dropped regarding the member of parliament, Clay's own reaction was more overt. He reared back, stepping away from O'Callaghan and turning a horrified expression on the man.

'What di… what did you… what did you do?' he stammered, the colour having leached from his face.

His long-time friend gave Clay a shocked blank stare. 'I don't know what you're talking about, Robbo. What are you saying? You think I topped Cal?'

Virtually spitting his derision, Clay said, 'I know you did. You threatened him just the other day, and now you've gone and carried out that threat.'

Bliss was studying O'Callaghan's reaction this time. He hoped the increasing volume of the sirens meant the calvary were going to arrive before things got out of hand, but moments later he realised it was already too late for that. The ex-armed forces man brushed aside his jacket, snapped open a holster and whipped out a gun.

'You fucking disloyal piece of shit!' he cried, glaring venomously at Clay and ignoring the anxious pleas from Bliss and Greenhill to put the weapon down. 'How long have we known each other? All that time, all that devotion I've shown you and your ambitions. Then you go and murder our friend and try pinning it on me. Well, you're not getting away with it, Robbo! No fucking way. I mean it.'

Clay responded by raising his hands, terror written in his eyes and in every complex feature of his face. Bliss looked between the two men with mounting astonishment and realised he had got everything completely backwards.

'Mr O'Callaghan,' he said sharply, trying to snag the furious man's attention. 'Brendan. Look at me. Please, look at me.'

As the man turned, so did the weapon in his hand. Bliss swallowed and continued. 'You hear that phaser in the distance but growing ever louder, Brendan? Well, it's not the Starship-fucking-Enterprise. That's an Armed Response Vehicle. I know who you are and what you did for your country. I don't think this is the way you want to go out.'

O'Callaghan's frown deepened, but he made no reply.

Bliss nodded encouragingly. 'Yes. I know the kind of man you are. And this is not how you want things to end.'

'You don't know the first thing about what I've done and seen,' O'Callaghan snapped back in a fine spray of spittle. 'So don't pretend we're all in this together.'

'Okay. Fair enough. But I refuse to believe you really want to end it all this way.'

'You keep saying shit like that,' O'Callaghan said with a shake of the head. 'What makes you think I won't come out on top?'

'Sheer weight of numbers,' Bliss said. He kept one eye on the politician, making sure he didn't attempt to slink away. From the corner of his own eye, O'Callaghan was doing the same. 'Brendan, any second now there are going to be so many red dots on you people will think you broke out in a rash of measles. You might nail Clay before you go down, but you will go down and I, for one, don't want to see that happen.'

Just at that moment, the siren abruptly cut off. Bliss heard tyres screeching as the ARV slewed to a halt only yards away. 'Come on, Brendan,' he said urgently. 'Lower your weapon. We had the wrong idea at first, but I think we all know what's gone on here now. Clay won't get away with it. I mean that.'

His words prompted O'Callaghan to shift the barrel of the gun back to his friend, who stood perfectly still. The gun jerked as O'Callaghan snarled at him. 'Tell them, Robbo. Tell them what you did. Tell them all. These cops. The people standing around using their phones to film us. Tell everybody what you did and maybe, just maybe, you get to live.'

As he clocked the firearms team racing from their vehicle, Bliss caught their attention with a raised hand which he slowly moved up and down in a calming motion. He feared their target would get off a round before they ended his life, and with the gun wavering he couldn't be certain who might get shot. But just as he thought everything hung in the balance, the terrified MP surprised them all by lunging forward and reaching for the weapon. As the two men grappled with it, Bliss practically threw Greenhill to the ground before stooping to cover her like a human shield. He never once took his eyes off the weapon, which was now jammed between Clay and O'Callaghan, the barrel constantly changing direction as the two men fought for control over the gun.

Behind them, the armed police officers took the opportunity to scurry closer and position themselves in an improved formation. Many of the people who had attended the ceremony had found their way back to the site but were now being kept back by the response teams that had arrived in the wake of the ARV. From a distance, the scuffle taking place might have looked relatively harmless, but Bliss was wary of an accidental firearm discharge.

'Get them further back!' he called out. 'Get everyone the fuck out of here.' He knew the firearms officers would not intervene until they felt they had no alternative, and would do nothing while the fight between the two men continued.

Seconds later, O'Callaghan's left foot got snagged up in a rut in the rutted soil, causing his leg to buckle. In doing so, he lost his balance, and as he tumbled to the floor it was Clay who emerged with the pistol clutched in both hands. Bliss realised the firearms team had no idea which of the two men posed the greater risk, and he sensed them relax believing the gunman had been disarmed. He knew then he had no option but to act.

'Robert,' he said, clambering to his feet but making sure he remained in front of Beth Greenhill, who reflexively rolled herself up into a ball to make herself a smaller target. 'Take it easy. You heard what I told Brendan. If I point the finger at you now instead, those armed officers will put you down. You pose a threat to life, and they won't hesitate. Right now they're a bit confused. They know somebody here is a wrong'un, but if they recognise you, they won't think you're our suspect. Use that in your favour.'

Clay shook his head, his eyes wild and staring almost maniacally. 'No,' he said. 'It's already too late for me now. You know too much and you'll eventually discover everything. I can't go to prison. I won't survive inside.'

'I'm not about to pretend, Robert. No playing games here. This is real. This is life and death. You point that gun at any of us, and you really are finished.'

Now kneeling on the ground, O'Callaghan cried, 'Go on, Robbo. Stick the barrel in your mouth and pull the trigger. Or aim it at me if that makes you feel better about yourself. Either way, you'll be dead. You fucking betrayed me, you treacherous bastard!'

Nodding to himself, tears spilling down both cheeks, Clay looked down at his friend and whispered, 'I know. I hear you. But Cal was always going to be the weak link. He'd have given me up in a heartbeat if it meant saving his own skin. After removing him from the equation this morning, I had to decide what to do about you. When this lot bumbled along and fingered you for the shooting, I panicked. I thought I could buy some time for myself by throwing you under the bus. I'm sorry.'

O'Callaghan was having none of it. 'Stick your fucking apology.'

'I understand your anger. With Cal, it was easier. He always implied that he'd hired the gunman all those years ago. He never thought I had it in me, but I was confident he didn't, either. So, we exchanged our pathetic lies and allowed it to sit between us for decades. I sort of realised it had to be you, but I could never bring myself to ask. And in the end, with the police reinvestigating and this time making some real headway, I couldn't trust him not to tell them everything. I had to make sure he never got the chance.'

'Well, what are best mates for? Look, just do us all a favour and blow your own brains out.'

'No, I won't do that,' Clay said in a flat and even voice. Then he swivelled and levelled the gun at his friend. 'But I will do this.'

All Bliss heard for what seemed like minutes afterwards was the sound of gunfire. He snapped his eyes closed, not wanting to witness the inevitable result. When he opened them again, Robert Clay lay sprawled out in the dirt with his eyes wide open, his friend kneeling by his side. O'Callaghan's lips moved but he spoke so softly Bliss could not hear a word of it. Drained and relieved, he glanced behind him, reached out a hand to a shocked and trembling Greenhill. He hauled his new partner to her feet, feeling her body shudder and her legs quake. He pulled her close, hugged her tight.

'It's okay, Beth,' he whispered softly in her ear. 'It's okay. It's all over now.'

FIFTY-FOUR

THAT EVENING, BLISS TOOK both his old and new teams for a post-work drink. Seeing that Beth Greenhill still felt shaky following their close encounter with a loaded gun, he asked Chandler to share a few war stories with her. The two of them hit it off within minutes and soon got into the swing of the occasion.

The mood amongst them was not one of triumph as some might have expected, nor was it particularly euphoric. Instead, there was a shared sense of relief at having resolved their disparate cases – for the most part, successfully. Each carried the burden of knowing there was always something they could have done better or quicker or instead of. So as day turned to night inside the Woodman pub, the teams reflected on how they might have improved on their separate wins. And as ever, thoughts inevitably turned to the victims.

Bliss first discussed the cold case with his investigation partners, and while they were enthusiastic about their ultimate achievements, he knew none of them would forget how they got there and why. The path towards their success had begun with Justin Nolan losing his life at the hands of a gunman. For more than two decades, he had remained the only victim of that first terrible crime, but now two more people had subsequently lost their lives. Callum Davey was, as Bliss had believed all along, the instigator behind Nolan's murder. But he had not hired the gunman. Brendan O'Callaghan had earlier confessed to having carried out the hit as a favour for his two friends and was on remand having been charged with murder. Davey, he told them, had insisted that the only way any of them would benefit was if someone removed the human barrier to success. O'Callaghan had duly obliged.

As for Robert Clay, the investigators assumed he was the reason Davey had pulled over while on his way to work, why the tech billionaire had allowed his killer to get so close. Perhaps the MP had persuaded his friend to call in to say he had decided to work from home, or maybe Clay had placed that call himself using Davey's mobile. A subsequent search of the minister's own vehicle had yielded no clues, but the same team later discovered a handgun in the Jaguar's glove compartment. To the team, this all but confirmed Clay's intention to murder his private secretary, as well. At the end, his career and reputation in tatters, his life completely ruined, Clay had chosen to end it all by aiming his pistol and showing intent to use it, knowing the surrounding armed police officers would fire upon him. Suicide by cop, some called it. Cowardice was the right term in Bliss's opinion.

Contemplating the murder of two young boys in the drugs case left him with a sour taste in his mouth. While there was a measure of satisfaction in charging the two men responsible, the loss of two young lives misled by their own naivety and the greed and dispassionate nature of the drugs business left in its wake a burning anger. Life meant nothing to the people who enjoyed lavish lifestyles paid for from the business of drugs. Such people were happy to use and abuse others provided they all contributed to the wealth, and their disregard for the pain and chaos their employees caused sickened Bliss. Two lads in their mid-teens ought not to have been ripped from this world so cruelly, leaving such gaping holes in the lives of their loved ones.

But as with every case before these latest two, Bliss also understood the need to take all the positives from the win and let them feed the hunger and desire to do it all again the next time the call came in. He always found this aspect one of the more difficult to deal with, but he joined in with the laughter and good cheer throughout.

After inevitably being cajoled into delivering a speech, Bliss thanked everybody for their wonderful efforts. He enforced the nature and value of teamwork and was happy to praise others rather than bask in the glow of their appreciation of his own leadership.

'More than ever,' he said. 'This past week or so has been about how we all work as one. We don't always agree, and nor should we. I try to lead by example, but I don't always get it right. That's why I trust and rely on the people around me to help steer us in the right direction. Not everybody agrees with the way I do things, but again I appreciate it when they care enough about the job to tell me and put me in my place. Penny Chandler is one who has always enjoyed doing just that, and I have a feeling Beth Greenhill will not be backwards in coming forwards when doing the same. Whatever our contrasts, it's our similarities that make us successful. We do this job to make a difference. And long may it continue.'

He finished by taking a long pull of his Guinness, the cheers and applause ringing nicely in his ears. Chandler stood and raised a hand for quiet. 'Thank you for that, Jimmy. I think I speak for everyone here when I say how well you took command this past week or so and led us to achieve these results. On a personal level, I couldn't be happier to see you back where you belong. And on that note, this feels like the ideal time to tell my unit colleagues the news I recently shared with you.'

'You're in the club?' Bishop called out, raising a swell of laughter.

'No, but thanks for playing. In fact, as some of you are aware, I had talks with DCS Fletcher last week and decided to take her up on the offer she made. With Jimmy gone, we've been waiting for a new DI, and all secretly fearing it might be Bentley from CID. Well, I'm here to tell you it's not going to be him. It's far worse than that, I'm afraid, because it's me. I'm stepping up to acting DI while I go through the training programme.'

As one, Chandler's colleagues rose to celebrate her announcement. Caught in the spotlight, she squirmed and blushed, gave a mock curtsy before shaking all the congratulatory hands and gratefully accepting many pats on the back. When they were done, only Bliss remained standing by her side. Although delighted for his friend, he couldn't help but wonder if the role was more of a poisoned chalice than a great opportunity. Mia Short had taken on the position only to lose her life. Bish had removed himself from the job and later endured a mental breakdown for which he was still undergoing therapy.

And now Chandler.

His heart was bursting with pride, but also trepidation.

'I can't begin to tell you how delighted I am with that news,' he said, raising his voice to be heard above the din. 'I've been encouraging Pen to make this move for as long as I can remember. I still recall the days when I urged her to go for DS, only to have her eventually do so when my back was turned. This time she's waited for me to move on before finally taking my advice, something we'll have words about later. But the truth is we all know she'll do a cracking job filling my shoes, and at the very least Pen's unit colleagues can take comfort knowing she is a better option than DI Bentley. Now, before I get back to my beer, Phil has asked to have a word.'

DC Gratton rose from his chair and walked across the room to take centre stage. He cleared his throat a couple of times and clenched his hands into fists. 'I have some news of my own to share with you all. Those of you in the unit are aware I've been going through my firearms training. Well, over the weekend I passed my exams with flying colours.'

More hearty congratulations spilled over, but Gratton wasn't through. 'As you'll also be aware, my original aim was to take up a slot at HQ in Huntingdon. But after many discussions and a great deal of thought, I've decided to go for a position with the Met's counter-terrorism command.'

After a few vociferous protests, Gratton waved them aside. 'The more I've got involved with the firearms side of policing, the more I realised what a unique role it is. When I looked around and started to evaluate what each branch meant in terms of importance, I decided working counter-terrorism was where I wanted to be. It might be a while before a suitable post crops up, but I hope you all wish me well.'

The reception he received when he stood down surely convinced him how much he meant to his colleagues. After settling everybody down again, Bliss said, 'Listen up, people. Let's not be sad at the thought of losing a good friend, a damn fine person, and a bloody good copper. Let's be happy for Phil because this is obviously something he truly believes in. The Met's reputation has not always been a good one, but their firearms teams are among the best of the best and in uncertain times it's counter-terrorism we look to more and more. Please, raise your glasses and three cheers to Pen and Phil.'

Before leaving, Bliss separately took both Greenhill and Chandler to one side. He encouraged Beth to seek help if the shooting continued to play on her mind and warned her not to allow it to fester in the darker corners of her psyche. But she was an experienced copper, and he thought she'd be fine within a day or two. For her part, Greenhill was grateful to him, especially for his actions when O'Callaghan first pulled the gun.

'I was waiting for you to accuse me of acting like a misogynist,' he replied with an easy grin. 'Believe me, I didn't intend to demean you by protecting you because you're a woman. If it had been Ben or Guy standing beside me I'd've done the exact same thing.'

'Don't be so bloody stupid,' she chided. 'What you did was instinctive and believe me it told me an awful lot about you, Jimmy Bliss. You basically used yourself as a shield to protect me, and I'll never forget that.'

'Pen and a few of the others tell me I react without thinking, which is why I get myself into so many scrapes.'

Greenhill squeezed his forearm, offering a warm smile. 'Well, I want to thank you, anyway. I would have frozen and made a target of myself, so who knows what might have happened if you hadn't thrown me to the floor and then dropped over me?'

'That sounds intriguing,' Chandler said as she approached cautiously. 'You never miss a trick do you, Jimmy? Always looking for a chance to cop a feel.'

'Yeah,' he said. 'It's scandalous. I'm a sexist for not wanting Beth to get shot. And congratulations again. I'm thrilled you finally took my advice.'

Chandler turned to him and pecked his cheek. 'You gave me the confidence.'

'Plus, you'd rather not have Bentley for a boss.'

'There's that as well.'

He grinned and winked. 'The team is lucky to have you. Just don't lead by my example. Do it your way.'

'Fat chance,' she scoffed. 'Behind my back they already call me the female Bliss. Some of them have even referred to me as the Blissette.'

'You could do an awful lot worse from what I've seen and heard,' Greenhill told her.

Chandler laughed and turned to Bliss, her eyes wide and sparkling. 'Get your coat, Jimmy,' she said. 'I think you've pulled.'

*

Later that night, as Bliss was fussing over Max and wrestling with the dog over a chew toy, he took a call from Munday. The MI5 man told him the security services had moved on and no longer had any interest in him. They understood and accepted the circumstances under which Robert Clay had died, deciding Bliss was not to blame and had not acted against their wishes as far as they could tell.

'You live on fine margins, Bliss,' he said. 'It's a balancing act you've yet to fall foul of, but you won't always be quite so fortunate.'

'Mine is not a political game,' Bliss said defiantly. 'In fact, it's not a game at all. It's about good and bad, right and wrong. I chose my side long ago, and I'm sticking to it.'

'Did you ever think that perhaps you get to hold the moral high ground because there are others who don't have that luxury? Personally, I believe Robert Clay would have been no more than an afterthought for those above my pay grade. But there are other Robert Clays out there, Bliss. Men in or soon to be in positions of great power and influence, working at levels of government, law, and order beyond anything you or I can imagine. The security services need to work with such people, and in some cases to have them work with us. It's often a filthy job, but someone has to do it.'

'And I respect those who step up,' Bliss told him. 'I just prefer to get on with doing my job, Munday. I don't like being dictated to from the shadows.'

'Nor should you. But I live and work in the real world, whereas you live and work in the one people like me allow to filter through the cracks. I wish you a long and happy retirement, Bliss. And despite my grudging admiration for you, I do hope our paths will not cross again.'

FIFTY-FIVE

SHORTLY BEFORE MIDNIGHT, BLISS began to feel the accrued after-effects of managing his condition and decided on an early night after taking Max for his last walk of the day. The following morning, he attended a breakfast meeting at the Hinchingbrooke area headquarters, once again finding himself surrounded by the familiar trio of Detective Chief Superintendent Fletcher, Superintendent Edwards, and DCI Diane Warburton, in addition to the Chief Constable himself.

After the niceties, coffee, and pastries, the five sat in a circle to discuss the eventual outcomes of the two investigations Bliss had worked.

'Even by your standards it's been quite a few days, Jimmy,' Fletcher said.

Bliss could only agree, but instead of doing so, he remained silent.

'It's difficult to know where to begin, but I think our county lines murder enquiry is as good a place as any. Please, feel free to have your say.'

'From my perspective, it's a clear win,' Bliss said without needing to consider his response.

Fletcher gestured with one hand. 'Feel free to elaborate.'

'Happily. Going in, we had two murders on our hands and three lines vying to be top dogs in the city, suggesting things were about to get tasty out there on the streets. We've emerged with two men charged with those murders, we've also dispersed two of those lines, while at the same time nabbing a large consignment of drugs belonging to the third. Not to mention bagging a shedload of their cash and making a significant number of arrests. Yes, we're still in the position of having a line operating in Peterborough, but nothing we did was ever going to change that.'

'I find myself in full agreement,' Wood-Lewis said, dressed in the crispest of white shirts and leaning forward in his chair. Bliss noticed the CC's cufflinks bore images of Labrador dogs, which made him admire the man even more. 'The situation in Peterborough was on the verge of spiralling out of control, whereas we now know the strengths and weaknesses of the only player and so are more able to adapt in terms of resources. There is, however, the matter of this meeting you arranged with one of our suspects, Jimmy. I gather you don't particularly regard that as an issue.'

'Not much of one, no,' Bliss said. 'In my estimation, reducing that inevitable encounter to a one-on-one confrontation took the sting out of it.' He, of course, made no mention of Danielle Halford and her backup arriving at the scene. 'Confronting him with weight of numbers, and armed at that, could well have got messy for everybody concerned. I believed I could nullify that considerably with a different approach.'

'Yet you went with a dawn raid when you believed Morrison and Tapper were together inside the same house. What was so different about that?'

'The potential demeanour of the specific individual. In my estimation, if Morrison knew someone had ratted him out, and that we'd already arrested his mate, he'd feel trapped and on edge.

I thought he'd be far more likely to come out all guns blazing under those circumstances.'

'Hmm. I think that's open to debate,' DCS Fletcher observed. 'However, I take your point. That said, I think perhaps your active pursuit yesterday of a man believed to be armed is more difficult to talk your way out of, though I have no doubt you're about to try.'

Bliss remained calm. 'I realise it was a risk. But to be frank, I'm not sure I had much of a choice, ma'am.'

'You decided to go in without waiting for armed backup. I'd say that was a choice, Jimmy.'

'If you look at it as a one-off situation minus full context, then yes, you're probably right. But believing O'Callaghan to be armed and looking for an opportunity to use the weapon is the very reason I chose to act. I was confident that he had already killed one person that morning. There was no doubt in my mind that he also intended to take out Robert Clay. When I saw them both walking towards Clay's car, I evaluated the circumstances and decided it was potentially the last drive the two men would ever take together. Things were falling apart very quickly at that point, with Callum Davey having been murdered earlier that day. I'd called for an ARV, but it hadn't arrived. Even so, I couldn't let that car drive off with those two men inside.'

'The difference between this incident and your previous encounter with a suspect is that last time you were on your own, putting only yourself at risk,' Edwards said, though neither her tone nor manner were unkind. 'This time you had Investigator Greenhill with you. I have to ask, did her presence feature in your thought process? Did you ask her what she thought you should do?'

'Yes, to the first. Very much so. Did I ask? Not in so many words. You have to bear in mind, we didn't go there looking to confront the pair before the ARV arrived. But Beth willingly accompanied me after I pointed out that we couldn't let them leave. I realise that's not exactly what you want to hear, but in the moment, I felt Beth was with me and agreed with the decision. If I misread the situation, then I will apologise to her later.'

'There won't be any need for that,' Wood-Lewis told him. 'Investigator Greenhill insists she would have reached the exact same conclusion you did, even if she'd been on her own. She agreed with you and never once considered holding back. She was also at pains to point out how you reacted when the two men started grappling with the weapon, and how you protected her and put yourself in the line of fire. Jimmy, nobody is seeking to blame you here. We're just looking for some reassuring noises that you recognised the dangers and took them into account.'

Bliss spread his hands. 'I don't believe I was gung-ho about it, if that's what you're asking. I processed each situation and took the decisions I considered necessary. To my mind, we were not in any immediate or direct danger, because this fight was between the two men we were looking to keep contained until firearms arrived.'

Fletcher chuckled. 'I think your definition of a Health & Safety Risk Analysis differs from our own. The outcome of your deliberations, at least. But I also like to think that any one of us here in this room would have acted as you did, Jimmy. Not, perhaps, by the modern play book, but aligned with the ethos we all signed up to. What we cannot ignore, though, is the death of Robert Clay. However well-intentioned, your decisions and resulting actions inadvertently led to our firearms officers taking the life of this city's MP.'

'A man we believe took one life and fully intended to take another,' Bliss said. 'I feel for those firearms officers, but I did my best to talk him down. Him and O'Callaghan, for that matter.'

'If the evidence backs you up, that will help dissipate the fallout.'

'It will. Nonetheless, I take full responsibility for my actions. Given the exact same set of circumstances, I'm not sure I would change any of them.'

Nodding, DCS Fletcher said, 'As the Chief Constable previously alluded to, there will be no formal reprimand. You did what you felt you had to do at the time. Hindsight is a wonderful thing, but it changes nothing. It was a risk, but both you and Investigator Greenhill were willing to take it. And don't concern yourself with the PCC and the media. Between us, we'll take care of them.'

Bliss hadn't even considered the Police and Crime Commissioner. The media would do their worst, but their waning powers held no fears for him. 'It's definitely more activity than I had anticipated for my first two ops in these new roles,' he admitted. 'And I got it badly wrong determining who killed Callum Davey, an error that could have been more costly than it ended up being. I hold my hands up to that and I understand if there's a price to pay for my poor judgement.'

DCI Warburton spoke for the first time. 'Nobody is blaming you for that error, Jimmy. You can be forgiven for thinking it had to be O'Callaghan, especially given his military background. The most logical conclusion happened to be wrong on this occasion. But it's a mistake most of us would have made, given the same circumstantial evidence and information. And we should all bear in mind that, ultimately, he was the first man to brandish a weapon.'

Looking around the table, Bliss saw only nods of agreement. 'So, we're good here?' he asked. 'Everyone satisfied with the outcomes, if not quite how we achieved them?'

'I think we can safely say that, yes,' the CC said.

'I've spoken with Beth, Guy, and Ben,' Edwards told him. 'They're all perfectly happy with how their first unsolved reinvestigation unfolded. Working without being micromanaged was a pleasurable experience, and each felt they played their part in gathering fresh leads. The death of Robert Clay is unfortunate, but there's no doubt in my mind this was a big win.'

'I'm very glad to hear it,' Bliss said. 'And I'm grateful for the support. Genuinely I am. It's uncommon these days. It's not unusual for us to see good men and women tossed aside because those in command close ranks. You each have my respect and gratitude for not taking the easy way out. I know I've not always been the easiest person to work with. So, for my part, I'll try my best to steer clear of trouble in future.'

'That's good to hear,' Fletcher said. 'These new jobs of yours might yet work out after all.'

FIFTY-SIX

BLISS WAS PUTTING THE finishing touches to his SIO policy book when Beth Greenhill popped her head around the door. 'Still hard at it, I see,' she said. 'No rest for the wicked, I suppose.'

'Hi, Beth,' he said with a puzzled frown. 'I wasn't expecting to see you here today. You did know we'd been given the day off, yes?'

'I did. But you're still here.'

'Yeah, I had to attend a debriefing, after which I popped over to Fotheringhay to speak with Mrs Nolan. I felt she deserved a personal explanation of what happened to her husband, and why.'

'That was a nice touch. I'm sure she appreciated it. So how come you ended up here?'

'I thought I'd catch up on some paperwork and all the administrative rubbish that goes with the job. I was just finishing up before heading off home. Were you wanting a word with me?'

She gave a sheepish shake of the head. 'No, no. You've had a long enough day. It can wait.'

Bliss turned in his seat to give Greenhill his full attention. 'No, go on. Please. You must have had a good reason to drive all the way here. What did you want to say or ask?'

'Mainly, I just wanted to make sure your case review meeting went okay. I hope – think – I said all the right things when DCS Fletcher asked me to comment.'

'I couldn't have asked for more from you,' he told her. 'You supported me at the time, then backed me afterwards. I'm grateful to you for both. I don't expect all our unsolved cases to be quite as hazardous, but I think we came through it as a bona fide solid team.'

Still leaning against the door frame, Greenhill said, 'I completely agree. I felt we all worked well together throughout the entire investigation. I admit things got a bit frantic yesterday, but the job is the job, right?'

'Absolutely. And to answer your original question, the meeting went well, thank you. Not even a minor bollocking.' He paused to smile. 'Which makes for a pleasant change.'

'That's good to know. I'm relieved. I couldn't wait for tomorrow to find out how it turned out.'

'You could have called.'

Greenhill unfolded her arms and looked hard at him. 'Yes. I could have. I didn't want to.'

'Okay. Was there something else?'

'Actually, there was. I was wondering if you felt like grabbing a drink and a spot of dinner. My treat this time.'

Bliss wasn't entirely sure if Beth had made the offer out of gratitude or if she genuinely wanted to spend more time with him. He thought about it for a moment, took in her expectant face, before deciding that it didn't matter either way.

'I'm sorry,' he said with a shake of the head. 'I've had a rough few days and they've taken their toll on me. Physically, you understand. I'm not at my best and I wouldn't be good company. Another time, perhaps.'

She regarded him for a moment or two before nodding. 'Of course. I should have realised you'd be knackered after everything you've been through. I'll be off. See you bright and early tomorrow. And thanks again for… well, you know what for.'

'My pleasure,' he said. 'Take care.'

Barely seconds after Greenhill had left the room, Penny Chandler marched in. She said nothing. Instead, she strode purposefully across the room, planted her feet squarely in front of him, held out a hand, and flicked him hard in the centre of his forehead. Bliss blinked twice and jerked his head back.

'What the fuck…?'

'You are a complete moron,' she snapped at him, her chin thrust forward. 'Maybe not even a complete one. There's probably something missing in you even as a moron.'

He looked up at her in astonishment. 'What are you banging on about, you daft biddy?'

Chandler gestured towards the open doorway. 'I overheard you and Beth talking.'

'And? So?'

'And so, that delightful woman didn't drive all the way here today to chat about work, Jimmy. You know she didn't. And she definitely didn't ask you to dinner as a colleague who had just protected her so heroically. She was asking you on a date, you moron.'

'Stop calling me that,' he said. 'And anyway, that's not how I read the conversation.'

'Hence my branding you a moron.'

'Was it really so obvious?'

'To anyone but a moron, yes. But to Jimmy Bliss, the cretinous oaf, I suppose not.'

Bliss took a beat. Chandler was right. Subconsciously, he had noticed but had bottled out. He told himself it was because Beth Greenhill was a new colleague, but he knew he was deflecting.

'Come to think of it,' he said. 'I did wonder why she'd come in on the off chance that I'd still be here.'

'She didn't. She called me first to ask. I told her you were still hard at it, and the reason I came over here was to stall you until she turned up. That's when I overhead the conversation. You moron.'

'If you don't stop calling me that, I'll…' Bliss clenched his fist in frustration.

Chandler stuck her chin out further and pointed at it. 'You'll what? Come on, big man. You go ahead and chin me if you think you're hard enough. Moron. Idiot. Fool.'

'All right, all right,' he muttered in defeat. 'But she's gone now. I can't change what just happened. Besides, I really am exhausted.'

His friend shook her head in resignation and said, 'I just don't understand you, Jimmy. Beth is lovely. Attractive. Classy. Just your type, but way, way out of your league. And yet for reasons beyond my comprehension, she's interested in you.'

'I said all right. Let it go, will you?'

Chandler puffed out her lips. 'Okay. Consider it let go. Anyhow, what I also came over here to say was that was a great result yesterday. It's the first time I've had a chance to speak with you on your own. Having a loaded gun waving about must have got the old ticker pumping hard.'

'And then some,' Bliss answered. 'That and the old dirt box popping like a fish's mouth at feeding time.'

Chandler laughed at the image he'd conjured up. 'And why am I not surprised to find you still here? I was told you and your team had been given the day off given everything you went through yesterday, but I had a small bet with myself that you'd be in. I'd just spotted your motor in the car park when Beth called me, so I won my bet.'

'Good for you. You'll be both richer and poorer for it. Look, I just wanted to catch up on my paperwork while nobody else was around. Fat chance of that, it seems. It's busier than Piccadilly Circus around here, so I'm headed home any moment now.'

'Good. You make sure you do. By the way, and this is the last time I'm going to mention it, you genuinely seem to have a fan in Beth.'

'You think?' he asked, still a little uncertain.

'No doubt. You're her hero. As you heard yesterday, I tried to convince her that you flinging yourself on top of her was your clumsy way of getting closer, but she wouldn't have any of it. As it goes, she got a bit flustered talking about it. I told her I wouldn't fancy your sagging body lying on top of me sweating and heaving, but she seemed to think it was chivalrous of you.' Chandler shrugged. 'Takes all sorts, I suppose.'

'You're a cheeky mare.'

'I learned from the best.'

'You off home soon?' Bliss asked.

Chandler gave an exaggerated yawn. 'I am. Had a few too many late nights recently and I need to catch up on my beauty sleep.'

'I couldn't agree more.'

She gave him a playful slap on the arm. 'Up yours, old man. And don't call… oh, you didn't call me anything. Bugger.'

They both laughed. He waited for her to wave goodbye on her way out of the office and start off down the corridor before calling out, 'Night, Pen.'

'Yeah. Fuck you, too,' came her distant reply.

Bliss smiled to himself as he wrote the last couple of lines in the policy book. He decided to save the unsolved case report for the following morning. He was bushed and just wanted to go home, take Max for a walk, put his feet up in the garden, grab a couple of beers, listen to some music, and get another early night after demolishing a takeaway. As he switched the lights off and left the office, he virtually bumped into Chandler coming back the other way.

'Did you forget something?' he asked. 'Some insult you neglected to throw my way?'

'No,' she said. 'When it comes to you, I'm never stuck for offensive things to say. Truth is, I got halfway down the corridor and changed my mind. I realised I didn't really want to go home yet to my lonely flat, plus I suddenly realised I was bloody famished. You fancy some dinner and a beer?'

He brightened. 'You just said the magic word.'

'Yeah. But didn't you tell Beth you were knackered? Aren't you exhausted after all your heroics? I thought you weren't up for having dinner out.'

Bliss gave some thought to the offers both women had made. 'That,' he said eventually, 'depends entirely on who's asking.'

AUTHOR'S NOTE

P EOPLE OFTEN ASK ME about my book titles. The truth is, they come to me in all kinds of ways. Mostly they occur to me in the writing, either from a line I've written, or a theme included in the book. Sometimes they're obvious, and on occasion dredging them out of my subconscious is excruciating. My Jimmy Bliss book, *The Death of Justice*, was definitely the latter. I must have gone through half a dozen different attempts before that one stuck. On the other hand, the entire book, *Fifteen Coffins*, was written around a title that came to me out of the blue.

Something More To Say is from a Pink Floyd song, *Time*, which I first heard fifty-one years ago on the album 'Dark Side of the Moon'. I've always loved the lyric, and in fact I'd intended it to be the title of Bliss #11, but in finding my way through the end of his career as a police officer and into the start of another chapter of his life, I knew it worked better for the first book in what will be his last hurrah.

One bright spark reader noted that the title of my first Bliss book was also a song lyric, *Bad to the Bone*, and wondered if this was my subtle way of bookending the series. I can put that theory to bed now, because the next book is well under way and I'm really looking forward to you reading that one.

Although I'm obviously comfortable with the main characters in this series, it's never easy writing a new Bliss. You have to introduce new elements, or you stagnate, and the series dies away rather than ends naturally. The three new UCT colleagues here came as a breath of fresh air to me, and if you were paying attention you'll be prepared for another slight staffing shuffle around next time. Finally, I thank you for your interest, but once again I can confirm that I simply do not know when the Bliss story will conclude. I don't like odd numbers, so book #13 is unlikely to be the last. While admittedly my enthusiasm for the business of writing is on the wane, my desire and eagerness to write is not. The two are very different things, and being able to juggle both is the key to longevity. I hope that I will know when it's time to call it quits, as opposed to loyal readers drifting away because the quality has nosedived. But that day has not yet come around, and so hopefully we'll meet again next year.

ACKNOWLEDGEMENT

First on this list of people to thank is Kath Middleton, one of my beta readers. When I sent out the beta version I had the overwhelming sensation that I had used the early part of the book as a bit of an 'info dump' to explain the staffing changes and the setup of the Unsolved Cases Team. Kath not only has a sharp eye and a keen mind, but she is also honest, and she told me that even though she really enjoyed the book, she felt the first part dragged a bit for the reasons I just mentioned. That was all the confirmation I needed. Hopefully you won't see where or how in the finished version, but I made some major cuts in those early chapters and reshaped the entire opening of the UCT. If it reads well now, that's mainly due to Kath. If it doesn't, well, that's down to me. Oh, and I must also thank Kath for the word 'spalling' when describing the condition of some of the churchyard gravestones. I'd never heard it, but liked it, and also liked the idea of other puzzled readers reaching for the dictionary :-).

As mentioned in my last book, a conversation with Graham Bartlett led me to Jimmy Bliss having these two new roles, and I wanted to thank him again for his guidance on getting the balance just right. Also, to Dorothy Laney and Lynda Checkley, I extend my usual thanks for their time and ability to spot typos during their beta reads. A special mention here for Ruth Murphy who made some great calls during her ARC read, and to Jo Copping for sorting out my Goodreads debacle. To my expanding Facebook group, ARC readers, page followers, and readers everywhere, I thank you for your continued support. I get lots of people thanking me for writing Jimmy Bliss, but as I always tell them, this is a combined effort, and I am thankful for and grateful to my readers.

Jimmy Bliss has served me well. My other books are not quite as popular, though they are still read in dozens of countries. But it's Bliss who made the desired impact, Bliss who keeps me going, and who previously allowed me the space in which to write other things and create other characters. So, yes, I'm thankful for and grateful to him, also. Next time we're together in the pub, I'll buy him a Guinness or several.

Cheers.

Tony
August 2024

Printed in Dunstable, United Kingdom